Witchfire

Witchfire

A CONNOR HAWTHORNE MYSTERY

by Lauren Maddison

alyson books
los angeles | new york

MANUFACTURED IN THE UNITED STATES OF AMERICA.

THIS TRADE PAPERBACK ORIGINAL IS PUBLISHED BY ALYSON PUBLICATIONS, P.O. BOX 4371, LOS ANGELES, CA 90078-4371.
DISTRIBUTION IN THE UNITED KINGDOM BY
TURNAROUND PUBLISHER SERVICES LTD.,
UNIT 3, OLYMPIA TRADING ESTATE, COBURG ROAD, WOOD GREEN,
LONDON N22 6TZ ENGLAND.

FIRST EDITION: MAY 2001

01 02 03 04 05 **a** 10 9 8 7 6 5 4 3 2 1

ISBN: 1-55583-595-3

LIBRARY OF CONGRESS CATALOGING-IN-PUBLICATION DATA
MADDISON, LAUREN.
    WITCHFIRE : A CONNOR HAWTHORNE MYSTERY / BY LAUREN MADDISON.—
1ST ED.
    ISBN 1-55583-595-3
    1. AMERICANS—ENGLAND—FICTION. 2. WOMEN NOVELISTS—FICTION.
3. LESBIANS—FICTION. 4. ENGLAND—FICTION. I. TITLE.
PS3563.A33942 W58 2001
813'.54—DC21   2001018813

COVER DESIGN BY PHILIP PIROLO.
COVER PHOTOGRAPHY BY LAUREN MADDISON.

FOR SANDRA

YOU ARE MY PASSION,
MY SERENITY,
MY LOVE.

Acknowledgments

With utmost appreciation to:

Debra Elston and Sandra Satterwhite, two women who love my work and love me enough to read it critically.

Katherine Missell, for her invaluable advice, support, and her incredible library of rare books to aid my research.

Pamela Perry, of Great Britain, who generously volunteered to ensure that my "English" was correct.

Mel Nortcliffe and Alex Laberge for their friendship, their hospitality, and, most of all, Mel's anecdotes on all that is British.

God bless them every one.

Prologue

Peace is in the grave.
The grave hides all things beautiful and good.
I am God and cannot find it there.
—Percy Bysshe Shelley
Prometheus Unbound
Act 1, Scene 1

Darkness crept along under the trees, scattering a patchwork of tenebrous shadow in the faded moonlight. In the deepest hours of night, in the space between sleeping and waking, Philip Janks, the vicar, turned restlessly in his bed. But whatever sound or sensation had disturbed his slumber was no match for the profound fatigue brought on by his latest vigil with old and undeniably mean-spirited Mrs. Rathman who (he almost dared hope) would join her Creator sooner rather than later.

A few hundred yards away from the vicarage, in the shadow of St. Dunstan's church, the noises came again, stealthy yet unmistakable—metal on stone, sibilant whispers, and the cascading of soil tossed at random. Just out of range of windows that might overlook the spot, a shaded lantern perched on a small hummock of grass beside an open grave. Two men stood in the yawning hole, leaning on their shovels while on the headstone another man sat, arms crossed over his chest.

"I'm not paying you fifty quid to stand there and do nothing," he hissed at the diggers. "Have you reached the coffin yet?"

The older of the laborers nodded and tapped his shovel gently on the surface beneath his feet. The wooden lid of the casket answered with a thud. "We're a standin' on it, guv'nor."

"Then stop standing on it, and open it!"

The grave digger shrugged and tossed the shovel onto the grass. "Step to the end there, Collin, and give a hand." The younger man dug out one more clump of earth to give himself a place to plant his feet and threw his shovel over his head. It landed with a clank. The man above them rose from the headstone. "Quiet, you fool! We'll have every damn person in the village down here."

"Who the hell does this blighter think he is?" Collin snarled. "I ain't a doin' no more jobs with you, Fred, if I gotta listen to the likes of his lordship there."

"We're almost done, Col, let's just get the bleedin' box open, and then yer can be gettin' home to the wife."

Collin favored the man with a baleful glance, then shifted himself to stand at the far end of the grave. Fred took a chisel from his pocket and made short work of the clasps that secured the lid of the ebony casket. "Musta been a rich one paid for this burying," he mused softly, glancing up at the headstone. But the carving was hidden by the long dark overcoat of the man who was paying them. "There, that oughter do it," he said, straightening his back with a grunt. "Let's open 'er up."

Together the two men heaved at the coffin lid and broke it loose from the surrounding dirt. "Well, I'll be blowed," said Fred.

"All this for...that," added Collin, who was positively amused, if the jiggling of his belly were any indication.

The man above them peered over the edge of the pit. "What is it? Do you see the body?"

"Body?" chuckled Fred. "Not unless the dear departed was one o' them rock monsters on *Dr. Who*."

"What the devil are you talking about?" said the man as he held the lantern down into the hole.

"This here box's filled with stones, guv'nor...just a bunch o' stones."

"That's impossible!" he snapped.

"Then look for yourself, your majesty," added Collin, beginning to see even more humor in the situation. "T'ain't nothin' but bits o' granite."

Transfixed, the man in the dark coat peered into the casket and saw for himself that it was true. No body and certainly not the item he expected to find buried with it.

"Bloody hell!" he growled. "Then where is the old bitch?"

Fred and Collin were snorting, trying to suppress the urge to laugh out loud. "Don't suppose you're thinkin' you don't have to pay us," Fred reminded him. "You said dig, and we dug. Not our fault if there's no corpus delicti," he added, with an air of putting one over on the man with the money and the fancy way of talking.

The man in question drew himself up to his full and considerable height. "Of course you'll be paid...everything you have coming."

From beneath his coat, he pulled out not a wallet but a gun. Even in the dim light of the lantern, Fred and Collin instantly recognized their peril.

Fred stepped back, almost knocking Collin over. "Now, no need to take it personal, guv'nor. We was just having a bit o' fun with you, that's all. If you don't want to pay us, then forget about it. We'll forget about it...everything we seen here."

"Of course you will," said the man, and pulled the trigger once, then again. The muffled reports of the silenced pistol were not loud enough to disturb the slumber of the vicar, let alone the repose of the dead. Two shots to the heart, two kills. Fred and Collin sagged against each other and collapsed atop the wooden coffin. The man stood looking at them for only a second, satisfied they were dead, and then tossed the lantern into the grave. It landed on its side, its open shutter starkly illuminating the bodies of the two would-be grave robbers.

Their erstwhile employer made no attempt to cover up the bodies or fill in the grave. He turned and walked briskly away until he reached the low stone wall and climbed over it. A hundred yards away a gray sedan waited along the dark side of the road. He opened the rear door, climbed in, and tapped on the partition between the passenger and driver. The engine coughed once, then turned over, and the car slid swiftly away from the cemetery. Within moments there was nothing to break the silence but the trickle of dirt from the edges of a brand new grave.

Chapter One

Confusion now hath made his masterpiece!
Most sacrilegious murder hath broken ope
The Lord's anointed temple, and stole thence
The life o' the building.
—William Shakespeare
Macbeth, Act 2, Scene 3

Santa Fe, New Mexico

Connor Hawthorne impatiently thrust aside the galley of her latest book. There always came a time in this painstaking process when she was quite sure she could not bear the thought of reading her own work even one more time. The words she'd committed to paper more than a year earlier, now typeset in an elegant Baskerville, had in the process of repeated proofreading, segued (at least in her perception) from original and literate to trite and mundane. The preliminary cover design stared back at her with its abstract suggestions of mayhem, murder, and courtroom drama. She sighed. It *was* a good book. That much she knew. And just as she'd promised herself a year earlier, it was different this time; it didn't follow the pattern she'd established in her first four books. Still, everything about the novel had begun to grate on her, and she impulsively tossed it halfway across the room, more or less toward her desk.

Connor was restless, her insides unsettled, the proverbial cat on a hot tin roof, she thought, wondering just how often cats were stupid enough to cross a tin roof in broad daylight. Try as she might, she couldn't sit still and, worse, couldn't fathom the reason. Up until the last couple of days, the elegant little casita she'd rented in Santa Fe, with its whitewashed walls, Spanish tile floors, and comfortable, overstuffed furniture, had felt like a haven from the worrisome energy of the outside world. She'd finished all the author's alterations on the book, and spent the rest of the time reading, hiking, and tooling around the area on a Honda Gold Wing she'd bought shortly after her arrival. The bike's 1100 cc engine had taken her along the "high road" to Taos, to Red River, to Chimayo, and to Bandelier. She'd covered a thousand miles or more in northern New Mexico, though not daring to venture back to the Navajo reservation, at least not yet, not while painful memories were still fresh.

She was consciously aware that the serenity of her stay in the "Land of Enchantment" had been extraordinarily healing for her, but now the peace and tranquility were more of an annoyance than a comfort. She had the distinct sensation that something was wrong...somewhere.

A soft knock at the door. It could only herald a visit from her landlord, Freddy.

"Come in."

The elderly man who slipped through the door stood no more than five and a half feet tall. His proportions were that of a porcelain doll. Freddy beamed at her in his usual "I love the world" sort of way. "Connor, my dear. What keeps you indoors on such a day as this?" His extravagant gesture toward the window drew Connor's eyes to the clear light flooding the courtyard in the late afternoon.

"Freddy, every day here is like that," she countered, knowing he would be honor bound to defend his adopted hometown.

"Not true, Connor. Each and every day is unique."

"Mmm, I don't know. Deep blue sky, bright sun, crystal-clear air, warm days, cool nights. Lots of adobe, lots of brown. Looks pretty much like that to me every time I go out the door."

Apparently Freddy had learned his lesson, for he refused to incite any further teasing about his devotion to Santa Fe. "Oh, all right. I'd think authors would have more imagination than that. So how's the book coming along? Or isn't it?" His bright, inquisitive eyes had already taken in the galley lying face down with some of its pages crumpled up.

Connor followed his glance and shrugged. "It's fine. I think I'm just tired of it."

"Small wonder. You've hardly done a thing but work on that book for the last few months. Any chance your daughter will be coming back again for another visit?"

"I think four weeks with Mom was just about her limit. Twenty-year-olds these days are remarkably independent."

"So she's back in England?"

"Yes, the term started at Oxford, and she's in her last year there. I think she's finally starting to get depressed about that."

"Real world starting to press in? Well, at least you had a good long visit, and you sounded as if you were having fun down here."

"We weren't that noisy, were we?"

"No, I was just eavesdropping out of sheer jealousy. My children are half a world away geographically and light years away any other way you look at it." He sighed and glanced again at the galley. "So your work is finally done?"

"It's about as done as it will ever be." She smiled at him. "So what brings you down from the main house, Your Highness?"

"One has to visit one's subjects from time to time," he grinned. No one who met him would have guessed that Freddy was royalty. The name "Freddy" was an irreverent foreshortening of Friedrich von Kraal, and he was the last of a long line of Prussian dukes. He often said that he was probably not only the last, but arguably the shortest. According to Freddy, some of the medieval swords in the family's collection were longer than he was. Fortunately for his acquaintances, the elderly man was not prone to taking his blue blood too seriously.

Unlike his grandfather, who had relinquished the perquisites of nobility with intense resentment, Freddy embraced democracy in general and liberal politics in particular. He also reveled in having sired four daughters, none of whom would be saddled with a title.

"So are you here to confer favor upon me?" Connor asked, with a mock bow in his direction.

"Only my usual blessing," he answered. "The real reason for this intrusion is that this letter was misdelivered to my box."

"Now there's a surprise," she said, taking the letter from his outstretched hand. What is it with the postal service these days?"

"Don't ask," Freddy rolled his eyes. "It's a small wonder we get as much mail as we do. Last fall they lost three packages sent to me by friends in the East. Well, I'd best be off. Costanza is waiting tea for me."

Connor walked with him to the door and waved at Costanza, the live-in cook, housekeeper, and general majordomo, who was indeed waiting on the terrace of the main house above the casita. Freddy paused. "Sure you don't want to pop in for just one scone and a cuppa.

Connor smiled. "If I keep having afternoon tea with you, Freddy, I'll become addicted to clotted cream. Now be off with you, Your Royal Dukeness."

She watched him walk briskly up the path, marveling as always that at the ripe old age of eighty-two, the man moved with the grace and ease of a panther...well, a small panther.

Closing the door behind her, Connor looked at the letter in her hand. The postmark was blurred, but the stamps were British. She would not have been surprised to receive a letter from her daughter, Katy, or her great-aunt Jessica, but the bold block printing on the pale blue paper was unfamiliar.

Carefully slitting open the thin airmail paper along the end fold, she sat down at her desk.

Dear Ms. Hawthorne,
I am sorry to express my deepest regret over the most unfortunate occurrence here in St. Giles. The authorities cannot begin to imagine how such

an atrocity could be committed in our little village. And I, quite frankly, bear some guilt in not having awakened to the sounds of the crime being committed, as I might thereby have been able to avert the subsequent happenings.

Will he never get to the point? Connor thought, her pulse ratcheting upward. What atrocity? And what did it have to do with her? St. Giles had been her Grandmother Broadhurst's home for more than six decades, but Mrs. Broadhurst was gone now.

To be honest, the desecration of graves is, as I understand it, not altogether uncommon, but in this instance, when not only is a grave opened and robbed, but two men are murdered and left within the grave itself, well, it does not bear thinking about. Still, I want to assure you that everything is being done that can be done. I myself am most anxious to learn the whereabouts of your grandmother's remains so that they can be once more laid properly to rest. Please inform me if there is any way in which I can be of assistance.

Faithfully,
Philip Janks, Vicar of Saint Dunstan's Church

Connor had to sit down. What on earth was going on in St. Giles? The vicar wrote as if Connor must already be in possession of the details of this sordid event. Yet she had no idea at all. True, she did know that her grandmother was not buried in the plot at the churchyard, for reasons that were all too complicated to explain to someone like the vicar. But the masquerade she and her father had engineered in order to protect her grandmother's secret and reputation had been successfully carried off—a funeral, a burial, and a headstone to mark the spot. But it would appear they had not fooled everyone.

Or had they? Whoever opened the grave might have been looking for the body itself or something other than the body. But what? And two men had been *murdered*? *Dear God,* she thought, *will it never end?* Between her former job as an assistant district attorney in Washington and her more recent but more life-threatening experiences as a private citizen, Connor had seen enough of death.

She snatched up the cordless phone and took it to the patio, where she could soak up the last few drops of sunlight. Dialing her father's number in Maryland, Connor waited, eyes closed. After four rings there was a delay while the call was forwarded to another phone, then a brief moment of static before she heard his voice.

"Benjamin Hawthorne."

"Dad, it's Connor."

"Hi, sweetheart, it's good to hear your voice. You still in Santa Fe?"

"Yes."

"How's the book coming along."

"It's done for the most part, but I didn't really call to chat."

"Oh?" His tone was more guarded.

"I just got the strangest letter from England."

"It's about the incident in St. Giles, isn't it?"

"You mean, you already knew and you didn't tell me?" Her voice took on a sharp edge.

"Now don't get all bent out of shape. I was informed through some of my sources at Scotland Yard, but I wanted to find out exactly what this was all about before I mentioned it to you. For all we know, the incident might not be connected at all to...other matters."

She could tell he was reluctant to be more specific over a phone that was vulnerable to eavesdropping.

"And just how likely is it, Dad, that this 'incident' is just some sort of weird coincidence? And surely someone is questioning the contents of the...er...container." Unwillingly, Connor heard herself using the same absurd double-talk on her end of the conversation. She still hated cloak-and-dagger stuff, even when it was necessary. It was her father's far-reaching powers as a presidential advisor and "troubleshooter" that had saved their lives, as well as a few others. Now, even as a private citizen, he still had his contacts and there were always loose ends in need of his attention. She would respect his caution, but she didn't have to like playing the game.

"Yes, the authorities there are somewhat puzzled, but I haven't had to address their questions directly—at least not yet."

"All right, Dad. This doublespeak is giving me a headache. I'm finished here for the moment, and there's no reason why I can't come back east for a few days...so we can talk like regular people."

Benjamin laughed. "Sorry. You just get used to this after so many years. It's a hard habit to break."

"It's probably just as well. I tend to think it keeps you safer."

"A definite possibility. So, when are you coming?"

"I'll get a flight out tomorrow."

"What about Laura? Will she be coming with you?"

Connor's hesitation stretched into an uncomfortable silence. "I wouldn't think so. She's staying at the hogan she built near her grandmother's house on the reservation."

"Is something wrong between you two?"

"No...of course not. I mean...there's nothing...let's just drop the subject. Laura and I are good friends, and we have our own lives. We've been through a lot together, but we both needed to put that behind us."

It was Benjamin's turn to opt for silence. Several heartbeats passed before he said, "Sure, I didn't mean anything by it. And I'm looking forward to seeing you tomorrow. I'll send a car to the airport. Just let me know when your flight lands, and which airport."

"Thanks, Dad. Bye."

During their conversation, the sun had reached its nadir in the evening sky. Great splashes of orange, yellow, gold, and magenta dripped down the horizon and melded into the high desert. Taking a deep breath, Connor briefly considered dialing another number, but she changed her mind. She didn't need to drag Laura into another bizarre situation, and she was uncomfortable asking. Much that lay between them was still unspoken—it might never be spoken—and Connor sometimes thought that was how it should be. Other times, though, she missed everything about Laura—her strength, her wit, her gentle teasing, and not least of all, her wisdom. Connor wasn't entirely sure why she resisted the long-term invitation implicit in the way Laura looked at her. They certainly weren't strangers. They'd come close to dying together in the desert; they'd saved each other's lives.

Hell, Laura had almost died trying to protect Connor.

But the resolution of those painful events, and the ones that had led up to Connor's flight across the Navajo reservation, had left scars. She wasn't still mourning Ariana. That was one emotional issue that had finally been put to rest along with the man who had murdered her. And Laura had been the one who carried out the death sentence while defending them both from a vicious attack. Laura was an ally, a friend, an incredibly courageous human being—and very easy on the eyes too. So why did Connor balk at the thought of a relationship? What was she afraid of? Why, after a couple of idyllic weeks together when Connor returned from her long European sabbatical, had Connor run away? That was the only way to describe her sudden flight; anyone as precise in thought as she was could not characterize it any other way. She'd looked across the breakfast table at Laura one morning, felt her heart pound, and suddenly made up a thousand reasons in her mind why she couldn't stay. Then, to make matters infinitely worse, she'd left without saying a word to Laura.

Connor squinted at the sky again. The noisy crows circling high above her weren't volunteering any answers to any of her questions, even though Laura had told her the sleek black birds were considered messengers by some Native Americans. If they were talking to Connor, she decided her grasp of "crow" must be too limited. So she put the debate aside, as always, for another time, another place, and went inside to pack a suitcase. That night she cleaned out the fridge, left the next month's rent check for Freddy, and took out the trash. One of the niggling little hunches she sometimes had told her she wasn't going to be back for a while.

Chapter Two

*For man walketh in a vain shadow, and disquieteth himself in vain:
he heapeth up riches, and cannot tell who will gather them.*
—The Book of Common Prayer

England
County of Somerset

"Darling, we'll be late."

Gerald turned away from the mirror in which he'd been carefully adjusting his formal tie. "We're never late, Gillian. Whenever we arrive is precisely the right time."

"You do love to make an entrance, don't you, darling?" she laughed. "You're worse than that silly old Mathilda."

"I don't think referring to Lady Hevenham as silly old Mathilda would endear you to our circle of friends, my dear," he said, prissily picking at his shirt cuffs and turning back to the mirror. He noted with concern the increasing number of gray strands mingled among the carefully cut blond hair and the slight paunch mostly disguised by a well-cut dinner jacket. But he was still pleased with his face in general.

Blue-gray eyes wide set, aquiline nose, perfectly even teeth, and the family chin; yes, he'd inherited the strong Fenwycke chin with just a hint of cleft.

"We're all peers of the realm, Gerald," she retorted, in both senses of the word.

"Not precisely 'we,' Gillian. *I'm* the one with a title, moldy as it may be."

"Only because your elder brother decided to blow his brains out," she retorted. "Otherwise you'd be the penniless Lord Gerald, and not the very wealthy Lord Fenwycke."

"And you'd be living in some tiny bed-sit in Bloomsbury, working as a clerk. Best you keep in mind that I sit in the House of Lords. Last time I checked, there were no 'ladies' sitting in the upper chamber."

She favored him with a belligerent look and plucked her wrap from the chair in the entrance hall. "Not that the House of Lords is anything to brag about," she said loftily. "More like a bunch of impotent old men sitting around doing nothing."

Gerald felt an unexpected torrent of anger erupt within him. This, of course, was the one comment guaranteed to infuriate him, the one issue that had monopolized his thoughts far too often in recent years. He and his fellow peers of the realm were just what Gillian described— impotent. And in the past two years, they had been mostly divested of even their limited authority. What the devil was wrong with this country and its people? Where was their sense of tradition, of what was proper and what wasn't? Gerald shoved his arms into the sleeves of his black cashmere overcoat and yanked the door open savagely. For that matter, he thought, where the hell was a footman when one was needed to open a door? If he heard even one more piece of cost-saving advice from his odious accountants, one more item that he "really couldn't afford," he'd throttle the lot of them.

Neither of them spoke on the way to Bannister House, the massive and elegant edifice a few miles distant from their own more modest dwelling. Sitting in the back of the vintage Deusenberg with Richard, the chauffeur/gardener at the wheel (Gerald was damned if he'd arrive driving his own car), they both stared straight ahead. Finally, Gerald, in glancing out the side window, let his gaze linger on his wife. She was still extraordinarily beautiful, he thought. Her light brown hair was professionally streaked with golden highlights, her makeup flawlessly applied over pale skin. Yes, Gillian was very satisfactory in appearance and a good match for him, Gerald had decided when they first met. Her 5 feet 7 inches of lithe, well-toned body complimented his 6-foot 2-inch frame. That had certainly been one of the factors in his decision to propose marriage. He generally regarded his wife as suitably ornamental, except on those rare occasions when he caught her unawares and the look in her eyes, one of calculating shrewdness, gave him pause. But Gerald was not given to excessive analysis of human motivations or of anything in life. He remained comfortably ensconced in a world of his own modest delusions of grandeur. If he ever considered that such a beautiful woman had married him only for a title and an estate, he didn't dwell on it.

In the midst of these ruminations, Gerald chanced to take note of his wife's elegant satin-skirted evening gown. "By God, Gillian, don't tell me you've bought yet another bit of fluff that'll set me back a thousand pounds."

"And what if I have?" she answered archly. "Surely you don't expect me to wear something that 'our circle of friends,' as you call them, have already seen. Besides, it's not as if we're poor, darling. You know as well as I do that you're simply rolling in it."

"Hardly 'rolling'. And the way you spend it."

"Then why don't we get rid of that monstrosity of a house and move into the city, where there's actually some life?"

"Sell Haslemere? You're joking, of course. That house has been in my family for more than 300 years."

Gillian airily dismissed his indignation with the wave of a bejeweled hand. "And I think the plumbing is at least that old. Good God, Gerald, it's just a big, drafty barn that consumes money."

Gerald spoke through clenched teeth. "Consider this subject closed, Gillian. I will never sell Haslemere."

"Never say never, darling."

"I mean it, Gillian. Over my dead body!"

"Don't tempt me, darling."

At that moment the car drew up in front of the portico, and a well-turned-out manservant opened the door of their car. Mentally Gerald scowled. His host had no trouble keeping enough servants.

They joined the line of guests streaming into the grand foyer of the sixteenth-century manor house, where other servants quickly divested the new arrivals of wraps, coats, and hats. Gillian turned and walked briskly down the corridor to visit the powder room and check her face. Gerald never understood how a woman could fear some makeup calamity had occurred during a fifteen-minute car ride, but he'd gotten used to her vanity. After allowing himself a brief glance in one of the pair of Louise XIV gilt mirrors that flanked the entrance hall, he set himself to the task of casually encountering their host, Lord William Carlisle. Across the ballroom he spotted William and his wife, Ellen, chatting amiably with a small group of guests. While he pondered how to insinuate himself into that little clique without appearing to do so, he felt a hand on his shoulder.

"My dear Lord Fenwycke. What a pleasure to see you here."

Gerald turned and looked into the beady-eyed countenance of Clarence Newbury, tabloid reporter and all-around pest. The women naturally called him Clare, but the absurdly unctuous little man didn't seem to mind. Nor could Gerald understand what attraction the pudgy, red-faced shrimp held for the women who were always dragging him to parties where he didn't belong.

"What the devil are you doing here, Newbury?" Gerald inquired, trying to keep an eye on the progress of conversation in William's group.

"Soaking up the free liquor, of course. And keeping my hand in. I always like to know who's doing what to whom."

"Since when do hacks like you make the guest list at Bannister House?"

"Oh, let's just say I have my ways," he snickered. "A journalist's secret, don't you know."

His attempts at playing the mysterious spy were transparent as could be, thought Gerald, particularly since he had only to follow the direction of Newbury's flickering glances to solve this particular mystery. Lady Hevenham, the one Gillian kept calling "silly old Mathilda," just to chafe him, was looking Newbury's way. *So*, Gerald thought, *it's true about the old lady liking some young entertainment.* He saw her turn and begin tacking through the crowd in his general direction. She was the last person he wanted cornering him here; he shook off the reporter's hand and turned away abruptly. He was only a few paces away when he heard the grating, high-pitched voice behind him. "Now, Clare, darling, what have you been doing? The orchestra is playing my favorite melody."

Gerald allowed a fleeting sympathetic thought for old Newbury. "Hope he's at least getting paid well."

Another survey of the vast room told him that he had missed a chance to speak to their host, but he did spot Gillian deep in conversation with a man whose back was to Gerald. A moment later, though, the man turned to gesture at something, and Gerald's heart sank. Conrad Thackeray had everything Gerald coveted from a material perspective—seemingly endless wealth, excellent taste, and sleek, blond patrician looks that made even the most jaded women stop and take notice. Still, there was one consolation. Thackeray, for all his money, did not have a title...well, not a real title. He had one of those economically inspired knightships, the sort that went to various and sundry men who had performed some service to Her Majesty and were not hereditary titles that could be passed on to later generations. In his case, the "Sir" probably had something to do with the activities of one or more of his companies. It certainly wouldn't have been conferred for conspicuous altruism. Conrad's ruthlessness in business and his mockery of "bleeding heart" liberals was common knowledge.

Observing his wife and Thackeray standing so close together, Gerald had the uncomfortable feeling he was missing more than the exchange of social pleasantries. But Gerald being Gerald, he told himself that it was his paranoia talking. Thackeray had a reputation for getting what he wanted. And he had even gone so far as to hint to Gerald that there was nothing in the world he *couldn't* have. Surely if Gillian were available, she would be interested. Several million pounds constituted a powerful lure to someone as consistently and obsessively well-dressed as Lady Fenwycke.

Thus it was with some reluctance that Gerald moved through the noise of a hundred voices talking all at once and took his place beside his wife. Thackeray stuck out his hand and smiled. "Gerald, old man. Good to see you here. Just talking to your distaff side. Understand you're thinking of selling Haslemere."

Gerald caught the glint in his wife's eyes and fought to control his emotions. No sense in letting this social-climbing poacher learn more than need be about how things were in the Fenwycke family. Casually, Gerald slipped his hands into the pockets of his trousers. "So that's what my wife's been up to," he said with a tiny smile. "And she no doubt told you that we should live in the city."

"Yes, Gillian was only just mentioning that possibility. And I would be very interested in buying the place from you. It would be a perfect weekend retreat for me. And you've got a lot of land, room to do some shooting. I understand the quail and other game birds are pretty much thick on the ground there."

"Indeed," Gerald replied, his face a mask. "One of the many reasons I would never even consider selling. Haslemere is part of my family and will remain so."

Thackeray didn't look the least bit put off by Gerald's adamant refusal. "That's quite all right. No need to explain. It's your castle now, isn't it? Nothing like tradition to perk up an old Englishman." He laughed uproariously at his own weak joke, and Gerald found himself wondering once again just where Conrad Thackeray had come from. There was nothing in print that explained where he was born, precisely how he got to be a billionaire, or why, as one of England's most eligible bachelors, he had remained single.

Gerald took his wife's elbow firmly. "If you'll excuse us, Conrad, we should be making the rounds."

"Want to chat up old Carlisle, eh?" Thackeray's smile was almost a sneer, and Gerald was uncomfortable with how close to the truth the man had come. Could he know just how badly off Gerald's finances were? That he, the last of the Fenwycke line, had squandered most of his family's fortune and had every intention of appealing to William Carlisle, a distant cousin to Gerald? If he could only get William alone, make the request for a luncheon appointment seem casual.

"I'd like to see several of the guests here," Gerald replied sharply. "Come along, Gillian."

His wife, however, proved entirely uncooperative and firmly shook off her husband's hand. "You do as you wish, darling. I'm quite enjoying myself with Sir Conrad." Her subtle emphasis on the "Sir" was not lost on Gerald. Perhaps a minor title that came with a great deal of money was worth more to Gillian than a genuine peerage with a faltering bank balance.

Mustering all the dignity within his power, he nodded. "As you wish, dear." He nodded to Thackeray and turned on his heel, narrowly avoiding a collision with a champagne laden tray. Now that, he thought, would have been humiliating.

Bannister House was a sprawling edifice dating from the 1500s and in the intervening centuries, generation after generation had undertaken to add on and modernize the place. Fortunately these earlier Carlisles had demonstrated both taste and restraint, so that there had been little of the uglification that plagued some of England's oldest homes. But centuries of improvement had resulted in the expansion of the main house to more than thirty rooms, a dozen of which were on the ground floor. As was their usual custom, the Carlisles had not limited guest access to any parts of the house; thus it took Gerald more than half an hour to locate William Carlisle in the large, multibayed library, talking to a small group of friends about his recent acquisition of a rare manuscript. The room was breathtaking, measuring as it did more than seventy-five feet in length and almost forty feet in width. Above the ground floor bays ran a gallery which completely encircled the room and gave access to more shelves. Gerald wondered why anyone would want to own thousands of books.

He couldn't really follow the conversation, but he waited, glass in hand, on the fringe of the group, for an opening where he might draw William aside. Just as he saw that moment finally arrive and sidestepped closer to the doorway through which William would pass as he exited the library, Gerald heard a booming shout from the other end of the room. This was followed immediately by a scream so shrill it pierced the hubbub in the adjoining reception hall. A heartbeat's length of silence was engulfed by a babble of voices raised in alarm. There were more screams, and guests began pouring into the library. Lord Carlisle pushed his way through the crowd, asking everyone to stay put and keep calm.

Without thinking, Gerald followed in his wake, and people stood aside for him as well, apparently assuming he was with William for a reason. At the far end of the library, in the darkest corner, they were drawn no longer by screams, but by a heavy silence that contrasted sharply with the cacophony of alarmed guests behind them. William firmly but politely parted the spectators and strode into the narrow walkway beside the last bay. Gerald, trying unsuccessfully to peer over the shoulder of the 6-foot-4 Lord Carlisle, could not at first see what egregious spectacle had set the faces of nearby spectators in masks of shock and distaste. One woman had turned away from whatever was there, her face buried in her companion's waistcoat, her shoulders heaving with emotion.

In that instant Gerald actually walked right into William's broad back, yet William did not turn around to see who had shoved him. He stood still as a statue, and Gerald was finally able to move sideways and forward so that he, too, could see. He immediately wished he hadn't. He wished that he'd never followed William, that he'd never come to Bannister House, for he knew he would always remember, in gruesome detail, the horrifying "thing" that dangled obscenely from the tall mahogany library ladder. It was a "thing" to him, for his brain simply could not process the information his senses provided. In his frame of reference, human beings, even deceased ones, were supposed to have heads, for God's sake.

W

The seeker slowly turned the pages of the ancient book for at least the hundredth time. Reverently, carefully, but with growing frustration. But the answers remained elusive, for there were parts of this masterful creation that the average mortal could not yet comprehend. The most important element was still missing, the element that ensured complete mastery. The seeker was not, in most matters, ignorant. A thorough education had been achieved at sometimes painful cost, a prominent place in the world achieved with careful planning. But even to rule absolutely over the tiny fiefdom of one's life was not enough. It was in another realm the seeker wished to dominate, for in that realm fate could be bent to one's desires and one's ambitions. Power was a commodity unlike any other, for it promised immortality in ways the ignorant could not comprehend.

But all this was still purely academic, for the knowledge had been hidden away. It did not lie hidden in the final resting place of Gwendolyn Broadhurst. More puzzling, of course, was that Gwendolyn was not there either. "Stones!" the seeker muttered, "A coffin full of bloody stones!"

Chapter Three

I am going a long way
With these thou seest—if indeed I go
(For all my mind is clouded with a doubt)—
To the island valley of Avilion.
—Alfred, Lord Tennyson
The Idylls of the King, "The Passing of Arthur"

Washington, D.C.

The streetlamps had just flickered on when Connor knocked at the door of the graceful old brick townhouse in Georgetown. When the door swung open, there stood one of her favorite people on earth, Malcolm Jefferson. His broad face beamed at her. "Well, it's about time," he said, drawing her into a bear hug. "Eva's been fussing around here all afternoon trying to get things just right. I knew she wouldn't stop until you actually got here."

Connor could easily imagine Malcolm's older sister fussing. She was a holy terror when it came to dirt, disorder, and misbehavior...from anyone. Returning her friend's embrace, she said,

"You didn't have to go to any trouble. It's just dinner, isn't it?"

"Yes, and good plain cooking too. But you haven't been back here since last year. And she wanted the place to look nice, the way you always had it." He stepped back into the foyer and took Connor's jacket.

"It looks perfect, and I wish you'd both stop worrying about it. This is your house now, and you can do anything you want. Paint the walls, put up a jungle gym in the dining room...just be happy here."

A frown creased Malcolm's handsome features. "That's something we still haven't settled to my satisfaction, Ms. Hawthorne. We'd been here for almost a year before I found out we weren't just house-sitting. You actually put this place in my name."

"Yes, so?"

"You just don't go around handing out million-dollar pieces of real estate. And you should have asked me first."

"And have you getting your back up about the whole thing. I had this strong sense that your steel-sided pride would deprive Eve and your kids from having a great home, great schools, the whole nine yards. Besides, is there a law against giving someone a gift, *Captain* Jefferson? Since you're a cop, you'd be the expert."

Malcolm snorted. "Don't get sarcastic. You know more law than I do, and when you were in the business, you prosecuted as many criminals as I've ever arrested. But that's not the point. It's too big a gift."

"I didn't know size or dollar value was the deciding factor in whether a gift was appropriate. As far as I'm concerned, for the man who saved my life, this isn't much at all by way of saying thank-you."

"That isn't something you need to pay me back for. We're pretty much even on that score." Malcolm's eyes grew darker for a moment, recalling that his friend had talked him out of eating his gun at the lowest point in his life, when his wife had been murdered.

She smiled. "You're a stubborn man, my friend, but this time I'm not backing down. I could never live here again, not after everything that happened. But I couldn't bear the thought of total strangers sitting in these rooms, walking up and down those stairs. So, it's really not what you think, that I was doing you some big favor. We're helping each other. And I bet the kids love it."

"They think they live in a palace now, and it's a good thing Eve's around to keep them from getting all spoiled. Their school is great, though they're in the minority by a long shot."

"That's what comes of movin' uptown, child," Eve's voice rang out from the dining room. "You gotta take the bad with the good." Malcolm's sister emerged from the doorway and gave Connor another hug, this one a warm, mothering, soft embrace that always made her melt a little. Hugs weren't something she could count on when she was growing up, at least not from her mother. "Now why y'all standin' out here in the hall...I'm sorry...in the *fo-yay* 'stead of settin' down in the parlor like civilized folk." Connor was gratified to see that Eve hadn't changed one bit from her down-to-earth self. Where Malcolm had fought to rid himself of every trace of the deep South in his voice, Eve flaunted her Southern-ness, her dialect, and her philosophy. If you didn't like it, too bad.

"I can't get past your brother, Eve. He's still bent out of shape about the house."

Eve fixed her brother with a stern glance. "I thought we'd been through all this mister. You thinkin' no self-respectin' grown-up man'd accept such a thing. You'd rather be back over there on 16th Street, with them children dodgin' pushers and pimps on the way to school?"

"No, Eve, that's not the point."

"It sure as heck is the point. What Connor did she did out of the goodness of her heart. And lookin' down on a gift is shameful. If our momma was alive, she'd tan your hide. I won't have it, you hear me...I will not have it."

Connor listened to the exchange with some amusement, though for Malcolm's sake she tried not to smile. There was no enmity in their hearts or in their words. These were two people who had been disagreeing amicably for a lifetime. And Eve was used to having the last word. "So," Connor interjected, "do we get to eat now or should I come back in an hour or two when everything's settled?"

Malcolm smiled sheepishly. "Oh, it's settled. My sister has spoken."

"Darn right, boy. And don't you forget it." Eve patted his head, not an easy task for most people, considering Malcolm stood an imposing

6 foot 6 and tipped the scales at 265 pounds. But Eve resembled him in more than just facial characteristics, topping out only a couple of inches below her brother. "Connor, honey, why don't you go freshen up? I'm about to put the pies in the oven, and as soon as your daddy gets here, we'll sit down to supper."

Connor had wandered into the kitchen when she heard the doorbell and Malcolm's voice in the hall. A moment later Benjamin appeared in the kitchen door. "Hi, sweetheart," he said, grinning broadly. Connor met him halfway across the floor and hugged him hard. "Seems like ages since I've seen you."

"It's only been about four months, Dad."

"Oh, well, when you're old, time just crawls along."

"Stop it," she chided him playfully. "You'll never get old, and you know it."

Connor did note, however, the signs of fatigue around his clear blue eyes—eyes the same somewhat unusual color as her own. His hair, once a lush, almost-black shade of brown, and still as thick as his daughter's, was shot through with an entirely new crop of gray hair. Even for a man in his late sixties, he was in remarkable shape, but she worried about him anyway, and for the first time in her life she sensed a potential frailty in him belied by his upright carriage and broad shoulders.

"I like to think I won't," he said, "but time has a way of balancing the books for all of us."

"Sounds awfully philosophical coming from an ex-politician. Now let me introduce you Eve Jefferson, Malcolm's sister."

Benjamin stepped forward to offer his hand. "Ms. Jefferson, I've heard so much about you from Malcolm. It's a pleasure."

Eve favored Benjamin with a warm smile. "And likewise I'm sure, Senator. There were times months back when I heard your name a whole lot around our house."

"Please no titles anymore, ma'am. Just Benjamin."

"Well, then, 'Just Benjamin,' I'm Eve, and let's keep it on a first-name basis. I don't put much stock in all that Washington nonsense myself. Now y'all sit down in the dining room, and I'll bring in the plates. It's chicken and dumplin's, so I'll spoon it up right here."

Since Eve would brook no offers of help, Connor, Malcolm, and Benjamin filed into the dining room. It was a lovely room, with its dark wainscoting and maroon-patterned wallpaper. The long Regency dining table was covered with an ecru damask cloth, and candles adorned both ends of the table. But, given the small number of guests, the places were set only at the end of the table nearest the kitchen. Connor saw that there were five places laid, not four. Just as she was about to ask why, the bell rang again. She thought she detected a somewhat startled look on Malcolm's face, but why would he be surprised by the arrival of an expected guest? She felt a twinge of disappointment. She'd sort of wanted this reunion to be private, just family, so to speak. For a fleeting moment she wondered if by some horrible miscarriage of divine justice, her mother had been invited, but she immediately discarded the thought. Malcolm and her father loved her too much to spring that sort of surprise.

"You two sit down. I'll get the door," said Malcolm, quickly pushing back his chair.

Connor picked up her napkin as Benjamin began pouring deep ruby claret from a bottle standing on the sideboard. Malcolm had remembered that in direct contravention of accepted social practice, she drank red wine with everything, including fish and chicken. Connor was just reaching for her glass when she glanced up at the archway to the front hall. In the next instant, over went her glass, and wine streaked across the white cloth. She didn't even notice because her attention was entirely elsewhere.

"Laura," she whispered.

No one spoke for a several heartbeats. Malcolm squirmed, clearly unsure this was a good idea, and Benjamin contented himself with observing his daughter and Laura, his former employee, like a scientist evaluating the outcome of a particularly important experiment. The silence might have gone on forever if not for the incredible "curative" powers of Eve Jefferson. She came bustling through the swinging door, plates in hand and took in the scene at a glance.

"You must be Laura Nez," she smiled. "I'm Eve Jefferson. I think you know the rest of these tongue-tied guests. So sit down right there beside my chair and dig in. I'll be right back with the other plates. Malcolm, come with me and get some salt for that tablecloth. I want to soak up the wine before it sets. Benjamin, you can help carry the salad." She left the room, flapping her apron and shooing the men ahead of her like chickens in a barnyard.

"I take it you didn't expect me." Laura was the first to break the silence.

"Um...no, I didn't. I thought you were busy with finishing the hogan and helping the Chee family with their new house."

"I was. And I've been doing some other things too."

"Such as."

Laura slipped off her soft suede jacket and draped it over the back of the chair Eve had indicated and sat down. "Errands, research, keeping an eye on things. "

"For my father?"

"Mostly. He may be officially retired, but you know he still likes to keep his hand in. He may not be the president's advisor anymore, but a lot of people look to him when they need help." She brushed back her long, jet-black hair and shrugged slightly in a gesture Connor had come to know so well. "It's always something different."

Connor nodded. Her father knew too much about international intelligence gathering and, more importantly, too much about where the bodies were buried to ever be completely out of the "game." "I figured as much. He doesn't really talk about it, but after what happened in the mountain, I guess he feels like he's got to keep trying to clean up the world."

"And I sometimes end up playing Sancho Panza to his Don Quixote," Laura smiled. But it didn't reach all the way to her deep brown eyes. Connor saw the puzzlement and hurt reflected there and flinched away from the challenge of admitting it.

Instead, she kept it light. "I think my father has one up on the Man of La Mancha. Dad knows when the windmills really are monsters that need slaying."

An awkward silence suddenly fell between them, as if a knife had cut the connection. Connor thought it strange that she was suddenly unable to muster up some small talk to fill the gap. And while she wracked her brain, she left an opening for Laura to ask the inevitable question.

"What happened, Connor? It's been weeks and not a word from you." Laura's expression was carefully neutral, her low, resonant voice carrying no hint of remonstrance, no anger, no challenge. Connor desperately wished she had an answer that wouldn't sound absurdly trite. But sitting there looking at Laura, remembering the way her long, thick hair swirled around her, the copper skin of her shoulders in the new light of dawn...Connor had to shake herself to clear a path through those dangerous thoughts.

"I...it isn't that I...look, let's talk about this later on, please."

"That's fine with me. As long as you don't run off again without letting me know why."

"I won't. I promise."

"Since I know you're a woman of your word, I'll rely on it."

Moments later, Eve, Benjamin, and Malcolm came back with the rest of the food. Once they were seated, Eve asked her brother to say grace.

"Dear God, thank you for this food and these people around me right now. These are my friends as well as my family. I thank you for this house we live in and the blessings I receive every day of my life. Amen."

For no reason she could fathom, Connor felt tears pricking at the back of her eyelids as Malcolm completed his simple prayer. Perhaps it was his mention of family. These people were indeed her family. Along with her daughter, Katy, and her great-aunt Jessica, both living in England, these were the core of her life, the human beings who gave it fullness and meaning. These past few months spent alone, she had forgotten that not-so-small truth about herself.

As she looked up from the "amen," she found Laura looking directly at her. Connor swallowed hard and reached for her fork.

Benjamin tasted a couple of healthy bites. "Good Lord, Eve. I had no idea chicken and dumplings could taste this good."

Eve regarded him with a smile. "I don't reckon you eat much chicken and dumplin's, mister senator. You probably get stuck eatin' all that fancy French cookin' they's all so fond of in these parts."

"Are you kidding? I know the location of every diner in the Washington metropolitan area. I keep tabs on when they serve my favorites, and this is one of 'em. Don't suppose you make meat loaf too?"

"You *ought* to have a woman lookin' after yo' needs, a good wife to cook and keep house. What's a fine specimen of man like you doin' livin' in that club Malcolm told me about?"

Benjamin allowed himself a good-humored sigh. "You're probably right, Eve, but I'm a little old to start over again. Besides, my divorce from Connor's mother isn't quite final yet. So I'm not shopping around, if you know what I mean."

"Don't you worry none. I wasn't thinkin' of matchmakin' or somethin' like that. But a man needs home cookin', and you come on by here any time you want. No need to wait to get yo'self invited. If I left that up to my brother, we'd never see anyone."

"That's not true, Eve. Why, just last month we had Fitch and his wife over."

"That was almost three months ago. Now eat up."

For the next few minutes a companionable silence reigned as the five of them tucked in to Eve's marvelous cooking. Then bits of small talk darted back and forth across the table. Benjamin asked after Malcolm's children, who had been strongly encouraged to have an overnight at a cousin's house so that the adults could have a little peace and quiet. Malcolm dutifully reported on their height, grades, and general attitudes. He said his eldest son was starting to give him a little trouble, but Malcolm, who had managed to survive some difficult teen years of his own, was ready for it.

Eve talked about her work at the A.M.E. Church. Laura explained the significance of a hogan to the Navajo culture. Connor briefly outlined the plot of her latest book. Eventually the rhythm of forks on plates slowed to a halt, and each of them declared himself or herself to be absolutely full. Eve stood to clear the table, refusing offers of assistance, and suggested they all go into the parlor, as she called it, in defiance of modern terminology.

It wasn't until they were all seated near the fireplace of the comfortable room, furnished with tapestry-upholstered chairs and sofa to complement the mahogany wainscoting, that Connor finally asked her father about the situation in England. It was obvious within minutes that Laura already knew of the attempted grave robbing and the murdered men left behind. Malcolm, on the other hand, had not heard any of it.

Benjamin briefly explained about the opening of Gwendolyn Broadhurst's grave and the fact that two bodies were discovered in the open site the next morning. Malcolm looked as if he'd swallowed something unpleasant. They all knew there was a great deal more to Gwendolyn's death than anyone supposed, just as they knew it must remain a secret.

"What I don't understand is why you didn't let me know about it right away," Connor griped. "It isn't as if I weren't involved in this."

Her father leaned forward in his chair. "Of course not. And I didn't intend to leave you out of the loop indefinitely. But I was trying to get more details, get a little clearer on what is actually going on. I'm trying to figure out if this is a bizarre coincidence, or whether it has anything to do with the other situation, with what happened on the reservation."

Each of them was silent, thoughtful. It had been over a year now since Connor and Laura had been forced to flee across the Navajo reservation with a killer trailing close behind. First Malcolm had come after them, then Benjamin. They had all converged at the sacred mountain, with Connor injured and Laura a heartbeat away from the next world. Inside that mountain they had seen strange things so strange, in fact, that they were still difficult to fathom. The old Navajo woman, Grandmother Klah, had taught them some of what they needed to learn. And finally Gwendolyn had arrived from England, drawn by a deep psychic connection with her granddaughter. She had come there, already profoundly ill with cancer, and had been granted a way to leave this world and, in a sense, take her body with her.

The rest of them knew it was logically impossible, but they had seen it with their own eyes. And they also knew that no one else could ever be allowed to learn the secret of what lay inside the mountain. A great many people had died because of one psychotic man's lust for power, and although he had been thwarted by Benjamin, there were others equally greedy for supremacy who would try to exploit the secret of the mountain.

As a result, Mrs. Broadhurst's coffin had been secretly filled with stones, sealed, and shipped back to England for burial. Only the ones in this room, and a wise and reticent Navajo tribal cop in Tuba City, were privy to the truth. At least until now. Someone else had now learned that there was no body in that grave.

Connor broke the silence. "What could anyone want with my grandmother's remains? It doesn't make a lot of sense. And why kill two people and leave them there to attract attention?"

Malcolm spoke up. "Usually when a perp leaves his mess right out in front of God and everybody, there's a message in it."

"A message to whom?" Connor asked.

"I'm assuming it's for Gwendolyn's family, which would be you and your dad, Amanda, Katy, and your Aunt Jess."

"But if we don't understand what the hell the message is, then it didn't work very well, did it?"

Laura spoke up. "Perhaps it's not so much a message as it is bait."

Benjamin stared at her for a moment. "You mean someone leaves those bodies and waits to see who turns up to investigate, other than the local constabulary."

"Exactly," she replied. "What better way to draw out whoever's responsible for the empty casket and the whole funeral charade?"

Connor nodded her agreement. "That makes sense. And that might mean we'd be wiser to stay away. But it would seem perfectly normal if family members were concerned about the desecration and they showed up to see what was being done about it." She consulted her father with a glance.

"I agree. But before anyone goes running off to investigate, I should share some other information I've received in the past couple of days. I have people who keep tabs on unusual occurrences around the world.

And the desecration of Gwendolyn's grave, even with the two murders, pales in comparison to some recent news."

"What is it, Dad?"

"A couple of days ago, the son of an old friend of your grandmother's gave a party at his home several miles from Glastonbury, place called Bannister House. His name is Lord William Carlisle. I don't know if you'll remember him or not."

Connor shook her head. "The name seems familiar, but if I've met him, I don't recall anything about it."

"Well, there were about seventy-five or a hundred people there, and somehow, in the midst of this crowd, one of the serving maids was murdered."

Malcolm frowned. "And why does that qualify as bizarre? Murder is restricted to the dead of night in empty houses? People get killed in public places all the time."

"Of course," replied the former senator. "But how many people are stabbed a dozen times and then decapitated within earshot of a hundred people?"

"My God," breathed Connor. The image came as a shock to her, not because it was incomprehensible, but rather because it *wasn't*. As a prosecutor she'd seen crime scenes that left her with nightmares, horrible images that woke her in the night with the sweat of fear soaking the bed sheets. It was partly those images that had finally led her in a different direction entirely, from criminal prosecutor to crime novelist, a profession where she alone would control the outcome.

"It actually happened during the party?" Laura asked, her tone brisk and businesslike.

"Or shortly before it began. Whoever did it had draped something over the body as it hung on a library ladder. And then someone bumped into the ladder, the cloth fell, and there she was, hanging upside down, her feet tied to the top rung."

"But the decapitation," Connor said. "Where was the head?"

Benjamin shook his head. "Don't know and apparently neither do the police. It isn't there, and no one left the premises after the body was found. Lord Carlisle immediately sealed off the grounds and telephoned for the police. More than fifty officers searched every inch of the estate but didn't turn up a single piece of evidence or a likely suspect."

"But the killer could have left before the body was discovered," Connor countered. For years she'd had to stay one step ahead of defense attorneys, which meant searching for the flaws in any theory her investigators presented. "And he could have been several miles away with his 'trophy' before anyone was the wiser."

Laura spoke up. "Is this the connection you feel, Benjamin? That there's something tying this butchery to the opening of Gwendolyn's grave?"

"It seems tenuous at best," he said, nodding. "But when you say 'feel,' that's exactly how I'd put it. I feel something is connected here. Two murdered men in Gwendolyn's grave. Then someone leaves a body in the middle of a reception at Lord Carlisle's home."

"Also a message?" Malcolm interjected.

"A pretty gory one, but, yes, a message of some sort. William is inclined to agree with me. I spoke with him earlier today."

"You say William's father and my grandmother were friends?" Connor asked her father. "And did William himself know the Broadhursts?"

"Yes, he did, although he's younger than I am, probably no more than early fifties. It was his father, James, who was great friends with your grandparents, particularly Gwendolyn. When your grandfather received his knighthood, James Carlisle threw a big party for them. Your mother was a child then."

Connor found it hard to imagine Amanda having ever been anything but full grown and exceedingly temperamental. Besides, even though Amanda had been born in England, her accent had metamorphosed into a curious mélange of Philadelphia O's and Boston long A's, which Amanda no doubt equated with high social standing. Connor put thoughts of her mother aside, thoughts that almost invariably led to opening up old wounds for her father or herself. "Still, Dad, the connection is pretty thin. Grave robbing, even when it turns into a homicide, is pretty far removed from what happened at Lord Carlisle's house. The only connection I see is that William Carlisle knew my grandmother." She paused. "Or is there something else you haven't shared?"

Benjamin looked a little uncomfortable. "When I said that William's father, James, had been close to your grandparents, especially Gwendolyn, I meant that James also shared your grandmother's keen interest in...um...the spiritual realm."

Connor looked at him narrowly. "You don't have to beat around the bush. We all know my grandmother said she was descended from a long line of Celtic witches and that she had some pretty amazing powers of intuition."

Laura, who had had the honor of meeting Gwendolyn Broadhurst, if only too briefly, held up her hand. "I'd call it more than intuition, Connor, and I think you would too."

The room was silent, and Connor fought against the impulse to snap at Laura for broaching the subject with which she was most uncomfortable. She could not deny that what Laura had said was true or that Mrs. Broadhurst had appeared to have remarkable powers of seeing what others could not see and knowing what others could not know. Yet the whole idea was exceptionally discomfiting to Connor, particularly since Mrs. Broadhurst had made it exceedingly clear that Connor was guilty of ignoring her own emerging spiritual intuition, or magical talents, whatever they were supposed to be. Gwendolyn had insisted that Connor would not find it possible to shirk her destiny or her birthright, an assertion she fervently hoped had been nothing more than an old lady's fancy.

"All right," she said, the strain evident in her voice. "Let's assume that Gwendolyn was more than intuitive, and that she practiced these 'arts of the craft' or whatever you want to call it."

"White magic?" Laura ventured.

Connor glared at her. "Or whatever. And let's say for the sake of argument that James Carlisle was doing something along the same lines."

Benjamin nodded. "It would make sense. There are close-knit groups of people who follow the old religions, and she and James may have been part of such a group."

"So assuming that connection, which we can't really confirm at this point," Connor warmed to her role as devil's advocate, "there is a slim possibility that the crime committed at William's house is connected to the opening of Gwendolyn's grave and the two bodies that were left there. But that's just it—slim. You haven't said that William is also involved in these 'spiritual' activities."

Malcolm was watching Benjamin closely. He, too, thought that the former senator had leaped to somewhat tenuous conclusions, and yet he knew that was not Benjamin's style. If anything, the retired spymaster was fastidious in his analysis of any situation. "Is there something else you're not telling us?" Malcolm asked.

"No, but I'm not entirely comfortable playing such an outlandish hunch, and I know my lawyer daughter probably finds this leap of logic a little absurd, but there it is. I know in my gut that something serious is going on, and we're just seeing the tip of it."

Connor didn't entirely disagree. "Assuming your hunch is right, the question is, what can we do about it?"

Malcolm sat forward. "Well, even though your sources are generally better than mine, Benjamin, I still have a little pull in cop world. I once did a law enforcement exchange program with Scotland Yard, spent three weeks there studying their methods and trying not to get underfoot."

"Which is hard for a guy your size," Connor grinned.

Malcolm swatted at her playfully. "Yeah, but sometimes size comes in handy."

"Like when you had to carry me on a stretcher for miles through the desert?" Laura reminded him.

"Well, yeah. But that was no big deal." Laura started to protest, but he quickly continued. "Anyway, I got to know one of the detectives a little bit, gave him a few ideas about a case he ended up solving, and he said if I ever needed a favor to let him know. I've never had any reason to call in that marker, but this might be the time."

Benjamin nodded. "Good, that'll give us more of an idea of what the local CID thinks of the murders at the cemetery."

"CID?" asked Laura. "Remind me what that stands for."

"Criminal Investigations Division," said Benjamin.

"They're more or less analogous to our detective divisions," added Malcolm, "as opposed to uniformed officers."

"My source might be too high up in the hierarchy to get an inside track on the actual investigation without making waves," said Benjamin. "But Malcolm and I can pool our resources and see what we come up with."

"For my part, I think it's time I finally went and settled my grandmother's estate," said Connor. "I've been putting it off because I couldn't face the thought of going back there to her house. I didn't even go after the funeral. Without her there, it's..." Connor's voice trailed off, and she took a deep breath. It still hurt, and she still missed the incredible old lady.

"That's an excellent idea, honey. She left it for you," Benjamin quickly responded. Connor had the distinct impression that he would have suggested the trip if she hadn't. Then she saw in his eyes that there was more.

"What is it, Dad?"

"I want you to keep in mind that this may have more to do with who your grandmother *was* than with who we are or with what happened last year."

"That doesn't make any sense," Connor said, her expression one of puzzlement. "What do you mean by who she *was*? We all know she was an eccentric old lady with a..."

"With what, Connor? I'm not sure you've ever really come to grips with that—or even with your own abilities." Benjamin's expression was a mixture of concern, curiosity, and something else—intensity.

Connor sighed. She hated all this stuff, this insistence on her accepting that in some way she was Gwendolyn's spiritual heir. Yes, Connor had had visions; yes, she'd experienced frustratingly inexplicable events both inside herself and all around her while she'd been in New Mexico. And there was no longer any doubt in her mind that these phenomena were real. But that didn't mean she had to like it or pay any attention to it now that Gwendolyn was gone. Except for the occasional dream, she was sure that whatever connection they'd had was ended when her grandmother went away.

"Dad, I'm not denigrating these 'abilities' you and Laura keep talking about. It's just that I don't want to live my life pursuing that sort of knowledge. I'm not a psychic or whatever they're calling it these days. My grandmother may have been the descendant of a long line of Celtic witches, but that doesn't mean I'm the least bit interested in following in her footsteps. Besides, my mother obviously wasn't tempted in that direction." She saw the corners of Benjamin's mouth twitch. "Well, all right," she admitted with smile, "my mother *can* be a real witch sometimes, but somehow I can't picture her chanting away in an oak grove."

"I think you're confusing witches with Druids," Laura said, chuckling softly.

"Probably, but it's all pretty much the same to me. What I don't understand is what my father is trying to get at."

Benjamin shrugged. "Nothing specific. I simply think you have to be more open to understanding the truth about your grandmother and what sort of influence she may have wielded."

"Influence over whom? To what purpose?"

"I don't think there's any way to explain it to you, and, to be honest, I don't entirely understand it myself. But she led me to believe that there were facts about her you would someday need to know and that she would make sure you learned those facts. I'm assuming that's why she left the house and all her personal belongings to you."

"Why didn't you mention this before?"

"You weren't ready to revisit the past. You made that clear on several occasions, starting right after the funeral. And then you traveled and worked on a new book. I knew that when the time was right, you'd go."

"And now I guess it is." Having made the decision, Connor's voice took on its faintly prosecutorial tone. "So tomorrow evening I'll fly to London, hire a car, and . . ." She paused, her expression that of a person who's just seen an idea emerge. "I'd decided to skip the London Book Fair this year, even though my publisher has been ragging on me to put in an appearance. If I do that first, then it would appear I had a reason to go to England *aside* from investigating the cemetery incident in St. Giles."

Benjamin nodded. "If someone is that interested in our family's reaction to the grave robbing, the fact that you're carrying on business as usual might make them think that we're just as baffled as everyone else about the empty casket and have no idea what to do about it."

"At least it won't seem as if I'm rushing to the scene to investigate. But I can promise you that when I get down to St. Giles, if there's anything to find, I'll find it."

Benjamin favored his daughter with a warm smile. "I have no doubt of that. But I don't like the idea of you going alone. We have no idea what is motivating these outrages. And if there *is* something significant brewing, it might stir the pot too much if I show up there too. You have good reasons—the Book Fair and settling your grandmother's estate—but I don't."

The silence was heavy with unspoken issues, no one voicing the obvious solution. Connor stared straight ahead at nothing in particular. Laura studied her cuticles. Finally, Benjamin grew impatient. "Connor, I don't know what's been bothering you lately or what's going on in your private life. That's none of my business. But you said that you and Laura are friends, and she and Malcolm here are the only two people in the world I would count on to stand by you in some sort of emergency."

"You think I need someone to protect me from the bad guys?" she snapped, immediately regretting how puerile she sounded.

Benjamin took a deep breath. "No, I'm not assuming there's any situation you couldn't handle, nor am I assuming that any such situation will arise. But I happen to know, after a lot of years out in the field, it was a damn good thing to have someone watching my back. That's all I'm saying. I want Laura to be there to watch your back."

Connor swung her gaze to Laura. "What do you think about all this? It isn't as if you have to take orders from my father. You don't really work for him anymore...or *do* you?"

Laura's warm brown eyes locked with the clear blue ones challenging her from across the coffee table. "I don't have to be ordered to do what's right," she said softly, but with a definite edge to her tone. "And as long as we're on the subject, I don't have to be ordered to look out for someone I love."

With that startling statement, Laura Nez rose from her chair and left the room. The next noise they heard was the front door slamming.

Malcolm looked over at his dearest friend and let out a long sigh. "You know, Connor, you really have a way with women."

Chapter Four

Truth will come to light;
murder cannot be hid long.
—William Shakespeare
The Merchant of Venice, Act 2, Scene 2

England
County of Somerset

Lord William Carlisle sighed deeply as he firmly closed the door behind Detective Chief Inspector Foulsham. He felt as though he had virtually lived with the crew of police officers for weeks on end. Not that he begrudged them a chance to solve the hideous murder that had taken place in William's ancestral home, but so far Foulsham had gotten nowhere with his investigations and questions and searches. Although William had allowed the police to set up an incident room on the property in what had once been a large stable and had cooperated by providing detailed lists of guests, servants, catering staff, and so forth, not one solid clue had been unearthed to explain the death of Patricia Frome. A thorough investigation into the young woman's background had revealed nothing of particular interest. If anything, it would seem that her gruesome death had been the highlight of an almost depressingly mundane and colorless existence.

Patricia, aged twenty-two at the time of her death, had been an average child of average suburban London parents who had little to say of her beyond, "She was always a good girl, no larking about with the boys and such, never gave us no trouble, did Trish." Further interviews with what few friends Patricia Frome could claim yielded no fresh insight. She had no steady boyfriend, although she visited the local pub on occasion along with other people employed at Bannister House. She had been hired a year earlier through an employment agency and, despite her less than focused attitude, had somehow managed to perform adequately under the critical eyes of Mrs. Hutchins, the Carlisle's formidable housekeeper.

While Nicholas Foulsham found the circumstances of Patricia's life frustratingly devoid of any deviations from routine that might have explained her death, William was saddened by the girl's colorless existence. To have lived more than two decades of one's life and left not a single deep impression on anyone. To have begun and ended without anything of note happening in between. Well, not precisely, he thought, for at some point in her latter days, Patricia had met the person who killed her. But did she know her killer before she died, or did someone take her life so quickly she never even knew who had done it or why? The possibility that the culprit had been among his own guests or a member of his staff was more than distasteful for William. He was a man of intense scruples who prided himself on dealing honorably with every human being no matter their station. He also felt a strong protectiveness toward those in his employ. It was, he knew, an obsolete attitude, no longer justifiable in this day and age, but there it was. Patricia Frome had died under his roof, under what should have been his protection.

Which brought him to another consideration: the awareness that he had heretofore considered Bannister House and the grounds upon which it sat to be sacrosanct, immune to the evils that pervaded the world outside its borders. Just as his father and grandfather before him, William was a master of the white arts, the magic of light and faith handed down through his family for generations. And this power, nurtured within the family line, had always protected those within their influence. Now someone had breached not only the physical defenses of Bannister House, but the metaphysical defenses of the Carlisle family as well. William surmised there was more to the grisly murder than the taking of one innocent girl's life. The time and place had been chosen for maximum effect, maximum publicity, and minimum subtlety. Someone either harbored a serious grudge against the Carlisle family, and wanted to inflict extreme embarrassment, or, more likely, this was but the opening gambit in a *danse macabre* for which the perpetrator was calling the tune. William had no desire to join the waltz, but he doubted he had much choice.

"Woolgathering, my love, or trying to work out the concerns of the world?" Ellen's voice startled him from his reverie in front of the fireplace in his private study. Unlike much of Bannister House, which was meticulously furnished in accordance with traditional expectations and historical accuracy, this was his room, his refuge. Some of the pieces were antique, but they'd been chosen for utility and comfort rather than to satisfy nitpicking interior designers. The old leather chairs, cracked in dozens of places, the massive writing desk with a welter of scrapes and stains on its smooth leather top, a faded oriental carpet worn almost through to the floorboards in spots, and the overstuffed footstool that didn't particularly match anything—he loved this room.

He looked up at his wife's smiling face. "Trying to work out something...but whether it concerns the world or not is a matter of conceit, I should think."

"I've never known you to act on conceit, William, so I can't imagine you starting now, even with this decapitation business in our library." Ellen tucked a lock of dark blond hair behind one ear. "That poor girl," she said, "and no one even seeming to care much that she's gone."

He reached for her hand. "We care, darling. And that counts for something."

Ellen sat down across from him, perching on the old footstool. "Yes, I suppose it does. But I'm rather more concerned as to why this happened, and—"

"Why it happened *here*," he finished the sentence for her.

"Exactly. And I'm furious that someone used that girl to convey some sort of warning or, even worse, a challenge to us."

"So you see it that way too."

"Of course," she nodded. "I know we haven't had much chance to discuss it, but I wanted to leave you alone with your thoughts, and let us each come to our own conclusions."

William frowned. "I can't say I've reached any definitive conclusions. It's all too vague. Still, we're not the only ones who see more to this than a bizarre murder."

Ellen looked at him sharply. "Surely not that Foulsham chap, with all his police procedures and time-line charts." They'd both been fascinated as well as amused with the officer's heavy reliance on diagrams, graphs, and data analysis to evaluate the possible suspects in the crime.

"No, of course not. I think he's got it into his head that this is some sort of psychotic episode, a one-off. And I'm not going to try diverting him from that course, at least not yet. No, the newly interested party is Benjamin Hawthorne."

"Gwen's son-in-law, the one who works in the American government?"

"Yes. Although he's semiretired now. Or at least he doesn't hold an active post in the government. Still, he's got contacts everywhere, and he heard what's going on."

"You've heard from him then?"

"He rang me up this morning while you were in the village. Very polite, very subtle. Didn't come right out and say anything specific, as if he were afraid of wiretaps and whatnot."

"Probably an old habit," she smiled.

"True, but I found myself thinking that perhaps he was right to be cautious."

"Surely you don't see some international plot in all this," she asked.

"Not precisely in the sense of political goings-on," William said. "But this situation does make me think in terms of conspiracy. And Benjamin has already guessed that there may be some connection with the incident in St. Giles."

"The opening of Gwen's grave."

"Hmm," he nodded. "I have the impression he wanted to explain to me about the stones in her casket."

"I wish someone would explain it. I take it he wasn't forthcoming, though."

"No, but he did mention that Gwen's granddaughter would be arriving shortly to settle up the estate."

"Interesting...what was the child's name?"

"Connor. And hardly a child, Ellen. She's over forty now, I should think. Only ten or twelve years younger than we are."

"Of course, you're right. How odd that we tend to get people fixed in our minds at a certain age and forget they're growing older right along with the rest of us."

"Indeed. And she's led a full life, though not an entirely happy one."

"True. The letters we've had from Gwen's sister, Jessica, alluded to some sort of tragedy, and somehow it was all related to Gwen's suddenly dashing off to America and never coming back."

William frowned slightly. "That too is something I hope Connor will clear up for us."

"Odd name for a woman," observed Ellen. "Isn't her given name something different?"

"Lydia, I believe, after her great grandmother, but it's not a name that pleased her, I imagine. Connor is her middle name."

"'Lydia' is a bit old-fashioned," she agreed. "And I've read a couple of her books. They're excellent, but very...unrelentingly realistic, I should say. Not the sort of books a 'Lydia' would write. Or at least that's what I imagine *she* thinks."

"Perhaps so. But, names aside, there's likely a great deal more to this young woman than meets the eye. At least I'm quite sure Gwendolyn thought so. She told me more than once that Connor was her true heir."

"What about Gwen's daughter, Amanda?" asked Ellen.

"I suppose the gift skips a generation sometimes. At least it appeared to have in Amanda's case. Gwendolyn was saddened that her daughter had turned into a somewhat bitter woman and ended up with a drinking problem and a family that more or less keeps its distance from her."

"Didn't Jessica say something about Connor's lover having been killed?"

"Yes. And although she didn't share all the details, Gwendolyn confided in her before she left that Connor had taken it very, very hard and that Amanda had been no help at all."

Ellen lifted an eyebrow. "I seem to recall Gwendolyn mentioning that Amanda was always obsessively concerned with appearances. I can't imagine having a daughter who turned out to be a lesbian quite suited her."

William smiled. "No, I don't think it did. Gwendolyn always said that Amanda often failed to identify true substance. But I know Gwendolyn could not have cared less about her granddaughter's preferences in the bedroom. From what I understand of Benjamin, he too is only concerned with his daughter's happiness. He also mentioned that she would be traveling here with a companion, a Miss Laura Nez."

"If I'm not mistaken, that's a Native American surname...Navajo, I believe."

"You never cease to amaze me, my love, with your storehouse of knowledge."

"I've read Tony Hillerman," she said with a grin. "And I found the books quite educational. We sometimes forget that we're not the only ones with a long history of sacred spiritual traditions that don't quite fit the Judeo-Christian norm."

"And we're not the only ones who have secrets either," he replied, his expression thoughtful. "I'm hoping Connor will trust us enough to explain where our Gwendolyn got to on her trip to the States."

"And I'm hoping she'll trust herself enough to help us figure out what's going on here."

"If she's half the mage her grandmother believed, Connor Hawthorne could put a stop to whatever is going on here and restore the balance," William said, his expression brightening for a moment. "On the other hand, if she's completely resistant, she could be a perfect pawn for the others."

"Do you really suppose it's come to that after all these years? That evil is rearing its ugly head once more?"

He shook his head. "I don't care to assume any such thing, but if—and I'm only saying *if* all this is related—the opening of Gwen's grave and the two murders in the graveyard, and the murder of Patricia Frome..." his voice trailed off.

"Then someone is orchestrating it, and perhaps someone is trying to discover a way to attack our circle."

"But that in itself isn't unusual, Ellen. You know as well as I do that there is always a seeking of equilibrium between Light and Dark. The pendulum swings both ways before it returns to center. The question is, why now? And why in this way? I can't help but think that someone has come into possession of knowledge that will prove dangerous to us. They seem to know that Gwendolyn possessed the key to much that we hold sacred. Why else open her grave? And why make a public spectacle of cold-blooded killing?"

Ellen stood and took her husband's hand. "If what you suspect is true, then we shall have to be especially vigilant and perhaps prepare to convene the circle. Gwendolyn never did anything without a good reason. If she chose not to leave us any hints about where the key could be found, then she must have had good reason. Perhaps she foresaw some of what is now happening and planned in advance that our defensive strategy would take on a different format than what we're accustomed to."

"Or that it would involve different people," he said. "Connor Hawthorne, for example."

Ellen sighed. "And someone else, I think. Someone else has emerged among our enemies. But I find myself sorely wishing I were as wise as Gwendolyn Broadhurst, bless her soul, wherever she is. I do wonder if perhaps this Laura Nez is somehow destined to be instrumental in all this. Do you know if Miss Nez is Connor's paramour as well as companion?"

"Benjamin didn't say, and I didn't like to ask. But I don't think we should assume anything. Jessica said Connor had taken the murder of her lover the year before last very hard. Laura Nez may be some sort of bodyguard for all we know."

"Did Benjamin say when they were coming?"

"Next day or two, I would imagine. Once again I had the sense he was being a little cagey about mentioning specifics over an open line."

"That reminds me, William: You should check your E-mail. You've got two encrypted messages waiting."

"You could have opened them, darling," he shrugged.

"What, and discover that you're having a torrid affair with a film star?" she laughed.

"You know perfectly well that no self-respecting film star would have me," he retorted, pulling her into his lap. "And besides, whatever in the world would I do without you, my love?"

For a few moments, Lord and Lady Carlisle, nestled in the depths of the high-back wing chair, engaged in some spontaneous affection of the sort teenagers once called necking. But the sound of steps in the hall jerked them back to reality, and Ellen quickly arose from the chair and smoothed her hair. Romance was delightful after more than twenty-five years of marriage, but even so, she retained a sense of propriety about public displays of affection.

Their butler and general factotum, Gilmore, arrived to announce a visitor. "Lord Fenwycke is in your study waiting to have a word, m'lord."

William suppressed a smile. Despite the arrival of the twenty-first century, his manservant clung rigidly to the old ways. A simple "sir" would not do when addressing "his lordship," and no amount of coaxing would change the elderly man's mind. His sense of proper form had also been impressed upon the entire household staff and not one of them would risk Gilmore's wrath by refusing to follow his example.

"Thank you, Gilmore. I'll attend to Gerald directly." He turned to Ellen as Filmore melted away into the hall. "I can anticipate the reason for this visit," he frowned.

"An appeal to your better nature," she quipped, "or, more precisely, your pocketbook?"

"Rumor abounds that dear Gerald has been most foolish in his business dealings."

"Surely he can't have gone through all of the Fenwycke money."

He shrugged. "Hard to believe considering the way his father built up the family's enterprises, but the word is that he's been borrowing heavily and has Haslemere mortgaged to the hilt."

"I imagine Gillian has had a hand in that," Ellen retorted. "Anne Waverly told me the other day that the woman's accounts at dressmakers are nothing short of obscene."

William smiled at his wife, struck yet again by the sparks of amber light in her steel-gray eyes. "Then I am blessed to have a wife who manages to look stunning without spending a small fortune on silks and ruffles."

Ellen poked him playfully. "If I didn't know you better, my love, I'd say you were a regular chauvinist."

"Hardly possible, now is it? You never let me pay for a blessed thing you buy, even when I insist. Perhaps I should be even more grateful that my wife is a veritable wizard at working the stock and bonds markets."

"Hush, you silly old thing. And go deal with Gerald. What are you going to tell him?"

"Well, I'm not going to bail him out. I backed a loan for him three years ago, and I daresay I'll be stuck with that as it is. No, I think I'm going to offer him a different kind of help, more on the lines of solid advice on how to get himself out of this jam."

"People in need rarely take well to advice from those who have a lot of the ready but won't come across with it, darling."

"That's as may be," he said firmly, "but that's all Gerald is going to get today." He paused. "And speaking of nuisances, if you see that so-called journalist Clarence Newbury around here again, have him thrown off the property. Caught him skulking about the stables trying to get a look into the incident room."

"Wasn't he here the night of the murder?"

"Yes, and you'd have thought he'd seen enough then. I know I did." William stalked off in a mood of righteous indignation, and Ellen almost felt sorry for poor Gerald.

Chapter Five

A naked thinking heart, that makes no show,
Is to a woman but a kind of ghost.
—John Donne
"The Blossom"

Connor walked into La Madeleine and immediately spotted Laura sitting at a table near the fireplace. Despite the emotional ambivalence just being near her caused, Connor had to admit that Laura would stand out in any crowd with her long, luxuriously thick dark hair and a face that just about anyone would call beautiful—and slightly exotic. And that was only one of the aspects of being around Laura that made Connor so damned crazy.

At that instant Laura looked up as though she felt herself being observed. Her eyes met Connor's, and a smile made a brief appearance, then vanished. Clearly, Laura was as unsure of Connor's feelings as Connor herself. Which was absurd, really. A grown woman, survivor of some of the worst that life had to offer, and she couldn't come to terms with her emotions where Laura Nez was concerned.

"You're right on time," Laura said, without glancing at her watch.

"I didn't think visiting my mother would take much time, and I was right."

Laura frowned. "She hasn't changed, has she?"

"You mean about me or in just being herself? Actually, in either case, the answer is no, she hasn't changed at all. If her looks are any indication, her drinking is even worse. And now she's added my father to her list of people to hate, along with my grandmother for deserting her, and me for being, and I quote, 'a goddamned queer,' and humiliating her, besmirching the family name, and..." Connor stopped in mid-sentence, her voice choked with emotion.

Laura put her hand over Connor's. "You didn't really expect much to have changed, though, did you?"

Connor sighed and blinked back the glimmer of tears. "No, I suppose not when I thought about it rationally. But there's always that part of you that wants things to be different even when you know perfectly well that nothing will ever change for some people." She squeezed Laura's hand, then pulled away. "I guess I'd better order something. We should be leaving for the airport before long."

"I already ordered. Since it's Sunday, they serve brunch late." She motioned to the square wooden block on the table. "Two French country breakfasts, two café au laits, and this other orange juice on the table is yours."

Connor smiled. "Why is it you seem to know me better than I do sometimes?"

"Maybe because I do," Laura answered. "Though obviously I don't know everything, or your sudden departure wouldn't have surprised me so much."

"I left you a note," Connor retorted, unable to keep the defensiveness out of her voice. The fact that Laura didn't respond made the excuse sound all the more lame. They both sat for several moments in silence, sipping orange juice and listening to the hissing of the fireplace and the sloshing of the big water wheel on the other side of the restaurant.

"All right, maybe the note wasn't really adequate."

One of Laura's eyebrows, perhaps the most expressive part of her face, went skyward. "I don't think there's any note you could possibly write that would have been adequate under those circumstances. And in this case I believe the exact wording was, 'I'm sorry, Laura, but I need more time. It's hard to explain, and I do care about you, but I'm begging you to understand that I can't make this kind of commitment, at least not now.' Does that sound familiar?"

Connor was taken aback. "That's all I said?"

"Yes, that would be the extent of the explanation for your leaving before dawn one morning and not calling me for months."

"You knew I had to finish the corrections on my book, that I wanted to get a place in Santa Fe."

Connor was pleading for an out, appealing to Laura's instinctive generosity of spirit, but apparently Laura wasn't giving any quarter this time. "Yes, I knew all that, but I also had the impression that you and I were falling in love."

There it was, out in the open, and the words hung in the air between them.

"You certainly don't mince words, do you?" Connor said, torn between the urge to run out the door and an equally strong impulse to put her arms around Laura and beg to be forgiven.

"Not when the subject is this important. All I want is the truth, Connor. I've been hurt, and so have you. When I lost Jocelyn to cancer, I grieved for a long time. And when Ariana was murdered, you needed time to heal. I understood that. You went away to Europe for six months, and I didn't hear a word from you. I didn't even dare hope you had those feelings for me. But when you came back to New Mexico, you came back to *me*. And the day I turned around and saw you standing in the door of the hogan, I felt...well, my old grandmother would have called it 'feeling your heart fly with the eagles.' I'd call it sheer joy."

Connor could not meet Laura's intense gaze, and she found herself staring at the beads of moisture on the glass of orange juice, trying to formulate words to explain what she'd done, and why. Not for the first time she wondered how a best-selling author could be completely bereft of words when they were most needed. And with that uncanny knack for mind reading, Laura said, "It doesn't matter if all the words are exactly right, Connor. What matters is that you tell me how you feel, from the heart, not from that brilliant head of yours."

Connor almost opened her mouth but was granted a momentary reprieve as the waiter dashed up and plunked down two plates and two enormous, soup-bowl-size cups of café au lait. Reclaiming the wooden block, the waiter asked whether they needed anything else, didn't wait for an answer, and dashed off again.

Neither of them spoke. Connor reached for the coffee, thought better of it, and pulled her hand back.

"The truth is that what I feel scares the hell out of me."

Laura was silent, digesting the revelation. "Okay, that's honest. But do you mind telling me first what it is you feel, and second, why it scares you? Then maybe I—or we—can deal with it."

Looking into Laura's eyes, Connor began to believe that she could be honest, that perhaps, just perhaps, she could be her true self and Laura would actually understand. This was fairly new ground for her. In some ways Connor knew she had not always been completely open with Ariana because Ariana was so vulnerable, so sensitive, so easily hurt. Or at least that's how Connor had always perceived her. Not until much later did Connor truly understand Ariana's fears and dreams, the same fears and dreams that helped destroy her. Laura, on the other hand, was not a woman who would ever be dependent or irrationally jealous or given to flights of fancy. No, she wanted the truth, even if it hurt, even if it were unpleasant as hell. And she wouldn't cave in and die of disappointment. If Connor didn't want her, Laura would walk away with her dignity intact and go on with her life. That realization was a great relief in some incomprehensible way. And Connor felt something inside her shift.

"All right," she said. "I'll tell you everything, but would you mind if we ate our breakfast first? I just realized I'm starving."

Laura was clearly taken aback for an instant. Then she shrugged and even mustered one of her patented smiles. "Deal. And I'm hungry too. Besides, I figure if I finish my potato galette first, I can have yours."

It took less than ten minutes for the two hungry women to finish off their excellent breakfasts. Popping the last morsel of buttery croissant into her mouth, Connor heaved a satisfied sigh and pushed away her plate. Laura sat back in her chair and waited. Connor knew it would be easier to direct her comments to the coffee cup in front of her, but once she'd made up her mind, she didn't shirk the difficulties.

Looking Laura right in the eyes, she said, "I guess you know I love you."

This obviously wasn't what Laura was expecting to hear, because, for the first time since she'd known her, Connor saw that she was completely speechless. She decided to take advantage of the lack of interruption. "And I suppose you also have at least guessed that being in love, caring this much for another human being, is what terrifies me, because I don't think I could stand to go through what I went through with Ariana."

"You mean because she died and left you, or because she was unfaithful to you at the end?"

"Both."

"And you can't help thinking I could also hurt you in some way, leave you or cheat on you or—"

"No, that isn't it, not really, but—"

"But what? Those are your fears, and if loving me is frightening you, then the logical explanation is that you predict a painful outcome."

"But I don't think that of you."

Laura's voice was deceptively gentle. "So you've said. But you also didn't believe Ariana would ever betray, and she did. So now you believe you have no way of realistically predicting anyone's behavior. You assume that you're prone to being gullible and don't want to be made a fool of or plunged into mourning ever again. Does that about cover the whole gamut of objections, Ms. Hawthorne?"

Connor, her expression one of abject misery, could only nod her agreement. Laura's tone had become a shade sarcastic, and Connor knew, as only an attorney who has been on the losing side can know, that her arguments were about to be annihilated in the full-blown double whammy of Laura Nez's logical mind and passionate spirit.

"Then let me set you straight on a few points. First and foremost, I'm not Ariana, nor am I saying anything against her. I couldn't compete with a dead, and therefore marginally martyred, ex-fashion model, so I'm not going to try. I'm me, Connor. Do you get that? I'm the person I've claimed to be since the beginning. I give as much or more as I receive. I don't make myself a burden, nor do I want to be with anyone who does. I don't necessarily believe in fate, but I do believe that when you recognize a soul mate, you don't screw around wondering if it's the right thing to do. We're both smart enough to acknowledge our feelings, and since you've said it, let me add my vote. I love you too, Connor Hawthorne, and I'll be damned if I'll let you wallow in all this fear and keep us from having one hell of a good time together."

Laura ended her brief tirade, which, for all its having been delivered in a low voice, had lost none of its impact. She sat back, eyes blazing with a mixture of emotions—anger, passion, desire, and even perhaps a hint of fear. Connor understood all of them, especially the fear. She didn't know if she could withstand any more loss in her life. She wrapped her fingers tightly around her coffee cup.

"I'm sorry," was all she could manage.

After several seconds of silence, Laura reached for Connor's hand once more, unfazed by the curious glances of the elderly couple at the next table. "Don't apologize to me, Connor. Part of this is my fault anyway. I thought when you showed up in New Mexico last summer that you'd conquered all your demons, so I didn't look closely enough. I was too busy being incredibly happy. Besides, you must know I'd forgive you just about anything." She paused. "Anything but not being true to yourself and honest with me. What I want to know right now is if you're willing to let the past go and give us a chance at a future together."

Connor released her death grip on the cup and placed her hand on top of Laura's, clasping it between her own. "I should have talked to you instead of running. But the night before I left, I woke up in a cold sweat. We were back in the desert, after you got shot. And all I could think about was how afraid I'd been then, that you were going to die. You see...it was really then that I realized there was something happening between us, something really remarkable. And you were bleeding to death right in front of me, and it seemed as if right at the moment I was beginning to feel something for you, I was going to lose you, just as I'd lost Ariana. Death was going to deprive me of any chance of happiness. And I knew there'd be nothing but this empty hole inside me that nothing would ever really fill. So we said good-bye at the airport, and I went looking for...something."

"I know that, Connor. I also knew that you hadn't had enough time to grieve for Ariana, to make peace with what happened between the two of you before she died. I didn't begrudge you those months, not for a moment. But I did miss you."

"I was pretty sure I was missing you too. And once I'd spent all that time wandering around the world, working and thinking and grieving, I sort of forgot that horrible sensation of paranoia over being hurt, and I came straight back—to you."

"But you'd buried the fear," Laura prodded gently.

"I guess I did. But then that nightmare brought it all back. And when I looked at you the next morning lying there asleep, so alive, so beautiful...I felt as if my world could shatter in an instant. So I ran away, and I couldn't even let myself think about why I'd done it. I just buried myself in work twelve hours a day and—"

"Tried to go it alone."

Connor nodded miserably.

"But don't you see that life is all about cycles of winning and losing, and even when there are no guarantees, we have to keep reaching for happiness where we find it?"

"I used to think that, before my lover was stabbed to death and someone planted a bomb in my home and then tried to kill both of us, and shot you, and you came so close to dying, and—"

"Whoa there, woman," Laura said with an ironic smile blossoming on her face. "Considering everything that's happened to us, isn't it about time you admitted that we're both lucky to be alive, and maybe we ought to take advantage of *that* fact?"

For a long beat, Connor said nothing. Then, with the warmth of Laura's hand in hers and the love in Laura's eyes penetrating her heart, Connor felt something inside her give way, break loose, as if a long pent-up river of emotion had been liberated. Tears flowed down her cheeks. Out of the corner of her eye, she saw the female half of the elderly couple lean even closer, trying to make sense of this "scene" at the neighboring table. If she leaned much more, she would topple right out of her chair and into Connor's lap. Somehow the woman's sheer nosiness tickled Connor. And as sheer joy bubbled up inside her, the last barriers were washed away. She turned and looked the conversational intruder right in the eye. "Isn't it wonderful?" she asked. "My girlfriend just proposed to me, and I think I'm going to say yes." The expression on the old busybody's face was priceless, and Connor's mirth became joy, and her joy turned to laughter.

Laura grinned, regarded her with something akin to awe. "Gee, when you let go, you really let go, don't you?"

Connor got herself under control, but didn't bother to lower her voice. "I suppose I do. Amanda always said I was stubborn, but once I make up my mind...Now, what do you say we go to England and investigate some murders, some witchcraft, and a castle or two?"

Leaving their breakfast companions positively speechless, Connor and Laura strolled out the door, arm in arm.

W

The next few hours were spent in hasty preparation to depart. Benjamin had booked seats on the evening flight to London, which meant that, given the time difference, they would arrive about ten hours later. They would land at Heathrow early Monday morning.

Laura knocked on the door of Connor's suite at the Georgetown Inn shortly after three o'clock. Connor answered, and experienced more than a slight twinge of desire as Laura walked in, clad in her favorite ensemble of dark jeans, low-heeled boots, and a soft leather jacket. Her long hair was braided and fell down her back. Sterling silver and turquoise earrings dangled from her earlobes. Over her white turtleneck lay a stunning miniature squash-blossom necklace, handcrafted in silver, lapis, and gold. Laura noted Connor's fascination with the necklace. "Grandmother Klah gave it to me several years ago," she said, referring to the ancient Navajo medicine woman who had been both mentor and savior to Laura. "I don't know why I haven't worn it before this, but she said I would know when the time was right. Apparently it is."

"It's almost as lovely as you are," Connor whispered, struck almost dumb by the intensity of her feelings for this woman.

"As Eliza Doolittle once said, 'If you're on fire, show me.' "

And Connor did just that, closing the distance between them in two long strides.

A few moments later, Connor said somewhat breathlessly, "Since when did you start quoting Lerner and Loew in casual conversation?"

"Since I first saw a musical when I was almost twenty years old. And I figure if someone has gone to all the trouble of coming up with a perfect line, why not use it?"

Connor grinned. "I can see the logic in that, but don't expect me to start playing Professor Higgins to your Eliza."

"You mean you won't teach me to act like a proper lai-dy when we goes to England, perfesser?" said Laura, in a perfectly horrible rendition of a Cockney accent.

Connor laughed. "There isn't a thing in this world that I could teach you. You're perfect in every way."

"I think that's overkill, Ms. Hawthorne. As an author you should know better."

"Humor me, Eliza."

$$\mathcal{W}$$

Laura and Connor took the elevator to the lobby level. Having spied a rare parking place on the street beside the Georgetown Inn, Connor had slotted her Lexus into the tight space rather than parking in the underground garage. She and Laura didn't have a great deal of luggage, so there was no need for a bellman and a cart.

As they emerged from the inn, a strange tableau confronted them. Crouched beside Connor's car, a man in ragged jeans and a denim jacket had his hands over his head, attempting to ward off the blows of a furled umbrella wielded by an indignant little old man in a tweed suit.

Instinctively, Connor dropped her luggage and darted toward the car with Laura right behind her. The elderly man saw her coming and stepped back abruptly. The one who had been crouching beside the car, and who, on closer inspection, was much younger than she'd originally thought, took the opportunity to escape, roughly shoving between Connor and Laura before either could get a grip on him.

They both turned, and Laura seriously considered giving chase as he broke into a dead run, but a voice behind them delayed her response. "Terribly sorry, ladies, for not having collared the delinquent." The accent was crisp and undeniably Irish. Connor and Laura swung around to face the diminutive gentleman who stood beside the car, one hand on his umbrella, which now stood at approximately parade rest.

"What exactly was he doing?" Connor asked, puzzled by the man's cheerful demeanor.

"I daresay he was trying to make off with your lovely automobile," said the man, "at least that's what it appeared—the way he was monkeying about with the door there." Laura looked closely and could indeed see fresh scratches on the paint.

"And you decided to intervene?" Laura asked, with the barest hint of incredulity. In her experience, urban dwellers did not become actively involved in thwarting car thefts, other than perhaps using their cell phones to dial 911. Besides, she doubted if this man could claim a full five feet. He wasn't exactly the hero type.

"Thought it was my duty really," he said, appearing puzzled at her skepticism. "Can't let someone get away with crime in broad daylight, right in front of witnesses, now can you?"

"It happens rather frequently here," Connor said. "But I should thank you for coming to the rescue, so to speak."

"Not at all," he said, cocking his head to one side in a curiously bird-like gesture, as if studying them both. "Damsels in distress are my speciality. And now, if you'll excuse me, I'd best be getting on."

"Wait," said Laura, stepping obliquely in front of him. "We haven't even gotten your name. I'm Laura Nez, and this is Connor Hawthorne."

She knew Connor would recognize the strategy. The man might

refuse to simply give his name when asked, pleading to remain anonymous for his good deed. But by offering their own names first, Laura made it difficult for him to refuse without seeming exceptionally rude. And her ploy worked.

The man stopped in his tracks, lifted his hat an inch above his head to reveal a shiny bald island of skin surrounded by white fringe, looking for all the world like a monk's tonsure. "The name's O'Rourke, ladies, Sean O'Rourke. And if I may ever be of assistance, it would be a pleasure. Good day to you both." He skipped nimbly around Laura and was out of sight around the corner in a heartbeat.

"What was that all about?" Laura asked as she started back toward the luggage.

"He was a little odd, wasn't he? But it's probably just what he said...some hophead wanted a car and Mr. O'Rourke decided to play Good Samaritan."

But Laura thought the expression on Connor's face belied the certainty in her tone. "Since when did leprechauns take up law enforcement?"

Connor shook her head, wanting to brush off the incident. "I guess since the INS started letting them visit."

"Or since you decided to go to England," Laura reminded her. When Connor didn't rise to the bait, Laura decided to keep her suspicions to herself. "Want to pop the trunk so we can put the luggage in the car? It's getting late."

Chapter Six

In tragic life, God wot,
No villain need be!
Passions spin the plot:
We are betray'd by what is false within.
—George Meredith
Modern Love, 43rd Sonnet

England
County of Somerset

Gerald Fenwycke's foul mood was not helped in the least by the appearance of Conrad Thackeray in the drawing room at Haslemere when he returned home. The source of his mood could be traced directly to his conversation with William Carlisle. The superior, snide bastard had as much as told him that he, Gerald, was a damn fool for having squandered his inheritance and assets on high-risk stock deals, tenuous ventures, race horses, and his wife's shopping habits. On top of it all, William had flatly refused him a loan or any other assistance. Even an appeal to their familial relationship had not swayed the balance.

"As much as it would pain me to see you lose everything, Gerald," he'd said, "maybe it would do you and Gillian some good to experience life in the real world. You're a smart man, and you have a good head for business when you apply yourself. I suggest you sit down with your wife and devise ways to cut your expenses. You can't keep on paying a staff and operating Haslemere as if it were the self-sufficient fiefdom it was 200 years ago."

Gerald hadn't waited to hear the rest of his cousin's advice. It was all he could do not to yank a sword off one of the walls and cut off the man's head. He shivered as the memory of Patricia Frome's body reasserted itself. No, he didn't really mean he would behead someone, nothing so grotesque as that, but it would have been nice to knock him right on his backside.

And now, on top of everything else, he arrived to find not the comfort of hearth and home and wife, but the smirking countenance of Sir Conrad, who was clearly enjoying the fawning attentions of Gerald's wife. Frankly, it was just about the last straw.

"So what brings you here, Thackeray?" he asked without the slightest pretense of courtesy.

"Gerald!" his wife protested. "You've left your manners elsewhere, I see."

"And you've left your discretion in the same place," he retorted angrily. "Now what the devil is he doing here?"

"If you must know, I invited Sir Conrad to talk over a business proposition he happened to mention the other night during the party."

Gerald's eyes narrowed. "What sort of proposition, Thackeray? It had better not have anything to do with selling this house or my land. If that's your intention, then you can just clear off now. And you can leave my wife the hell out of it. Don't think I can't see what you're playing at."

A trace of anger flitted across Thackeray's face but was instantly replaced by as pleasant an expression as the man was capable of producing. "Now see here, old man, no reason to get all in a dither or impugn the character of your lovely wife."

"My wife is no concern of yours," Gerald snapped. "Unless there's more going on here than meets the eye."

Thackeray ignored Gerald's outburst completely. "I'm not here to ask you to sell me Haslemere; I quite see that you couldn't bear to part with the place. No, what I had in mind is a bit more temporary and, I should think, extremely profitable for you."

Against his better judgment, the word *profitable* caught Gerald's attention, but he had no intention of appearing anxious. Instead of answering, he went to the tantalus that sat on a long mahogany console table and selected a cut-glass decanter. The sterling silver tag hanging around its neck read "Scotch," and he poured himself a stiff peg. "Suppose you get to the point, Thackeray."

His uninvited guest sat back in the wing chair and crossed his legs. "It's a simple business proposition. I need storage space for some valuable experimental seed and a couple of acres to make some test plantings."

Gerald looked at him in disbelief. "Oh, come now! Don't tell me there isn't a single place in the whole of England where you can build your own research facility."

"Of course not. But in this instance, secrecy is vital. Some of my more unscrupulous competitors have done everything but bug my office. I know my various facilities are watched, and there have been several attempts at bribing my employees. It occurred to me that no matter how I go about acquiring a facility and setting up a small laboratory, they'll know about it in a matter of days, and then it's back to the old cloak-and-dagger routine. But, on the other hand, if I had access to some established farmland, and I could bring in my materials say, at night, in unmarked vans, leave only a technician or two on site to monitor the progress of my little experiment, then I'd have the luxury of finishing the tests and presenting my findings to the government without outside interference."

"The government? What's the government got to do with it?"

Thackeray looked surprised. "Well, obviously, old man, if this project is successful, the government will want to be involved from the start. This could mean drastic changes in how food is produced in this country. England could rely a great deal less on imports. Means a great deal to the balance of payments."

Gerald, though he would not admit it, did not quite see how all this was supposed to work, or why, if this was so hush-hush, Thackeray had not been given space at a secure government facility in which to carry out his work. But for all he knew, perhaps this was the way it worked in those circles. Perhaps the government did not become involved until the tests had proved successful. And much as he distrusted Conrad Thackeray, the man had been given a knighthood for some reason. Perhaps it had been in recognition of some other secret work he'd carried out, in which case Gerald's political stock could only increase in value if he were somehow associated with the successful completion of some startling advance in agricultural science.

Still, he was not inclined to give in so easily. And Gillian was being uncharacteristically quiet, contributing nothing from her spot in the window seat to which she'd retreated. "Why should I let you in here, disturbing my land, interfering with farm tenants, and making a general nuisance of yourself?"

"Nothing to fear there, old man, hardly any disturbance at all. For that matter the project won't take long. Only a few weeks at most. And that old stone barn that sits on the mill road running through Haslemere will work perfectly. My vans won't need to come through the front gates or pass anywhere near the house. We'll be perfectly quiet and well behaved, and your tenants won't even know we're there."

"They'll know if you start planting something."

"We only need a small plot to begin with, just a few square feet. When we're ready to go to phase two, then you and I can discuss how much acreage I can use. Surely that's fair."

Gerald still hesitated, not so much because he cared what the man did with his silly plants, but because he hated giving in to him on any point. Still, there was the potential for income. He considered the dozen bills on his desk and requests for payment from people who had loaned him substantial sums of money. He wondered just how high Thackeray was willing to go to obtain his little secret enclave.

Thackeray seemed to read his mind. "Of course, I'm willing to pay for the privilege of setting up shop here for a few weeks," he said, "and pay handsomely. Although I hadn't settled on a figure yet, Gillian suggested a nice round sum of 100,000 pounds to secure a short lease and, say, 10,000 a week for the use of the land and water and whatnot."

Gerald had to grip his glass to steady himself. Had the man said 100,000 pounds? Good God! That would be enough to bail him out of his immediate troubles and keep the Inland Revenue men away from his door. And if the weekly payments went on long enough... Plus he could charge more if Thackeray wanted more land. His mind raced. Acquiescence was on his lips when his eyes fell on Gillian, and the Scotch soured in his stomach. She looked too...pleased. And her eyes never left Thackeray. Surely there was more to this arrangement than he'd been told, some sort of added benefit that had remained unspoken. One hundred thousand pounds was a great deal of money, after all, and Thackeray was not known for parting with a single pence without good reason. And yet, didn't he trust his wife? Despite everything else, she'd been faithful to him all these years. But would she continue to be? Would she stand by her titled but bankrupt Lord Fenwycke? Gerald wasn't sure he wanted to know the answer, but he ventured one last objection, at least for appearances' sake, to show that he wasn't going blindly to the role of cuckold if that was indeed what Gillian and Thackeray had in mind.

"Just how much time will be you spending here, Thackeray, whilst all this is going on?"

"Glad you mentioned that, Gerald, since you and I don't seem to get on well. As it happens, I'll be busy elsewhere most of the time. I have a manufacturing concern down Somerset way that needs my attention. You'll hardly see me at all, something which I should think you'd appreciate. So, tell me, do we have an agreement? If so, I can have my bookkeeper prepare a bank draft for the initial 100,000 and have it delivered to you, or we can wire the money to your account."

For several long moments, Sir Conrad's question hung in the air between them. Gerald had only to nod, to reach out his hand, and financial salvation was his. And yet he knew in his heart of hearts that once he had given in, there was no going back; once he had given this opportunist, money-grubbing commoner a toehold at Haslemere, nothing would ever be the same. But William Carlisle had abandoned him, cut him adrift despite the kinship of their two families for generations. Gerald had no choice, and he had a feeling Thackeray knew it.

"Very well then," he growled. "Since you insist that your work is in the service of Her Majesty's government, I don't see how I can properly refuse you. But rest assured that were it not for the altruistic ends that you claim, I'd rather see you in hell."

Thackeray smiled and stood up, offering his hand to Gerald, who pointedly ignored the gesture. Thackeray showed no signs of reacting to the snub. "I've always thought one should be careful for what one wishes, old man. Who knows which of us will end up in hell...and when?" He paused and looked over his shoulder to acknowledge Gillian. "Lady Fenwycke, it's been a pleasure." Then he turned back to Gerald. "You'll have your bank draft by special messenger this afternoon, and I'll have my solicitors draw up an agreement."

His footsteps echoed down the corridor, and Gerald heard the front door open and close. He refilled his glass from the Scotch decanter and circled around the chair in which Thackeray had been sitting, unwilling to allow even so distant a connection between them, all the while wondering if he and that man might not be in danger of sharing something much closer to them both.

Gillian rose from her seat and circled the room, slowly examining the art on the walls as if for the first time. "You know, Gerald darling, you needn't behave in such a beastly fashion with Conrad. He's only doing us an enormous favor."

Gerald felt the pulse in his forehead pounding out the anger that surged through him. "Favor? He's doing us a favor? I should have thought it was the other way round. It sounded as if he was pretty keen on setting up his little laboratory at Haslemere."

"Oh, be sensible, darling." Gillian's brittle laughter echoed from wall to wall. "He could have done it any number of places. Surely you can see that. He mentioned he was looking for a building and a bit of land to use, and I suggested he do the work here."

"But why? You know how I feel about Conrad Thackeray."

"Well, yes, darling, but that's hardly the point, now is it?"

"Then, by God, what is?"

Gillian whirled on him, looking more like a caged tiger than a loving wife. "The point is, Gerald, that my dressmaker, Madame Dussault, called this morning—personally, I might add—to see if I was unhappy with my last two dresses, since neither of them had been paid for. Naturally, I told her I would clear up the matter at once. A little research through your papers convinced me I'd better cast about for solutions to your insolvency." She ignored his outraged expression. "You've been naughty, Gerald, but as you can see, I've found a way out of our current situation, at least for the moment. Naturally, there may be other alternatives farther down the path. We'll just have to see, won't we?"

Gillian started for the door. "Oh, and I should tell you that I'll be going away next week for a few days. I've been feeling the need for some time on my own."

"But where..." Gerald, consumed as he was by anger and frustration, couldn't manage to finish the sentence.

"Oh, just a little place near Glastonbury. I've taken a cottage for a couple of weeks. I'm sure now that I've rescued you from public humiliation, you'll be a good chap and not bother me while I'm there."

Before Gerald could utter a word, she was gone. And really, when he thought about it, what could he have said? The plain, unvarnished truth was that Conrad Thackeray had just paid Gerald 100,000 pounds sterling for the privilege of bedding his wife whenever and wherever he wanted. Sadly, Gerald wasn't quite man enough to do anything about it, other than cash the check.

Chapter Seven

Visionary power attends the
motions of the viewless winds,
Embodied in the mystery of words.
—William Wordsworth
The Prelude

England

"So, who's going to drive?" Connor asked as they stood in line at the Hertz rental counter.

Laura smiled. "I've only been here once before, for about twelve hours, and I didn't do any driving. Just one quick trip at night in a taxi."

"It's been a few years since I've driven myself, but I've hired a car to go down to my grandmother's house a few times. There's something a little unnerving about driving on the 'wrong' side of the road."

"And driving from the 'wrong' side of the car," Laura added.

"London streets are pretty well marked. Lots of directional arrows pointing at the lane you're supposed to be in. They get so many visitors here, they try to keep it simple. And the traffic is lighter in the country, even if the roads are narrower."

"Then we'll switch off. You take the city, and then I can experience the challenge of country lanes."

Whey they reached the counter, they discovered that Connor's father had reserved a Volvo Estate Wagon for them, but she asked the clerk to change it to something smaller. "I'd like something more along the lines of a Renault Clio or a two-door Citroën...with a stick shift." The clerk looked puzzled. Laura decided that he'd pegged these two customers with their Gold Club reservation and British Air Club Class baggage tags as well-heeled, certainly not bargain hunters.

The clerk scurried back to the key board in the rear office and exchanged the Volvo keys for another set. He'd almost reached the counter when he threw up his hands and said, "Oh, wait, I almost forgot. There's a package for you."

He went back to a row of cubbyholes and pulled out a small rectangular package, explaining that it had been delivered by a local company the night before. At the counter again, he was handing Connor the keys and the package when he suddenly seemed mesmerized by the bold printing of her name on the brown paper. Instead of letting go of the package, he yanked it back, and said breathlessly, "Why, you're *the* Connor Hawthorne, the writer. Oh, my lord, I can't believe it. I've read every one of your books. And," he said, leaning forward and lowering his voice to a conspiratorial whisper, "my partner, James, is your second-biggest fan, after me of course." He clasped his hand over his heart as if the experience were too much to take in. "I can't believe I'm actually meeting you and..." His voice trailed off as he regarded Laura with undisguised curiosity.

Clearly he was dying to make the obvious assumption. Laura, of course, knew that he knew. But she had no idea how Connor wanted to handle such situations. Connor had displayed a consistent unwillingness to discuss her personal life while Ariana was alive, not because she was ashamed of her eleven-year relationship, but because she was an intensely private person. Given that attitude, the next words that came out of Connor's mouth surprised the hell out of her.

Looking at the clerk's name tag, she reached over the counter and said, "Trevor, it's a pleasure to meet you, and this is my...partner, Laura Nez." There had been only the slightest hesitation before that previously unthinkable word *partner,* and the implications of the bold declaration set Laura's mind reeling. But she kept her confusion to herself and shook Trevor's hand as Connor signed the last of the rental papers.

"Oh, Ms. Hawthorne," he sighed. "I do so wish I had one of your books here with me. Not that I'd really be allowed to ask for your autograph anyway. Company policy, don't you know. We aren't really supposed to..."

Connor waved away his concerns. "Trevor, not to worry. Do you have a business card or something with your mailing address?"

The young man snatched a rental contract envelope from its display stand and quickly scribbled his name and address on the inside of it, then, darting apprehensive glances at his fellow clerks, he slipped it across the counter with all the subtlety of a mole passing classified information to a secret agent.

Connor slid it into her shoulder bag and smiled at him. "I promise I'll send you an autographed copy," she whispered. "Would you like it made out to both you and James?"

Laura thought he would swoon from pure delight, and not for the first time she marveled at how gracefully Connor dealt with her celebrity status, how kindly she treated people who had become fans.

"Yes, oh, that would be marvelous, absolutely marvelous. I mean, only if you have the time, of course. Wouldn't want to be a bother." He glanced again at his coworkers.

"Not in the least, Trevor. You've been most helpful and I can't think of a better way to thank you. Now, if I could just have the keys and that package."

With a start, he apparently realized he still had those items behind the counter and thrust them into her hands. She glanced at the package and dropped it in her brief case. "Rental cell phone," she told Laura. "Leave it to Dad to think of everything."

Bidding farewell to the celebrity-struck Trevor, they stopped at a Barclay's cash point for a supply of British pounds, then followed the signs to the car park and found the little blue Renault in its assigned space. Tossing her baggage in the back, Laura surveyed the diminutive car with obvious skepticism. "Doesn't seem very secure," she ventured. "In an accident, we'd be toast."

"Let's not plan on any accidents," Connor replied. "I know you'd prefer a big, safe, bulletproof Mercedes." Their eyes met. For an instant, Laura was caught in the grip of visceral memory. Her hands fighting the steering wheel as the big silver car careened off the road, rolling over...a man, a bringer of death, running toward them, raking the windshield with bullets. She shook herself slightly as if to physically dislodge the image, and felt Connor's hand on her arm. "I'm sorry. I shouldn't have brought that up."

"No, it's all right. I know you were trying to get me to lighten up a little, and I should. Even Benjamin thinks I have a tendency to look for conspiracy and danger around every corner."

"I'm thankful for your borderline paranoia, sweetheart. Otherwise, I wouldn't be here right now. But let's leave the past in the past and go have some adventures."

They got into the car, with Connor in the right-hand driver's seat, and she fumbled with finding the ignition, then awkwardly ran through the gears, shifting with her left hand.

"Why do I think our first adventure is going to be getting out of this parking lot?" Laura grinned.

"Gee, thanks for the vote of confidence," retorted Connor. "Just you wait 'til I get the feel of this thing."

True to her word, Connor was shifting smoothly by the time they headed out of the airport and plunged into the first of many round-abouts. As they flew around the traffic pattern—clockwise—and shot down a ramp onto a multilane motorway, with its jungle of unfamiliar traffic signs and warnings, Laura had the distinct impression that they'd gone through the looking glass and everything was backward. It wouldn't have particularly surprised her to see a tall white rabbit pop its head over the backseat. But she felt considerably less ill at ease when Connor reached out and squeezed her hand. At that moment she realized she didn't particularly care *where* they were as long as they were together.

W

The hum of several thousand voices speaking a dozen different languages billowed through the vast exhibition hall at Olympia where the London International Book Fair was in full swing. Laura and Connor stopped at the inquiry desk to collect two badges left for them by Connor's publisher. On a display inside the main door, Connor caught sight of the daily edition of the show's newspaper. There was her publicity photo and a medium-size headline announcing her appearance at a book signing that afternoon. Clearly, the staff from her British publisher who were attending the show had moved quickly upon learning that one of their most well-known authors would be available to promote her books. Connor grimaced as Laura picked up a copy of the newspaper. "Makes it a little hard to keep a low profile," Connor said.

"Nothing wrong with that. The more everyone thinks you're here to pump sales, the less chance that someone in particular thinks otherwise."

"I suppose," replied Connor. "But I'm never comfortable with all the hoopla around doing tours and book signings."

"Then why do you do it at all? It isn't as if you really need to do much promotion. Your books sell in the hundreds of thousands now, as soon as they're released."

Connor paused to purchase a Book Fair catalogue from the information stand near the door, and plunked down her fifteen pounds before answering the question.

"It's true, my books seem to sell pretty well. But I mainly do it because I think authors owe something to their readers."

"Refreshing attitude coming from a celebrity," Laura smiled.

Connor gave her one of those "oh, please" looks. "I'm hardly a celebrity. I guess some authors probably get to the point where they don't care about the one-on-one anymore, or they're too famous to venture out often. But there are lots of us who won't forget that our success came about because thousands and thousands of people plunked down their twenty-five dollars for a hardcover or seven bucks for a paperback, and the least we can do is acknowledge them when the opportunity presents itself."

"So you really don't mind it?'

"No, except that I don't particularly like notoriety. I hated it when the press in Washington used to dog my footsteps through the courthouse looking for tasty quotes to make me look foolish. But this is different. Book fans stand in line because they love your work, not because they want to tear it apart."

"You must have signed a million books by now. It's a wonder you can still write," Laura grinned. "But I happen to know your hands work extremely well."

Connor, caught off guard by the allusion to intimacy, blushed slightly. "You're incorrigible, you know?"

"Absolutely," Laura answered, tucking her arm through Connor's. "Now let's do a little exploring before I surrender you to hordes of fans."

For more than an hour, they wandered the aisles, stopping at various stands to check out the offerings of an international array of publishers. Laura marveled at the sheer number of people packed into some of the displays, and that many of the people in the hall were wandering about with cigarettes in hand.

"Are they a little behind the times in banning smoking in public places?" asked Laura, as they fanned their way through a cloud near a large standing ashtray on the perimeter.

"No, they're not behind at all. The British have a definite resistance to being told what to do. And they'll only put up with so much regulation. There's no smoking in places that people *must* go, like government buildings, the Tube stations, the buses, and so forth. And private businesses can decide for themselves whether to allow smoking.

"What about bars and restaurants?"

"Most pubs have set aside a nonsmoking section if they have a dining room, for instance, and most tea shops and bakeries are nonsmoking, for obvious reasons. But events like this, well, smoking is optional."

"You sound as if you approve."

"I do, but that's only because I still miss the habit."

They paused to look at a display of New Age books at the Llewellyn Publishing stand. Connor explained that this particular publisher was quite well known for its list of spiritual books. Laura was fingering a copy of the Shaman's Calendar when a young woman tapped her. "If you're interested, miss, we have one of our authors here today doing readings."

"Readings?"

"Yes, quite fascinating really. They're astrological readings based on ancient Celtic traditions."

Laura instantly felt a shiver run up her spine and glanced quickly to see if Connor had been listening. Her face was devoid of expression. Laura looked over the young woman's shoulder to the table a few feet away where the author sat, and was instantly reassured. Helena Paterson was an attractive, middle-aged woman dressed in a wool skirt and tweed blazer. The author glanced up and caught Laura's eye. The woman had a kind smile and an unassuming manner.

On an impulse, Laura caught Connor by the arm and asked the assistant, "Would it be possible for us both to have a reading?"

The young woman led them over to the table and introduced them to Helena. Laura immediately sat down in one of the guest chairs. Her intuition detected Connor's reluctance, and apparently Helena was equally tuned in, for she gestured to the other chair and addressed Connor. "Perhaps you'd like to listen while I do a reading for your friend. Then you could decide if you'd like one too."

Helena immediately turned her attention to Laura and asked her birth date. She wrote it down, whereupon Laura asked if the time of birth mattered.

"Not to begin with. In general, astrological readings do depend on the exact time, but in this case, we'll simply begin with your date of birth."

She flipped through her *Handbook of Celtic Astrology* until she came to the chapter corresponding to Laura's sign. "Ah," she said, "this is quite interesting." And for the next few minutes, she described Laura's temperament and character in amazingly accurate terms.

From there, she went on to consult her ephemeris, then pointed out certain planetary conjunctions that had been significant in the past and some that would be of influence in the immediate future.

"Does this make sense for you?" she asked Laura, as she concluded her brief but perceptive analysis.

"It does," said Laura. "Some of the dates you mentioned correspond with recent events in my life." She turned to consult her lover with a glance. Had Connor noticed the correlation between the dates Helena had mentioned and the life-altering events of the past two years?

Connor had indeed noticed. And she'd grown increasingly intrigued with the almost pinpoint accuracy of Helena's reading. At the beginning, she'd angled her body away from the table, scanning the shelves of books as if seeking some occupation for her mind. But as various pieces fell into place, Connor's attention had been drawn back to the soft-spoken woman who sat across from them, meeting Connor's gaze with frankness.

"Now, did you wish a reading for yourself?" she asked Connor, in a neutral tone that neither prodded nor discouraged, but was kind all the same.

Connor felt Laura squeeze her hand beneath the table. "I suppose it couldn't hurt." She looked at her watch. "I do need to get some lunch before I meet with my publisher. If it doesn't take any longer than Laura's, it should be fine."

Helena immediately consulted her own watch and then flipped open her book. "I'm only on until noon anyway. Then I must be some-where else. So, what is your birthdate?"

Connor's response prompted Helena to announce that Connor's was the oak. "It's a powerful sign," she said, and spent the next few min-utes explaining. Her take on Connor was just as intriguingly on the money as Laura's reading. Connor was actually smiling and relaxed by the time it was over.

Laura and Connor were gathering up their shoulder bags when Helena placed a hand on Connor's arm. "I don't usually get what you might call clear psychic messages, but ever since you sat down, I've had the oddest urge to warn you to be careful."

"Careful of what?" Connor scowled, and Laura saw the old skepti-cism welling up in her partner's eyes.

Helena, however, was unperturbed. "I haven't the foggiest notion. It might be something quite minor, of course, though I don't think so. But I simply couldn't ignore it. I wish I could be more specific. I know vague warnings are quite useless, but perhaps you'll be a bit more vigilant. Whatever it is will happen quite soon, I should think. Anyway, I must run. I hope you enjoyed the readings. When you get a chance, read the whole book. I think you'll find some information of use to you both."

In a twinkling, the author was gone, and Connor stood staring after her. "I hate that 'beware of a tall dark stranger' mumbo jumbo," said Connor, half under her breath.

Laura poked her. "She did not say one thing about a tall dark stranger, and you're just being your usual skeptical self. She only said you should be careful. And she was following her hunches, which is something you do all the time whether you admit it or not."

"And if that isn't a generality, I've never heard one. That way if I get hit by a car or fall off a mountain, or forget to 'mind the gap' when I'm disembarking the Tube, the warning pretty much covers it all."

"You're impossible," said Laura, with mock exasperation. "If you'd been paying any attention to that lovely woman, you'd have realized that she's not only intelligent and well-versed in her subject, but she's also true to her work. She wouldn't lie about her intuitive impressions."

"You can tell all that about her in five minutes, I suppose."

"As a matter of fact, I usually can," smiled Laura. "I liked you from the first time I saw you in the Albuquerque airport."

"But you couldn't have *known* what kind of person I was."

"Yes, I could...and I did."

Having no immediate comeback to claims of outright clairvoyance, Connor suggested they climb the stairs to the gallery, which hung beneath the glass roof of the Victorian-era building, and have something to eat.

W

"We can grab a sandwich or soup and a pint if you like."

"A pint? Won't the fans question beer breath?" Laura teased.

"You know, it's a funny thing. I don't drink that much as a rule, but a pint of lager with lunch and dinner just *feels* right when I'm in England. Besides, that's what breath mints are for."

They picked up a couple of sandwiches, once Connor explained that the word *salad* on the labels meant the garnish. "Where we'd say, 'ham sandwich with lettuce and tomato,' they would say, 'ham salad' or 'ham with salad.'"

"But what if you want an egg salad sandwich?" inquired Laura, with only moderate seriousness.

"Then you order an 'egg mayonnaise' on whatever bread you'd like."

"Don't get too far from me until I learn how to forage for food," Laura quipped. "I might end up with something very strange to eat."

"Stranger than chorizo sausage breakfast burritos smothered in green chile sauce, washed down with a Dr Pepper at eight o'clock in the morning?"

Laura held her chin high in mock indignance. "There's nothing strange about plain old, home-cooked soul food."

"Dr Pepper is soul food?"

"Oh, shush, and pick out a sandwich for me. I'll go over to the bar and get us both a pint."

They took their food and drinks to a table overlooking the wrought iron railing that separated them from the commercial extravaganza going on below. From above, the interlocking stands and displays resembled a maze built for testing the intelligence of small mammals, which in a sense, Connor thought, it was. People scurried up and down the aisles, and knots of human traffic snarled the intersections of horizontal and vertical rows. Laura asked Connor if all book conventions were pretty much like this one.

"No, each one has its own character. Believe it or not, this is fairly subdued compared to the one in the States, the Book Expo, which is considerably larger and more high energy. Take the author book signings as an example. Here, it's fairly low key. People come around to the publisher's stand and politely wait for a signed book, and there aren't that many signings in the first place. But at BEA, there's an entire section of the convention halls set aside for dozens of signing tables with long, roped-off lines for each author. There are sometimes more than a hundred people waiting to get a book signed by their favorite writer, and the books are free with a modest donation to the Literacy Project."

Laura shrugged. "Even though I hate standing in line, I'd do it for one of your books."

Connor smiled. "You definitely don't have to stand in line, my love. And that's another Brit-ism you'll have to change. Here they don't stand in line, they 'queue up.'"

"I kind of like that one. And putting together some of what I've learned today, I think I'll eat the last crisp in the bag," said Laura, suiting her actions to the words, "finish my pint, and go queue up for the loo."

"And I'll go along to my publisher's stand before they start to get nervous that I'm not going to show up. You can meet me at the Booksellers Association stand where they've set up for the signing in about half an hour."

Connor descended the stairs and made her way up and across the main hall to arrive at her publisher's stand halfway down the *M* row. Fletcher Phillips, the managing director of the U.K. office, looked delighted to see her.

"Quite a shock you've given us," he grinned. "Took some doing to get the announcement in the daily news for the fair, but we managed."

"I appreciate that, Fletcher. I really did make the decision to come at the last moment, or I would have given you some lead time."

"Not to worry. If I've learned anything over the years, it's that creative people tend to be unpredictable."

Connor assumed he meant this as some sort of compliment, though she tended to equate "unpredictable" with "unreliable" or perhaps even "flaky"" She was none of these, or hoped she wasn't.

"Well, I'm ready to go and set up."

"Certainly. Two of the staff are already taking care of that. You'll just have to sit down and sign books. It isn't a huge crowd or anything, since we didn't have time to get any press releases out to the media."

Connor heard just the tinge of accusation in his voice. She recalled that he considered himself a master of marketing. It must have killed him to have so little time to mount a full-scale media blitz. She opted for sympathy. "Just as well, really. You know I'm not really crazy about fanfare. This will be properly low key."

Fletcher sighed. Apparently low key was not in his marketing vocabulary. "Not much choice anyway. But shall we go on up?"

They moved out into the aisle, and Connor started to walk away, when Fletcher let out a subdued yelp. "Wait! I almost forgot. There's a package here for you. We've been holding it until you arrived."

"A package?" asked Connor, puzzled that anyone would send something to her at the fair in care of her publisher.

"Yes, some mail we've received at our offices—some letters, a couple of items of what's probably junk mail, but we thought we'd let you decide."

"Oh," shrugged Connor, relieved that there was no mystery to it after all. When Fletcher handed her the manila envelope, she shoved it into the plastic carry bag she'd been handed by someone at the front door. "I'll look at it later."

Upstairs, all was in readiness. A queue had formed along the balcony railing where perhaps two dozen people waited patiently. Connor caught sight of Laura talking to a short, balding man who was laying out pens on a small table. Fletcher introduced Connor to Francis Cuddahy, his assistant, and Connor introduced Fletcher to Laura.

"A pleasure to meet you, Ms. Nez," he purred, bowing ever so slightly over her hand. "Have you been to Connor's book signings before?"

"No, this is my first opportunity." She took in the people who were waiting. "Doesn't seem like a crowd, though."

Fletcher looked positively pained. "It's just that with so little notice, and so many events going on here today, well..." He hunched his shoulders into an eloquent shrug of apology.

"Don't worry about it, Fletcher." Connor patted his arm. "Besides, if I'm not mistaken, here come some more potential customers."

The other three turned and saw that indeed there was a group of seven or eight people headed their way. These new arrivals spied the queue and immediately joined the end, causing Laura to comment that people in England seemed quite courteous on the issue of whose turn it was.

"They do it at bus stops too," Connor informed her. "Even though it's no longer an official policy, people still usually form a line as soon as they see the bus coming."

Laura caught Fletcher's eye. "Is she just putting me on, do you think?"

He smiled. "No, our Ms. Hawthorne is quite the Anglophile. Sometimes I think she knows more about our customs than we do. And we do still queue up for buses, though it's more apt to be the older folk who keep up the practice."

"Sounds suspiciously civilized," Laura commented.

"We are fairly civilized," Fletcher added, "except at football games. Then all bets are off in regard to behavior."

"That's soccer here, isn't it?" inquired Laura.

"Ah, yes. American football is an entirely different sport, more like rugby, of course, though our lads don't wear helmets and all that padding. Makes rugby a bit more challenging, I should say."

Laura, an avid football fan, didn't argue. "I've seen rugby and Australian-rules football. I don't think they're courageous; I think they're nuts."

"Quite," replied Fletcher. "Wouldn't catch me doing anything more strenuous than cricket. Now, we'd best get started. We're already a minute behind."

Fletcher went to talk to the patrons, and immediately a young woman approached the table and proffered her own hardcover copy of Connor's last book.

"To whom would you like this personalized?" asked Connor, opening the book to the title page and looking up expectantly.

The young woman blushed. "If it isn't too much trouble, then…"

"No, of course not," Connor said encouragingly.

"Well, if you could make it for my mum. She's a real fan of yours, but she doesn't get about much these days, what with the arthritis and all. I work at a bookshop…that's why I'm here today, to help my manager.

Then I saw the Book Fair newspaper and asked couldn't I have my lunch break while you were signing books."

A thought struck Connor as she looked down at the book. "But how did you happen to have this with you?"

"Oh, but I didn't. Soon as I saw that paper, I called my brother. He works delivering packages and such, you know, on a motorbike. He stopped at our flat, grabbed the book, and brought it here, right to the front door."

Connor smiled at the girl, and after inquiring after her mum's name, carefully and legibly wrote: *For Sylvia, best wishes to one of my most loyal fans. Many thanks, Connor Hawthorne.*

The young woman walked away beaming, and Laura, who'd overheard the exchange, stepped closer to Connor and asked, "Do you always take so much time over each one?"

"Not usually. Most people are in a hurry and don't want to stand in line forever. But this one was special. Do you realize how much trouble that girl and her brother went to just to get me to sign that book? That deserved a little extra effort."

"I keep finding new reasons every day why I love you," Laura smiled. "Here comes your next customer."

Connor nodded pleasantly to a middle-aged man, thin to the point of emaciation. Francis handed her a book, opened to the title page and Connor and inscribed the man's name, Theodore, and her own, then handed it back. He didn't say a word, simply looked at the signature suspiciously, then tucked the book under his arm.

"You see," Connor said over her shoulder. "Some people get a signature, and that's about it."

Even though a number of people joined the queue, all the books had been signed within an hour, and Connor pulled out a chair, motioning Laura to sit down.

"You know something," she said. "I sat right here at this table last year talking to P.D. James."

Laura's eyebrow went up. "You're kidding me. She was here?"

"Right here. She was supposed to give a talk, but the way the promoters had set it up, no one could hear her over the background noise.

So she sat down at a table and invited people to come up and talk with her one-on-one.

"I'd love to have been there. She's one of the greatest mystery writers who's ever lived."

"Don't I know it. Just talking to her made me feel like a rank amateur all over again. But she was so gracious to everyone, and she even signed a book for me, congratulated me, and wished me luck with my work."

"Must have been a kick," said Laura.

"One of those thrills of a lifetime. So, shall we be going? I think I've had just about enough of wall-to-wall people for one day. Besides, I'd like to get an early start for the country tomorrow."

Laura slipped her leather bag over her shoulder and handed Connor hers. As they were about to leave, Connor remembered the envelope Fletcher had given her, and turned back to the table for the plastic carry bag. But she saw no sign of it. She stooped and looked beneath, lifted the edge of the drape that formed the back wall of the stand. Nothing.

"What are you looking for?" asked Laura, as soon as she realized Connor was not behind her.

"That plastic bag someone handed me when we came in. I'd put a manila envelope of some fan mail and form letters and stuff that Fletcher had been holding for me. But I can't understand where it's gone. I sat it down right here, leaning against this post."

They both looked again at the only places within reach, and found nothing. Laura was the first to notice that there was a sort of passageway behind the drapery wall, and stepped into it. On the floor was the plastic bag and an empty manila envelope. "Is this it?" she asked, stepping back through the opening.

Connor peered at it. "Yep. Has my name on it. But it's empty."

"I guess someone only wanted what was inside it."

"But there was nothing important," Connor frowned.

"Maybe our thief didn't know that."

"Thief?"

"How else did it get six feet away, not to mention empty, unless someone grabbed it from where you put it down?"

"But it still doesn't make any sense."

"Nothing about this situation does, Connor. That's why we're here. But I don't think there's anything more we can do about it. Someone must have seen Fletcher give you the envelope."

"I suppose. I'll call him tomorrow and ask if he or his staff can remember exactly what was in it."

They descended the stairs and plowed their way through the crowds to the main entrance. There wasn't a cab in sight.

"Want to take the Tube instead?" asked Connor. We can find a taxi outside the Earl's Court station."

"I'm always ready for a new experience," smiled Laura. "Let's do it."

The two women dashed across the street, and after pausing at a vending machine to purchase tickets, they trotted to the platform just as a train was approaching the station.

"We'll have to wait a few minutes," Connor explained as they took their seats. "This route only operates when there's a fair here at Olympia. So the train runs back and forth every twenty minutes or so."

While they waited, Laura practiced her usual hobby of watching and analyzing people. It amused her to look for clues in their dress and appearance that might give hints as to what their lives were like. Focused on the other riders in their car, she almost missed another, rather unexpected passenger—a tiny man with a fringe of white hair around his bald pate, who looked extremely familiar. He was trotting down the platform to a farther car, and was out of sight before it came to Laura. "Connor! That man," she said, trying not to point, a practice considered extremely rude by the Navajo.

"What man," Connor asked, following the direction of Laura's intent gaze.

"You can't see him now, but I'd swear it was that guy from Washington, the one outside the hotel who caught that kid trying to steal your car."

"The Irish guy? The one who looked like a leprechaun?"

"I'd swear he's in a car ahead of us."

Connor shrugged. "I suppose it's possible. We never asked him what he did for a living. He could have been on his way to the Book Fair."

"Maybe," Laura admitted, but Connor could tell from the tiny frown line in the middle of her forehead that she wasn't inclined to the coincidence theory.

"We'll look for him when we get off the train at Earl's Court. If it's the same man, we can try and strike up a conversation about what a small world it is."

"Too small sometimes," said Laura, "and sometimes, too big."

With that cryptic remark, she lapsed into silence and Connor decided to leave her alone with her thoughts. As for Connor, her mind was already more than a hundred miles away, in the tiny village of St. Giles on Wyndle.

When the train pulled into the station, Laura dashed for the door, and down the platform to the stairs leading to the Warwick Road exit. Connor watched her scanning the crowd, and was almost tempted to be amused by Laura's obsession with spotting the stranger. Within a couple of minutes, the platform had cleared and Laura came back down the stairs to rejoin Connor, who led them the other way, toward the Earl's Court Road exit.

"No luck, I assume" said Connor.

Laura shook her head. "He dematerialized as far as I can tell. But, on the other hand, he was pretty short. I may have just missed him in the crowd. Still..."

Connor took Laura's arm. "Hey, don't worry about it right now. If we see him again, I promise I'll help you chase him down. For now, let's go get some really good curry for dinner."

Chapter Eight

Lady, the stars are falling pale and small,
Lady, we will not live if life be all,
Forgetting those good stars in heaven hung;
When all the world was young.
For more than gold was in a ring,
And love was not a little thing
Between the trees in Ivywood,
When all the world was young.
—Gilbert Keith Chesterton
The Flying Inn

After checking out of their London hotel, Connor introduced Laura to the phenomenon known as the full English breakfast, traditionally comprising eggs, sausages, bacon of the center-cut, smoked variety, kippers, fried tomato, beans, mushrooms, and fried bread or toast.

"I can't believe I ate every bite," Laura groaned, reaching for the car door handle.

"Neither can I," said Connor. "Although I noticed you carefully avoided the kippers. And unless you've decided to drive, you might want to go around to the other side."

Laura realized she was standing on the right side of the car. "Oops, force of habit," Connor laughed. "Don't worry. We'll both do it a few times before our brains change over."

"Seriously, though," said Laura as they buckled their seat belts, "does everyone eat that much breakfast?"

"No, not at all. Visitors love the idea, but I imagine the average person here would only have that sort of breakfast on weekends. And the breakfast you get in most tea shops is simpler—just eggs, sausage, beans, and toast.

"I don't get the whole kippers thing," Laura grimaced. "Those oily little fish for breakfast, ick!"

"As someone who eats fiery breakfast burritos on a regular basis, you have no room for criticism."

"You're right," Laura agreed, "but I'm still not eating any kippers."

They made good time on the M4, which Connor informed her was roughly the equivalent of an American interstate highway, though not perhaps as wide or well-maintained. "Highways aren't as much of a priority here," she explained. "You won't see those big, wide ribbons of blacktop like we have back home. Except for the motorways, or the 'M' roads, and what they call the 'dual carriageways,' you travel through most of the country on two-lane roads with the occasional passing zone."

"Does that mean people tend to be a little more sedate in their driving habits?" Laura queried hopefully.

Connor shook her head and grinned. "Not exactly."

About thirty-five miles west of the airport, Connor turned off the motorway and headed south on the A346. Laura, who had been studying the large scale book of "ordnance survey" maps, frowned slightly. "It seems as if we'd make better time staying on the highway until the..." her finger traced across the page, "A46, I think. Then we could go south toward Bath."

Connor nodded, downshifting for another roundabout. "We could, but I'm inspired on this rare sunny day to take the scenic route, and show you one of my favorite tea shops along the way, in Marlborough."

"Tea?" Laura's expression was a mixture of amusement and puzzlement.

"Of course. We are now in England, where the official cure for everything from minor difficulties to major disasters is a good hot cup of tea. All visitors are expected to consume tea a minimum of twice per day, either by itself or in company with afternoon snacks. Thus, you will also be experiencing scones, crumpets, clotted cream, and homemade strawberry conserve."

Laura looked at Connor in wonder. What had happened to the tense and apprehensive woman who'd stared at her defiantly across a dinner table just two nights ago? It was as if their reunion had lifted a heavy weight that hung over Connor and shrouded her in old sadness. But here, as they sped through the unfamiliar countryside, Connor's energy was bright and lively, her spirit tangible to Laura's inner senses.

"So," she said. "What other culinary delights may I expect? Malcolm mentioned that he thought the food here was pretty bad."

Connor smiled. "That depends entirely on where you eat and what you eat. There's awful food everywhere in the world but also excellent choices. You've already experienced the joys of breakfast. Lunch ingredients depend on whether you're in a restaurant or a pub, where you get mostly simple food, a ploughman's with bread, cheese, pickle, and such, and there's usually something hot, like a steak-and-kidney pie."

Laura shook her head. "Hmm...kidneys. Sounds tantalizing."

"Hey, you introduced me to Frito pie."

"Where else but New Mexico could you get a meal you can eat out right out of a bag within seconds of ordering it? Slit open a little sack of Fritos, pour in chile, beans, jalapenos, cheese, maybe a little sour cream. And all you need is a spoon."

"And I appreciated the novelty," said Connor, "except for the jalapenos. I could have skipped most of them."

"Sorry about that," Laura chuckled. "But you were pretty brave."

"Thank you, and now it's your turn to be brave, even when faced with steak-and-kidney pie."

Recalling what a good sport Connor had been when first confronted not only with the spicy delights of traditional New Mexican cooking, but the more dubious charms of Frito pies and corn dogs, Laura resigned herself to doing likewise. "All right," she agreed, "but I *still* draw the line at kippers."

W

The cream tea at Polly's Tea Room in Marlborough was everything Connor had predicted. They started with quiche, then proceeded to the scones, clotted cream and jam, and copious quantities of tea. Laura went to the front of the shop to pay while Connor retreated into the deserted back room and used the cell phone to check in with her father.

"Hi, Dad."

"Connor, where are you?"

She was taken aback at his abrupt tone. "We're in Marlborough, why?"

"So you're not far from St. Giles?"

"Maybe an hour, hour and a half. What's going on? You sound upset."

"Amanda called me this morning."

"That's a surprise. Another drunken outburst?"

"Oddly enough, she sounded perfectly sober and insisted that she'd only called because she had neglected to tell me something."

"And what was it?"

"She'd gotten a phone call from the local constabulary in St. Giles, as well as a telegram."

"More news about Gwendolyn's grave?"

"The police were reporting a break-in at your grandmother's house. They found Amanda's phone number on a list stuck to a memo board and called her, but she wasn't home and didn't get the messages right away."

"Why didn't they call you too?"

"I'm not actually a relative anymore, and Amanda assured them she would pass the news along to you. I checked with the records of the telegraph company and got a copy of the wire."

"How *do* you do that, Dad?"

"Finesse, my child. Anyway, the wire was sent because the sergeant, who knew Gwendolyn personally, was aware that she'd left the property to her granddaughter. He actually sent the telegram to you in care of Amanda."

"So why didn't she mention it to me when I saw her yesterday morning?"

She heard Benjamin sigh. "It sounds a little crazy, but Amanda swears she had a dream last night and that her mother ordered her to call me."

Connor considered for a moment, listening to the hiss of the trans-Atlantic connection. "So it's either a bad case of the DTs or maybe Gran's up to her old tricks again."

"Well, you have to admit, honey, we don't actually *know* where Gwendolyn went...I mean..." He wasn't able to find an ending for the thought and she fully empathized with his uncertainty.

"No, Dad, there's a lot we don't know. And I'm not sure I really want to. But someone is after something of my grandmother's, and they're willing to not only break into her house, but dig up her grave. So whatever it is, it must be significant enough to justify committing crimes."

"And there's the matter of the murders."

Laura came through the door and Connor motioned for her to wait for a minute. "I don't know that I'm convinced there's a connection. Maybe we've just seen too many strange things, Dad. Maybe that makes us all tend to see form in shadows that are really just shadows."

"I hope you're right, hon, but if I learned anything inside that mountain in New Mexico, it's that nothing would surprise me. And if by some bizarre chance your grandmother is, or was, involved in all this, I think you should be ready for anything."

"When you say, 'is' involved, why do I get the feeling that you're expecting Gwendolyn to be hovering around here somewhere?"

There was a long pause. "Okay, I wasn't going to mention this, at least not yet, but Amanda isn't the only one who's been having dreams."

Connor sat with a stunned expression, then motioned for Laura to lean closer and held the cell phone between them. "Dad, you know how much this stuff makes me nuts, but tell me anyway. What kind of dreams?"

"Nothing dramatic. Just a clear image of your grandmother's face telling me to make sure nothing happens to you, and that you find what you're looking for."

"But I'm not looking for anything," Connor protested.

"Or you don't know you are," her father replied. "If I were you, I'd take a good look around that house. The only other image I can recall is Gwendolyn standing in front of the fireplace in her library. Maybe that's significant."

"Or not," Connor retorted.

"Or not," he agreed quietly.

Immediately she regretted her irritation. "I'm sorry, Dad. It's just that I'm not really comfortable with..." she lowered her voice as she saw a patron passing by on her way to the loo, regarding them with curiosity, "with this spooky stuff, and it took a long time to accept that my grandmother was gone."

"Maybe we all need to reassess what 'gone' means, Connor. Despite what we saw and felt and experienced, I don't think any of us, not even Laura, are quite up to speed with what's really..." he paused, searching for the right words, "out there."

"I've got to tell you, Dad. It worries me when even you and I can't agree on a solid definition of reality."

"I have a funny feeling there's no such thing as objective reality, daughter of mine, or else the definition keeps expanding."

"Nothing like flexibility, I suppose. Well, we'd better get moving then."

"You have the keys to the house?"

"Gwendolyn's lawyer, make that solicitor, sent them to me months ago."

"Good. And how's Laura?"

Momentarily embarrassed that Benjamin didn't realize she was listening in, Laura quickly leaned back, away from the phone. Connor grinned at her. "Well, Dad, I'd have to say that having a bodyguard isn't half as annoying as I'd expected."

He laughed. "I can't tell you how glad I am to hear that. Now the both of you be careful. Oh, and there's one other thing..."

Benjamin's voice faded in a hiss of static and the connection was broken. Connor was dismayed to see the battery indicator was blinking. "Damn. I can't understand why the battery is already drained. I guess it wasn't charged all the way. He was right in the middle of a sentence." She put the phone back in her bag. "Remind me to plug this into charger when we get back to the car. So what did you think of all that? Suppose we're chasing 'ghaesties and ghoulies,' as someone once called them?"

Laura appeared to take the question quite seriously, and Connor poked her side gently. "Hey, I was only kidding."

"Maybe not," Laura replied. "After all, 'There are more things in heaven and earth, Horatio, than are dreamt of in your philosophy.'"

Instantly, Connor was transported back to that cavern, hidden deep within the sacred mountain and Grandmother Klah was regarding her with shrewd assessment. Connor blinked, and the image was gone. "That's what your Grandmother said to us, when we first got to the cavern, and saw..."

"I know. And I have a feeling she was telling us that that was just the beginning."

W

Connor and Laura wound their way through the west of England. Small villages rose up suddenly before them—ASHTON COMMON WELCOMES SAFE DRIVERS—and just as quickly disappeared—THANK YOU FOR DRIVING SAFELY IN OUR VILLAGE.

"Have you noticed how polite the signs are here?" Laura asked.

"There's a tradition of courtesy in England, even though modern realities have caught up with most of it. Still, people are generally very nice, especially in the country."

"What's your grandmother's village like, St. Giles on Wyndle?"

"A little larger than some we've been through. There's a commercial center along the High Street and some nice lanes within walking distance of shops. That's where the house is, on one of the lanes. There's also a beautiful old church, sixteenth-century, with a vicarage and cemetery."

"And what, pray tell, is a Wyndle, and why is St. Giles on it?"

Connor chuckled. "That's one of the oddities of life here. Once a place gets a name, there is little likelihood it will ever be changed. According to most ancient historians of the village, there used to be a branch of the River Brue called the Wyndle and in England, the towns near rivers sometimes include the name of the river in the town name."

"As in Stratford-upon-Avon?" Laura asked.

"Exactly. Except in this case, there's no longer any Wyndle. But the name stuck."

Laura continued watching the countryside. "It's incredibly green even at this time of year, although the hedges are still pretty brown. When does spring weather really show up here?"

Connor glanced at her. "Why all this intense interest in town names and meteorology? You've hardly said a thing about why we're here. As I recall, you're pretty fond of planning and theorizing."

Laura thought about the question for several ticks of the odometer. "I suppose it's because I feel a little out of my element here."

"Just as I did in New Mexico, when we were traveling around the reservation? That was more home to you."

"Yes, but it's more than the scenery and the road signs and the unusual traffic patterns," she said. "It's the energy. The closer we get to our destination, the more apprehensive I feel."

Connor frowned slightly. "You feel threatened by something?"

"Not exactly, but I do feel as if we're nearing the center of something very powerful, some kind of spiritual energy maybe."

"Sure you aren't just being influenced by the fact that we're near Stonehenge?"

"Oh, stop it," Laura admonished her with a smile. "No, and it's not because we're only fifty miles or so from the Glastonbury Tor, which by the way has a pretty fascinating history. No, this is just something I sense inside, and it's a lot different than what I feel when I'm on tribal land, the home of the People. This feels entirely, I don't know, foreign." Connor raised one eyebrow, and Laura laughed again. "That sounded absurd, didn't it? We *are* in a foreign country after all. But you know what I mean."

"I think I do. Places really do have a feeling to them. Being near and inside the sacred mountain just about terrified me because the whole idea of animal messengers and dreams having meaning and spirits communicating with you was beyond my comprehension. Plus, I'd never spent any time in the high desert, never understood the kind of magic that exists there if you know where to look. And I'm still a little uncertain about everything that happened. But here, I don't know...it's more like home to me. I know that doesn't sound quite logical since I've spent much more of my life in the States, but coming here always felt very much like coming home."

Laura looked at her closely. "Then this is probably your spiritual home," she said. "We all have one, and I think it may depend on where we've spent other lifetimes, maybe the last lifetime. I'm not up on all the reincarnation theory, but I do know somehow that your soul belongs here, belongs to this energy here."

Connor felt a shiver run down her spine. "I don't know about that, but I have a feeling that wherever you are, that's where I belong."

Laura smiled and put her hand on Connor's knee. "A romantic turn of phrase. I'm beginning to understand that there are a lot of facets to you I have yet to experience."

"Let's hope so. I wouldn't want you to get bored."

"Not likely," said Laura, moving her hand so that Connor could downshift for the twenty-sixth small village on their route. "And are we there yet?"

W

Connor insisted they should stop to visit the henge of Avebury where, unlike at Stonehenge, visitors are allowed to freely wander amongst the stones, touch them, or simply commune with them as they choose. Connor and Laura sat in the sunshine for a while, their backs against one of the tall, irregularly shaped stones.

"Hear anything?" asked Connor.

Laura smiled. "Not really. But then I'm not a 'channel' the way some people are. I have a friend in California who would probably be taking dictation from this rock if she were sitting here. But I just get impressions, feelings, things like that. Never any words. How about you?"

Connor tilted her head back to feel the sun. "Nothing from the stones, but I'd have to say my dreams are pretty vivid sometimes. And out in the desert, when we were hiking, I had some kind of weird visions, I guess you'd call them. And I have heard my grandmother speaking to me, in dreams anyway."

The two of them basked in the sunlight for almost an hour before Connor mentioned they'd better be going. "Let's visit the gift shop first, though. I'm sort of a sucker for souvenirs. And no, not tacky ones..." she exclaimed in response to Laura's arched eyebrow, "cool ones."

They wandered into the gift shop and ended up browsing in separate rooms until Connor appeared at Laura's elbow. "I want you to look at something," she whispered, and led the way back into the center room, and over to a small Plexiglas jewelry case. Connor leaned in close. "I don't know. Maybe you'll think this is pretty damn presumptuous of me, and it's not something I'd even considered, but I saw them, and if you don't want to, just tell me, and..."

"Sweetheart," Laura whispered, "would you like to tell me what you're talking about?"

Connor reddened slightly. "Sorry. But you see those rings right there in the corner. I, um, that is, I thought we might buy them."

Laura was dumbfounded. Following Connor's pointing finger, she located the two rings nestled into green velvet ring boxes. "They're—"

"It's too much," said Connor. "Isn't it?" And she began to turn away.

Laura grabbed her arm. "No, it isn't. And don't jump to conclusions when I haven't even had a chance to say anything. They're beautiful."

"But would you want to wear one? Not now, of course. But someday."

"You mean when we're married?" said Laura, a smile tickling the edges of her mouth.

Connor blushed furiously. "I didn't imagine you'd want anything that formal, but we could have our own, well, ceremony, I guess...someday."

"Let's look at them," said Laura. "I'll ask the shopkeeper."

Leaving Connor to compose herself, Laura found the woman with the keys to the jewelry case. Up close, the rings were even more spectacular. Each of the quarter-inch-wide rings consisted of a golden circle of joined Celtic knots, triangular shapes fitted one to the other, side to side. There were only two of them, a larger and a smaller.

"What does the symbol mean?" asked Laura.

"It's a sacred sign," Connor replied before the clerk had a chance. "One of the things it represents is infinity. You see the way the knot is formed, no beginning and no end. Celtic spirituality didn't recognize separateness."

Sensing Connor's hesitation and sensitive to the fact that the clerk hovered nearby, Laura plucked the smaller ring from the box and slid it onto her left hand. In one swift motion, she handed the larger one to Connor. Both rings fit perfectly. Their eyes met for a moment, and Connor cleared her throat. "We'll take both of them," she said, replacing her ring in its box as Laura did likewise.

At the cash register, Laura reached for the box containing Connor's ring. "I'll pay for this one," she said. "And you can buy the other."

The clerk, whose advanced age perhaps explained her lack of understanding, said, in a cheerful voice. "Isn't that sweet. Two friends getting matching souvenirs of their visit to Avebury. Something you'll always treasure."

"You could say that," said Connor.

W

They motored gently into St. Giles just after four o'clock. Connor was aiming for another tea shop, but Laura insisted she wasn't ready for more scones yet. They turned off High Street and down Wisteria Lane. Another quarter mile brought them to a small wooden sign that read ROSEWOOD HOUSE. When they pulled into the driveway past the open gate, Laura's jaw dropped. She turned on Connor. "*This* is what you call a house?"

Connor couldn't suppress a grin. "In England, people use that term a little differently than in the U.S. They don't throw around the term *mansion* the way Americans do."

"But that place must have at least ten rooms," Laura argued.

"Twelve to be precise, and you'll be happy to know that although my grandmother was old-fashioned in a lot of ways, she was a great believer in first-rate plumbing."

"Is that unusual here?"

"Let's just say that water pressure is not a priority in this country, and actual bathrooms had to be added in rather ingenious ways to these old houses. Gwendolyn went to a great deal of trouble and expense to have 'en suite' facilities installed in a home that dates from around 1650, I think. There are actually three full bathrooms to go with the six bedrooms."

"Six bedrooms. But I thought she lived alone."

"Since my grandfather died, and my mother married Dad and went to America, she was on her own sometimes. But her sister, my great-aunt Jessica, lived here much of the year. And my daughter and I have spent lots of vacations here."

"Which reminds me," Laura asked, her tone betraying some tension. "Will Katy be coming down to visit?"

Connor completed the turn around the circular gravel driveway that ran under a modest portico and turned off the motor. "I hope so. At least once we get this situation cleared up...whatever this situation is. Why? Is that making you nervous?"

"It's just that I haven't met her. And you told me she didn't get on well with Ariana once she got to be a teenager. And then she felt really guilty that Ariana died before they had a chance to reconcile. I don't know how she's going to feel about there being someone new in your life."

"She'd better feel fine about it," Connor said, a bit snappishly, but then she sighed. "Look, I know it could be a little awkward, but I honestly believe you and Katy are going to get along fine. She's grown up a lot, and she keeps nagging me to be happy. And I mentioned you in a couple of my letters to her. So I don't see any reason why we wouldn't have her blessing. She'll see that I'm happy."

"All right. But I have to tell you that my experience with young people is a little limited."

"Don't worry about that. I don't 'grok' the music, the clothes, the politics, or anything about them. And she doesn't get the concept of 'grokking' because she refuses to read *Stranger in a Strange Land*, but I still manage to get along with my daughter most of the time, and you will too. Now, what say we get the car unloaded."

W

The musty agedness of the old house assailed them when Connor finally got the old key to turn the tumblers of the reluctant lock, although on first inspection everything looked extremely clean and tidy. She decided they would probably have to get fires going in the library and the drawing room to get air circulating. But her plans changed as soon as she caught sight of the library. It was a shambles, and she simply stood in the doorway gaping at the mess. Somehow, when her father had mentioned a break-in, she hadn't envisioned a swath of destruction. She had assumed the thief or thieves had been looking for valuables to steal, not objects to destroy. It reminded her uncomfortably of what someone had done to her townhouse in Georgetown not that long ago. The sense of violation she'd felt then rose up in chest and throat again, this time on Gwendolyn's behalf.

"Not good," was Laura's reaction. "Your average burglars did not do this."

For a full minute, they surveyed the remains of the library. "This was her special place," Connor said, her voice tight with emotion. "When I was little, I used to peek in here and find grandmother poring over some big leather-bound book or studying the globe that...well, it used to be over on that shelf. And later on, when I got older, I'd tiptoe in, just in case she was napping in front of the fireplace in that big wing chair."

The chair was as war-torn as the rest of the room, its leather upholstery shredded. But the worst disaster, in Connor's eyes, was what had befallen her grandmother's unparalleled collection of books. In this room she had gathered not only the history of the world, but also an exhaustive array of books on every conceivable religious and spiritual tradition. The selections were often esoteric in the extreme and rare beyond description. Yet here they lay, some damaged beyond restoration.

Laura stooped to retrieve one of the books. "Given the fact that every one of these has been pulled down and apparently looked at, I'd say that someone wanted a book, a particular book, very badly."

Connor stared at her. "Why just a particular book?"

"I don't know a great deal about book collecting," she replied, "but I would imagine that a lot of these are rare and valuable. So why not take them? Why wreck so many unless they were looking for one specific book and only glanced between the covers of each one before tossing it aside. A lot of these are leather bound with nothing on the spines. So you'd have to look inside." Laura held up a copy of *Malleus Malleficorum*, the handbook of the Inquisitors in their search for witches to burn. "Some pretty intense reading. Did Gwendolyn actually read Latin?"

Connor nodded. "Yes, she did, as well as Greek, French, Italian, and German." An unexpected smile flitted across her lips. "She couldn't pronounce any of them worth a damn, but she could read them all."

"I wish I could have gotten to know her better," Laura said, her tone wistful.

"I wish you could have too. I wish there had been time."

There followed a long silence as Laura began picking up the books and stacking them on the library table. "You know she said something to me, right before she...left."

Connor looked at Laura, puzzled by the turn in the conversation. "I remember she said something to each of us, Malcolm, Dad, Albert Tsosie, and she thanked you, said you were exceedingly wise."

"Yes, she said that, but there was something else, something she whispered." Laura looked slightly uncomfortable. "I hadn't really thought about it until right now."

"What was it then?" Impatience had crept into Connor's voice.

"She said, 'When the time comes, you will see me again. You are her *anam cara*.'"

"*Anam cara*? I've heard that, but I can't remember where. What does it mean?"

"That's just it, I don't know. That's probably why I forgot about it, filed it away. I figured someday the meaning would become clear."

"You're a lot more patient than I am."

"Well, it isn't as if I could ask her, at least not directly or in any way I know how. And Grandmother Klah is never any help on things like this. She just tells you to figure it out for yourself."

"I knew there was a reason those two old ladies got along so well," Connor sighed. "They both used the same lines."

"So do you know what it means? Or do you suppose we can find the answer in one of these books?"

Connor shrugged. "Maybe. I guess there's no reason to put off the job. We may as well start stacking the books on the two tables. Then we can sort them out into subject categories."

Laura bent down for more books. "I don't know about you, but my classical Greek is a little rusty. Can you read these titles?"

"No, I can muddle my way through in French and Italian, and I have a vague memory of prep school Latin, but Greek is out of the question. Just put all the Greek ones over here in the corner. Maybe I can find someone in the village or in London who can help us catalogue them."

"I believe there's a Mrs. Folkes over in Shepton Mallet who has studied the classical languages." The intrusion of this unexpected advice uttered by a strange voice caused Connor to trip over a lampshade, and Laura almost dropped the stack of books she had gathered.

Connor was first to find her voice. "And just who are you?"

"So sorry," said the tall, lean man who emerged from the shadow of the doorway. "Didn't mean to startle you. But I heard from the local PC that someone might be mucking about in here who didn't belong."

"I can assure you I do belong," Connor answered, her tone uncharacteristically sharp in an effort to mask the degree to which she'd been startled.

"I can see that," he said. "I have surmised that you are probably Mrs. Broadhurst's granddaughter, Connor Hawthorne, also I believe a popular author in America."

"Then you have the advantage of me," said Connor, with the same degree of formality. "I have no idea who you are or why you are in this house."

He stepped farther into the room, and in the light from the tall Palladian windows, they could see that he was nattily dressed in a dark three-piece suit, white shirt, and striped tie. He had a definite air of the undertaker about him. "As to the first question, I'm Detective Chief Inspector Nicholas Foulsham. And the reason I'm here is because, as you can see, there have been some nasty little offenses committed such as burglary and the destruction of private property."

Connor eyed him narrowly. "You have some identification, no doubt."

The man nodded and produced a leather folder with his warrant card. Connor inspected it closely and handed it to Laura, who did likewise before returning it.

"So, aside from the fact that you are a police officer, what is the actual reason for your presence in my grandmother's house?"

"As I said Miss Hawthorne, the criminal trespass and—"

"Spare us the runaround, Inspector. It hasn't been my experience that DCIs investigate village burglaries. That would hardly be a wise use of your time, now would it?"

He smiled and spread his fingers in front of him in a pose of surrender. "I see the acorn doesn't fall far from the tree. Mrs. Broadhurst would have questioned my presence with equal asperity. To be honest, this incident is only of interest to me insofar as it may be related to the murders in the cemetery where your grandmother's grave was opened."

"You believe then, that there is some significance to the fact that it was Gwendolyn's grave that was opened, or you see a connection between my grandmother and the two men whose bodies you found in the grave?"

"Yes, perhaps, although I'm equally puzzled about the one body I didn't find in it." His dark eyes swept from Connor to Laura and back again. "Don't suppose you could enlighten me on that point?"

Fortunately, Connor had prepared for this question since Benjamin had been certain that it would be asked, more than once. "No, I can't.

My grandmother's body *should* be in that grave, and I have no idea why it isn't."

The detective's eyes came to rest on Laura, who returned his gaze without a flicker of anxiety. "And you, Miss . . .?"

"Nez. Laura Nez. I'm a friend of Connor's, and I've come to help her get things in order here. Naturally we had no idea there would be so much that was *out* of order."

"I didn't mean to pry into why you were here, Miss Nez, but whether you had any ideas about the disappearance of Mrs. Broadhurst's, er, remains."

"You know, I can't honestly say where she is at the moment," Laura replied, with deep conviction, and Connor had to bite her tongue to keep from laughing at her lover's bold admission of truth, which went right over the policeman's head.

"I don't suppose I must remind either of you that we rather frown on murder here. And it isn't a joking matter."

Connor stepped forward, matching her 5 foot 9 against the inspector's 6-foot frame. "Despite America having produced Al Capone, Son of Sam, and Ted Bundy, we 'rather frown on murder' too. Now, if you haven't anything else to ask, and no other reason to be in my house, perhaps you would excuse us." Connor's tone left no doubt as to her understanding that Foulsham had insufficient grounds for being there without her permission.

"Yes, of course. There is just one more small matter, though."

"And what is that?" Connor asked, still clearly annoyed.

"Well, it occurred to us that perhaps the thieves weren't looking for a body to steal, but had perhaps expected to find something of value in the coffin. Could you imagine what that might be?"

Connor was caught slightly off guard. She hadn't considered that possibility. Her guilty knowledge of having knowingly attended a sort of "mock" funeral had kept her focused on someone simply wanting to confirm Gwendolyn's death. That they might have actually been searching for something, well, that opened up a whole new can of worms. But she wasn't about to invite a cop to join her investigation.

"No, Mr. Foulsham, I can't. This isn't Egypt, and we don't bury our dead with treasures for the next lifetime. So it seems a pretty implausible theory."

He smiled thinly. "Hardly even a theory, at least not yet. But surely in your former career as a prosecutor you encountered some implausible motivations for criminal behavior."

"You're quite well informed, Chief Inspector."

"I make it a habit to be informed, Miss Hawthorne, though it's hardly difficult in your case, considering your celebrity as an author. A quick glance at one of your book jackets can tell someone a great deal." He stepped toward the doorway. "I'll be in touch, though, if anything else comes to mind. Perhaps you would do likewise, that is, if anything should occur to you that would shed light on this rather difficult situation."

"By all means," she said, curtly. "Good day, Chief Inspector."

They watched him walk down the driveway to where he'd parked his car outside the gate, which explained why they hadn't heard him approach. Connor found this disturbing. Why had he made a point of entering the house so silently? Surely he would have known that would-be burglars did not park in the front of the house in broad daylight and leave the front door standing open with luggage piled in the hall. Apparently Laura shared her misgivings. "So how much of our discussion do you think he heard?"

"I have no idea," Connor said, shaking her head, "but if he heard any of it, that would explain why he questioned us both so pointedly about Gwendolyn's whereabouts. Still, he may only be guessing. So let's not worry about him for the moment."

"We still haven't talked much about why her grave was opened, though. And why there were two bodies in it."

"That's because I don't have any good theories. We'll just have to see what we can find."

"There's something here for you to find," Laura announced abruptly.

"What's that supposed to mean?"

"Haven't a clue," she said, her face a study in bafflement. "That just came to me all of a sudden. That there *is* something here for you to find."

"You mean, there *was* something, before our gang of so-called thieves paid a visit."

"No...I mean the present tense...*is* something here. I'm inclined to take it on good authority. Maybe Gwendolyn's found a way to whisper in my ear or something."

"Oh, great. I should have known this would have to get spooky. We couldn't just have normal crimes and normal culprits and..." Connor took a deep breath, "okay, so what am I looking for?"

"You're going to hate the answer, but I think we'll know what it is when we find it."

"If this book weren't a family heirloom, I'd seriously consider throwing it at you," Connor said with mock severity. "But as it is, I think I'll go find the brandy."

"Not without me, you won't."

Chapter Nine

The world is made up, for the most part, of fools and knaves.
—George Villiers,
Second Duke of Buckingham

Lady Gillian rolled over in the warm, cozy bed and reached out to find an empty pillow next to her head. She lay there for a moment, listening for sounds from elsewhere in the cottage. All was silent, yet she smelled the aroma of cherry pipe tobacco seeping up through the rafters from somewhere below her. She felt deliciously satisfied in a way that poor, stupid Gerald had never accomplished with his staid lovemaking. No, she thought, this was a significant improvement, and one she should have hit on much sooner. Brief trysts with servants, both male and female, had been much less satisfactory, if only because she was quite understandably always the one in charge. That little serving maid Patricia had been a perfect example. Young, nubile, eager to please. Pity she'd had to come to an end so soon. Yes, she'd been an interesting diversion, but not a challenge, and better off dead than alive really.

Conrad, on the other hand, was anything but subservient. He was a world unto himself in many ways, and she had now experienced his dominance firsthand. Much as Gillian liked being in control, there was something extraordinarily seductive about Conrad Thackeray's offhanded acceptance of Gillian's acquiescence, however disingenuous, as if it were no more than his just due.

She'd hoped for a repeat performance this morning, but apparently Conrad had other ideas. Descending the narrow stairs of the cottage, she found him seated in an old leather wing chair, clad in a dressing gown, his head wreathed in rings of tobacco smoke.

"Good morning, darling," she announced brightly.

"Mmm," he replied, taking little notice of her scantily clad figure.

"It's positively freezing in here," she said. "Why don't I turn up the electric fire?"

"As you wish."

She dialed the heater knob to its highest setting and reached for a lap robe to wrap around her. "Is something wrong, Conrad?"

He finally focused on her, and she had the uncomfortable sensation of being examined critically and found wanting. Something in his eyes.

"Why do you ask, Gillian?"

"You seem, well, different than you did last night."

"Once you know me a little better, Gillian, you'll learn that I keep my interests in their proper perspective, and pursue my amusements at the proper time."

"Surely our amusements needn't cease simply because it's morning. After all, we have this place to ourselves. We can do anything we want, darling." Gillian stood and let fall first the lap robe, then her nightgown. Slowly she sank onto Conrad's lap and began nuzzling his neck. Her hand reached beneath his dressing gown, flesh seeking flesh.

In the next instant she was seated on the floor, her legs in a decidedly ungraceful tangle. "What on earth d—" she began. But her protest stopped in mid syllable as Conrad's strong hand encircled her throat.

"A few ground rules, my lovely Gillian. I don't like my women to act coquettish, and I certainly don't like being disobeyed. If you cannot grasp these simple facts, you will quickly cease to be an amusement. Is that clear?"

Gillian nodded.

"Good. Now since you've started something," he flung open the dressing gown to reveal his tumescence, "you can finish it." She saw the menace in his eyes and found herself caught up in both fear and arousal. She knew he expected her to service him, and the half of her that was indignant was no match for the half of her that was aroused. She did as she was bidden.

"You know, Gillian, you're especially lovely when viewed from this perspective." He sighed. "And when you've finished, there are some things we need to discuss about Gerald."

W

The feckless Gerald Fenwycke, unaware that his name was on the lips of the man he'd come to despise more than he thought possible, had taken it upon himself to learn more about Conrad Thackeray's little "experiment." Riding across the open fields, it occurred to him that this was when and where he felt most at home, most like the liege lord he often imagined himself to be. Trapped in the mystique of centuries past, Gerald liked the view from the saddle of his tall thoroughbred, Blazing Star. Unlike his ancestors, however, Gerald had no vast land holdings peopled with suitably humble serfs, no soldiers who leaped to do his bidding. What remained of his domain was but a shadow of what had been. Typically, Gerald gave not a thought whatsoever to the poverty and disease and hopelessness that had plagued those who had served the nobility. For him there was only a hazy, dreamlike vision of riding through his little kingdom as faithful minions tipped their caps and lowered their eyes.

Not that anyone tipped a cap today, he thought angrily, as he reined in his horse near the fence of one of his tenant farmers who was working the fields today. The man barely nodded an acknowledgment of Gerald's presence and went on with his work. Determined to get some satisfaction, Gerald sidled his horse closer to the fence and shouted at the man, "Oy, Carson. Have a word with you?"

The man looked up as if debating whether to accede to the barely polite request, further annoying his landlord. Finally the farmer plodded over the rows of turned earth to the fence. "And what would be the problem, then, *sir*?" he asked, pointedly omitting Gerald's title.

Boiling inside with righteous indignation, Gerald tried to keep his voice steady. "I've leased out some land over by the old barns. Wondered if you'd seen anyone coming or going. They'd have to use this road."

The man took off his hat and mopped his brow. "Reckon I've seen them then," he said. "Figured they have summat to do with the electric."

Gerald looked at him quizzically. "The electric. Why on earth would you think that?"

"Them vans they be driving, all dark gray with writing on the sides. Too far away to read, but reckoned they was a fixin' of something up there."

"There is nothing being repaired. All the wires are in good order." Gerald was exasperated with the slow-witted bumpkin. "Just how many vans have you seen on the road?"

"Hmm, hard to say what with 'em goin' up and down the road. Could be the same one makin' a lot o' trips, could be ten each makin' one trip. See what I mean?"

Gerald sighed. Clearly he was going to have to find out for himself what Conrad Thackeray was doing. "All right then, Carson. I'll let you get back to your work. Good day."

Gerald hesitated a moment before turning his horse, and was rewarded with the sight of Carson touching the brim of his cap. Almost gleeful, Gerald snapped the reins and was gone, too late to see that the farmer had only been removing his hat to mop his brow once more.

Twenty minutes later, Gerald approached the section of land on which stood the old stone barns. Ranged along the largest building were four vans. So Carson had been partly right. There was more than one on the site. He walked his horse slowly up the road toward the buildings, intending to see what was being stored here that was so incredibly important it must be hidden from Thackeray's competitors. Then, almost as if by magic, a figure materialized in the road ahead of him, so suddenly that his horse shied and reared up. Gerald, whose horsemanship may have constituted his only real talent, quickly brought the animal under control. The man, dressed in dark pants and jacket, never flinched, even when the horse's hooves swung up near his face. In his hand he carried what looked to Gerald for all the world like a police truncheon. He gaped at it in astonishment.

"What can I do for you, sir?" said the man, a hint of aggression in his tone. That hint was enough to set Gerald off.

"Do for *me*, young man? I'll thank you not to patronize me on my own land, not to mention startling my horse."

"Your land, sir?"

"Yes. You're standing on my property, and I'll thank you to clear the way and let me pass."

Gerald spurred his horse forward, but the man didn't budge. "Well, now, sir, as I understand it, this here land is under lease to my employer, Sir Conrad, so that he can do work on certain confidential projects. And, that bein' the case, he wants people kept away. And what he wants, he gets, if you take my meaning, sir."

"I do indeed take your meaning, but perhaps you will take mine when I tell you that lease or no lease, all this acreage is mine, and I have no intention of allowing activities to be carried on here unless I am clear about their purpose and their effect on my property. Now, move away."

Once more, Gerald moved Blazing Star forward, and once more, the man did not stand aside. This time, however, he also grabbed at the horse's bridle, an action that further infuriated Gerald. He raised his riding crop, fully intending to lash the man's face with it, but at that moment another figure emerged from a gap in the hedgerow, a man dressed identically to the first one, also carrying a truncheon. He strode up to stand beside his cohort. Gerald lowered his arm. "Release my horse this instant, you bloody fool!" he yelled, anger suffusing his flushed red face.

"Now, now, sir," said the new arrival. "No need for such language. If you'll just turn this handsome animal around and head back where you came from, there won't be any trouble, sir."

"*You're* giving *me* orders," Gerald choked on the words. "Why, you presumptuous toad..."

The man's eyes narrowed, and Gerald, even in the throes of fury, could not mistake the cold cruelty that shone there. "It would be all for the best, sir, if you would turn your horse around and leave. No one is permitted beyond this point by orders of Sir Conrad. If you have a dispute with that, it would be best you take it up with him."

Gerald, almost against his will, found himself backing his horse away. The first man released his grip on the bridle. Gerald shouted at them both. "You're damned right, I'll take it up with Conrad. And I'll soon set him straight." The men smirked, which only served to increase Gerald's belligerence even further. In a rage, he yanked Blazing Star's reins and spurred the big horse back down the way he had come. His heart was pounding in his chest so loudly he could hear it in his ears, even over the steady thump of Star's hooves on the hard packed dirt. What the devil was going on back there?

Sensing his mount's labored breathing, he finally slowed to a walk,and pondered this bizarre state of affairs. He could not fathom the behavior of the two men on the road. Even if Thackeray's project were top secret, he'd already explained it to Gerald. And surely he would have informed his men that Gerald was privy to the nature of the work. Then a cheering thought came to him. Perhaps Thackeray hadn't confided in his hired thugs. That made more sense, and that would explain why they acted like such idiots. They were probably too stupid to exercise any discretion. Thus they would take orders literally. No one was allowed in. They had no way of knowing that Gerald had a right to be there. The entire incident could be chalked up to the ignorance of the lower classes.

With this rationale a balm to his shredded nerves, Lord Fenwycke returned to his stables. The one remaining stable boy cum groom arrived with reasonable alacrity to take his horse, and this small efficiency further improved Gerald's state of mind. Entering through the rear of his house, he availed himself of the boot jack to remove his tall riding boots, then slipped on a pair of soft shoes, and decided to retreat to his library and figure up the best possible disposition of Thackeray's 100,000 pounds. As long as he kept his mind on that and away from any thoughts about what his wife might be up to, he'd be fine. Besides, there was a chance, albeit small, that he'd been entirely wrong about Thackeray's motives. Now that he'd seen the flurry of activity at the old barns, it was easier to imagine that perhaps the man wanted something other than Gillian. Unfortunately, as Gerald was smart enough to understand, Conrad Thackeray's shopping list did not have to be limited to any one item.

W

Gillian sat alone in the lounge of the local pub. Conrad had gone to purchase more pipe tobacco at the shop next door, leaving her alone to ponder all he had said that afternoon. He was expecting her full agreement and cooperation. In truth, she was willing to give both as long as it benefited her, but she didn't think it good form to give in without some pretense of thought. Her face grew warm as she recalled what she had already given in to these past twenty-four hours, but whether the warmth was due to shame or pleasure remained an unanswered question in her mind.

She wondered if, at that very moment, her husband were actively pondering whether or not his wife would venture to be unfaithful. The thought made her smile. Not only venture, she thought, but succeed. Whether Gerald cared was of little import, but it pleased her to think he might be angry or, better, devastated by her infidelity. Hers was the perverse nature of a genuinely cruel woman; perhaps that was why she fit so well with Conrad.

Gillian did not even possess a kind side. In her "nicest" moments, she was haughty, manipulative, or demanding. Nor did she care what anyone thought about her actions. There was only one yardstick by which she evaluated her choices, what they would do for Gillian. At least that had been the case until now. She suspected that a new element had been dropped into a formerly simple equation. Conrad Thackeray actually seemed to matter to Gillian. This caused her some consternation, but not enough to send her running back to Gerald. No, there was more to be had here than a romp round the bedroom, though that had been exquisitely entertaining. As long as she kept her wits about her and let Conrad believe he had subdued her completely, there would be many opportunities for a smart woman like Gillian.

"Wool-gathering, darling?" his voice knifed through her reverie.

"What, oh, no, just thinking about...everything."

"By that I assume you've been considering my proposal." Conrad lowered himself into the chair next to hers, and laid his pipe on the table.

"Quite. Just wondering about a few details of course," she replied.

"Good. It reminds me that you're no simpleton. Frankly, I couldn't abide that. I've had plenty of women who could provide only one thing with any degree of consistency." He leaned closer. "Though you're not bad at that either." She rewarded him with a modest blush. "No, I'd say you have the perfect combination of brains and..." his eyes dropped to her chest, and she suddenly felt completely naked, an odd sensation to be having in the Fox and Dove Public House, "other attributes."

"Good," she said, clearing her throat twice, "then let me understand just what you're about. It isn't that I much mind getting rid of poor old Gerald, but I want to be sure that my position as Lady Fenwycke is entirely secure."

"How could it be anything else?" he asked, an ironic smile quirking at the corners of his mouth. "You're childless, which is all the better. There's no young heir waiting in the wings to deprive you of your lawful inheritance. Gerald's elder brother is dead, and his sister is living a somewhat jaded existence in Paris. She had no claim on the estate anyway. And your husband has, in any event, made a will in your favor. There isn't anything that could threaten you."

"Except the lack of money, Conrad. You know full well that Haslemere is like a bottomless well. Gerald's never been able to make a go of the place, just keeps pouring money into it. Without some other assets besides my clothes and jewelry, owning Haslemere is hardly a blessing. It's rather more of a curse."

"Just so," Thackeray smiled. "And that is where I come in, Gillian dear. I have more than enough resources to completely renovate Haslemere, modernize it, and turn it into some sort of profitable commercial concern. Then you and I can do as we wish."

Gillian's lips formed into a vicious smile. "I do hope I can be the one to tell him that Haslemere is destined to be Somerset's next bed and breakfast, overrun with tourists and their sticky-fingered children."

"I think that can be arranged."

"But what you haven't quite specified, Conrad, is precisely how you intend to rid me—or should I say, rid us—of Gerald. Anything that draws suspicion to me would naturally tend to attach to you as well."

Thackeray's face darkened for a moment, and Gillian noted with some gratification that he hadn't missed her subtle threat. If she ended up in any trouble, she had no intention of facing it alone. She held his gaze without flinching to be sure he didn't entirely underestimate her resolve, and was rewarded with a small, thin smile.

"Quite understood, Gillian. But I have something rather special in mind, something I think you will rather enjoy. And I've already designed a way for us to carry it off without anyone the wiser."

He looked about to assure himself they were well out of earshot in their little corner table. "You wouldn't mind seeing old Gerald suffer a bit, would you?"

Chapter Ten

*We have seen the best of our time: machinations, hollowness, treachery,
and all ruinous disorders, follow us quietly to our grave.*
—William Shakespeare
King Lear, Act 1, Scene 2

Benjamin Hawthorne rolled his chair back from the state-of-the-art communications center he'd had built into the home office of his apartment during his years of government service. His retirement, however, had rendered him no less informed about events around the world, on a day-to-day basis (hour to hour if necessary). While he reflected that his life was sometimes lonely, given the divorce and the fact that he no longer journeyed to the Old Executive Office Building every day, there were compensations. He had more time to think, to analyze, and to make sense of the emerging patterns of behavior on the part of various governments and international agencies. He believed, as did those who often came to him for advice, that there was a degree of logic, however convoluted, in almost any decision made in the halls of government. He had an uncanny ability to decipher both the logic and the motivations involved. Sometimes his conclusions led him to suggest specific actions that others would be wise to take. More often, he simply amassed information and correlated it for his own edification.

It was this disciplined practice that had led him to more fully investigate the activities of one multinational corporation whose corporate decisions were puzzling in light of the world's economic situation. Branches of the company were trading in markets that ordinarily should not concern them. What's more, they were buying or selling when current economic conditions dictated the reverse. His research had also uncovered what to him seemed an unusual movement of gold bullion in international trading. With careful research he had traced most of these transactions. Benjamin knew that if current trends continued, economic power would be concentrated in a very few hands within the next few decades. He thought it prudent to have some idea whose hands those might be.

The laser printer at his side continued to spit out the reports he had requested from a number of agencies around the world who specialized in data gathering. Just as he was collating the last of it, the buzzer on his desk sounded, an internal call from the doorman of his private club. It was gratifying to hear the cheerful tones of young Robert, who had replaced the surly old army veteran, Hendry. He'd been a man almost impossible to fire, yet equally impossible to tolerate, so rude was he to anyone to whom he took a dislike (excepting the members, of course, since he was not entirely stupid). But when Hendry had gone to his just reward, the hiring committee had settled on Robert Vittorio, a sober, hard-working family man who fully appreciated the salary and the benefits of his job, which included a small apartment in the building next to the club.

"Gentleman to see you, Mr. Hawthorne. A Mr. Jefferson."

"Thank you, Robert. Please send him up."

In less than a minute, Benjamin heard the click of the door to the hallway. "Come in," he shouted over his shoulder. "Make yourself at home. Help yourself to a drink if you want—the bar's open all night."

"Thanks, but I won't be staying that long."

Benjamin whirled around at the sound of the unfamiliar voice. The figure in the doorway was difficult to make out, but the gun in the man's hand was clear enough. Benjamin kept his torso perfectly still, but his foot slid toward the alarm button under his desk.

The man moved the gun slightly. "No need to summon assistance, Mr. Hawthorne. I said I wouldn't be staying."

"What do you want?" Benjamin's voice was ice cold. Facing the wrong end of a gun was hardly a new experience for him, but he certainly hadn't expected it here and now when he'd been out of the game for so long. Adrenaline surged through his body.

"I'm only here to deliver a brief message."

"From whom?"

"Hardly relevant," replied the intruder. "Just be aware that you've been prying into matters best left alone. Your research into corporations involved in legitimate business enterprises will cease right now."

Benjamin's mind was racing. If he could keep the man talking another few seconds. "What possible harm can be done by research, unless, of course, it will flush out the sort of criminals who hide behind legitimate businesses? And for that matter, precisely which research has attracted so much attention? I look into a great many matters for a variety of reasons. So why don't you go back and tell whoever sent you that their errand boy has not been taken seriously."

The man's annoyance was obvious. He moved forward slightly, the gun now pointed directly at Benjamin's chest. "So you're a real wiseass. Well, maybe I'll just advance the timetable on dealing with you." He raised the revolver slightly, and Benjamin saw, with that special clarity inspired by impending death, each action in agonizingly slow motion: the finger beginning to squeeze the trigger, the hammer beginning its backward motion, the cylinder turning in millimeters. But the man had savored the potential kill a moment too long. There was a blur of motion behind him, and within seconds the would-be messenger/assassin lay face down on the floor with Malcolm's size 14-EEE foot planted on the back of his neck. In Malcolm's hand was the man's gun.

"So what else do you do for fun around here, Benjamin?"

The former senator took a deep breath and exhaled slowly, allowing his pulse to slow to a normal pace. "Well, next I thought we'd swim with some crocodiles."

W

It took two hours for Malcolm to get the perpetrator processed through Central Booking and lodged in a jail cell before he could return to Benjamin's club. In the meantime, the distraught doorman, Robert, had been questioned by not only the police, but by every club member who had learned of the incident while sitting in the clubroom bar. By the time Benjamin talked to him, the man was completely convinced he was going to lose his job, his apartment, and his reputation. Benjamin had no intention of letting any such thing happen. He called for the evening doorman to come in early, and took Robert up to his apartment, where he gave him a stiff drink and firmly explained that the incident had not been Robert's fault.

In fact, it hadn't. The intruder had certainly not gained entrance through the main door of the club, as a quick check of the security tapes had proven. Robert had never been away from his post during his duty period, except for one bathroom break when the assistant manager had stood directly in front of the entrance.

What Benjamin did ask Robert was if anyone had called to see him when Benjamin wasn't at home. The doorman thought about that for a moment and said that yes, there had been two people in the past week. One said he was delivering a package, and he seemed irritated when Robert told the stranger he was authorized to sign for all deliveries and that no delivery people were allowed inside unless they were accompanied by a member. The man had insisted that the package contained items of very high value that could only be delivered to the addressee. Robert was adamant about the rules, and the delivery man had refused to leave the package.

The second caller had been two days later. This man was dressed well, in a suit, and carrying a briefcase. He said he was doing some work for Benjamin Hawthorne and even produced some sort of government credentials. He merely wanted to slide an envelope of confidential documents under the apartment door. True to his principles, and with an eye to his job, Robert had remained unswayed by any and all blandishments, including a fifty-dollar bill waved under his nose. In fact, it was the money that convinced him the man could not possibly be associated with Mr. Hawthorne.

Benjamin, after determining that the encounters had taken place outside on the steps, beyond the range of the security cameras, asked Robert to think back and recall as many details about the two men—height, weight, hair color, eye color, accent, mannerisms—as possible. Robert closed his eyes and concentrated with all his might. Bit by bit, he built a picture in his mind of the delivery man and the bogus government agent. And not surprisingly to Benjamin, the descriptions were remarkably similar. Eventually, even Robert caught on to the fact that he had probably been dealing with the same man both times. He was astounded.

A few minutes later, the door buzzer sounded, signaling Malcolm's return from the police station. Benjamin told Robert to go home and get a good night's sleep and reminded him that he had done Benjamin a great service by sticking to his guns and refusing both money and a variety of convincing explanations. "I won't forget this, Robert. If you ever need anything, don't hesitate to come to me."

"Thank you, Senator. I appreciate that. So you don't think they'll fire me over this?"

"Absolutely not. I wouldn't stand for it. Now go home."

Robert saw Malcolm standing in the doorway. "Is there anything else you wanted to ask me, Captain?"

"Nope. We got all we need. If something else comes up, the detectives'll let you know."

Robert fled down the hallway, relief written on his features.

"So," said Malcolm, closing the door behind him. "Want to tell me what this was really all about?"

"You got back pretty quickly, considering the red tape downtown."

"Being a police captain has its advantages sometimes. And one of them is that you get to push in line, in front of the guys who are just booking pimps and hookers."

"Get anything out of him?"

"Not even name, rank, and serial number. No ID on him, no labels in the clothes, no serial number on the gun. Of course, we can send that to the lab and probably raise one, but it'll turn out to be from some ten-year-old crime, or stolen in a robbery, just the sort of information that gets us nowhere. A lot of guns keep floating from buyer to buyer."

"Did he ask for a lawyer?"

"No, and he didn't make any phone calls, and he didn't say a single word."

"Unusual."

"Sure is. These guys always have something to say, even if it's just a threat or a curse, know what I mean? So...once again. Are you going to answer my first question, or is this going to involve that stupid, classified, 'need to know' bullshit?"

Benjamin laughed. "No, and I'm sorry I've had to pull that one on you before. But you know I'm out of all that now." Malcolm raised an eyebrow. "Oh, all right, I'm pretty much out of it. But seriously, I haven't been involved with any heavy-duty operations in a long time. If you can believe it, this guy was here to tell me to stop playing on the Internet."

Malcolm looked even more skeptical. "What, you haven't paid your dues to CompuServe? Or you've been trading dirty pictures?"

Benjamin shook his head. "Okay, okay. Let me show you exactly what this guy did and said."

"You've taken up character acting, and you're going to do an instant replay?"

"Don't you wish. No...I'm going to use a handy device I had installed a couple of months ago. There are two foot switches under my desk. One is the alarm, which I let him see me aiming for, and the other activates a video camera, which covers the entire room from up there." Benjamin pointed at a wall sconce that looked exactly like a wall sconce. Even knowing what it was, Malcolm couldn't determine where the lens had been placed. He expressed his admiration and thought, not for the first time, that he was glad to be one of those Benjamin considered a friend. Benjamin Hawthorne's enemies were de facto members of an endangered species.

"So, I have on tape the entire incident with our anonymous messenger," said Benjamin, "but I haven't found anything on it."

For the next half hour, they watched the tape over and over. Neither of them could make anything of the brief incident. The man had no discernible accent, and there was nothing unusual about his speech patterns. He was roughly in his thirties, had oddly shaped scars on both wrists, and was right-handed. There ended the analysis.

"So what exactly are you researching that has someone pissing in his pants?"

Benjamin leaned back in his chair. "To be honest, I look into a lot of different things. But I do have a hunch. And there's a certain irony to the fact that this particular matter was actively on my mind, and on my desk, when this bastard dropped in." He gestured at the image on the video monitor.

"You think you know who sent him?"

"Not precisely, no. But the last few weeks or so, I've been keeping a close eye on a major corporation that seems to be involved in unusual transactions."

"Such as?"

"Amassing gold bullion for one, by..." Benjamin reached for a stack of papers on his desk, "purchasing very large quantities of armaments through a series of well-disguised dummy companies."

"Anything illegal?"

"Nothing that would justify law enforcement getting involved, at least not yet. It's almost as if someone, or several someones, are putting long-range plans into effect. It wouldn't be visible to most intelligence agencies because it's so diversified and spread out all over the globe. It's just this mania I have for analysis on a global scale that brought it to my attention in the first place.

"What sort of plans?" Malcolm asked. "Another power-hungry dictator plotting to take over the world?" He started to smile, then sobered instantly. They'd recently dealt with a man who'd been insane enough to want to do just that. It had ceased to be a joking matter. Benjamin, recognizing Malcolm's sudden reticence, answered the question seriously.

"No, I don't think goes that far. But I suspect I've only uncovered the tip of the iceberg. It's virtually impossible to get solid evidence on the types of transactions that would be illegal, such as the sale of hot-listed weapons, nuclear devices, that sort of thing, but my instincts tell me that something like that is going on. And someone is getting very wealthy in the process."

Malcolm shivered. "Sometimes I think I've got it easy in my job. I only have to deal with murderers, drug dealers, rapists, and psychos. They're dangerous, but they don't generally threaten the lives of thousands of people. What you're talking about, black market nukes and shit like that..." He shook his head. "Now that's truly scary."

Benjamin nodded. "You're right. It is. That's one reason I try to keep an eye on things. Not as if I'm the only one, of course. We've got whole teams of handpicked investigators and agents and hundreds of inform-ants keeping their eyes and ears open for these kinds of deals where weapons of mass destruction change hands. But we miss some. It's inevitable."

"And that means someday one of those things will end up here, doesn't it?" Malcolm was deadly serious, and Benjamin decided to be honest with him.

"Already has. Last year our people nailed two men who'd slipped across the Canadian border with a device the size of a suitcase. They were planning on detonating it inside the Lincoln Memorial."

The room was silent. Benjamin knew what Malcolm was thinking. If that had happened, most of Washington, D.C., would have been vaporized, along with his entire family. It was almost too much for a sane man to contemplate.

"Maybe it's time to move on," Malcolm said softly. "I've thought sometimes about going back down south. This kind of thing makes me think it's time."

"Do what you need to, my friend. Sell the townhouse and pull up stakes and settle anywhere. I'll be happy to make sure you get top rec-ommendations...not that you couldn't on your own, but in a town of politicians, a little extra 'grease' never hurts." He paused. "Still, I'd hate to see you go. I realize D.C. is a prime target for every class of enemy, but you've done good work here. You're a helluva cop. You've risen above the corruption and the bullshit and made your mark on this police force. I'd like to see you make it all the way to the top. We need good people here, too, you know."

They contemplated the man on the video screen for a while, each lost in his thoughts. Benjamin got up and refilled their brandy glasses. "Now, to get back to these multinationals, I've got one worry I want to share with you, but you'll have to promise me you won't go running off half-cocked until we work out a strategy."

Malcolm frowned. "Why would this involve me, and why would I...wait a second. Does this have something to do with Connor and what's going on over there in England?" He sat forward in his chair, all signs of fatigue banished by worry.

"See, I knew you'd react that way. Just the way you went flying off to New Mexico without so much as a plan. Now granted," he added, raising his hand to ward off Malcolm's defense, "if you hadn't, my daughter would be dead, and Laura Nez would be dead, and a lot of things would be different...in a very bad way. So I can't thank you enough for being an impulsive maniac. Which reminds me, have I thanked you yet for saving my life tonight?"

"I sort of took it as a given."

"You would. But thank you anyway. That's two I owe you."

"Don't owe me a thing. You and Connor, you're family to me."

Benjamin felt a quick rush of emotion surge through his chest as he looked at the earnest man who sat across from him. "You're one amazing human being, Malcolm, and I'm damn lucky to know you." He cleared his throat, having been about as sentimental as he ever got. "Okay, this is what I've found out or at least extrapolated from all this information. Much of it has come in only recently because it's from slightly 'unofficial' sources in different parts of the world." Benjamin stood and brought a world globe to the coffee table. He spun it slowly, ticking off locations from which he'd gathered information. "Nairobi, Algiers, Taipei, Buenos Aires, Vancouver, Sydney, and Miami—movements of stockpiles of weapons and equipment. Now that's just some of them. I can't be sure of who is involved, but the core of the pattern, the source that all these reports can be linked back to, is right here." He spun the globe and stopped it with his index finger on the little island nation that figured so largely in the affairs of the world—England.

Malcolm leaned forward and frowned. "I'm not doubting your conclusions, but even if England is small by our land mass standards, it's still a pretty big country. How could you possibly find a link between this business with Mrs. Broadhurst's grave and that bizarre murder and some possible international conspiracy?"

Benjamin sighed. He had to admit the question was perfectly reasonable. He hadn't quite worked out all the details himself. But it was a nagging hunch. And his mother-in-law, Gwendolyn Broadhurst, had put a lot of stock in hunches. "All right, let me give you the last few pieces, even though I can't absolutely swear they're a hundred percent confirmed."

He rifled through the stack of papers once more. "It was kind of a long shot, but I ran down the lists of shareholders in the subsidiaries of this multinational corporation. Actually, I didn't do all the work. This involved hours of searching for hidden threads and dummy companies—well, you know the drill. When people don't want to be connected to something, it's generally hard work to find the links. But eventually my research people compiled a list of every single shareholder, board member, and corporate officer involved with any of these subsidiaries, at least as far back in the web of ownership as we could go."

"I have a feeling you're about to tell me that someone we know is on it."

"Not exactly, but close. Purely on a hunch, and this is where I probably should thank someone else who isn't exactly *here* right now, or at least I don't think she is..." he glanced around the room almost involuntarily and was amused and relieved to see Malcolm doing the same. "Even though it seemed crazy, I ran the list of several hundred people against another much shorter list, and I hit pay dirt."

"Okay, I'll bite. What was the other list?"

"I asked William Carlisle to send it to me yesterday—a list of all the guests invited to the party where that girl was murdered."

Malcolm stared at him. "You said 'matches'...plural. How many?"

Benjamin's voice had a choked quality to it. "That's what strikes me as so weird. What are the odds that there would be *any*? And I found *three*?" Malcolm waited for the other shoe to drop. "And Lord William Carlisle is one of them."

Chapter Eleven

Attempt the end, and never stand to doubt;
Nothing's so hard, but search will find it out.
—Robert Herrick
Seek and Find

"The wind is really blustering this morning," Laura commented from the vicinity of the bedroom's window seat.

Connor buried her head in the plump feather pillow and struggled to get her bearings. For all her world traveling, she'd never gotten used to the effects of jet lag.

"Umgg," she said.

Laura chuckled. "Is that a new language you're speaking, or have you lost the use of your vocal chords?"

"Both. In this new language that means wake me tomorrow." Connor peered over the down comforter. "And how is it that you're so chipper this morning?"

"Twirling. I already did mine."

Connor looked at Laura as if she had completely come unhinged. "Excuse me?"

"Twirling. I read a little book about it a couple of years ago. Sounds silly, but it works like a charm."

"Is this some sort of whirling dervish ceremonial dance or something?" Connor asked, clutching the bedclothes tighter. "Because if it is, I'm not up for it."

Laura advanced on her, a determined look in her eye. "No, it isn't a dance, and we should have done it as soon as we got here. But I couldn't find the directions until this morning."

"You're serious, aren't you?"

"Look, it isn't all mumbo jumbo. It's actually rather scientific. Your body has an electromagnetic field, and so does the Earth. Generally, they're sort of in synch with each other. But when you move quickly from one part of the world to another, flying especially, your body doesn't have time to adjust."

"This is one of those circadian rhythm things, isn't it?"

"Sort of. But this is advice direct from a guru."

Connor groaned. "Oh, please!"

"Hey, I would think, after all we've been through, that you wouldn't be quite so skeptical of new ideas."

Connor sighed. "Oh, all right. So who is this alleged..." catching the look in Laura's eye, she amended the question. "Who is this guru?"

Laura picked up the little booklet from the nightstand. "Da Avabhasa. And the guy who put together this guide is Bill Gottlieb. You might even want to read it sometime. Get the whole explanation."

"For the moment, could you just hit the highlights for me?"

"Okay. We traveled from west to east, so we twirl the opposite direction, from east to west, to compensate. So since your left hand is east, and your right hand is west, you twirl left over right, or toward your west hand."

"Could you say that again in English, for the sleep-deprived?"

Laura grinned. "How about if I just tell you clockwise?"

"That I can grasp. And I have to do this twirling right now?"

"The sooner the better."

"But it's bound to make me dizzy. I can't go on amusement park rides, even that teacup thing." Laura yanked back the comforter, and Connor yelped. "It's freezing in here."

"You'll be back in your bed in just a minute. Remember, you get to lie down flat on your back and relax after you do it. Now, come on."

Protesting all the way to the center of the room, Connor, at Laura's direction, assumed the "twirling" position, arms extended straight out from her sides. "This feels incredibly silly," she muttered.

"No one's here to see it but me. Now, put your right palm up and your left palm down."

"And you do the hokey pokey and you turn yourself around."

"Connor! Would you be serious?"

"Okay, okay. When do I start?"

"Right now. Just keep turning at a moderate pace and keep breathing, and when you get too dizzy, lie down immediately on the bed and relax."

Laura was surprised at how many revolutions Connor was able to complete before breaking off and stumbling toward the bed where she flopped down on her back.

"Whoa! Stop the world, I want to get off," she mumbled.

"Shush. You're supposed to relax your whole body and contemplate peace."

"Any minute now, I may be contemplating my dinner from last night."

Laura laughed. "You're incorrigible. Just lie there and be quiet."

"Care to join me?" Connor asked, her hand reaching for Laura.

"You may not have noticed, sweetheart, but I'm already dressed."

Connor peeked through slitted eyelids so as not to disturb the relaxation phase of the treatment. "Um, yes you are. Why so early?"

"I'm going to take the car and drive down to that market we passed yesterday. We need some coffee and tea and some food."

"I'll get dressed, and we'll eat in the village."

"We can't run go to a restaurant every time we want a cup of coffee. And besides, I like stocking up."

Connor smiled. "You're nesting, aren't you? This is some sort of domestic impulse, isn't it?"

Laura swatted her gently. "Probably, but don't even think about making fun of it." She rose and headed for the door. "Be back in no time."

"I think 'no time' only exists in quantum physics," Connor called after her.

A paperback novel came flying across the room and landed against the headboard with a thunk. "Not a family heirloom," Laura explained, as her steps quickly receded down the hallway.

Connor laughed and snuggled herself into the warm bed.

W

When she awoke an hour later, feeling surprisingly refreshed, the silence of the old house told her Laura wasn't back yet. Connor padded to the bathroom and contemplated the old-fashioned sink, reflecting on the vagaries of British plumbing. Why couldn't they have the cold *and* hot water coming out of the same tap? She supposed there was some reason she had yet to learn. But in the meantime the situation made brushing one's teeth and washing one's hands potentially painful—the choices being icy cold or boiling hot. She opted for a quick tooth brushing with cold water, and a long bath in the claw-foot tub.

Even after a leisurely soak, she still heard no sound in the house and felt a little niggling of worry in the pit of her stomach. She pushed it away, though, since she reminded herself that Laura was a grown woman, it was broad daylight, and this was perhaps one of the safest places in the world. Determined to embark on something useful, Connor descended to the ground floor and went back to work on organizing the library. It still infuriated her that someone had felt the need to cause so much wanton destruction, but the more she worked, the more she became convinced that there had been a method in the madness.

She and Laura had piled up many of the books near where they had fallen, and at length it occurred to her that many of the volumes had not been found lying near the shelves where they were housed. Few other people would have been able to reach that conclusion, but Connor was one of those blessed with some form of photographic memory. She had been in the library hundreds of times growing up, and she'd examined many of the books, gliding along on the tall ladder that ran on tracks in the floor and on the upper shelves. When she closed her eyes and let a mental picture of the room form, she could recall her grandmother's eccentric yet logical system of organization.

Gwendolyn had sorted her books on these floor-to-ceiling shelves by topic, content, and her estimation of the relevance of that content. Her opinion of a book could be learned simply by observing its placement. The work of authors she found trite, mundane, badly written, or, worst of all, to be of poor scholarship, were relegated to the topmost, least accessible shelves.

The greater part of Gwendolyn's library had been devoted to fairly arcane treatments of theology, religion, and just about every spiritual practice known to humankind, from animism to Zen Buddhism, along with a solid collection of classical history, literature, and reference materials. Connor recalled more than a dozen versions of the Bible, as well as the Gnostic Gospels and other fragments of Christian texts that had been excised from the Bible by various religious authorities over the centuries for purely political reasons. It was here that Connor had first been introduced to the texts of the other major religions—the Baghavad Gita, the Vedas, the Torah and Talmud, the Koran, the Book of Kells, the Dead Sea Scrolls—and anything she could get her hands on.

Then there were what Gwendolyn had explained were lesser known, yet equally important sources of knowledge—often consisting of hand-sewn bundles of parchment packed carefully into leather-wrapped wooden boxes, the outside edges of which were decorated much like the spines of normal books. These individual document vaults, each a work of art in itself, thus blended in on the shelves. And the first fact that registered with Connor, after she had inventoried her memory for what should be there, was that all of those parchment bundles were gone.

She took a quick but thorough tour around the room, examining each stack of books and noting their position relative to the shelves. She was right. None of those rare compilations of ancient manuscripts was anywhere to be found. A trickle of fear rolled up her spine as the ramifications of her discovery began to sink in. She'd already known that this was not a simple case of vandalism or crime of opportunity. Now she realized there was a cunning mind at work here, the mind of someone who was looking for something far more valuable than mere objects. The person who had been here was seeking knowledge. But of what, she asked herself.

After throwing a blanket over the damaged upholstery of her grandmother's favorite chair, she sat down with a pad and pencil and carefully drew a diagram based on her memories. She knew she couldn't be absolutely accurate, but even a general outline might tell her what she needed to know. Shelf by shelf, bay by bay, the library as it had been came to life under her pencil. Thanks to her remarkable memory for detail, there were few blanks when she was done.

With a sudden start, she checked her watch. Almost three hours had passed since Laura had gone to a store less than a mile away. Connor decided that being a mature adult about it was giving her a headache. She was worried, and that's all there was to it. But just as she started for the hall to collect her jacket and set off walking down to the village, she heard the crunch of tires on gravel. The little blue Renault slid to a halt under the portico. It was all Connor could do to keep from rushing outside and saying something parental, something along the lines of "Where have you been?" and "Do you know what time it is?" She'd heard them when she was young, said them to Katy about ten years later, and really didn't think her fully grown-up lover would appreciate the sentiment.

As it was, the urge to be annoyed died a quick death when she saw Laura come through the door laden with a dozen plastic shopping bags, her hair swirled around the shoulders of her jacket, a broad smile of greeting on her face. Connor wondered if it would always be like this, if her heart would always skip a beat at the sight of Laura Nez.

"I'll bet you didn't know that this is a village holiday in honor of someone who performed some remarkable feat of bravery a hundred years ago today—never did catch the name. But at any rate, the shops are all closed, and there was nowhere to buy food until I got to

Glastonbury, where I eventually tracked down a real live supermarket, a Safeway, if you can believe it, and I indulged in all sorts of treats and delicacies."

Connor surveyed the collection of bags. "Looks as if there's enough here to feed a platoon."

"Funny you should mention that," Laura said, heading toward the kitchen. "I took the cell phone with me so it wouldn't wake you. Your Dad called, and it seems we'll be having guests shortly."

"Guests?"

"Yes, it's beginning to look like a regimental reunion. Benjamin and Malcolm will be here tomorrow night."

"But I thought he was concerned about us appearing to be overly concerned with what's happened. Weren't you at the same dinner? Just a few nights ago he said it might draw too much attention if he came too."

Laura pursed her lips and leaned against the counter. "Yes, I was there, although I admit I was a little distracted by your presence. And I do recall Benjamin's logic. He felt that since you had a legitimate reason for being in England, and a pressing responsibility to look after your inheritance from Gwendolyn, you could also poke into other matters without attracting unwelcome interest."

"Good, then I'm not crazy. Now I'm wondering about my father."

"No. As always, I tend to think Benjamin Hawthorne is crazy like a fox. He didn't go into a lot of detail. Just said there'd been some trouble there, but Malcolm had been in the right place at the right time. And he said he'd received some new information that was rather disturbing. I also got the impression that he'd almost been willing to hold off coming for a little while, but a certain really tall D.C. cop was ready to commandeer an aircraft at gunpoint and have them drop him by parachute right over St. Giles so he wouldn't have to waste any time on land transportation."

Connor burst into laughter. The image was absurd but not out of character for Malcolm Jefferson. He counted himself as one of her guardian angels, and so he had proven to be. For her, the best part about their relationship was that Malcolm's protectiveness didn't stem from male chauvinism. He considered Connor an absolute equal, knew that she could take care of herself under most circumstances. But he owed her his life twice over, and in the same way he might reckon up a debt of honor between men, he didn't think saving hers just once made them even. She doubted he would ever consider that they were even.

"I've never asked why that guy is like a one-man SWAT team when it comes to you being in danger." When Connor hesitated, she hastened to add, "but don't if it's personal between the two of you."

"No, well, part of it is maybe, but I don't intend to have any secrets from you. I know you'll keep it to yourself, and not discuss it with him unless he chooses to talk about it." Connor put groceries away as she spoke. "Several years ago, when I was still a prosecutor, Malcolm Jefferson caught a hoodlum who snatched my purse. I was so impressed by his attitude that I took an interest in him and put in a word here and there. Later, he and his wife, Marie Louise, got to be friends with Ariana and me." Connor paused, but Laura displayed no reaction beyond genuine interest. Connor wondered when was she going to stop feeling awkward every time she mentioned Ariana."

"So, a couple of years after that, just before I quit the D.A.'s office, Marie Louise was killed in the course of a bank robbery. It was a fluke thing, she went to get money for their vacation and tried to protect some elderly customer. The robbers shot her down without a moment's hesitation, and Malcolm saw every bit of it replayed on the security-camera video. Anyway, he went through a really, really rough time, and one night I went looking for him because I had a very bad feeling about where he was emotionally. Turns out it was a good thing I did. He was close to the edge." She took a deep breath. "Then, a few weeks later when he and his partner finally ID'd the perps from the bank, I managed to get to the suspects' address just after Malcolm did and convince him not to shoot them where they stood. I demanded that he hand me his gun. God, I know how badly he wanted to see them suffer, and I think his partner would have backed him no matter what happened. But I also knew he had too much integrity to live with himself if he killed them in cold blood. Then his kids would have ended up without any parents at all." She slid a package of spaghetti into the larder. "And that's about it. He's been my knight in shining armor and regular all-around avenging angel ever since."

"With good reason, I think. And I like having him around. There's something about that man that makes me feel extremely safe."

Connor snorted. "Oh, right. Like you need someone to protect you. Don't forget I've seen you in action, rolling out of a wrecked car with a machine gun cradled in your arms like Bruce Willis on one of his most pissed-off days."

"Bruce Willis? I think I'd prefer Kathleen Turner in *Undercover Blues*. You know, deadly but with a devastating sense of humor."

"How about Sigourney Weaver in *Alien?*"

Laura mulled that over for a second or two. "No. I couldn't deal with that much slime."

Connor looked at her and smiled. "I think you could deal with just about anything."

"Except figuring out what's *in* some of the packages in the grocery store meat department. This cultural exchange is going to take a little more research." She glanced at Connor. "Okay, what's going through that mind of yours?"

"I'd completely forgotten about what I was doing when you came home."

"And what was that?"

"A little research. That's what reminded me. I started working in the library again, and I realized there was something wrong with the picture."

"Aside from the fact that it's a mess?"

"That's sort of the point really. If you didn't know how the library was before, it would look as if someone pulled all the books off the shelves for pure devilment. But some of the books are nowhere near where they were shelved in the first place."

Laura frowned, trying to see where Connor was going with all this. "But that may just be the result of a random act of vandalism?"

"Almost, but not quite. You see, I was just starting to discover that some material is completely missing, and...let's go back in there. I want to check a few other things."

They trooped back to the library, now flooded with light and warmth from the early afternoon sun, one reason Gwendolyn had always loved the room. Connor moved to the stack of books nearest the first of the tall front windows. She ran her finger down the spines. She went quickly to the books heaped up near the other front window, and after a few moments, she said, "It's just as I thought."

"What is?" asked Laura, still puzzled.

"All of these books deal more or less with the same subject area, at least from Gwendolyn's point of view. And all of them are from those shelves at the far end of the room, nearest my grandmother's writing desk."

Laura looked from the books to the shelves and back to Connor. "Considering the size of the room, someone would have had to fling those particular books all from that one section at least thirty feet and take a lot of care with their aim."

"Exactly. And not one of them is seriously damaged, even though most of them are fairly old. Hitting the walls or the floor that hard would have torn the covers off half of them."

With growing comprehension, Laura summarized. "Ergo, someone carried these particular books over to the window..." Her eyes took in the window seat and the bright light streaming through the glass. "Where it was easiest to look through them, and then he, or she, tossed them aside, one by one. They would have sat down at Gwendolyn's desk, but it was too dark when they were here." She looked at Connor. "But you also said some books were missing, though I can't imagine how you figured that out so quickly without taking an inventory. There must be more than a thousand books here."

"That's because they weren't books in the modern sense. These were rolled up, or in some cases, hand-sewn manuscripts on fairly brittle parchment paper. My grandmother had an old man in the village, a cabinetmaker, fashion containers for them, wooden boxes like magazine storage containers, except these were covered in fine tooled leather and their edges made to look like the spines of books."

Laura scanned the room. "And they're all gone?"

"Every one of them, unless I've overlooked a stack."

"Any chance someone else moved them or borrowed them?"

"Mrs. Gwydden wouldn't dream of changing the location of a single item in this house."

"Mrs. Gwydden?"

"My grandmother's housekeeper for about twenty years. I wrote to her last year and asked her to keep coming in as many times a week as necessary to keep the place up."

"I noticed when we first arrived that the house didn't have that unlived-in smell or feel to it," Laura commented. "Just a little mustiness."

"Not much gets past you, does it?"

"Oh, I'm as fallible as the next person."

Connor's expression announced she didn't believe it for an instant. "At any rate, I know she wouldn't have moved those manuscripts."

"All right, then. How about the second theory? That she loaned them to someone?"

Connor thought about it for a moment. "Doesn't seem likely, considering their importance to her, but there is just the slimmest possibility she was having them restored or preserved or something like that. I'll give Watkins a call tomorrow and check."

"Watkins?"

"Fine old bookshop in London. They helped my grandmother build this collection. If she'd wanted any restoration done, she'd look to them for advice on who could do it."

"All right," Laura nodded. "That's a place to start. But what was so important about those papers and these books that someone not only broke in, but spent some time diligently searching for something so specific?"

Connor sighed. "To answer your second question first, these books, as I said, are primarily about a couple of specific subjects that are, not to put too fine a point on it, witchcraft and pagan religions."

"I see. And since Gwendolyn was the descendant of some pretty powerful Celtic witches, I'm guessing the missing documents are in the same vein."

"That's what really bothers me, though," Connor frowned. Most of those papers shouldn't have been of any interest to someone outside the family. A lot of it was the work of past generations of Broadhurst women on the family's genealogy and their involvement in sacred circles—what some people would call covens, except that word carries such a negative connotation for most people."

"Not for me. Don't forget I'm an equal opportunity believer and an equal opportunity skeptic," Laura reminded her. "My grandmother taught me well. She said there were many traditions of belief in the world, and it would be my job to discern which were based in wisdom and 'of the spirit,' as she said, and which were nothing more than elaborate theater for the weak of mind. It was a long time before I really understood what she meant."

"So she wouldn't tell you which ones had her stamp of approval?"

"No," Laura said, "and it used to annoy me back when I wanted someone to give me a book with all the right answers so I could memorize them and get an A-plus on the life test. Of course, even then I understood she was proud of her own tradition of Navajo spirituality and the path she'd chosen. I knew long ago that she was an amazingly powerful woman, just like Gwendolyn."

Connor looked at her quizzically. "You really think that? I mean that Gwendolyn was like Grandmother Klah?"

"Well, of course. Why else would she have sent for Gwendolyn to come to the mountain? I could tell at once that they 'knew' each other, if you understand what I'm trying to say."

"True," Connor agreed. "It was like watching a reunion of old friends, even though they had never met, at least not in this world."

"But they shared something profound, some kind of wisdom that crossed the boundaries between Celtic witch and Navajo shaman. And I'm certain they had met in other realms, so to speak."

Another shiver crawled up Connor's spine. "It's those 'other realms' and..." her arm swept the room to encompass its contents, "all of this that scares the hell out of me. I don't like even thinking about it."

Laura's expression conveyed an understanding of Connor's confusion. "Okay, let's sit down for a minute and get a few things straight. Now, first of all, as far as I'm concerned, I refuse to be scared of any place or idea or practice, no matter how hard to fathom, that has the approval of Grandmother Klah, or your Grandmother Broadhurst. They are incredible women. Of course, I can still visit my grandmother in the flesh, and yours sort of hopped the transcendental express to points unknown, which makes it harder to get good advice or a home-cooked meal. But, and this is my point, I can't imagine that two such beings are going to completely abandon us to the whims of evil people."

"So you think that means we can't fail at figuring out what's going here? We've got some sort of metaphysical golden parachute?"

Laura sighed and shook her head in mild exasperation. "No. We're not invincible just because we've got some spirit guides and magic-wielding people rooting for us. Our lives are still our lives. If we make mistakes, we'll live with the consequences...or die with them. I don't know which, though I'm feeling pretty enthused about living these days." She reached for Connor's hand. "All I'm saying is that there's nothing to be afraid of when it comes to knowledge and understanding. The more we know, the better off we'll be. Besides, we have reinforcements coming, and for all we know, there could be whole platoons of invisible watchdogs just itching to help us out."

"Sort of like an army of friendly Casper the Ghost types?"

"I don't know, this is England. I'm thinking more along the lines of the Canterville Ghost."

Connor finally let herself laugh. "Are you ever serious about this stuff?'

"Not unless someone drags me to a big Catholic church and there's a priest staring at me from the pulpit. Then I try to contain my amusement. But that's because Grandmother Klah also taught me respect for other people's beliefs. Now, I have a feeling that your grandmother wouldn't have left anything of vital importance where it could be so easily stolen. And she specifically left this house to you, not to your mother or your aunt. She wanted you to have it, and she wanted you to have what was in it."

Connor looked around the room again. "I tend to agree. She knew I didn't need it from a financial perspective. And even though I have fond memories of the place, I wasn't going to pine away if it were sold or it if it went to someone else. So she had a specific intention. But you've seen the size of this place. Any hunches about where we start looking?"

Laura jumped to her feet. "No hunches or incoming communications from points elsewhere. So, my brilliant suggestion is that we start at one end and search the good old-fashioned way."

"Not knowing what we're looking for tends to cramp my style. How about yours?" Connor inquired.

Laura shrugged. "That makes it harder, I suppose, but not impossible."

Connor pushed aside a stack of books that teetered near the edge of a table. "Then lead on, MacDuff. I'm ready to explore strange new worlds."

"What's strange," replied Laura, "is mixing Shakespeare and *Star Trek.*"

Chapter Twelve

Nature is often hidden,
sometimes overcome,
seldom extinguished.
—Sir Francis Bacon
Of Nature in Men

Lady Carlisle pushed aside her breakfast plate as her husband strode into the dining room and poured himself a cup of coffee from the urn on the sideboard. "Morning, love," she murmured, her smile fading when she took note of his unusually somber expression. "You don't look as if you're bearing good news."

He sat in one of the Queen Anne walnut dining chairs, which creaked dangerously under his tall frame. "Don't really know," he said, "and that irritates me more than anything. I read those E-mail messages. Both were from Benjamin Hawthorne, and he asked more questions than he gave information. Wants to know what we make of the murder here and the bodies they found in Gwendolyn's grave."

"He had no theories of his own?"

"None he was willing to share. Cagey old bird, I should think, still very much the spymaster and all."

"And no enlightenment on the subject of our dear Gwendolyn, like where she's got to exactly?"

"Toward the end of the second note, he sounded as if his next E-mail would offer up some sort of explanation to that little mystery, but I just got it, and there was a decided change of tone. I shouldn't call it hostile, precisely, but very cautious and almost, suspicious, if you like."

"That doesn't make sense. Surely he thinks of us as allies."

"One would have thought so. But we may be wrong."

They heard the mellow tones of the bell, signaling a visitor at the front door.

"Oh, hell," snapped William. "Who's here at this time of the morning?"

W

"If I might have a word with you, Lord Carlisle." Foulsham's mournful intonation might have been alarming, suited as it was to either announcing a death, or inviting one to come have a look at a corpse, except that William had learned from experience that this was the policeman's only tone of voice.

"Of course. Please do sit down."

Foulsham arranged himself in an armchair and steepled his fingers in front of his nose. "As I'm sure you are aware, we've been pursuing every possible line of investigation in the death of Miss Frome." He paused as if this gem of non-information required acknowledgment, but William refused to rise to the bait. He sat back in his own chair, legs crossed, and waited.

"In the course of our enquiries, we've learned less than I'd hoped, but we have turned up a few bits and pieces, as they say." Another pregnant pause. "Were you aware of Miss Frome's visits to Haslemere?"

Coming out of the blue as it was, this odd tidbit surprised William in the extreme. "Haslemere?" he echoed, realizing too late that he'd broken his vow of silence.

"Yes, Lord Fenwycke's place. Not too far from here, you know. And we've got hold of a girl there, does day cleaning, who came to us with a story about Miss Frome and...er..."

"And what?" William snapped impatiently. "Get on with it, man!"

"Well, Miss Frome was visiting Haslemere on her days out and we quickly ascertained that she wasn't walking out with one of the servants there."

William was almost tempted to smile at Foulsham's use of the old-fashioned euphemism for dating, but he restrained himself. "So what *was* she doing there?" he asked, but Foulsham remained silent, staring at William as a scientist might examine a new specimen. "If it wasn't some gardener or other..." his mind flew toward an obvious solution, but it seemed absurd, given Gerald's unmitigated snobbery. "Surely you don't mean she was having assignations with Lord Fenwycke, of all people."

Foulsham's mouth bent into what could have been a smile or a sneer, depending on one's perspective. "Well, not to put too fine a point on it, my lord, but the assignation as you say wasn't with Lord Fenwycke...it was Lady Fenwycke."

The policeman left this revelation hanging between them, and for an instant, William felt something dark and sinister weighing in upon him, as if all light had been extinguished in the sphere around him. Then, just as quickly, the sensation passed and he was aware of Foulsham's eyes boring into him.

"Were you aware of this little, er, arrangement between the lady and your maid?" he asked, emphasizing the possessive pronoun. "Or perhaps you thought it was none of your business."

William bristled visibly. He did, indeed, entertain some rather old-fashioned notions, particularly about how gentlemen behaved in the matter of keeping private matters private; prying into someone's affairs was boorish in the extreme. However, that Foulsham would assume him capable of withholding information from the police in a murder investigation irritated him enormously.

"I certainly was not aware of such a liaison," he said simply. William frowned, trying to make room for a completely different picture of the

Fenwycke household. His first thought was of Gerald. Did the man know what his wife was up to? Condone the extramarital affair? Or was he ignorant as usual? William surveyed Foulsham dispassionately. "So what do you make of this, Chief Inspector? Is it your contention that this matrimonial infidelity is in some way related to Miss Frome's murder?"

A look of sheer cunning swept over Foulsham's face. "I don't think I said that, now did I, my lord? Is that how you see it? There's always the possibility that someone was not happy with the situation—Lady Fenwycke carrying on with a serving maid in broad daylight."

In broad daylight? William stifled his amusement at the sheer absurdity of Foulsham's statement. Would the woman in question have been less censured if she'd restricted her dalliance to the evening hours? He doubted it. "No, Foulsham, that is not how I see it. The facts as you present them need not be related at all to the death of the young woman. Naturally, it's unfortunate that this matter should be brought out under such circumstances, but what people do in the privacy of their homes is just that, private. Have you discussed this with Lord Fenwycke?"

"Not yet, although I'm due there straightaway. You will, of course, be kind enough to keep what I've told you in confidence, my lord, until things are a bit clearer, what?"

William was almost glad the man had asked specifically for confidentiality. Otherwise, he wasn't sure how he would have balanced what he saw as two opposing duties, both points of honor. On the one hand, he would have been disposed to break the news of Gillian's affair to Gerald personally, so that he need not hear it from the likes of Nicholas Foulsham. On the other, he was not unaware that he bore a duty to the police to not obstruct their investigation in any way. Taxing Gerald with this revelation, and observing the man's first reaction, was part of their investigatory technique.

William ushered the officer to the door, with a terse assurance that he had no intention of discussing these revelations with Gerald, or anyone at Haslemere. "Good day, Chief Inspector. Keep me informed, please." He closed the door and reflected on how many times of late he'd had to show this man out.

W

He found Ellen still occupying the dining room, her face buried in the morning paper. When he came in, she folded it neatly, as was her habit, and asked him what Foulsham had wanted. "Another round of pointless questions, darling?"

"No, for once the DCI was giving information rather than seeking it." In a subdued voice, he quickly related the news of Gillian Fenwycke's indiscretion.

Ellen raised an eyebrow. "Really. I wouldn't have thought it of Gillian for some reason."

"Why? You think she's too straitlaced?"

She chuckled. "Oh, not at all. There's nothing straitlaced about Gillian. I can't imagine how men can be so blind to a woman's true nature sometimes."

William blinked. "I guess I'd never really thought about it. But you said you were surprised by this."

Ellen shrugged. "Only by the nature of the indiscretion. I wouldn't put much past Gillian, on the basis of scruples, since she clearly hasn't any to speak of. But I'd sooner suspect her of lying, cheating, and stealing than to do something so plainly human as to have an affair. I wonder if she had any feeling for the girl at all?" Her expression was sad.

William, too, hoped there had been some real emotion in Patricia's last relationship, but he doubted it. He examined his fingernails thoughtfully, turning the matter over in his mind, and when he looked up, his wife was staring at him, the light of comprehension dawning in her eyes.

"So, that walking ghoul, Foulsham, came here to see if you knew whether Gillian was having a romp with Patricia and therefore might have tipped Gerald to the affair. Which would give him or Gillian supposedly a motive for murder. Hmm. Perhaps he's not as stolidly unimaginative as he seems."

"Perhaps not," William nodded, "but where were we when the ghoul so rudely interrupted us?"

"You were telling me about Benjamin's E-mails. And I was about to tell you that I did have word this morning from one of our people in

St. Giles. Gwen's granddaughter and her friend are in residence at Rosewood House. And apparently there's been some commotion over a burglary there.

William frowned. "What was taken?"

"No news on that yet, I'm afraid. But you don't suppose someone actually found..."

"No, I can't imagine our erstwhile leader would ever have been so careless as to risk the integrity of our circle or its power."

Ellen finished off her juice and gently sat the goblet on the placemat. "Do you suppose it's time for us to call at Rosewood House?"

"I would have said yes if you'd asked me that yesterday. But I have the impression our visit would not be viewed in the best possible light by Mr. Hawthorne."

"But why?"

"This last message may have been brief, but he managed to convey that he and an associate were en route to England, and that he felt it best if he were present to effect introductions between his daughter and Gwendolyn's old friends."

"Sounds a trifle old-fashioned for someone his age, and a Yank besides."

"Does, doesn't it? Which leads me to believe he's warning me off in an oblique fashion. Telling me not to meddle where I'm not wanted until he's had a chance to sort me out in person."

Ellen nodded. "I see what you mean by the change in tone. Your conversation with him several days ago...didn't you say that was rather cordial?"

"Indeed it was. And something has changed his attitude. I think we ought to try and puzzle out just what that is."

"Surely he can't have just this moment twigged what we are, and what we do?" she asked.

"No, he isn't that dense. Gwendolyn told him a bit over the years, enough to keep him from interfering anyway. So whatever's made him get the wind up hasn't to do with the basic state of affairs. He's got hold of some information that makes us appear suspect. Problem is, suspect of what?"

Ellen walked over and put her hand on his shoulder. "You know, darling, it's time we started thinking about what needs to be done."

He twisted in his chair to look her in the face. "Surely you don't think you can take Gwendolyn's place? We've all agreed that until we could determine with certainty where she was—or is—we didn't dare convene the circle."

Ellen shook her head. "Not precisely, William. We've agreed to wait for more information, for greater understanding before undertaking any major tasks. But has it occurred to you that convening might be the best way to go about it? I don't have Gwendolyn's power, but I'm strong, William. Don't forget that it was I who knew from the moment her casket arrived in St. Giles that she was neither in it nor anywhere near it."

William mulled this bit of argument. "True. And that's the most baffling point of all. She should have communicated with us directly since then, and she hasn't. None of us has felt her presence in all these months. Yet if she were well and truly passed to the realm of the dead, we would know. I'm almost ready to believe there *is* such a place as limbo and that Gwendolyn's in it." He scowled at a spot beyond her shoulder, as if seeking confirmation of his theory.

Ellen brushed back the hair from his forehead. "I know, love. All I'm suggesting is that perhaps she's waiting for us to bring everyone together in order to become clear on how we are to proceed."

"For all I know, darling, you may be absolutely right. But it's vital that we not put a foot wrong here. We've both sensed the energy shifts and seen the shadows form during our meditations. We must tread carefully, Ellen. A huge shift in the balance could be disastrous."

Ellen sighed. "I know. I suppose I'm simply being impatient. But my dreams have been troubling of late, very troubling indeed."

He looked at her closely. "In what way, darling?" The expression on her face suddenly filled him with misgivings.

"The Tor," she said simply. "In every dream, I've seen the Tor."

Chapter Thirteen

Away! The moor is dark beneath the moon,
Rapid clouds have drank the last pale beam of even:
Away! The gathering winds will call the Darkness soon,
And profoundest midnight shroud the serene lights of heaven.
—Percy Bysshe Shelley
Stanzas–April 1814

Laura and Connor stood gazing up the steep grassy slope at the enormous tower rising from its crest.

"What exactly is a Tor?" Laura asked, shading her eyes from the midday sun.

"I believe it's an old word for a fairly high hill," replied Connor. "Thus I suppose it could be called Glastonbury Hill, but somehow that wouldn't quite do it justice."

Laura nodded. "I agree. It could only called be the Glastonbury Tor. So, are we going to climb up there or stand down here and think about it?" They both surveyed the steep incline and the hundreds of steps that wove a meandering path to the top.

"I've climbed it before. I have to warn you, it isn't all that easy."

"So, 'race you up there' would be a silly approach." Laura grinned.

"Only silly because you'd be racing yourself. I'm not sufficiently twirled, I guess. Just the thought of the climb makes me tired for some reason."

"We could do it another time," Laura said obligingly, though she was itching to see the tower up close. "For that matter, we probably should have stayed at the house and kept working on the library instead of playing tourist."

"No, we spent hours shelving books. We deserve some down time. Let's do it now. It's a beautiful day, and it's going to be dark fairly soon."

Adopting a fairly stately pace, the two women scaled the switch-back trail leading to the summit. Laura noticed that Connor appeared to slow down ever so gradually as they climbed. A little more than halfway, Connor stopped completely and dropped onto one of the benches thoughtfully placed for weary pilgrims. "Are you all right, hon?" Laura asked. "You look awfully pale." And indeed, she did. Laura noted with some alarm that all of the color had drained from Connor's face.

"No, I mean, yes, I'm all right. Just tired. Jeez, I must be getting old. The last time I came up here I was probably ten years younger. Now it feels like I'm carrying lead weights on my back."

"Did you feel like this before we started up?"

"Not exactly, no. I was just normally tired." She looked puzzled. "Now what is that supposed to mean...normally tired?"

Laura gazed at her, pondering. "I don't know, you said it. But maybe that's the simplest way of putting it. You felt the standard amount of everyday fatigue when we were down there, and the way you're feeling now—your instincts are telling you there's something more to this than jet lag combined with physical exertion."

Connor scowled, and Laura could tell she was prepared to argue the point. But at that instant, the sun disappeared behind a cloud. Not abnormal for England any time of year. But Laura had a clear memory of looking up at a perfectly cloudless sky only five minutes earlier. Now a turbulent mass of white-and-gray cotton wool hung just above the tower. In the shadow, Connor looked even paler.

"I have to go up," Connor muttered, rising unsteadily from the bench.

"Wait, you're not up to it. I think we should go back down. Besides, I have a feeling it's about to rain, and rain hard." Laura gently took her arm, but Connor yanked it away.

"No! I have to go up, now."

Laura looked around them, trying to assess the situation. She couldn't be sure what was going on with Connor, but her instincts told her it wasn't good. They also told her this wasn't about physical illness, and that it might be more psychologically threatening than life-threatening. But her protectiveness was in full gear, and she wasn't about to let anything happen to Connor. In this state, she was obviously not thinking clearly. It was only then, as Laura's practiced observer took in the entire site, that she realized everyone else had gone. But that was impossible. There had been at least a dozen people traipsing up and down the slope, and several more at the top. Where the hell were they? Surely they couldn't have disappeared so quickly.

In the few seconds that Laura had devoted to this internal debate, Connor had already moved another thirty yards up the hill. For some reason, she was now progressing faster than before, much faster, almost as if an invisible hand were tugging her along. Laura took the steps two at a time, trying to catch up. Half a minute later, thunder shattered the thick silence, and within seconds rain drenched her to the skin. She'd never experienced such a cloudburst, not even in the desert during a violent summer storm when she'd felt the entire Earth vibrating under her feet. This was worse beyond measure. Rain battered her face, stinging cold in her eyes. Up ahead, she'd completely lost sight of Connor; all she could do was follow. She had to climb and keep climbing. She thanked all the guardian spirits she could think of that her destination was uphill. Even blinded by this torrent, she couldn't fail to find the tower and, she prayed, Connor.

W°

Driven as she was to reach the summit of the Tor, Connor failed to notice that Laura was no longer beside her. And she paid only scant attention to the cold, pelting rain. The dreadful fatigue she'd felt only minutes before had evaporated, and in its place was a hunger she couldn't understand, but didn't question. Something was there, up there, something she needed to see or feel or know. But what? Her mind fogged with confusion, she kept running and ignored the tightness in her chest, the ache burrowing deep in her side. Without warning, the bulk of the tower loomed in front of her, the arched entrance just to her right. Connor fled inside as if chased by demons, and all was utter silence, though some rational part of her mind insisted she could still hear the driving rain slashing against the old stonework.

There, in the very center of the structure, she stopped and looked up. Above her rose the hollow center of the tower and beyond that, where the termination of the spire should be, where rain should still be pouring in, there was...nothing.

W

Less than a minute after Connor reached the tower, Laura ran almost full tilt into a painfully solid wall. Her reflexes being excellent, she flung up her hands in a fraction of a second and avoided doing serious damage to her face. Still, the impact hurt, and it occurred to her to wonder if she'd cracked something in her left wrist. Laura still couldn't see a foot in front of her. The rain continued unabated, and she clung to the stone facade to get her bearings in the darkness. The tower was square, she thought, and it had arches on two sides. All she needed to do was feel her way along the wall until she found an opening.

She went from left to right, secure in her logic that even if she'd moved away from one door, she need only navigate at most one blank wall and then a corner to locate another opening. Seconds passed as she slid her hands and feet along as fast as she dared. Yes, here was a corner of the structure. Around to her right...hands and feet...hands and feet...surely not more than another few yards. She tried to look up but was instantly blinded by the deluge of water sluicing down the sides of the tower. A punishing, fickle wind whipped her sodden hair from side to side, slapping her cheeks. Where was the opening? Where the *hell* was the opening? She was prepared to fall forward into an archway at any second, so it came as no surprise when her right hand slid off the edge into nothingness. She slid her feet over, then started forward, her left hand against the stone beside her as a guide, anxious to get out of the miserable rain.

But the rain didn't stop, and the howling wind did not abate. Instead, when a streak of lightning cleaved the darkness for an instant, Laura was horrified to discover she was still *outside* the tower, that what she had mistaken for a way in was yet another corner. Yet she knew that was impossible. She could not have passed over a six-foot wide entryway without virtually falling into it. This was wrong, all wrong! Laura fought the fear that had clamped a vise around her heart and lungs. She took deep breaths, struggled to find her center and let the energy flow into her spirit warrior soul. No matter the challenge, she had been taught to embrace normal human weakness and wrap it in the protective armor of spirit. In this way she could defy fear when need be.

But this was not garden variety fear, not the sort of pulse-racing scare you might get in a dark house on Halloween. No...the terror she felt was spawned by an atavistic horror of the evil without name that lay seething in the darkness all around her. In her mind's eye, she saw it rising up like some ungainly giant insect on countless legs, black-green slime dripping from pincered jaws, livid yellow eyes piercing the gloom, searching, searching for *her*. Her scream was swallowed up in the dark.

W

In the sanctuary of the tower, Connor had fallen to her knees, no longer willing to look into nothingness. Where walls should rise, stone on stone, all around her, there was only gray mist. It was as if she had fallen through a seam in the world and found herself surrounded by the primordial soup from which life itself had churned into existence. Connor shivered, but not as a reaction to stimulus from outside her body. For here there was neither heat nor cold, nor damp, nor dry;

there was no texture, no depth, no sense of up and down. Even the firm surface on which she'd knelt no longer pressed against her, as if the laws of gravity no longer functioned.

Minutes...or years passed. She opened her eyes again and blinked in the torchlight. She was both there and not there. Hooded figures chanted as they walked in a strangely quiet lock step through the doors on either side of her, a long procession of arms and legs passing around her and through her, a river of humanity that did not even sense her presence. She heard the sound of a bell tolling in the distance, and on the last stroke the walls melted away and stars shone fiercely in the sky above her. She stood alone on the summit of the Tor. Below her, bright threads of light shimmered down the hillside, crossing concentric rings of even brighter light encircling the Tor. She knew they were torches, held aloft to light the way of the priestesses who were even now converging on this sacred place. A tiny voice in her mind was asking unfathomable questions—*Who am I? What is this place?* But the voice was quelled by the sounds of battle.

Screams, and the third torch circle from the top broke apart. She watched in horror, her mind seeing what her eyes could not—a dark, fetid cloud rolled over the torchbearers, enveloped the priestesses of the South, and moved on toward the summit. In its path, nothing lived. Broken, charred bodies lay scattered in the wake of darkness. Her mind focused on the other priestesses. "Come quickly," she commanded. "The beast is upon us. It is in our midst."

She felt both their panic and their disciplined resolve to resist it. The torches to the east, west, and north bobbed wildly, drawing closer, as the warriors, alarmed by the screams, ran to protect the women. And yet the shadow moved faster, as if sensing the nearness of its prey. It would reach her as she stood alone on the Tor, before the others could take their places and cast the Circle of Light, before they gathered the strength to drive It back into its eternal resting place.

She turned to face the terror, knowing full well that even the talisman she wore, magical and powerful as it was, could not protect her from the full strength of the creature, fashioned as it was from fear and hatred and bloodlust, created by her mortal enemy and intent on death.

Her eyes never wavered from her foe as she loosed the precious links of metal from around her waist. It dangled in her hand for a moment, fire streaking from the quartz crystals embedded in the finely wrought gold. Then she flung the belt backward, over her head and down the slope behind her, unerringly sending it toward the two people she loved most—Daria, the priestess of the north and Caregyn, her chief among the warriors and valiant defender of the high priestess. Try as they might, she knew they would not reach her in time. There was no other way. She had chosen to sacrifice herself for those she loved. They would protect the talisman with their very lives, and it would return to the Light when the god of all gods ordained that it should.

She stared into the maw of the creature. It was "that which cannot be named" for it inflicted upon the human soul the only punishment of consequence—namelessness. This was the most horrifying of conditions, she knew. Her soul would, for all intents and purposes, cease to exist, lost in a place where it could not distinguish itself from the Darkness. The voice of the Lady whispered to her one last time, *Remember, my child, you are both the Light and the Darkness. Deny neither.*

She opened her arms and stepped forward to embrace the shadow.

$\mathcal{W}$

Laura! Listen to me, listen to the sound of my voice. You must turn and face it. Turn and face the beast. Part of it is you, my child. Do not run from it, you cannot escape, you can only vanquish the demons from within yourself.

"Grandmother?" Laura whispered. "Where are you? Help me?" But there was no answer, and she was alone. No, not quite alone. She sensed someone near, a loving presence. She half turned to face the thing that still stared at her malevolently. But it no longer loomed above her head. It had retreated a pace or two, and this, combined with the knowledge that she wasn't entirely on her own, gave her renewed courage. Then an image of Connor seared across her brain. Connor...wearing someone else's face...and yet... Now the beast was turning, turning to attack a woman in long white robes, the woman who was and wasn't Connor Hawthorne, and Laura roared with fury, flinging herself at the flanks of the enormous insect, pummeling it with her fists. "No," she screamed. "Fight me!"

W

She felt the sour hot breath panting in her face, looked into the shimmering many faceted eyes of the beast. Behind her Daria and Cargeyn were screaming her name. But it was too late. She would let time work its way with the balance of the universe. Tonight the moon was in Libra, but justice and balance would be delayed for a time, until she could be called back from the nothingness. She reached out her hand...

W

"Connor, sweetheart, please wake up. Please."

The sun blinded her until she tilted her head and could just make out the edges of Laura's face. "Where's that thing?"

Laura frowned. "What thing?"

Connor shook her head and sat up, her bones aching from prolonged contact with the damp stones. Through the archway the setting sun shone red against the horizon. She looked down at her clothes. They were completely soaked. A quick glance at Laura confirmed that her hair and jacket and pants were sodden.

"I don't know. I thought there was something attacking me, something big and dark, or maybe it just was dark outside, but...that can't be. It's still daylight. And...I must have fallen, hit my head when I rushed in here during the storm." Then she saw Laura's hands. The palms were scraped raw and bleeding in some spots. "My God, what happened. Did you fall or..." The look in Laura's eyes shocked Connor into a stunned into silence.

"Let's get out of here, and then we'll talk about it," said Laura, helping her up, and they stumbled out into the sunshine. Below them, small groups of tourists were making their way up the slope. One young couple had just reached the top and stared at the two women with undisguised curiosity. Connor wondered why, until she looked around with sufficient attention to realize that nothing else was wet, not the ground, not the stones, not other people. Just Connor and Laura, standing on the Tor, soaking wet from rain that had apparently not fallen on anyone or anything but them. She took Laura's arm and led her away from tower, down the first set of steps to a bench set into the hillside.

"Do you have any idea what happened here?" she asked in a low voice. "And how did you get hurt?"

Laura took a deep breath. "It's going to sound crazy, but I lost you in the rain and when I got to the tower, I couldn't find an entrance. I kept feeling my way along the walls...I guess that's where I got some of these scrapes...but no matter how hard I tried I couldn't get in. Then there was something..." She paused and swallowed hard. "There was something I guess I must have imagined, something right out of a Stephen King movie."

"What?" asked Connor, still able to conjure the image of an enormous, shadowy figure that had loomed over her.

"If I told you, I think you'd laugh."

"Nothing would surprise me, and at the moment, I don't find any of this even vaguely amusing."

"Okay, it was shaped like a huge bug." She raised her hand to forestall disbelief. "I said it would sound insane. But this thing was bigger than a Greyhound bus and a lot meaner. I thought it was going to attack me, and then I had the distinct impression it was going after you. Something told me—no, make that some*one* told me—to face it and fight it."

"Who?"

"Sounded a lot like my Grandmother Klah, to be honest. And it felt as if she might be somewhere nearby." Laura took another deep, shuddering breath, and Connor put an arm around her, oblivious of the passersby.

"Then what happened?"

"I started hammering on that big thing, whatever the hell it was, but suddenly I found myself hammering on the stone floor inside the tower, and there you were slumped down on your knees and reaching toward something I couldn't see. I grabbed your arm and kept shouting your name, and finally you looked at me, I mean really at *me*."

"What was I looking at before?" Connor asked, not sure whether to be puzzled or frightened.

"Damned if I know. Now, would you like to tell me what happened after you ran off? You must have come right into the tower despite not being able to see anything."

"But I could see," said Connor softly, and she told Laura everything she could remember about what had happened on Glastonbury Tor. The only problem was, she couldn't quite explain at what moment in the history of humankind this had all happened.

Chapter Fourteen

"It is my belief, Watson, founded upon my experience,
that the lowest and vilest of alleys in London
do not present a more dreadful record of sin
than does the smiling and beautiful countryside."
—Sir Arthur Conan Doyle
The Adventures of Sherlock Holmes (Copper Beeches)

DCI Foulsham slumped into his office chair and reflected on his highly unsatisfactory interview with Lord Gerald Fenwycke. Since Foulsham was not the sort to cater to anyone, regardless of class, and since Gerald lived somewhere in the highly class-conscious past, they had not gotten along at all well. Foulsham's bombshell regarding Lady Fenwycke's extramarital shenanigans hadn't done anything to endear the copper to his lordship, nor had her husband's reaction established any certainty in Foulsham's mind that Gerald had known. Quite the opposite, in fact.

Gerald's first response had been outrage, then indignation, then icy denial. Quite honestly, Foulsham doubted the man was that good an actor. When confronted with the statements made by one of his own servants, he'd dismissed the girl as a liar and a trollop. Foulsham wondered that anyone today would even use the word *trollop*. He knew Lord Fenwycke had every intention of sacking the girl, but he wasted no time on guilt. Sonja had made clear to him that she was sick of waiting on the Fenwyckes and would be handing in her month's notice anyway. While her attitude might have made her accusations suspect, there was a genuine ring of truth when she described the not-so-secret assignations.

Naturally, he'd sought substantiation and gotten it, more or less, from the cook. She'd been more concerned for her job and less forthcoming, but sufficiently self-righteous to highly disapprove of such carryings-on, especially among the gentry whom she believed should set a good example. Thus, although she avoided coming right out and saying what she'd seen, she did enough scowling, harrumphing, and cluck-clucking to obviate the need for specificity. She'd known all right, and that had been enough to send Foulsham sniffing after his lordship.

He had, of course, given passing thought to Gillian Fenwycke as a suspect, but the horrific nature of the crime tended to exonerate her in his estimation. Not that he was sexist when it came to hunting down criminals. He'd seen almost every type of violence that one human being could inflict on another in his more than twenty years with the police. And in his experience, women were capable of almost any crime. Had Patricia Frome only been stabbed, he would have been as anxious to thoroughly interview the girl's paramour as he was the cuckolded husband. But the decapitation, now that was another thing. Except for that story about Lizzie Borden over in the U.S., he'd never heard of a woman hacking off another one's head. To him that spelled male psychopath.

The problem was, he hadn't got anywhere at all really. There were no strong suspects on which to focus the enquiry. The report of the pathologist had been little help other than restating the obvious which was that the poor girl was missing her head, and that she had been identified by matching the fingerprints of the corpse with the fingerprints found in her room and on her personal possessions. Additionally, her parents had mentioned a childhood scar on the left calf, which had been confirmed.

Sergeant Peter Garrett sauntered into the office and slung himself into the chair opposite Foulsham's desk. The DCI was frequently annoyed with Garrett's lack of discipline, but always marveled at his ability to do the job. No matter how arduous or boring the task, Garrett never shirked an assignment and often surprised Foulsham with innovative theories. Today was no exception.

"You know, sir, I reckon this beheading's got to be tied to them other two murders."

Foulsham looked at him curiously. "What two murders?"

"The ones in the graveyard."

"But why?"

Garrett shrugged. "The girl knew young Collin personally, had a bit of a thing going with him when they were in school. So first he and his pal end up dead, then her. Stands to reason he must have told her something about what they were going to be up to that night. Then someone decides to shut her up too. Besides, before all this happened, they was all reasonably respectable village folk." His eyes took on a mischievous glint. "At least as far as that goes, these days. Don't reckon you can call what she was up to with the lady of the manor next door respectable, but you see what I mean. None of them ever been in trouble. Never been nicked. Never even been ticked off by a constable for drunk and disorderly in the pub. Least not as far as I've found out." He sat back, looking excessively self-satisfied at this lucent argument.

Foulsham raised one eyebrow, then the other. "Garrett, have you ever, in your twelve-year career, known a psychotic killer to simply murder some people the good old-fashioned way—shooting them and leaving them for dead—and then turn around and do a vicious stabbing and mutilation? And why shoot two men and then a woman?"

Garrett looked slightly less confident. "No, I haven't seen that. But then I never ran across one who wanted to keep a head as a souvenir. So what's there to say this villain ain't just as likely to pick a bloke as he would a girl? You're always tellin' me not to assume anything based on some egghead theory. So...here you go. I say hang the theory, and let's find someone who had to do with all three of these victims."

Foulsham's shoulders sagged with all the fatigue he felt. He didn't want to make his job any more difficult at this moment by trying to sell the idea to his superiors that these three murders, involving victims who had been killed in different ways, were related to each other. He stared at the stacks of paper on his desk. He was no further along today than he'd been a week ago. If he didn't make some progress soon, Patricia Frome would be handed off to someone else.

He was just about to question Garrett further on the connection with the St. Giles murders when Detective Constable Mary Fitch strode purposefully into the room and dropped a piece of paper on Foulsham's desk. "Memo from the superintendent, sir. Wants an update on the Frome case. Someone at the Met's asking after us."

Foulsham's face darkened. "And what does someone from the Metropolitan Police Force have to do with a Somerset homicide, if I may ask?"

DC Fitch's face remained impassive. "Wouldn't know, sir. But Sally, the clerk on the second floor says the super got a call from this bloke and they talked for a quarter of an hour. The super even got up and closed his office door like there was some big secret in the works. Next thing, she's handing me this memo and asking if I'd mind running it down to you."

Foulsham regarded the document sourly. Picking it up meant he'd have to read it. And once he'd read it, he'd be obliged to follow the directives outlined in it. If there was anything he hated, it was anyone treading on his patch. A thought came to him, and he pushed back from the desk. With a wink at his subordinates, he said, "Shame I wasn't here when you dropped by, Fitch. Perhaps you'll run into me later." Garrett and Fitch nodded approvingly. They weren't any more likely than Foulsham to tolerate meddling from outsiders.

With his strategy thus determined, Foulsham made haste to get out of the building before anyone else could cross his path. His haste, however, was his undoing. He arrived at the car park, stuck his hand in his pocket, and discovered he'd left his car keys on the desk. He went quickly around to the side entrance, intending to dash up the stairs, and ran smack into Superintendent Hollis.

"Foulsham, just the man I've been thinking of. Got my memo, did you?"

"Memo, sir?" said the DCI, mentally crossing his fingers to ward off bad luck.

Hollis's face creased with annoyance. "Sent it down to you almost an hour ago. Don't tell me this so-called interoffice communications scheme is broken down already?"

"I probably just missed it sir. I wasn't in my office the whole time."

"Well, I suppose. But I may as well put you in the picture. You won't have to trudge back up there and read it."

"Of course, sir."

"Chap in London, old friend of mine, works at the Met now, used to be attached to MI-6."

Foulsham's curiosity was piqued, despite himself. What did an ex-spy copper want with his piddling, if bizarre, little murder? He waited for Hollis to continue.

"A friend of his from the old days, pretty influential chap, I take it, ex-senator over in the States and all...got in touch with him about a couple of matters. One is that decapitation thing you and Garrett and Fitch are still working on..." Foulsham couldn't help but notice the slight emphasis on "still" as if he'd been sitting around doing nothing. "And that odd one in what was it, St. Giles on Wyndle, you know, the grave robbing and the two dead chaps bunged right down in the grave."

"I can't understand why an American is interested in either incident, sir. And why *both*? It isn't as if they're related." Foulsham held his breath, waiting to see if his superior held any specific views on the matter.

Hollis cocked his head to one side in a decidedly avian posture, a habit that had earned him some unkind nicknames in the uniform division, and regarded Foulsham with a penetrating glare. "So that's how you read it, Detective Chief Inspector?" Foulsham cringed. The use of one's full rank was never a good sign. "I'm sorry to hear that. Perhaps you can think of some connection. If not, let me know."

DCI Foulsham had taken the wrong tack and tried to quickly reverse course. "Sir, it isn't that I can't see any possible connection— I've already considered it. Still, I *am* concerned that someone outside the department sees one too. I'd rather like to know how they leapt to that conclusion. Sounds a bit fishy, if you take my meaning. Besides,

I don't see why anyone in London should be interested."

Superintendent Hollis's expression was uncharacteristically enigmatic. "If I were you, Nick, I wouldn't spend a lot of time worrying about why others are interested in these cases. But I would spend a lot of time trying to solve them. As I understand it from my friend at the Met, this American fellow is as good as they come. He's got the respect and admiration of every intelligence service on our side of the ledger, if you take *my* meaning. So if he's a trifle concerned that his mother-in-law's grave was disturbed, and two bodies were left in it, and he's also concerned that two of his friends, Lord and Lady Carlisle, found a headless body in their house, then we are going to be as obligingly helpful in addressing his concern as we can be."

There was an air of finality to all this that silenced Foulsham's objections. Besides, he had just begun to see the light. The person who had instigated this enquiry must be Benjamin Hawthorne, Connor Hawthorne's father and Gwendolyn Broadhurst's son-in-law. What he hadn't known was that Benjamin Hawthorne had that much influence on this side of the Atlantic. *Well,* he thought, *we'll just see about that.*

Hollis's gaze narrowed suddenly, and Foulsham had the uncomfortable sensation that his mind was an open book. Perhaps Hollis had simply been around for long enough to predict the behavior of his subordinates. "I don't suppose I'll need to remind you to tread gently with this American. Chap in London says Hawthorne's on his way here now with an American cop in tow who also has some friends at the Met. And Hawthorne's daughter's already in England." Foulsham didn't volunteer that he knew this last bit, or how he knew it. "So let's be as cooperative as possible, eh, Nick? I'll consider it a personal favor."

Superintendent Hollis continued to the car park and left Foulsham with one foot in and one foot out. He still needed his keys, but he also needed some time to think. He was both furious and intrigued, and he'd be damned if some amateur was going to trample all over his investigation. Senator, indeed. Like letting some fool of an M.P. start giving orders at the station. Given the time of day, a trip to the local was in order and within walking distance. That way he needn't worry about being over the limit. This was probably a three-pint problem.

W

Unaware that their inquiries and imminent arrival had caused so much consternation in the Somerset CID, Benjamin and Malcolm buckled their seat belts as requested and stared out the window at the rapidly approaching landscape. Malcolm stretched his exceptionally long legs into the extra space afforded business-class passengers and sighed appreciatively. "I usually have to fly coach," he explained. "The city budget doesn't allow for excessive expenditures on the part of its employees. I always feel like a pretzel by the time I get where I'm going."

Benjamin nodded. "The airlines have perfected the art of stuffing as many seats as possible into the coach section. But the one great equalizer is that we all get to breathe the same stale, recirculated air."

"Hmm. Since they banned smoking on planes, they've reduced the amount of fresh air sucked into the cabin. Increases fuel efficiency, I've heard."

"And gives everyone a chance to share," Benjamin added, glancing at the elderly gentleman across the aisle who'd been coughing and hacking pretty much throughout the six-hour flight. "At least it's almost over. We're about to land. I don't like flying unless I'm the one in the cockpit."

Having nothing to declare, they whisked through customs and quickly settled the formalities of car rental. When the shuttle dropped them at the parking lot, they quickly located the stall and the four-door Rover Benjamin had rented. Malcolm's expression was that of a Buick full-size-sedan man who'd just been sent to foreign-car purgatory. Benjamin laughed. "Don't worry, big guy, they're roomier inside than you'd think. And once you've seen the roads around St. Giles, you'll understand why we don't need a bigger car."

Malcolm looked less than convinced as he shoved his carry-on into the back of the car. "Did you notice the way that rental agent kept staring at you?"

"The blond kid?"

"Yeah. His name badge said Trevor something."

"No, I can't say as I noticed him staring. But he did seem kind of flustered, and he kept opening his mouth as if he were going to say something, and then he'd change his mind. But let's not start dissecting the behavior of everyone we meet. Otherwise we're going to turn completely paranoid."

Chapter Fifteen

Deep into that Darkness peering, long I stood there wondering, fearing
Doubting, dreaming dreams no mortal every dared to dream before.
—Edgar Allan Poe
"The Raven"

Connor and Laura were once more working in the library when they heard the now familiar crunch of tires on gravel. But the sound was not accompanied by a car engine, and Laura immediately went to investigate whether someone was attempting to roll stealthily into the driveway. She discovered instead a quickly departing delivery van, with the name of the local dairy emblazoned on the side.

She collected the milk, and then it dawned on her that the oddly quiet delivery van had an electric motor. "It was just the milkman," she called from the hallway, en route to the kitchen.

"Good old Mrs. Gwydden," she heard Connor say. "Might have known she'd get the deliveries started up right away."

Laura returned from the kitchen and found Connor perched high on the library ladder, shelving books. "I can't believe they still deliver milk right to the doorstep."

"Mail too," replied Connor, descending the ladder. "Even to the farmhouses that sit way back from the road. The mail carrier drives all the way to the house, gets out, and takes the post, as they call it, right to the door."

Laura shook her head. "Amazing. Are those the red trucks we've seen on the road—'Royal Mail,' et cetera."

"Yes, and that reminds me that we're going to have to give you an English lesson before we do another thing."

Laura looked at Connor in disbelief. "I may have been born Navajo, sweetheart, but my English is as good as yours."

Connor laughed. "It's probably better, actually. No, I meant you'll have to learn a few of the idioms so the locals will understand you. For example, small trucks are generally called vans. Bigger trucks, the sort movers would use, are called lorries. And semi-trucks or tractor trailers are called articulated lorries." She grinned. I just love that one...articulated lorries."

Laura laughed. "I suppose it does sound a little odd. Okay, what else?"

Connor thought about it for a moment. "Well, let's see. You hire cars, book tables at restaurants, leave your car in the car park, take tours on motor coaches instead of buses." She paused. "There are a few hundred more. Want me to go on?"

"Isn't there a handbook for tourists?" Laura asked plaintively. "Maybe if I studied, I could take an 'English Spoken Here' certification test."

Connor laughed and hugged her. "You don't need a handbook when you've got your own private tutor."

The phone rang and when Connor answered, she was delighted to hear her daughter's voice. "Hi, Mom. You all settled in at Rosewood House?"

"More or less, sweetheart. How's Oxford surviving?"

Laura made some charade-type gestures, which Connor translated as asking whether Laura should leave the room. She shook her head firmly to indicate she should stay, then turned her attention to the phone.

"You mean how is it surviving *me*," she heard Katy say with a chuckle. "Far as I know, Oxford can survive even its most unorthodox students. I'm working like mad on my Classics. Mrs. Plimpton is a horror when you misquote something during the one of the coachings."

"When will you be able to come down from school?" Connor asked. "I miss you."

"Oh, Mom. It hasn't been that long since I spent weeks with you in Santa Fe."

"I know, but at my advanced years, time seems to stretch out forever."

"Oh, right. You're in your forties, Mom. Now, that's old of course, but not completely ancient."

"Gee, thanks, honey. It makes my life easier knowing you aren't ready to have me mummified quite yet."

"Is that a bad pun or a last wish I should write down somewhere?"

"Did I ever tell you that you have a macabre sense of humor?"

"You didn't have to, Mom. I got it from you. Must be from over-hearing all those courtroom horror stories."

"I never told you horror stories..." Connor began, then stopped when she heard Katy laughing.

"You are so easy to get, mother dear. Anyway, I won't be free for a few more weeks, but if you're still on this side of the Atlantic in April, I'd love to see you. And Aunt Jessica sends her love."

Connor realized she hadn't talked to her grandmother's younger sister in months. "Is she there? Can you put her on the phone?"

"No, she had some sort of meeting at the Women's Institute. You know one of those church-lady things."

"Someday you'll probably end up a church lady, Katherine Vandervere."

"Bite your tongue, Mom. Like I'd ever wear tweed skirts and wellies at the same time."

Connor laughed and told Katy to give Jessica a hug for her and promised to leave word if she decided to go back to the States any time soon. "I'll probably be here for a while, though, and at the very least I'll swing by Oxford on my way back to London."

"Oxford isn't on the way to London," Katy teased.

"England isn't all that big a country," Connor shot back. "I think I could manage to drag these feeble old bones a few extra miles. And, besides..." Connor hesitated for a moment before plunging on. "Besides, Laura's never seen Oxford."

If she'd been expecting a negative reaction, she was pleasantly disappointed. "Then you've got to come. It's always great to show someone around who's never been here at all. You already know all the tourist spots and the ghost stories."

Without realizing it, Connor heaved a sigh of relief. "Then we'll make it up there as soon as we can. I need to clear up some things here first."

"No problem. I've got to log some serious time at the Bodleian. Be sure and give me a warning before you come."

"Why? So you can eliminate all evidence of a dissolute life?"

"Absolutely. You know, all the drugs, liquor bottles, discarded men's attire...should I go on?"

"Please don't. You're giving me gray hair as it is."

"Love you, Mom. Bye."

Connor hung up and turned to look at Laura, who was replacing more books.

"Katy's fine," she said, irrelevantly.

"I gathered. And is she okay with, um, well, with me?"

"She's fine. I guess I was a little more nervous about it than I let on."

"Only natural. Sometimes it's hard to combine the important people in your life. Sometimes they don't get along."

"But I have a feeling you two are going to be friends. And she keeps on growing up. Every time I turn around, she's a little wiser, a little more mature, and a whole lot more of a smart mouth."

"Kind of like her mother," said Laura with a smile.

"So I've been told from time to time. Now, where are we with all this?"

Laura surveyed the tidy shelves. "I can't believe we've gotten most of them back in place." She picked up a pad of lined paper from the desk. "Is this the final tally of what's missing?"

"Not much to the list. As far as I can tell, they took all of the loose manuscripts and eight or ten books at least." She looked at the list over Laura's shoulder. "I can't possibly remember the titles, of course, except one I happen to recall was bound in deep red leather with a lot of gold tooling on the spine. It was about the history of this area, something about the Vale of Avalon. Otherwise, the empty space on the shelves is entirely in the occult section."

Laura plopped down in a comfortable leather armchair. "Just how serious was Gwendolyn about the Celtic witchcraft stuff?"

Connor carefully arranged her face in what she hoped was a non-committal, disinterested expression and sought for a way to explain Gwendolyn. "My grandmother...it's hard to describe her, I suppose, to capture the person she was. Very complicated and yet very straightforward at the same time. You didn't get to spend much time with her when she came to New Mexico."

"But I fell in love with her anyway," Laura said softly. "She's one of the most amazingly perceptive and powerful women I've ever met. A lot like my own grandmother."

"I saw the resemblance too," Connor agreed thoughtfully. "They were like two sides of the same coin, weren't they?"

"But I get the impression you don't know as much about your grandmother's spiritual practices as I do about mine. Why? I can't imagine she didn't want to teach you."

Connor scowled. "That's just the problem. She did want to teach me, and I didn't want to hear it."

"Too weird for you?" Laura asked.

Connor sighed. "Maybe. I don't know. It's more that I was so caught up in the 'real' world, I didn't think I could waste any time on things I couldn't see, or touch, or taste. Does that make sense?"

"Sure. I remember how obnoxious I was to Grandmother Klah when I first came back to the rez as an adult. My life was falling apart. I'd had a bitter divorce, a checkered career, and Jocelyn had died. I couldn't imagine that there was anything else to consider other than cold, hard reality. Grandmother had to pretty much drag me kicking and screaming—well, figuratively anyway. I'd never known there was any other way to live, any other level of consciousness or awareness. At the time I didn't even fully understand what the Navajo meant by following the Way. For that matter, the words peace and harmony meant nothing to me. All I knew was pain."

Connor perched on the arm of the chair and stroked Laura's cheek. "I know all about that place. I spent some time there myself. My life was a series of what I considered typical heartbreaks. You know, the old 'life sucks sometimes, but so what?' My marriage was an utter farce, and my mother was furious when I divorced Alex and apoplectic when I met Ariana and she came to live with me at the townhouse."

"But what about your career? That must have meant something to you."

"My career as a prosecutor was successful but ultimately depressing. I was amazed that my first book sold so well, and then the next one. Ariana and I were happy, and I rode along taking all that for granted. I remember visiting here a few years ago, and Gran brought me in here and sat me down for a talk about my heritage."

"What did she tell you?"

"That's just it. I hardly listened. I didn't want to hear it. I was a jerk. I came out with this whole line of rationalist, intellectual bullshit about how all these pagan traditions were just footnotes in the quaint history of this part of England."

"And how did Gwendolyn take it?"

Connor was silent for a long moment. "I think she was hurt, but she was too stoic to let it show. She reminded me of all the lore and tradition she'd taught me and how much I'd enjoyed it when I was young."

" 'But I'm all grown up now, Grandmother,' I said, oh so loftily. I remember how she skewered me with one of those looks that said, *oh, really?* but I wasn't about to give in."

"You told me when we were in the desert in New Mexico that your grandmother had come to you in a dream."

"Hmm. Yes, and I think she was always dropping in from time to time. But I didn't want to see it as anything but random dreams for which some psychoanalyst or dream dictionary would have a logical explanation."

"What do you think now, after everything that's happened? Do you still think she was an eccentric old lady or..."

Laura left the question unfinished, but Connor heard the rest of it in her mind: *Or was she a witch?*

"I honestly don't know. There was a time when I would have laughed. But it isn't funny anymore, not funny at all." Her mind went instantly to the Tor and what had happened there.

Laura felt the shift in Connor's mood and sensed the reason. "We haven't talked much about what went on yesterday. I got the impression you were avoiding the subject."

Connor sighed. "I was. I guess I still am. Some part of me doesn't want to understand anything about it."

"But even for someone who likes solid evidence, we can't deny that our clothes were drenched, my hands were battered." She held them, palm up. "I might have been willing to concede that everything had happened on a different level, in the Dreamtime for instance, and what you'd probably say was all in our minds. But the soaking wet clothes and the injuries...not to mention the fact that we were both having visions of being in an entirely different place in time." She shrugged. "I can't find any way to rationalize it."

"So what's *your* explanation?" asked Connor, unable to keep the challenge out of her voice.

Laura didn't rise to the bait. "I don't have a coherent explanation that would convince you, considering how you feel about all this. But I think we stepped over a threshold, you especially. I think you were wit-nessing..." Laura paused uncomfortably, "or reliving some episode from the far distant past. And I *think* I was trapped on the borderline between this reality and another. Something was preventing me from reaching you in that past time."

"Reliving some episode? Then you're saying I *was* that person at some point. That this is proof of reincarnation?"

"I know you don't like the idea too much, but I suppose you realize that the majority of the world does believe in it."

Connor nodded glumly. "Yes, and I suppose it's possible. But why is it half the people who run around talking about it think they were Joan of Arc or Mary, Queen of Scots? If they're all telling the truth, Mary's body must have been the equivalent of Grand Central Station, with souls running in and out of it like crazed fireflies."

Laura burst out laughing. "Sort of like walk-ins, only with a much quicker turnaround?"

"Walk-ins?"

"Oh, never mind. It's just another one of those woo-woo terms you'd hate. But seriously, I wasn't talking about the reincarnation fanatics who are constantly putting themselves through past life regressions and regurgitating history instead of memory. Those are the ones you usually hear about. But there are a lot of other people who've had incredibly vivid flashbacks to other times; they've known things about the past that only someone who'd been there could know. There are some phonies out there, but a hundred times that number are real. At least I believe they are."

Connor wandered over to the window and ran her hand over the last few volumes still unshelved. "The problem is, I'm beginning to believe it too. But I don't really want to, because...because..."

"What is it, sweetheart? What's frightening you?" Laura got up and came to stand behind Connor.

"The Tor. What happened up there. I know perfectly well that you're right, that I'm tied to something that happened there God knows how many centuries ago. And I'm scared, Laura. I'm scared as hell. Every survival instinct I have is screaming at me to run, as far and as fast as I can."

"So why don't you? If that's what you want, we'll pack our bags and be out of here in an hour."

Connor turned to face Laura. "Because I can't." Her voice shook, and tears welled up in her eyes. "My grandmother told me I can't."

Laura stepped forward and took Connor in her arms. Connor held on for dear life.

W

The sun had almost dropped below the line of trees at the edge of the garden by the time Connor, bolstered with quantities of strong tea, had described her dream. She'd awakened in the night and been unable to go back to sleep. Not wanting her tossing and turning to disturb Laura, she'd come downstairs, fixed a cup of hot cocoa, and settled herself in the library to read in the big, soft wing chair that had been Gwendolyn's favorite. But she'd apparently dropped off almost immediately.

"At first I thought I must be awake. There was Gwendolyn, sitting across from me in the other chair. For a second I was sure that somehow she'd come back, through that place in the mountain in New Mexico. She didn't look at all sick, and I was glad of that, but then I realized she also didn't look as old. I mean, she wasn't forty again, but she didn't look eighty-three either. She sort of glowed around the edges."

Laura nodded, encouraging her to go on.

"She smiled and started talking to me. She was exactly like herself too. Brisk and getting right down to business. She said she was happy for me and that it was about time I'd gotten over all that foolish nonsense about commitment being too difficult and had taken up with 'that lovely young woman.'"

Laura felt herself blush slightly. "Gratifying to know I've got the unqualified support of the 'ghost' contingent." Laura had been trying to lighten up the situation a little, but she instantly realized Connor was in an utterly serious frame of mind that brooked no interjection of levity. "Sorry," she murmured.

"But she also said some things I didn't quite know how to take, that you and I were together in this place right now because we shared a common destiny, that we were intended to fulfill a role that had been taken from us long ago, and that you were going to see your way clearly this time." She turned a puzzled frown on Laura. "What does that *mean?*"

"I don't know. Well, at least I don't get the part about me seeing my way clearly this time. But I'm not particularly surprised that we're supposed to be together. It's felt like that to me almost since the first time I met you."

Connor regarded her fondly. "That part I completely agree with.

But she seemed to be telling me there's more to this than our being in love. She told me we both had a role to play, and she even referred to 'my friend, the policeman,' which seemed pretty strange."

"It's hard to imagine how Malcolm fits into all this. Did you ask her?"

"That's just it. She didn't respond directly to most of my questions. She almost seemed in a hurry, although I don't suppose that makes much sense either. Why should a ghost be in a hurry?"

Laura was slightly startled. "Why did you say 'ghost' just now?"

"I don't know what else to call her. Dream figure, phantasm,..for crying out loud, I don't even know *where* she is, let alone what!"

"Okay, so we can't nail that down for now. But what else did she have to say that made you think you can't leave here if you want to?"

"I didn't mean to make it sound as if she'd ordered me to stay. She'd never do that. And if she had, I'd have known it wasn't Gwendolyn. I'd have known someone or something was playing with my head. No, she was sitting there as real as you are right now and everything about her presence rang true."

"So she didn't insist that you had no choice in the matter of staying or not staying?"

"No, but she was crystal clear on the subject of debts of honor and family obligations."

"What do family obligations have to do with it?" Laura asked, beginning to think that perhaps Connor's dreaming consciousness had indeed gone off on some weird tangent.

"According to my grandmother, our family line, well, the females at least, have passed down a sacred trust from one generation to another. And this secret, whatever it is, has been passed along for centuries, waiting until the time was right for the...how did she put it, 'the reparation.'"

"And the time has arrived, I take it?"

"Apparently."

"One thing puzzles me, though. If this is supposed to be passed from one generation to the next, what about Amanda, or for that matter, her sister, your great-aunt?"

"I thought the same thing. And she answered the question without my even having to speak it aloud. She told me that sometimes the power of the witch failed to emerge in one of our lineage and when that happened, the elder woman had to wait for the next generation to appear before she could pass on the...mantle of authority, I guess."

"Did she happen to tell you what you're supposed to do with all this? I mean, are there any specific responsibilities that go with the job description?" Laura succeeded this time in making Connor smile.

"I guess I should have asked. But, as usual, Gwendolyn was short on details. She's always had this obsession with me figuring out things for myself. Even when I was little, she was forever pointing me toward a dictionary or an encyclopedia and telling me 'look it up, child.' She staunchly maintained I'd never learn anything if I didn't have to work at it."

"Wise woman. Of course, now she's left you with a puzzle that can't be solved with the aid of standard reference books. But what did she say about staying...the exact words?"

Connor closed her eyes, her brow furrowed with intense concentration. "She told me it was time for everything to be put right, and that only I could do what needed to be done. And if I chose not to, the consequences could be quite serious for those who would come after."

"That's all? She wasn't more specific?"

Connor sighed. "No. And I've wracked my brain trying to figure out what I might have missed. But there was no mistaking her tone. I don't know when I've ever seen her that deadly serious. Her eyes seemed to bore right into me, as if I were supposed to simply *know* something without being told."

"And that was it?"

"No, there was one more thing...the last phrase I remember her saying. Um...Remember, Connor, witches are priestesses.' "

Laura suppressed a shiver. "Interesting, if not elucidating. And then what? You found yourself still here?"

"The sun was just coming up, and I realized I'd been asleep—well, I thought I'd been asleep anyway. The room was cold, but I wasn't badly chilled or stiff, as if I'd been sitting in a chair half the night. So I didn't know what to think. I came back upstairs and got into bed. I must have fallen asleep instantly. If it hadn't been for that cup over there with hot chocolate dregs and the book on the floor that I'd been reading, I might have believed I'd never been down here at all."

Laura agreed, and was almost relieved to see the proof. Not that she didn't believe every word Connor had spoken. But Connor, Laura knew, was possessed of the sort of personality and intellect that required some grounding in physical reality, something tangible to latch onto. With everything that had happened since their arrival, Connor was under great emotional duress. Her predilection for sorting out fact from fiction with tenacious determination, and her unerring instinct for the truth, were useless. In a matter of days she'd been forced to discard the tools she'd relied on for a lifetime. Small wonder, Laura thought, that she looked exhausted.

"So at the very least you've had a vivid dream, and your grandmother wants to communicate with you. I think we ought to take this one step at a time. As a matter of fact, we can discuss it with your father and Malcolm when they get here. They're smart, rational people. In the meantime, I think we ought to be looking for something else."

"What?" asked Connor.

"I don't think for a moment that your grandmother intended to rely solely on dream chats to explain herself or what you're supposed to be doing here. She strikes me as too smart to leave anything important to chance. Wouldn't you agree?"

"I suppose, but what are you getting at?"

"If I were Gwendolyn, I'd want to help you all I could. And, if this secret is so all-fired important, I'd find a way to keep anyone else from getting hold of it." She swept her gaze over the shelves of books. "And I'd anticipate that someone might come along looking for something I didn't want them to have."

Connor followed her gaze, then locked eyes with Laura. "I'm beginning to get your drift. Gwendolyn would have left something for me."

"And I assume you didn't receive anything in the mail, no mysterious packages from her lawyer or anything."

"No, all I received were the papers about my inheritance. Naturally Amanda threw a fit when I got Rosewood House. But Gwendolyn's solicitor was admirably firm in telling her not to bother contesting the will. It was ironclad. He never hinted to me that there was anything else."

"Then I think we must assume that whatever instructions she had for you, she would have left here in this house."

Connor got one of those light-bulb-going-off expressions. "And that's why Aunt Jessica refused ever so politely to come down here and live when I asked her to. Gwendolyn must have told her the house should remain completely intact. I thought it was just obsessive courtesy when she told me she'd rather stay in her own house in Oxford until I'd had a chance to come here and look the place over. Besides, she and Katy get along so well, and I was glad to have someone keeping an eye on my daughter, ever so discreetly, of course."

Laura jumped up. "All right. Then where do we start looking?" He eyes inventoried the crowded room. Aside from the book shelves, there were writing tables, cabinets, bureaus, and, in pride of place, Gwendolyn's antique desk. Of course, there were also eleven other rooms to consider. "We can start in here. Why don't you look in your grandmother's desk again? I'll start with these built-in cupboards."

Connor started toward the desk, but looked back at Laura as if to say something. She never formed the words. Instead the sound that came out was a strangled yelp. Laura wheeled around and there, pressed against the leaded glass of the window, was a disembodied head with a flattened, distorted face.

W

With visions of psychopathic murderers lending wings to their feet, Connor and Laura raced toward the front door, almost tripping each other in the process. Connor reached the door first, yanked it open, and cannoned into a figure just mounting the front steps. Laura, close on her heels, only managed to avoid the sprawled bodies in front of her by means of an aerobatic leap that landed her several feet into the driveway, whereupon she, too, lost her balance and skidded across the gravel in a decidedly ungraceful and painful manner.

A moment later, the unmistakable sound of tut tutting came clearly from someone crushed beneath Connor's legs. She heaved herself off, and there, rising from the cloud of dust was a clearly frightened middle-aged man wearing black pants, a dark gray jacket, and, of all things, a white clerical collar.

Laura helped Connor to her feet and whispered. "Oh, this is just great. We've nabbed a priest." She lent a hand to the gentleman in question, while Connor stammered an apology.

"Well, well, quite unexpected, I must say. Didn't know I'd be getting such a workout." He inspected a tear in his jacket sleeve. "Wife won't be too pleased, I daresay, but she's wonderful with a darning needle. Don't seem to have my glasses, though. Didn't have 'em on. Were in my hand I think." He peered nearsightedly at the ground around him.

Laura nudged Connor. "He said 'wife.' Then he's not a priest."

"Priest did you say? Oh, certainly not. The village would be scandalized, now wouldn't they? Nothing popish about Saint Dunstan's. Old Mrs. Bindley wouldn't stand for it, now would she?"

The light began to dawn on Connor. "Sir," she began awkwardly, "are you by any chance Mr. Janks, the vicar who wrote to me recently about the incident at my grandmother's grave?"

"Why yes, I'm Philip Janks. You must be Mrs. Broadhurst's granddaughter. I have you down in the records as Lydia Connor Hawthorne, but I understood from Gwendolyn that you were to be called Connor. That is why I wrote to you by that name. I take it my letter reached you, then?"

"Yes, it did. And I appreciate your writing. I can't apologize enough for what happened just now. We've had a bit of trouble with—"

"Burglars," Laura interjected, earning a grateful smile from Connor.

"Yes, burglars. They made quite a mess in the house, and when we saw, er, we thought we saw a face...of sorts...looking through the window."

Mr. Janks looked just the least bit peeved. "Well, my wife does say I'm not extremely blessed with physical attractiveness, but I didn't think of myself as particularly scary."

"You were at the window," both women said, almost in unison.

"Well, yes. I tried the bell and no one answered. But I saw the car in the drive. And I did so want to offer my condolences in person. So I went to the library window...I know it's the library, you see, because of my many visits with Mrs. Broadhurst...so I went to the window and peeked in, after I took off my glasses, you understand, so as to reduce the glare, but I rather lost my balance in the ivy there, and leant a bit too far forward over the shrub, and pressed against the glass, and then I saw that I might have startled you. I came back to the front door immediately so that I might explain and then..." He raised his hands, palms up, as if lost for an explanation of the subsequent events.

Connor and Laura glanced at the wide clerical collar and exchanged embarrassed glances. The apparition was now completely debunked. The seemingly disembodied head had been an optical illusion because the white flowering shrubs in front of the window had blended so well with the vicar's collar. The distortion of features had been caused by his inadvertently mashing his face into the glass." They both felt ridiculous.

"Mr. Janks, please don't imply any insult. We were simply startled, and as I said, we've had the burglary and the desecration of my grand-mother's grave. It's been rather traumatic."

"Quite so, quite so," he murmured. "No offense taken. And no harm done really. If I could only find my glasses." He stepped back a pace, and they all heard the sound of crunching that could only be glass.

Laura said, in as grave a tone as she could muster, "I think you've found them, Mr. Janks."

Connor and Laura spent the next hour soothing the vicar. Though young for his job, he was old for his age. They fed him tea and cakes and propped him up in the library with a footstool. He insisted they were fussing too much, but they thought it was the least they could do under the circumstances. Connor, for her part, was dearly hoping Philip Janks was not a gossip. She doubted she could live down this sort of story if it ever got around the village. Besides, she wanted to make friends with the man eventually, on the chance that he had any insight to offer into Gwendolyn's last days before she left England.

All in all, by the time Mr. Janks had tut-tutted himself out the front door, he seemed completely composed and willing to let bygones be bygones. He had declined to let Connor pay for his glasses, pointing out that he himself had stepped on them. But she countered with a generous gift for the church restoration fund, which he graciously accepted, his eyes widening at the number of ten-pound notes she'd pressed into his hand.

"I might have guessed that you would take after your dear grandmother," he beamed. "She was one of our most generous members, always willing to help out with the children's spring fete or the jumble sale. Rest assured this will be put to good use."

"I'm sure it will, Mr. Janks. And please feel free to call on me anytime if there is a need."

"Quite so, quite so," said Mr. Janks, almost bowing at the waist. "For now, though, I shall bid you good day as my wife is no doubt preparing my tea."

He started down the driveway as Laura and Connor waved. "How much did you give him?" Laura said between clenched teeth. She intended to keep up the smile until he'd passed out of sight.

"I hope enough to prevent humiliating rumors and fend off an expensive lawsuit," answered Connor, without moving her lips.

Mr. Janks had just reached the gate at the end of the driveway and turned to the right when there came a screech of tires skidding on dirt. Connor and Laura fully expected to see their new friend hurtling back down the driveway, the sadly crushed victim of an auto-versus-pedestrian encounter. Thus they both almost giggled with relief when, after a moment's pause, they saw his head bobbing along above the hedge as he started home.

The vehicular noises were soon explained as Benjamin and Malcolm zipped up the drive and parked beside them.

"I see the village callers have begun," smiled Benjamin as he got out. "I believe the vicar is traditionally the first, but the others will follow."

"Not if they find out what happened to the vicar," Laura giggled, hugging Benjamin and then Malcolm, who had unfolded himself from the passenger seat.

"What have you been doing to that harmless man of the cloth?" asked Benjamin with mock sternness.

Interrupted by each other and hampered by bursts of uncontrollable laughter, the two women finally managed to explain the absurd incident. Malcolm looked from one to the other of them in disbelief and muttered something about getting the luggage.

Laura took Benjamin's carry-on and looped her arm through his. "I'm glad you're here." He glanced at her and saw that her comment wasn't purely social.

Connor came along behind them, Malcolm at her side. "You tackled a *priest?*"

"He's not a priest, he's a vicar."

"Okay, so you tackled a *vicar?*"

"Keep it up, kiddo, and you're not getting any tea."

"I hate tea."

"Shush. You want to get us kicked out of England?"

$$W$$

The four of them sat at the long kitchen table to exchange news and compare notes. Connor and Laura listened with interest to Benjamin's theories about the odd behavior of certain international businesses. Since his first discussion with Malcolm, he had received additional information on World Technology Partners. His hasty notes indicated that the parent company's offices were based in London. Its subsidiaries had been steadily acquiring controlling interest in certain European armaments manufacturers, advanced technology companies specializing in satellite communications and laser applications.

"But why do you think all this is significant, Dad? I mean, obviously there's a danger in any one entity controlling too much technology or weaponry, but I'm more concerned with what's happening here, or has happened here." She felt strange even saying it; the simple phrase 'what has happened here' now carried a hidden meaning, an uncomfortable subtext which she was not anxious to explain to her father or Malcolm. She caught Laura's eye from across the table. Laura understood.

"I wouldn't be concerned with any of this right now," Benjamin said, "except that I kept finding the same people involved as either shareholders or board members in so many of these companies. And when I boiled down the list and compared it against the people who were at the Carlisle party, I started to get worried. As I told Malcolm, there were three matches on the two lists."

"So that's what sent you dashing across the Atlantic," Laura observed with a smile, "along with your favorite sidekick."

Malcolm grinned. "I've been replaced as *her* favorite sidekick," he said, nodding his head in Connor's direction, "so I had to be reassigned."

Connor gave them both an "oh, be quiet" look and asked Benjamin the names of the individuals he'd found on the guest list.

"The one that stood out was William Carlisle. The others were Clarence Newbury and G. Fenwycke."

Connor stared at him for a moment. "You're suspicious of William Carlisle? But I thought his father and my grandparents were great friends. And Gwendolyn remained friends with William and his wife. Why would they be suspect?"

Benjamin shrugged. "I don't necessarily suspect them of anything. But the connection was there, and I'm not willing to overlook it until I get some sort of satisfactory explanation from William."

"And the other two names?"

Benjamin pulled his reading glasses from his coat pocket and flipped through the file until he found the page he was looking for. "Newbury is a journalist of the tabloid variety, and I don't have additional information yet on G. Fenwycke. That isn't an entirely unusual name here. Do they ring a bell with either of you?"

They both shook their heads, then Laura said, "We haven't had much chance to meet anyone yet. And other than the vicar, and that cop who was nosing around—"

"What cop?" Benjamin asked.

"I think his name was Foulsham," Laura replied. "A detective something or other."

"Detective Chief Inspector," Connor interjected. "He wanted us to believe he was looking into our burglary when he showed up. Which I knew was absurd, given his rank. Then he admitted he was also investigating the murders at the cemetery."

"And very likely the murder of Patricia Frome," added Benjamin. "Though I doubt he mentioned that aspect."

"No, he didn't. And I wasn't all that cordial since he just walked into the house without our knowing it."

"What was his excuse for that?" Malcolm asked, looking none too pleased.

"Oh, the usual line about the door being open and we didn't hear him knock."

"Did he ask specific questions?" asked Benjamin. "Or was he just fishing?"

"He did want to know if we had any idea what happened to Gwendolyn's body," she answered, looking at Laura for confirmation. "And we told him quite honestly that we had no idea."

"Sounds as if this Foulsham is trying to gather up enough threads to make sense of this, but we need to proceed cautiously. I don't know exactly whom we can trust here, except for a couple of people in London." He took another sip of his tea. "Have you found any clues as to what the supposed burglars were looking for?"

Connor and Laura exchanged glances, and Benjamin frowned. "All right, out with it," he said.

But Connor didn't answer. Instead, she stared at a spot somewhere over Benjamin's head. Malcolm focused on Connor, trying to decipher her expression. Finally Laura spoke up.

"It's kind of a long story. Why don't we go into the library and get comfortable?" They all trooped down the long center hallway and into the library. Connor curled up on the window seat, as if distancing herself from the proceedings. Benjamin looked at her quizzically for a moment but didn't press the matter. He seated himself in Gwendolyn's tattered chair, and Malcolm took the one facing him. Laura remained standing, leaning against the facing around the fireplace, but her attention was entirely on Connor, and neither of the men could fail to recognize the concern in her eyes.

Softly, Benjamin said. "So tell us what's happened here."

As succinctly as possible, with occasional glances at Connor for input which wasn't forthcoming, Laura explained their activities since they'd arrived. She summarized the results of their work in the library, the fact that the precious family documents were all missing, and the subject of the books that appeared to have been taken, although they had identified only one specific volume, the red leather-bound Glastonbury history. She finished up by explaining that they had just been about to embark on a thorough search when the vicar had shown up and set in motion that silly series of events. Laura didn't mention the Tor.

In the silence that followed her recitation, Laura debated explaining the rest. But she couldn't be sure that Connor wanted her to do so. And for the first time since they'd left the States, Laura felt disconnected from Connor, as if a wall had come down that she could not breach.

Malcolm was the one who finally spoke. His eyes had rarely left Connor while Laura talked, as if he were trying to see through her outer shell to the woman inside. "That isn't all of it." he said, his tone signifying a flat declaration, not a question. "There's something else that's bugging you both, but especially Connor."

Laura swept her eyes over all of them. She was surprised at Malcolm's conclusion, but then realized she shouldn't be. Who knew the woman better than Malcolm? They'd shared years of work and years of their lives together. Laura felt a twinge of jealousy; not one, but two people in the room knew her lover better than she did, had known every detail of her life for years. Why was that so difficult to accept? The answer was simple. In her heart of hearts, Laura felt as if she'd known Connor forever.

"Do you want me to tell them, or will you?" she asked. "I think it will make more sense if you do, because you remember the details, and I probably don't."

Connor turned a face to them that was, in some inexplicable way, not quite *her* face. They all stared, and Laura heard Benjamin's sharp intake of breath. Then the moment passed, and she was Connor again.

"You're right. I should be the one to tell this. It's just that it seems more absurd every time I go over it in my mind, and it sounds even less believable when I try to put it into words. But I'll try."

Little by little, with quiet encouragement from her three closest friends, Connor recounted the events as they had transpired on the Tor, both in the present and in whatever time zone she'd peered into. Benjamin and Malcolm, who were hearing it for the first time, sat transfixed. Laura, on the other hand, familiar with most of it, devoted herself to observing Connor closely. Yes, there was something odd going on. From Laura's perspective anyway, the air around Connor appeared to bend and cave inward periodically, as if drawn into a vortex. Then it would expand outward, shimmering at the edges. The only way she could think to describe it was that this would be the appearance of someone's aura *breathing*.

The effect was so subtle, Laura doubted anyone else saw it. But she changed her mind when, in stealing glances at Malcolm and Benjamin, she saw how Malcolm reacted, a frown passing over his face each time the phenomenon repeated itself. She wasn't sure he was even consciously aware of what he observed, but she knew he sensed it nonetheless. Curious, thought Laura, that she and Malcolm apparently shared this knowledge while Benjamin did not appear to register any of the shifts occurring around Connor, although his attention was riveted on his daughter.

When her story came to an end, Benjamin and Malcolm were silent. Laura had expected them to immediately begin firing questions at Connor. Apparently they couldn't think of any. She understood. At length, Malcolm turned to Laura.

"And where were you when all this was going on?"

There was just enough of an edge to his voice for Laura to become instantly defensive.

"I wasn't exactly sitting around filing my nails," she snapped. "I suppose you're already thinking you could have done a better job of protecting her. Why? Because you're a homicide cop?"

Malcolm's temper must have gotten the better of him, or the jet lag did. "Well, I wouldn't have left her alone in that damn tower."

"Left her? You think I left her? You don't think I tried—"

"That's enough! Both of you." Connor's voice sliced through the discord in the room and rendered the two combatants speechless. Laura felt for a fraction of a second that she was actually incapable of using her vocal cords. Malcolm had a surprised look on his face which she thought probably matched the one on hers.

Connor stood up and faced the three of them. "Malcolm, if you'd bothered to exercise your usually sharp powers of observation, you would have noticed the nasty cuts and bruises on Laura's hands. She got those trying to fight her way through an impenetrable barrier to get to me. I don't know why she couldn't get into the tower at the time, and neither does she. But I saw the look on her face when she finally did, and if I didn't know it before, I know it now—no one loves me more than she does, not even you, my old friend." She moved closer to him and put her hand on his shoulder.

Her gaze shifted to Laura. "You must understand that Malcolm has made himself my champion for a long time. It's hard for him to share that role with you or with my father or with anyone. Give him a chance, okay?" She held out her hand to Laura, who stepped forward and took it. "The two of you are tied to me, in ways you don't yet understand."

After a moment's silence, Connor turned and left the room.

Benjamin's eyes had taken on a strange quality, as if he were looking at something very far away. Laura, for her part, was trembling inside. The cause, she suspected, was not fear or anything else negative, but rather the presence of powerful energy in the room. She didn't know how else to explain the squirmy, electric feeling skittering around the insides of her mind and body.

Malcolm, never one to mince words, said, "What the hell was that all about? And why didn't that even sound like Connor talking?"

Benjamin's voice sounded old and rusty. "I'm not sure it was."

W

Two hours later, Connor appeared in the kitchen, where the rest of them were drinking coffee. She appeared her normal self, or at least the self they were generally accustomed to seeing. She said she'd had a terrific nap and felt better than she had in days. By unspoken agreement, none of them brought up the subject of what had happened in the library, and Connor either had no memory of it or had likewise chosen to ignore it.

"I say we drive into Glastonbury and have dinner at the pub."

"Isn't there a pub here in St. Giles?" Benjamin asked.

"Of course, but the food isn't all that good, and it's a little on the dark and grim side. Besides, I'm fond of the old 'Who'd A Thought It' in Glastonbury."

"That's the name of a bar?" Malcolm asked.

"Pub. And you'll soon discover that the pubs in England have a long and honored tradition of unusual names. Haven't you ever read Martha Grimes?"

"No, should I have?"

"They're great whodunits and most of them use pub names as titles—*The Man With a Load of Mischief* is a good example."

He smiled. "As long as they have food and beer, I don't care what they put on the sign over the door."

"Then let's get to it." On the way out she took her father's arm. "So, do you suppose we should introduce them to steak-and-kidney pie and spotted dick for dessert?"

Chapter Sixteen

When the Himalayan peasant meets the he-bear in his pride,
He shouts to scare the monster, who will often turn aside.
But the she-bear thus accosted rends the peasant tooth and nail,
For the female of the species is more deadly than the male.
—Rudyard Kipling
The Female of the Species

Gillian Fenwycke was annoyed, not frightened, a fact that Nicholas Foulsham would have filed under "Very Interesting." Unable to secure Gerald's help in tracking her down (though it didn't occur to him that Gerald actually did not know where his wife had got to) he'd put Mary Fitch on to calling all the B&B's and self-catering cottages within a hundred-mile radius of Haslemere. As it was, he'd spread the net too wide, for Gillian Fenwycke had turned up in a cottage not a dozen miles from her home. This was, in itself, an odd state of affairs, but given the circumstances, perhaps the Fenwyckes had had a falling out and she'd gone to the nearest refuge.

He soon learned, however, that there had been no falling out over Gillian's dalliance with little Patricia Frome, because Gillian insisted she had not been to Haslemere in three and a half days, having left well before Foulsham came to break the news to Gerald. She had left, she said, for personal reasons, to have some time to herself, to think some things through. The explanation sounded as if it might be true in a trendy, psychobabble sort of way, but Foulsham doubted it. Something else was going on here, and his observant eyes had already picked out indications that someone was staying there with Lady Fenwycke—two different brands of cigarette ends in the ashtray (not conclusive, but suggestive) and the faint aroma of aftershave. It rang a bell somewhere in his memory, but he couldn't quite put a name to the man who'd been wearing it. A quick trip to wash his hands yielded confirmation of his suspicions—men's whiskers stuck to the sides of the wash basin, and the fact that the feminine cosmetics were all pushed in a crowded clump to one side of the vanity table, leaving the perfect space for a men's toiletry kit.

He returned from his investigatory tangent to find Lady Fenwycke puffing away at yet another cigarette and still maintaining a studied irritation that was, quite frankly, irritating *him.*

"Perhaps I haven't been entirely clear, Lady Fenwycke. I am not disposed to consider what transpired between you and Miss Frome as necessarily connected to her murder, but surely you must see that as you failed to come forward with the information, that leaves me with certain, shall we say, rather pressing questions."

She flashed him a look that might have impaled a lesser man, but he did not allow her the satisfaction of any response to it. He simply waited until she stubbed out the cigarette angrily and went to stand in front of the large picture window overlooking the Mendips. Despite the relatively clear weather, the outlines of the hills were hazy as if the photographer in God had chosen soft focus for the scene.

Working it out, she is, thought Foulsham. She's deciding just how to approach this. He watched her closely, all the while working out the odds in his head, as to whether she'd admit the affair, deny it completely, or admit it with extenuating circumstances. She did none of them.

Turning from the window, she gave a first-rate impression of someone who has just encountered a particularly nasty insect in a kitchen drawer. "Why are you still here, Chief Inspector? I have nothing to say to you."

Foulsham was amazed. He felt almost a grudging respect for someone so self-assured she would simply decline to engage the subject he'd raised as delicately as possible. But respect or no, he wasn't going to let her dictate to him. "Lady Fenwycke, as unpleasant as you may find this interview, I assure you the setting is rather more comfortable than the police station. But if you'd prefer, my car is just outside." His expression remained neutral, with only the vaguest trace of menace, but she was sharp enough to see it.

"Then get on with it," she snapped. "But you're only wasting your time."

"That's as may be," he replied sententiously. "But as I'm the best judge of that, perhaps you will tell me when you last saw Patricia Frome."

Her expression was defiant. "I have no idea. I'm terrible with dates."

Foulsham made a show of consulting his notebook. "We have information that Miss Frome was seen at Haslemere late in the afternoon before she died. This would be the day before the party, which was on, let's see, yes, a Friday. Her regular day out being Thursday, she was absent until shortly before dinner was laid in the servant's hall at Bannister House. At dinner, she appeared somewhat distraught, and did not eat anything. She excused herself, and went to her room which, given the available number of servants quarters at Bannister House, she does not share with anyone. No one has been able to recall seeing Miss Frome after that." He looked up into the expressionless face of Lady Fenwycke. "Now, if you would be—"

"On whose information do you assume the girl was at Haslemere?"

Foulsham quelled his rising irritation. This woman was tough. Not that he was surprised. Lady Fenwycke's antecedents were not quite as impeccable, nor her blood as blue as she would like those in her social circle to believe.

"The source of this information is not in question, Lady Fenwycke. And, if you continue to avoid my questions, we certainly will have to continue this interview at the station. Now that I think of it, perhaps you *would* be more comfortable chatting with Superintendent Hollis."

He thought she turned just a shade paler. It might have been his imagination, of course, but he'd had a feeling she didn't want to find herself in an interview room with a police superintendent and a recording machine. His offer of Hollis was mainly bluff. He doubted the old man would agree to get involved in questioning anyone who could conceivably wield any clout that was not in his favor. Thus Hollis usually steered clear of the peerage. He swore that when you stepped on someone's toes in those circles, you never knew who would yell "ouch."

Apparently Lady Fenwycke was unaware of this and unsure of how much clout she could wield. Her affair with Patricia Frome had no doubt alienated her from her husband. Would he come to her defense? Would he send a solicitor if she needed one? He saw in her eyes she was unsure of the answers to these kinds of questions, and he knew instinctively she didn't want to leave the cottage, for reasons other than fear of the police.

She lit another cigarette and placed her gold lighter firmly on the side table. "Get on with it, Chief Inspector," she said, as if she'd been waiting patiently for hours to answer his questions.

"Of course," he replied, unruffled. "How long had you been having an intimate relationship with Miss Frome?"

"I don't believe I ever said I'd *had* an intimate relationship with her."

Foulsham smiled briefly. "No, I don't believe you've said precisely that. So perhaps we should begin again. Did you at any time conduct an intimate relationship with the victim?"

Lady Fenwycke sighed, and exhaled smoke in a long, thin stream into the air above her head. "Yes."

Well, he thought, this is like pulling teeth. "And was this relationship still active on the Thursday in question, when she was seen at Haslemere?"

"How precisely does one define 'active,' Chief Inspector?"

He sighed, this time letting his irritation show. "I think as intelligent adults, Lady Fenwycke, that we can agree on a definition without undue debate. However, if you prefer, I will phrase the question differently. Did you engage in sexual relations with Patricia Frome on the day before she died?"

There it was, the bald truth echoing off the stone walls of the little farm cottage. And he could see that Lady Fenwycke didn't like it one bit, not one little bit.

"No," she said, with astounding vehemence. "I did not."

Foulsham, who'd expected quite a different answer, was thrown off his rhythm, but not for long. He came at her from another angle.

"Was your husband aware of your affair with Miss Frome?"

She looked startled. Apparently she hadn't yet anticipated this question. But she soldiered on anyway. "You would have to ask him."

Good answer, he thought. Now let's see what you do with this one. "When is the last time you engaged in sexual relations with Miss Frome?"

"The previous Monday evening."

He referred to his notes. "That would be one of the victim's regular evenings out. I see here that Lord Carlisle is quite generous in the matter of time off from work. All the staff are permitted a full weekday, one evening during the week, and a day and evening at the weekend on a revolving schedule. Now...did Miss Frome spend all her free time in your company?"

"Certainly not."

"How often did you meet with Miss Frome?"

Lady Fenwycke had extinguished her cigarette. Without the prop, she'd ended up gripping the arms of her chair. He could see her white knuckles from ten feet away. "Perhaps once a week, no more."

He jumped to the inconsistency. "Then how is it that she was at Haslemere on the Monday evening and again on the Thursday?"

"I don't know why she was there. We had no...no prior plan to meet until the following week."

"But surely she must have told you why she'd come to be there."

Lady Fenwycke grew suddenly confident. "No, she did not, because I did not see Patricia Frome on Thursday at any time. The only person home at that hour was my husband. And I can prove it."

W

Despite the mental challenge involved, Nicholas Foulsham had to conclude that by and large, it was a colossal pain to deal with intelligent people. At the moment he was almost angry enough to ask for a transfer back to London where he could haul in stupid murderers who'd strangled their wives, or knifed their neighborhood drug connection, and get them tied up in their own lies in under an hour. Except for the occasional psychopath, life had been less complicated. Now he had all these damned blue-bloods to deal with. All brains and no brawn, he thought contemptuously. No doubt he'd soon be hearing from their solicitors, or more likely, Hollis would be hearing. And that wouldn't make the guv happy, not one bit.

Foulsham felt as though he were chasing his tail. First Gerald had denied knowing anything about the affair, and sounded extremely credible. Then when he was all set to pinion Lady Fenwycke, she not only claimed she wasn't there that day, but had an alibi as well. Of course, he would check on it. But he couldn't imagine she'd be stupid enough to give him one that wouldn't prove out.

So, if Gerald didn't see Patricia Frome that day, and Lady Fenwycke wasn't at home to rendezvous with the girl, what the devil was she doing there? And why had she been in the house at all? Sonja had been absolutely unshakeable on the times involved. Patricia hadn't left the house until after five o'clock, and she'd walked away down the lane toward Bannister House, which lay several miles away.

Foulsham swore vigorously as he swerved almost into a hedge to avoid an oncoming lorry was occupying two-thirds of the narrow road. His attention had also wandered, and he pulled over into the next layby to think. As he sat tapping his fingers on the steering wheel, it occurred to him that while Gerald had denied knowing about the affair, Foulsham had not asked him specifically whether or not he'd *seen* Patricia Frome. A man like Gerald would not necessarily take much notice of one of his own servants going about his or her business. But surely he would be concerned to encounter a stranger on the upper floors of his house, if indeed he had. Well, it was worth asking.

He swung the car around and started back down the A361. As he passed the turn-off that would take him toward Bannister House, he had yet another inspiration. Lady Carlisle had struck him as a shrewd and observant woman. He had yet to discuss this "affair" with her, but perhaps she kept tabs on the private lives of her staff to some extent. Or perhaps she could be persuaded to make them more forthcoming in their statements. He wasn't satisfied with the girl who'd described Patricia as "distraught." He wanted to know exactly how she was acting, and he wanted to know why. At the very least they could help him with the former.

W

Gillian Fenwycke's personal happiness was predicated upon two basic rules: There was only one acceptable way for events to unfold— her way; there was only one vote when it came to deciding what she could do—her vote. The interview with Foulsham had not adhered to either of these, and the result was predictable: Gillian was not happy.

Conrad Thackeray arrived late that evening to find Gillian still seated in the chair where she'd been for several hours. The ashtray was overflowing, and the cottage reeked of smoke. Beside her on the table was an empty wine bottle.

"For Christ's sake, Gillian. It's smells like a pub at closing time." He flung open a window, admitting the chill night air. She ignored his outburst, and he, for his part, ignored her as he set about pouring himself a whiskey from the drinks table. "Things are coming along splendidly at Haslemere. And Paul tells me old Gerald came nosing around down there on his thoroughbred stallion, acting like the lord of the manor." Conrad snorted at his own joke. "Well, I guess he is the lord, but mostly in his own mind. Paul sent him off with a flea in his ear. Bet you Gerald didn't like that one bloody bit, now did he?" As if it finally occurred to him that Gillian was not participating, Conrad broke off his monologue. "Well, then. You've been sitting here all day waiting for me?"

She flicked her eyes at him and correctly surmised that he'd stopped at the local pub on his way to the cottage. The glitter in his eyes was just a shade dimmer than absolutely dangerous.

"Hardly, darling. I've been unwillingly entertaining a gentleman caller."

"And who might that be?" he said, his jocular mood evaporating. "Don't tell me Gerald's been here."

"No. My visitor was Detective Chief Inspector Foulsham. You remember him. He was in charge of the task force office they set up at Bannister House. He must have questioned you."

"Foulsham, eh? Tall, skinny chap, rather corpselike?"

"I'm sure he'd appreciate the description, and yes, that's the one."

"What did he want?"

"Wanted to know how often I was having it off with little Miss Frome."

Conrad's eyes narrowed. "And what did you tell the chief inspector? You didn't admit it, certainly."

"Tried pretending he'd got it all wrong, darling. But he'd had it on good authority. Apparently the discretion of one's servants can't be counted on these days."

"So you up and told him all about it, did you? Give you a thrill, did it? All those juicy details."

She glared back at him. "Don't be absurd. You don't know sod-all about it."

This was the wrong thing to say to Conrad Thackeray. His current mood was unpleasant. Criticizing him was tantamount to lighting a match in a room full of dynamite.

He closed the distance between them in a heartbeat, and he yanked Gillian from the chair and pulled her face up to his. "I should think by now you'd know better than to demonstrate even the slightest disrespect for me. And if you do it again, who knows? You could end up just like the upstairs maid, or should I say, the upstairs lesbian." He snickered at his own inane joke and flung Gillian toward the stairs. "I'll be up directly," he said, retrieving his whiskey glass. "Make yourself presentable."

He turned his back, but Gillian didn't move. She spat out the words.

"What exactly do you know about Patricia's murder, Conrad?"

He drained his glass. "You're a bloody fool, Gillian, an absolute bloody fool."

If Conrad had seen the malevolent expression on Gillian's face, he might have reconsidered this evaluation.

Chapter Seventeen

And on her lover's arm she leant,
and round her waist she felt it fold,
And far across the hills they went,
In that new world which is the old.
—Alfred, Lord Tennyson
The Daydream, The Departure

The Who'd A Thought It was just beginning to fill up by the time they got there, but there was a table for four near the entrance, and Connor suggested they sit there as the main bar would get fairly smoky before long. "I quit years ago, and I'm still envious." They sat down in the sort of intermediate area between the quieter dining room near the small kitchen and the main bar just through an archway. Connor grabbed some menus from a rack on the wall and passed them out. "We order from the bar, and they'll bring out the food when it's ready," she explained.

After studying the menu, and another brief English lesson from Connor (chips are fries, crisps are chips) they all settled on roast beef sandwiches on whole meal with horseradish, two orders of chips to share, and pints all around. They sipped their ale, and Malcolm watched hungrily as plates of steaming food were set down at the table on the other side of the entrance door.

"You could have ordered a hot dinner," Connor told him. "It's not too late to change. They've got daily specials on the board, and the liver, bacon, and onions is always excellent. Why don't you go tell the barmaid?"

"No, the sandwich is fine, really."

Laura got the impression that Malcolm was acting a little odd or that he was unusually subdued. He hunched over his pint glass and didn't seem particularly interested in the good-natured chatter of the pub's patrons. She wondered if he was still peeved about their earlier argument, and was just on the verge of saying something to put him at ease when he abruptly asked Connor, "So, am I the only black guy in the county or what?"

They all looked surprised, and Laura saw he was instantly embarrassed by his outburst. By their confused expressions, it was obvious none of them had given any thought to the matter. To them, Malcolm was just...Malcolm. Connor reached across the table and put her hand over his. "No, you're not. But I will admit that the Glastonbury area is pretty damn pale compared to London. I never stopped to consider that you hadn't been out in the country. Would you be more comfortable if we left?"

"No, of course not. We've already ordered our dinner. It's just that I get the feeling everyone's staring at me, and it's annoying."

Laura caught his eye and smiled. "Did it ever occur to you that people stare because you're 6 foot 6 and the size of a left tackle?"

Malcolm laughed. "No, but that sounds good. I'm being sort of ridiculous, aren't I?"

Connor looked at him fondly. "No more so than the rest of us when we feel out of place. Now if you'll accompany me to the bar, we are going to add to our dinner order."

Malcolm and Connor were sitting in the "outside" seats, so it was easy enough for them to cross into the bar, a mere fifteen feet away, and catch the barmaid's eye. Connor smiled at her and asked if they could add two orders of the liver, bacon and onions.

Given the relatively short height of the bar's overhang, Malcolm had to lean over, with his elbows on the bar itself so as not to hit his head. The barmaid wrote down the new order and said she would add it to the bill. Then she looked right at Malcolm and favored him with a toothy smile. "My, you're a big one, aren't you? Don't get many blokes as don't fit under this." She reached up and tapped the beam above the bar. "Reckon you're ready for another pint."

Connor burst out laughing, and Malcolm couldn't help but follow suit. As they returned to their table, he with a new pint of Carlsberg in his hand, he said, "You paid her to say that, didn't you?"

"No, but I should have. Her timing couldn't have been better."

Soon the food arrived, and everyone tucked in to their meals with gusto, Connor not least of all. She quickly finished her sandwich and then ate Malcolm's, since he was busy devouring the enormous helping he'd received, which they all agreed was larger than Benjamin's. "They must think you're still growing," Laura teased, helping herself to another chip before Connor finished them off too.

"I like to think I am," he replied after swallowing the last bite. "But my sister tells me that the only part of me showing any progress is my waist size."

Within twenty minutes, there was not a scrap left. The woman who'd brought their food came back to collect the plates and expressed satisfaction that they'd finished their meals.

"Now," said Connor. "How about a sweet?"

While they were discussing the relative merits of items on the dessert board, Connor happened to glance toward the bar. Benjamin was the first to take notice of her startled expression. "What is it, honey?" he asked, following her gaze. Connor tapped Laura's arm. "Look over there," she said. "Isn't that the same guy we saw in Washington, you know, the guy who foiled the car thief?"

Laura leaned forward to see past Connor. "All I can see is his back now, but it does look like our leprechaun friend... Wait, he's turning. Yes, I'm sure of it."

"You know that man?" Benjamin demanded in a hoarse whisper.

Connor swiveled her head back toward her father. "Not to say 'know him,' but I'm sure he's the man who chased away a kid who was messing with my car in Washington. We saw him when we came out of the hotel. And Laura thinks she saw him again when we were leaving the Book Fair." Benjamin's expression was impassive, but Connor knew him too well. "What is it, Dad? Don't tell me you've seen him before."

"I'd almost swear that's the same odd little man who offered to buy me a drink in the bar at my club the day after you two left. He seemed harmless enough at the time. Talked my ear off about the 'troubles' in Ireland and the trials and tribulations of the 'wee' folk. I thought he must be an eccentric guest of someone, but when I asked the bartender, he wasn't sure. But I assumed the man had a legitimate reason for being there."

Connor and Laura stared at him, and Malcolm peered into the bar to get a fix on the person who had suddenly commandeered his friends' attention. "Which guy are you talking about?"

"He's gone," said Connor. "But he was there ten seconds ago, right in front of the bar." She jumped up, sloshing the beer on the table, and walked quickly to the archway, Laura hard on her heels. Both of them scanned the small crowd. Connor walked to her right to the end of the main room. It was not large, and there wasn't anywhere to sit or stand that was out of her sight. Laura went left around the corner to the small alcove near the fire. Here, too, there were no places of concealment. They both met at the arch. "Where the hell did he go?" Connor whispered. "He was standing right *here*."

They were both baffled. The little man gave every impression of having vanished into thin air, a possibility neither of them was willing to consider. There were no other public exits in sight except the door beside their table, and the only other way out of the main room was the passage from behind the long bar into the kitchen. They walked quickly through the dining room toward the kitchen, but the little man was nowhere to be seen.

They returned to the table where Benjamin and Malcolm were talking in hushed tones. "No sign of him?" Benjamin asked, though the answer was written on their faces.

"He must have gotten out through the kitchen, but why did he scram so fast?" Laura wondered aloud.

"My guess is that he saw us and wasn't too happy we saw *him*," said Connor, "but what I want to know is what he's doing here, 3,000 miles from where we first met him only a few days ago."

Benjamin nodded. "That would be my question also. Without a doubt, that's the man I met in Washington."

"Sean O'Rourke?"

"That's it, hard to forget a character like that. He even tipped his hat when he left, and he talked with an Irish brogue so thick it was hard to follow some of what he said."

The strange incident had put a damper on their collective mood, so they finished their drinks and left. Instead of going straight across the car park, Connor suggested they stroll along the High Street. All the shops were closed for the evening, and the only sign of activity was an enthusiastic group of young teenagers running their skateboards over the cement ramp formed by the base of the tall monument that stood on the sidewalk at the bend of the street. The crashing of wheels and boards, and the clamor of voices clashed with the peaceful appearance of the deserted street, but Connor assumed this was the only time they were allowed to use the area, and it also occurred to her that there wasn't much for kids to do in a town like this. Skateboarding seemed a harmless enough outlet. She led the little group past the teens and turned left up the High Street, past the George and Pilgrim Hotel, the Glastonbury Tourist Information Center housed in the centuries-old Tribunal building, and then she pointed out the interesting array of commercial enterprises—The Wicked Wax Co., The Gothic Image Bookstore, and The Glastonbury Experience (an enclave of bookshops, holistic healing practitioners, and gem-and-stone shops).

"Why all this New Age stuff?" Malcolm inquired.

Connor paused on the sidewalk. "This is a sacred place for a lot of people, on a lot of different spiritual paths. Some visitors tend to make fun of the bookstores and the vegetarian tea shops and the holistic healers, but they're just the modern version of what has always been here in some form or other. This town is in the shadow of the Tor, even though you can't quite see it from here. And over there, at the Abbey, that's where the bones of King Arthur and Queen Guinevere are said to have been buried." She indicated the tops of the Abbey ruins, which could be seen towering over the two-story shops lining the street.

"I thought King Arthur was a myth," Laura commented. "All that stuff about the Round Table and knights searching for the Grail."

Connor looked thoughtful. "Well, I don't think anyone really *knows*. Most acknowledged authorities believe the legend was built and embellished over the course of more than a thousand years by Mallory and Mary Stewart and others. The Welsh in the early centuries of the first millennium were pretty annoyed that early English monarchs appropriated Arthur and made him into something quite different from the pagan demigod of old Earth religions."

"Have you been sitting up reading in the library every night?" asked Laura. "Or have you always been an expert on legends of England?"

"Neither, actually," she answered cryptically.

Malcolm's expression indicated definite puzzlement. "So you're saying there *was* such a person as King Arthur?"

"Perhaps. Celtic tradition holds that Arthur did exist, and not only is he not really dead, but he'll be back one day to rebuild the kingdom he lost when he left this realm, if you will, toward the end of the fifth century."

"Will he be rebuilding it at Camelot?" Benjamin smiled.

"Or Caerleon, or Tintagel, or any number of other places. But some sources of historical conjecture say he will emerge, with the help of Merlin, from the gateway to the underworld."

"And where's that?" Laura asked.

"Underneath the Tor," replied Connor.

W

The night air having turned sharply cooler, they all agreed to continue their tour of Glastonbury another time. They walked through the George and Pilgrim, which had a rear exit to the car park. By mutual agreement, the driving was left to the person most familiar with the neighborhood. Thus Connor was behind the wheel as they swung around a series of roundabouts, turned right on Chilkwell Street and headed out of the town. Connor pointed out the entrance to the Chalice Well Gardens, and said they should certainly visit there. Less than thirty feet past that spot, she slammed on the brakes, nearly tossing Malcolm through the windshield. He'd been given the front seat by virtue of his height, and he almost regretted it as he slapped his palm against the dashboard to catch himself, even though the seat belt had already stopped his forward progress.

A chorus of mild protests erupted from the front and back seats, but Connor didn't appear to hear them. She turned sharply left, and started up a narrow road. NOT SUITABLE FOR MOTOR COACHES, the sign read at the bottom of the lane. "Doesn't exactly look suitable for cars either," muttered Malcolm as they squeezed between a stone wall on the left and a line of parked cars on the right.

"Where are we headed now?" Benjamin asked calmly, sitting forward a little in his seat. Still Connor didn't answer. She just kept driving, and in the dark they all knew she was going too fast for a one-lane road that accommodated two-way traffic. To their credit, however, none of them was foolish enough to try to stop Connor, or chide her for this inexplicable behavior. Laura spoke quietly, her voice tense. "This is the road up to the Tor. I guess we're having a little night tour."

A frightening minute later, Laura looked out the right window of the car and saw the Tor rising up in the blackness. It would have been invisible but for the waxing three-quarter moon now high in the sky. Near the wooden gate at the base of the pathway, Connor braked sharply to a halt, set the brake, turned off the engine, and got out of the car. Her companions set a speed record unfastening seat belts and exiting the car. Laura's account of losing Connor on the Tor was fresh in their minds. No one had any intention of letting it happen again.

Malcolm, Benjamin and Laura stood in a silent semicircle behind Connor. They looked at one other as if for some sort of hint or cue as to what they should do next. Minutes passed as Connor stared up at the tower on the summit, seeming to take no notice of the cold wind knifing through her light jacket. She took a few steps forward and put her hand on the top rail of the gate, as if to start through. Laura was beside her in an instant.

"Connor," she said softly. "It's too late to go up there now. There isn't enough light to see the steps."

"Enough light," Connor echoed. "Not enough light."

Laura shivered. A tingling sensation ran up her spine. She and Connor weren't having the same conversation. But perhaps she could get Connor to agree to leave, even if they each had entirely different reasons.

"So why not let it wait until a better time?"

A long silence followed. "The time isn't quite right," she said, "but it will be soon. I feel it coming." She turned to look at Laura, and her eyes were no longer quite the same. In the dark of night, they glowed, as if someone had struck a match behind them. "You feel it too, dearest Daria."

"Yes," said Laura, not entirely truthfully. "I do."

Connor moved to embrace her, and Laura, looking over her shoulder, saw two utterly baffled faces. She only shook her head slightly, but the message was clear: *I don't know why she's calling me that, or what's going on.*

W

The two women started down the road leading away from the Tor. Benjamin and Malcolm watched for a minute, then made a joint decision to follow slowly behind them in the car.

"Benjamin, I don't know what you're thinking, but it scares the hell out of me to see her acting like this. She's always been so...I don't know, level-headed."

Benjamin braked gently to let them get ahead of him again, and tried to get his voice under control. "Yes, she's always been just that. I used to tease her sometimes for being so incurably rational. And Gwendolyn would get so exasperated..."

"But she's acting totally weird. And this isn't the first time."

Benjamin glanced at his friend. "What do you mean?"

"This afternoon, when Laura and I got into that little...debate. The way Connor spoke to us. It was like...it didn't even sound like her talking. Then after she had a nap, she was herself again. And she didn't even mention it, as if she didn't even remember." He sighed. "I don't know. Maybe I'm wrong. But this, this is really weird. The way she drove up here, not listening to us and..."

"I know, but what can we do? I think Laura has the right idea, to just go along with her and see if she doesn't snap out of it." Benjamin moved the car forward again, seeing that Laura and Connor were nearly out of sight around the next bend.

"But what if she doesn't? What then? It must be this place. Maybe being at her grandmother's house. Maybe she's reacting to Gwendolyn being gone, but she doesn't really know it."

"Then you're saying you think my daughter is crazy." Benjamin wanted to be angry, hell—he *was* angry—but he couldn't find it in himself to spew it all over Malcolm. He knew the man adored Connor, would lay down his life for her. If even Malcolm thought she was going off the deep end? He took a deep breath. "I'm sorry. I know you didn't mean it that way."

"No, not exactly. But she might need some help. Maybe she's stressed about something. At the very least we've got to talk about it with Laura. She seems to know more about it than we do. At least she doesn't seem as freaked out as I am."

Benjamin sighed heavily and downshifted again. Laura and Connor had stopped at the edge of the road. "I hope so. Right now I'm damn glad Laura Nez had the moxy to set things straight with Connor and that they're back together. If Connor ever needed someone of her very own to love, it's now."

He rolled down the window as he let the car roll to a halt beside the two women. "Connor's feeling very tired," Laura called in an artificially cheerful tone, the sort that nurses use with patients. "I think we should ride the rest of the way home."

She bundled Connor into the backseat and wrapped her arms around the already dozing woman. "Let's go," she said. "And don't spare the horses."

"Glad to oblige," said Benjamin, revving the engine. "If you could tell me which way."

"This road comes back out on the same road, the A361. Take a left, and we'll be headed away from Glastonbury. There's signs after that. If we get lost, we'll ask someone the way to St. Giles on the nonexistent Wyndle."

They descended the last half mile as quickly as caution would allow and were soon back out onto a much wider road where the speed limit was fifty. Benjamin remembered more of the route than he'd thought and less than half an hour later they were rolling over the gravel and up the long drive.

Once they came to a stop, Malcolm jumped out of the car and opened the back door to help. Connor showed no signs of waking up. "Do you think she's all right?" he asked anxiously.

Laura, her face drawn into lines of worry, shook her head. "I wish I knew. Right now the only thing I do know is that I need a strong, able-bodied person to carry this girl up to bed."

Malcolm eagerly folded himself into the car to reach her. His eyes met Laura's and there was complete understanding between them. Whatever conflict had once threatened their friendship had been dissolved by the love they both felt for Connor Hawthorne. He scooped her up as if she weighed mere ounces and led a solemn and silent procession up the steps and through the door of Rosewood House.

Chapter Eighteen

For secrets are edged tools,
And must be kept from children and from fools.
—John Dryden
Sir Martin Mar-All, Act 2, Scene 2

Gerald had done much pacing through his house. He had done so because he was taken with the somewhat vague idea that gentlemen paced when they were highly disturbed by some event in their lives. They didn't throw breakables, and they didn't shout, except under extreme duress. He had determined that pacing, with an occasional bracing dram of whiskey, was about all that was left to a dying breed of noble, and therefore stoic, Britons.

Still, considering the duress under which he paced, the activity hardly seemed adequate. That impudent policeman had actually had the unmitigated gall to come into Gerald's home and give voice to hideously shameful accusations about Lady Fenwycke. Good God, this was his wife the man was talking about. How dared he to have even spoken about such things. Gillian would never, could never, well...Gerald stopped in midstride. He couldn't, in all good conscience, say that Gillian wouldn't perhaps, just as a sort of joke really, pretend she'd done an outrageous thing. And, he supposed, there were women who occasionally might experiment with that sapphic love he'd read about. But no, not Gillian. If for no other reason, she avoided scandal like the plague. Anything that could tarnish the Fenwycke family name was strictly against her admittedly peculiar code of ethics.

Though he'd been furious when she'd refused to give him the address of the cottage she'd let, now he was almost relieved she hadn't. Ignorance saved him from the distasteful responsibility of going immediately to Gillian and confronting her with the odious accusation. He despised a scene, and after fifteen years of marriage, he knew there certainly would be a scene. Gerald was not a man to wash the family's dirty linen in public, and he couldn't imagine having a row with his wife within hearing distance of any neighbors. No, better to wait until she returned to Haslemere, if she returned at all.

Gerald, of course, refused to admit to himself the real reason for not tracking down his wife at once and discussing the entire matter—he was reasonably sure she wasn't alone. Supposition was one degree of torment; actual knowledge was much worse. And besides, this current outrageous behavior with Conrad Thackeray had been almost eclipsed by the chief inspector's claims of yet another indiscretion with a servant of William Carlisle. On the other hand, if pressed, Gerald would be hard put to say which of these situations hurt his pride more.

W

Clarence Newbury, voice of the people, according to his byline in the *National Express Dispatch*, lived well beyond his means, at least those means that could be publicly acknowledged. The salary of a newspaper reporter, no matter how celebrated his career, did not run to a six-room flat in Knightsbridge, a late-model Jaguar, or a Savile Row tailor who skillfully altered his waistcoats to disguise a burgeoning paunch. Clarence had carefully nurtured a useful fiction among his acquaintances so that the majority of them believed he had benefited from the bequest of a favorite uncle who'd struck it rich in computer technology. There was, however, a small but growing minority of those who knew better. They contributed regularly to Clarence's upkeep in accordance with the rules of one of the oldest games in the book—blackmail. Clarence had set himself to learning these rules early in life, as soon as he discovered that information was a potent weapon if used properly. He was successful at the game because of what he liked to think was a unique combination of talent: ingenuity, tenacity, charm, callousness, and a restrained greed.

Clarence approached his avocation wisely. He was far too fond of golden eggs to inadvertently kill the geese. Thus he did not demand great sums from any one person and never more than the individual could part with comfortably. In this way, Clarence remained a nuisance more than a threat. He had spent years compiling and securely storing a thorough inventory of the various peccadilloes of the rich and the titled, though these were not necessarily one and the same. Naturally, it might be surmised that the gentry had more to lose in the face of scandal, but that was not uniformly true. It amused him that those with ample money and less social standing were rather more eager to avoid the disclosure of their sins than some peers of the realm who would bluster at him, "Publish and be damned." Clarence invariably did publish. The occasional breaking scandal was good for his reputation.

Over his morning egg and toast, he ran through a mental list of his current "accounts," as he called them. One, he thought, would have to be struck off, though it grieved him to lose so lucrative a source of income: Lady Gillian Fenwycke. It had just come to his attention that her secret was no longer his to keep. The police had somehow ferreted out her bedroom adventures with Patricia Frome. Of course, they wouldn't be able to keep their discovery secret for long. It was the nature of the beast, and Clarence had often used it to his advantage. He already knew, given his web of contacts, that Detective Chief Inspector Nicholas Foulsham had questioned both Gerald and Gillian Fenwycke as potential suspects in the girl's death. Based on prior experience, Clarence figured the lurid details would be on every front page within twenty-four hours.

He rather regretted it. He'd liked dealing with Lady Fenwycke. She didn't cry, or scream at him, or plead for mercy. She'd simply asked him how much and how often, whereupon he'd outlined his clever arrangement to have the money paid to a business that appeared on its surface to be a dressmaker's shop. He'd explained the elegance of the solution. "So often," he'd said, "ladies insist they couldn't make any payments without their husbands being the wiser. This way, all the gentlemen can do is complain about the size of the bills that come from that particular shop and ask why their wives need so many clothes."

"I don't imagine this is your only method of receiving payment," she said, and for a moment he thought he'd seen a hint of the feral in her gaze, as if she were calculating something beyond Clarence's imagination. But the moment passed, and he shrewdly offered no other information about his little business. No need for her to learn of all the ingenious ways in which he collected, and from whom. Utmost secrecy and cunning fail-safe methods were his protection against clients who had second thoughts about their payments or entertained hopes of turning the tables and sharing in his profits.

Besides, he thought it highly likely that Gillian would be annoyed to discover that she wasn't the only member of the family who was supporting Clarence's lifestyle, though for entirely different reasons. Gerald, though perhaps not directly guilty of any misdeed, had been quite anxious that one small, seemingly innocuous fact about his elder brother's death never be disclosed. Clarence, who had wisely followed up on what had been essentially a rumor, had uncovered some fire to the smoke—or at least a few embers sufficient to convince Gerald to contribute to Clarence's rapidly growing wealth.

This largesse was due in no small part to his investments with World Technology Partners, a company wholly owned by Conrad Thackeray. Everything Conrad touched turned to gold, either because he was extremely savvy or extremely ruthless, more likely both. In fact, Clarence had discovered evidence of some rather fresh skeletons in Thackeray's closet. But there was a menacing quality to Conrad that discouraged any thought of extortion. Clarence was fairly sure he'd end up another one of those skeletons, in the more literal sense. Instead, he opted for riding Thackeray's financial coattails, and the two men had, if not friendship, then an understanding between miscreants of the same stripe.

Despite his innate caution, though, Clarence was mulling over some rather odd information he'd received from someone inside WTP. First, Thackeray, who was obsessively punctual and kept office hours as if life itself depended upon his presence and supervision of the company's affairs, had grown positively erratic in his comings and goings. His assistant, who had always obliged Mr. Thackeray in fulfilling his every need, now never knew quite when to expect him. (Her annoyance over this state of affairs made her one of Clarence's most useful sources.) New employees had been added to the payroll without having been interviewed by the personnel manager or even seen in the office. Thackeray had set up overseas bank accounts for which he was the only signatory, thus bypassing WTP's entire accounting department. And midlevel managers had been calling to complain of electronic equipment they'd ordered from subsidiaries but had never received.

So, wondered Clarence, what was the old boy up to? And did it have anything to do with the sudden flurry of activity on the grounds of Haslemere? The lovely Sonja, he smiled. So terribly venal. He supposed he had her to blame for spilling the story about Gillian to the police. But he wasn't angry. In truth, the usefulness of that tidbit had about run its course anyway, what with the changing attitudes in the world at large. Clarence rather regretted the increasing tolerance of society, though his was a singularly "live and let live" attitude. He didn't much mind what other people did, only that public opinion was sufficiently opposed to their behavior that they would purchase his silence.

Clarence brushed a crumb of toast from his lapel, placed the dishes on the sideboard for the daily to clean up, and left his flat. With his furled umbrella in one hand, and his Burberry trench coat over the other, he looked for all the world like a successful banker, and he felt like one too. All was right in his world, and life could only get better.

W

Conrad Thackeray wasn't certain when he'd first had the sensation of being followed, but surely it hadn't been that long ago. He was positively paranoid about being vulnerable to his enemies, so it was with great care that he chose his routes, varied his routines, and regularly swept his home, offices, and vehicles for listening and tracking devices. Occasionally one would turn up, and Conrad wouldn't rest until he'd traced it back to its source one way or another. The responsible party was then given some "hands-on" instruction in how not to deal with Conrad Thackeray or World Technology Partners.

There had been nothing found in any sweep for several weeks. He was continually random in his choice of routes to and from the office. His driver was trained in defensive driving and eluding surveillance. The limousine was armor-plated and equipped with state-of-the-art communications, including signal-jamming devices. Rationally, there was no way anyone could be following him on a regular basis, and yet he *knew* there was. And he thought he even knew who it was, or at least what he looked liked, but the glimpses he'd caught were so brief he couldn't be sure a second later that the man had actually been there—the image that remained was of a tiny fellow, not five feet tall, with flowing white hair and huge bushy eyebrows. Not exactly the sort to blend into a crowd. But efforts by Conrad's chief of security to catch the culprit had been maddeningly fruitless. Conrad was almost tempted to think he'd been seeing things, that he might be losing his mind. Certainly his security chief had looked askance at him when he didn't think Conrad noticed. As he could not countenance the possibility of insanity, he clung to his belief that the man was real and his proof was forthcoming.

He left his office unusually late in the evening, choosing to walk the few blocks to one of the clubs to which he belonged. He'd scheduled a dinner meeting with the representative of a Middle Eastern syndicate seeking to purchase arms. The entire transaction would be illegal, but legalities were of little concern to Conrad. He had a cash buyer in hand, and the goods in a warehouse in Portugal. He frankly didn't care if they all blew each other to hell.

As he walked, he found himself involuntarily reflecting on how moody his assistant, Belinda, had become. He assumed it had something to do with the fact that he'd stopped shagging her. But what did it matter? Why did women always assume there had to be some meaningful emotion connected to sex? Good God, he paid her twice the going rate for secretaries, and she'd been more than willing to hike up her skirt, almost before he'd suggested it. Did she actually suppose that having it off on the couch in his office was tantamount to a marriage proposal? He would have to find some excuse to get rid of her. Conrad stopped to wait for the walk signal, and that's when he saw him. The little man stood on the opposite side of the street, next to the post of one of the Belicia beacons at the Zebra crossing, his eyes fixed on Conrad's, an odd smile playing across his face. Thackeray was consumed by a uncontrollable surge of anger. Despite the peril of the oncoming traffic, he dashed into the street. Horns blared. Brakes squealed. An off-duty cabbie yelled an obscenity.

Conrad ignored it all. His one goal was to reach the man without taking his eyes off him. For it was always in that instant when he glanced away that the man disappeared. He ran across three lanes and onto the center island. The little gray-haired figure hadn't moved an inch. Conrad could almost taste victory. He'd take hold of the damned spy and find out who he was, who he worked for. He started to run, but a crowd of pedestrians had stepped off the curb and was coming right at him. He tried to part the crowd with his arms, pushing and shoving, his eyes never leaving his quarry, and it was this mad determination that did him in. A tall hulk of a teenager who took issue with Conrad's rudeness had decided to shove back. His sheer strength knocked Conrad sideways and almost off his feet. He grabbed at someone's coat sleeve to catch himself and stared at the walk signal no more than ten yards way. The entire incident had taken a few seconds at most, and the man was gone. Conrad stared wildly up and down the street. There hadn't been enough time to get out of sight, even at a dead run, and the man was too old for that. Where the hell *was* he?

In his agitation, he dashed through the streets, peering into shops, his expression so alarming the ladies in a tea room shrank back from the window. It was then he realized he'd dropped his briefcase and his gloves, so he ran back to the corner. There in the street was the leather case, with the imprint of dozens of tires. Amazing, really, that no one had taken it. The gloves were gone, though. He allowed himself a moment to be annoyed. Eighty-five pounds they'd cost him. "Handmade," he snarled under his breath with all the anger of a man who'd grown up poor, as he waited for the signal to go out and retrieve his ravaged briefcase. Once on the other side, he stood panting against the wall of a building. The adrenaline had stopped coursing through his system, leaving him weak and trembling.

It wouldn't do at all if he showed up to the meeting in this state, so he turned into the nearest pub and ordered a shot of whiskey. Conrad drained it in one gulp and tossed a two-pound coin on the counter. Before he pulled away from the bar, however, the barman slapped down another drink in front of him and scooped up the coin. "I didn't order another," said Conrad, "and I'm not paying for it."

"No need," the barman shrugged. "Gent over there already paid for it. Said to deliver it with his compliments."

Conrad felt the pulse pounding in his ears. "What gent? Where is he?" In his panic, he reached over and grabbed the barman's arm.

"Hey, leave off, mate, or I'll toss you out o' here."

"Please, just tell me who bought the drink?"

The barman scanned the crowded room. "Reckon he's gone. T'was a little feller, no bigger than this," he indicated, holding his hand halfway up his chest, "and longish white hair." The barman stopped explaining as soon as he chanced to notice that Conrad was no longer listening; he was gone. "Barmy bastard," he muttered.

It wasn't until much later that night that Conrad noticed the contents of his briefcase had undergone a subtle alteration. In a side compartment, tucked away from the rest of his business documents, had been a set of photocopies of some very old unbound manuscript pages that had recently come into his possession. When he reached his home shortly after midnight, and pulled out the folder, all he found inside were blank pieces of white paper. His rage was only slightly mollified by the knowledge that the originals were safely locked in his personal vault.

Chapter Nineteen

Sweet is the lore which Nature brings;
Our meddling intellect mis-shapes the beauteous forms of things:
We murder to dissect.

Enough of science and of art;
Close up these barren leaves;
Come forth, and bring with you a heart
That watches and receives.
—William Wordsworth
"The Tables Turned"

"How you feeling, sweetheart?"

Connor opened her eyes and blinked in the strong sunlight. "Good Lord, what time is it? I can't believe I overslept."

"You didn't oversleep. We're not exactly on a timetable."

"I know, but there's a lot to do...I think."

"Any chance you might let me in on the plan?"

Connor frowned. "I didn't mean it like that, I...hell, I don't know what I mean."

"That's what got me kinda worried, darling. Last night was a little scary."

"Why? You mean about seeing our leprechaun at the bar?" asked Connor, pulling back the edge of the hand-tatted rose and white coverlet. "Since when does a weird coincidence scare you? I mean, it's something we should look into, but—"

"I don't mean that. I mean what happened at the Tor."

"But we've gone over and over that. I can't make any more sense of that than you can. I thought we were going to just leave it alone for the moment."

Laura took a deep breath. "I'm not talking about day before yesterday. I'm talking about the Tor last night."

"But we didn't go there last night. Why would we go there in the dark? You can't see anything." Connor sat upright, obviously annoyed, but Laura's expression remained neutral.

"That's what I've been trying to ask you because we *did* go there last night. You were driving us home, you stopped abruptly and turned up the road to the Tor without telling us why, and..." She stopped speaking as Connor's face went ashen. Laura reached for her hands. "Hey, don't panic. There's something going on here, and we just have to figure out what it is."

"But I don't remember any of this. I can't believe I could do all that and not know...my God, I must be losing my mind." Her voice trembled, and Laura moved close, wrapping her arms around Connor. "Shhh. You're not losing your mind, believe me. You're the sanest woman I've ever known."

"Is that a good thing?" Connor asked, with a trace of her old self.

"Sanity is somewhat overrated, but it beats the alternative. And that incredible mind of yours is just one reason I love you so much." She pulled back and took Connor's chin in her hand. "I don't know exactly what's at work here, but between you and me and your father and Malcolm, we're not going to let anything bad happen to you or to any of us. Okay?" Laura leaned in and gave Connor a quick, soft kiss.

Connor nodded, looking anything but convinced.

"Could I have a little more enthusiasm here?" Laura said, her eyebrows in full interrogatory mode.

"Oh, all right. Let me get dressed, and we'll hold a full council of war with the troops."

"That's better. Malcolm's burning some toast for us, and Benjamin is muttering about the lack of a decent omelette pan."

"I assume that means scrambled eggs then."

"Exactly."

W

Thirty minutes later, the four of them sat down to breakfast. True to Laura's prediction, the toast was singed on one side and inexplicably light on the other; the eggs were indeed scrambled.

Connor was tempted to tease her father over his omelette failure, but she felt suddenly very self-conscious. They too had witnessed her aberrant behavior the night before, and she still had no explanation for it. She sensed they were as uncomfortable as she was in even broaching the subject. The silence grew thick and awkward until Laura rescued the situation by suggesting they all go into the library and light a fire.

Twenty minutes later, when they were settled, Laura said with her usual candor, "So, I've talked to Connor and she has no memory at all of the events that took place once we started driving home."

Malcolm and Benjamin stared at Laura, then Connor, then at each other. From their expressions, Connor could tell they couldn't decide whether to be relieved or more worried.

"Laura's right. I don't remember anything about it. She explained what happened, that I drove you up there and then acted crazy, but the only thing I remember since we got into the car in the car park in Glastonbury is waking up in my bed this morning. That's it. No dreams, no nothing."

Benjamin pursed his lips thoughtfully. "But you seemed pretty normal while it was happening. You didn't act as if you were in a trance or anything. You had your mind made up, and you didn't seem worried about whether or not we listened to you...not that that's unusual." He paused to let his gentle teasing sink in.

Connor smiled in spite of herself. "Gee, thanks, Dad. To hear you tell it, people would think I'm a total shrew."

"Got you to smile, didn't I?" he said with a twinkle.

"Yes, you did," she admitted grudgingly. "But didn't anything about me seem odd?"

"Only that you were so focused on getting to the Tor, and you didn't respond directly to anything we said," Malcolm explained.

"Except that bit about there not being enough light," Laura reminded them. "You know, when I said to Connor that there was no reason to go up to the Tor because there wasn't enough light to see by."

Connor looked at Laura. "What did I say?"

"You repeated it once. You said 'not enough light.' And then I think you said that there would be soon, that you could feel it coming."

Connor had been watching Laura intently, as if looking for clues to what this might mean. Thus it was that she saw Laura's eyes flick away suddenly.

"There's something more," said Connor. "Something you're not telling me."

Laura sighed. "Right after you said you could feel it coming, you turned to me and asked if I could feel it too. And you called me Daria."

Connor felt a thousand tiny flickers of fire race up her spine as her stomach contracted into a knotted fist. "Daria," she whispered. "Daria. I know that name, but I...I couldn't know it. I've never heard it." Her breath was coming in shallow gasps.

Malcolm reached for Connor's hand. "Hey, don't zone out on us. We can't help you if you don't stick with us."

She focused on his soft brown eyes and made herself breathe again. "I'm still here. Though if I weren't, I can't imagine where I'd be." She shifted her gaze to Laura. "Did I *sound* like me when we had this conversation at the Tor?"

Laura thought about that for a moment or two. "Yes and no. I'm sorry that's such a wishy-washy answer. But even though it was your voice I heard, there was a quality to it that I didn't recognize, a sort of authoritarian tone, as if you were accustomed to being in charge."

"You mean I'm not?" joked Connor, and the ensuing ripple of quiet laughter took the edge off the tension in the room. "No, I understand what you're saying. It was my voice you were hearing, but not my thoughts. Is that it?"

"Yes, that's exactly what I meant, but I didn't know quite how to explain it."

"But it fits. Since I don't remember saying those things to you, or even driving to the Tor, it would seem I have some type of alternate personality capable of taking charge."

Malcolm frowned. "Are you saying this is some sort of mental problem, because if you are, I don't believe it for a minute."

"And neither do I," added Benjamin firmly. "I think there's another explanation entirely, but perhaps you don't want to consider it." His eyes met Laura's, and Connor suspected they both knew something she didn't, or they had discussed this theory in advance.

"Okay, I'll bite. What is it I don't want to consider?"

"That this is just another side of who you are," Benjamin began, but Connor interrupted him at once.

"Isn't that what I just said? That some split personality has emerged?"

"That isn't what I mean at all. And if this weren't so serious, I could almost be amused at how hard you fight to ignore the things your grandmother tried to teach you."

"What do you mean?"

"You'd actually rather diagnose yourself as having multiple personality disorder than admit to being in touch with your own past—a previous self from another lifetime."

Connor stared at him. Out of the corner of her eye, she saw Laura nodding with obvious approval of this outrageous conclusion. Malcolm simply looked thoughtful, as if he hadn't yet decided.

"A past life! Oh, come on, Dad. I mean, I'm not saying reincarnation definitely isn't true. I'll admit there's a certain amount of logic to it. But I don't believe we can *remember* other lives. It doesn't make sense. Our memories are all lodged in our minds, in our brains, the parts that turn to dust after we die. The soul is just...well, it's just the soul." Even she knew how lame the argument sounded, but she was determined to argue the point.

But Laura wasn't going to let her off the hook, however. "So show me where the mind is."

Connor shrugged and pointed at her head. "Somewhere in here."

"Where exactly?"

"I don't know. Different parts of the brain do different things."

"You mean different parts of the brain process input from our senses?"

"Okay," said Connor grudgingly. "Scientists know which parts correspond to sight and sound and so forth."

"And they have some idea where memory is stored."

"Yes, which is my point exactly."

"But could you point to where awareness is stored in there?" Laura asked, tapping the side of her skull.

"Awareness?"

"Sense of self, sense of identity, appreciation of your own existence. Where's all that?"

Connor scowled as she had the distinct sensation she'd been backed into a corner. "I don't know. Scientists haven't figured out the entire brain by any means, or even how it works, except in general terms."

"Energy," said Laura.

"What?"

"The brain works on principles of electricity, or energy. And I think the soul is pure energy made up of lifetimes of accumulated knowledge and wisdom. But most of the time when we're born, we don't remember who we've been; probably it's supposed to work that way, so as we don't think we're crazy as we're growing up. But it explains why children have a rich fantasy life and lots of people to talk to, even if the grown-ups can't see them. I think they're still aware of who they were, and maybe they can even see other life forms that we can't."

"Like aliens?" Malcolm frowned.

Laura poked his arm. "You've watched too many episodes of *The X-Files*. No, I'm talking about beings who aren't in a body at the moment. I can't say I know where they all hang out in between incarnations, but

I've traveled enough in the Dreamtime to know that they are often very near to us, even if we don't realize it. And some people have the ability to access their own storehouse of past knowledge. In Connor's case, though, it obviously wasn't by intentional effort, so I'm not sure where that leaves us." She took Connor's hand in hers. "If you're getting bleed-through from someone you were in a past life, I think it must have been triggered by the location, by being at the Tor. And that would tend to explain the weird experiences that we had the first time we went up there."

Connor was painfully aware that she would likely have to give up on her zealously guarded rationality, but it wouldn't be without a fight. "I'm not exactly anxious to be tossed into a rubber room, which is where I'll end up if this is some form of insanity. But I don't see how you can be so sure of your theories. Maybe the stress of the last year *has* just caught up with me."

Laura sat back in her chair. "Anyone else care to take this one?"

Benjamin inclined his head toward Laura. "I think you've been doing fine up to now. I'll only add that my daughter is completely sane...stubborn as hell, but sane."

"I'll second that on both counts," added Malcolm.

Laura smiled at Connor. "I believe we have a consensus so far. You, Connor Hawthorne, are definitely not crazy. But somewhere, possibly very long ago, you lived in this area, and you were affected by whatever occurred at the Tor."

Connor sank back in the chair. A consensus, Laura said, between her lover, her best friend, and her father. Apparently, they didn't think she was losing it. But the alternative, quite frankly, didn't bear thinking about. She'd avoided it all her life, that family "weirdness" that had been her grandmother's stock in trade. Even the events of more than a year ago had been firmly filed away under the catchall heading "Don't get it, don't need to."

Now "it," whatever the hell "it" was, had begun pressing in on her from all sides, invading not only her dreams, but also her waking hours, at least she thought she was awake, and not driving around the Tor taking her companions on impromptu night tours. No matter how you looked at it, she was acting like a nutcase, and she was left to choose between two almost equally distasteful explanations for her behavior—encroaching insanity or the influence of past lives.

With an increasing sense of helplessness, Connor turned to Malcolm, the one she was sure she could count on to point the search for an explanation in another direction, since he was a man most comfortable with the evidence of his senses. He wanted evidence he could put his hands on. "You don't really believe in all this, do you? I mean, this stuff about past lives or ancient events," she asked her old friend.

He closed his eyes for a moment, and Connor knew she was going to lose the argument the moment he opened his mouth. "The funny thing is, if you'd asked me that question a couple of years ago, I would have laughed about it. And don't get me wrong. I don't believe every crazy thing I hear about these days. And I wouldn't admit any of this to most of the people I know. But somehow, when I was chasing across the desert trying to find you, I got help when I most needed it. Something...or someone...showed me where you were before that son of a bitch could kill you both." He paused and smiled at Laura. "Then there was your Grandmother Klah," he said. "Now there's one formidable old lady. Not to mention *your* grandmother," he added, glancing at Connor. "Between the two of them, I learned some things. Most of all I learned not to question what I don't understand, and to keep an open mind." He shrugged. "I don't know squat about all this reincarnation business, but my gut tells me something is going on here we don't understand, at least not yet."

"But who knows if we ever will? What if nothing else happens, and I never know whether I'm having a breakdown or some damned mystical experience?" Connor protested.

Laura smiled grimly. "I don't think we have to worry about excessive peace and quiet suddenly settling over this area while we're here."

Benjamin looked at her curiously. "You think it's our presence, or at least yours and Connor's, that's somehow precipitating the events you've experienced?"

"Not entirely. I think we're here because something called us to be here, and that 'something' has been more awakened by the fact that we *are* here. Does that make sense?"

Malcolm nodded. "It's the chicken-and-egg thing, isn't it?"

Laura grinned. "Exactly. I have no idea what's causing what. Is the fact that we were at the Tor a couple of days ago when all the weirdness broke loose simply a coincidence that we got caught up in, or did it happen only because we showed up there?"

"If you accept that all events are interrelated, and that nothing happens for no reason at all, then there's truth in both statements," offered Benjamin. "Or we've got one big causality loop that defies analysis."

"And we're stuck in it," said Connor gloomily. "Either that damn hill is making me nuts, or..." She didn't know how to finish the statement.

"Or you're awakening something in that hill." Laura's eyes pierced Connor's miasma of confusion. "And we're going to find out what it is, sooner rather than later."

"But where do we start?" Malcolm asked. "You know I'd much rather be doing something than sitting around waiting for something to happen."

No one spoke for several moments. Finally, Benjamin cleared his throat. "I have a hunch Gwendolyn knew a lot more than she's ever told any of us. But she was pretty bent on Connor accepting the fact that she was destined to accept some higher calling."

"Jeez, Dad. You make it sound like I'm supposed to be headed for a nunnery."

Laura chuckled. "Somehow I don't think you'd do well with all those vows."

"Which ones in particular?" retorted Connor, with enough of a smile to let them know she was trying to reclaim her usual sense of humor.

"Obedience?" offered Laura, arching an eyebrow. "Poverty...um—"

"Don't even go there," Connor interrupted, punctuating the demand with a throw pillow aimed at Laura's head.

Laura ducked, and the pillow sailed on past. To Connor's dismay, however, she saw that an unsuspecting lamp was about to be victimized. But it was too late to jump up and deflect it. The antique celadon porcelain vase, which had been converted by some more eager than thoughtful designer into a large lamp with a silk shade, teetered backward as the pillow hit, wobbled for a moment, then, before Laura could grab for it, crashed to the floor. The sound left little doubt of its failure to survive the three-foot trip to the polished hardwoods.

"Oh, damn it!" Connor moaned as she knelt beside the pieces. "It's completely destroyed."

Laura hopped up and said, "I'll go find a broom and dustpan."

A second later, they all heard the sizzle as the lamp wiring sparked slightly. Malcolm immediately asked where the circuit breakers could be found. "Don't try to unplug it until I turn off the power," he said when Connor told him where to locate the circuit panel in the pantry.

Benjamin knelt beside her and began picking up the shards of porcelain, careful not to touch the metal pieces that were still in contact with the wiring. "It's just a lamp, sweetheart, and I don't think Gwendolyn would have lost any sleep over it. She always said that whoever ruined a perfectly good vase to make a moderately ugly lamp ought to be taken out and shot...or something to that effect."

"Then why did she keep it around? Come to think of it, I don't recall seeing it here before, at least not when I last stayed here two or three years ago."

"She only kept it because it was a present from your mother. Amanda had it made to order and sent it to her the Christmas before last."

Connor sighed. "Maybe we won't tell my mother that it's gone to that great lamp graveyard then. It would only upset her all over again."

"Funny thing, though," Benjamin said, picking up the larger pieces and depositing them in a wastebasket, "after the funeral, when you refused to come back here, Amanda insisted on coming. I told her she shouldn't since Gwendolyn had left you the house, but you know how she can be. She was about to make a huge scene in front of the townspeople."

Connor grimaced. "I know what *that's* like."

"Anyway, I finally said we could stop here on the way to the airport, and when she came in here and saw that lamp, she started to sob."

Connor had to swallow a lump in her throat. As much as she had every reason to be permanently angry with her bigoted, self-centered mother, she couldn't bear the thought of her being that sad.

Benjamin went on. "She really loved her mother despite all the times Gwendolyn took her to task. Standing there with her that day, I felt better about Amanda, knowing she hadn't gotten completely dried up inside. Of course, once she'd calmed down, she wanted to take the lamp back to the States with her and probably whatever else she felt entitled to, but I said she'd have to wait until you decided what to do with the place, and she'd have to ask you for the lamp."

"She must have hated that."

"She did. Started in on one of her tirades about being deprived of her rights as Gwendolyn's daughter and why would she be passed over...you know, all that stuff. She actually tried to defy me and snatch this silly lamp. But I hustled her out of the house before she could do a thing."

"Thanks, Dad. But I wouldn't have cared."

"No, but Gwendolyn would have. Her will says this house *and* everything in it are yours. She was damned specific about the contents being a part of your legacy. It's simply a bitter pill for Amanda to swallow, and I doubt she's gotten over it yet."

Connor sighed. "You think there's still a chance for her? That she'll really stay off the bottle?"

Benjamin shrugged. "I wish I knew, honey. Maybe I should have tried to stick with it, but after forty-five years of marriage, I couldn't do make myself go through the motions any longer. And when I quit my job, and stepped out of the limelight, Amanda didn't want to go through the motions anymore either."

Connor thought she detected a trace of tears glistening in her father's eyes. "Oh, Dad. I hate seeing you unhappy. I know you tried your best. But nothing was ever enough for her. Somehow she lost her happiness a long, long time ago, and nothing anyone else could do will ever bring it back."

The other lights in the room went out, indicating that Malcolm had flipped the right breaker. Benjamin immediately pulled the plug from the socket, glancing curiously at its enormous, British-style, rounded blades. Then he called to Malcolm that it was all clear to turn the power back on.

Laura returned at that moment with the requisite cleaning tools and set to work sweeping while Connor retrieved the lampshade from which the harp still dangled. Benjamin picked up the carved wooden base. "Most of these parts are fine," he said, with the enthusiasm of the hobbyist he'd always wanted to be, if he'd had the time. "You could use them to fix up another lamp." He turned the base over in his hands, and cocked his head to one side, a puzzled frown creasing his forehead. "Hmm, what's this?"

Laura, who had just finished sweeping up, moved closer to Benjamin to see what had drawn his attention. Connor joined them as Malcolm's voice boomed from the doorway. "What's everyone looking at?"

Benjamin gently poked his fingers into the recessed underside of the wooden base and pried at a piece of surgical tape which had been dyed the color of the mahogany base. He peeled it off and held it up so that the others could see. There, stuck fast to the tape, was a tiny, ornate key.

"I almost didn't see it, the way it blends in. But the light hit it just right, and I could see a lump where no lump should be."

"But what's it for?" Malcolm inquired, curious about the key, which was entirely unconventional in appearance. It obviously was not a door key, or made to fit any standard sort of lock.

Benjamin handed the key to Connor, who ran her hands over it thoughtfully. "I can't imagine."

Laura peered at it. "I guess we'll just have to do this the hard way."

Connor looked at her quizzically. "You mean—"

"Yep. Search every nook and cranny of this house until we find the lock that key is supposed to open."

Benjamin and Malcolm looked eager to start a search, and Connor suspected they were both getting tired of the inactivity of all this discussion and unfruitful theorizing. "All right then," she said. "Let's spread out and look. It's got to be something unusual and probably small, maybe a cupboard or a box or something. This key's only a little more than an inch and a half long. If anyone finds a possibility, holler and I'll come try it out."

Benjamin and Laura offered to go through the bedrooms on the first floor, while Malcolm and Connor stayed on the ground floor. "The house isn't all *that* big," said Connor. "If it's here, I can't imagine we won't be able to find it pretty quickly."

On that score, Connor was wrong. For almost two hours, the four of them hunted diligently. Given that the group consisted of a police officer, an ex-spy, a security specialist, and an ex-district attorney turned novelist, the search was about as thorough as any such operation ever conducted. If there was something to be discovered, they would have found it. But when they all returned to the library, the results were written on their faces. Laura was plucking a few cobwebs from her hair in a distracted fashion, and Connor had wrapped a handkerchief around the finger she'd cut open on a nail while fishing around in a cupboard in the small sitting room at the rear of the house.

"What are the chances that key doesn't fit anything in this house?" Laura asked, flopping down in one of the wing chairs.

"Then why keep it here?" Benjamin responded with his usual logic. "If it were a door key or a padlock key, then I'd say we'd have to extend our search to the grounds and possibly even further afield. But somehow I believe whatever we're looking for is right here."

Connor looked down at the key in her hand, saw the delicate tracery around the wards and the loop at the top. She glanced up at the shelves. "We've had almost all the books out of the shelves, and we didn't see anything behind them. But if the key was in this room, maybe..." Her voice trailed off, and the others turned to her. She saw the thinly veiled worry in their eyes.

"No," she said. "I'm not fading out on you again. But I was remembering something. It was a long time ago." Connor closed her eyes, concentrating. "It was summertime, and really warm. I'd been out playing, and I came back in here because...yes, I'd scraped my elbow on a tree or something. And I flung the door open and Grandma Gwendolyn was startled. She sort of jumped up..." Connor's eyes snapped open. "She was at the desk, and she did something...I don't know, the shape of it looked different, and I remember hearing the sound of it clicking or shutting. And she was between me and the desk so I couldn't see, but..."

In an instant they were all crowded around the antique, slant-front writing desk. There was already a key in the lock, quite unlike the one in her hand. So Connor tugged out the thin wooden slides on either side of the first drawer and then pulled the slant open, lowering it to rest on the slides so that it formed a writing surface. Within the desk all sorts of pigeonholes and compartments were now visible. But it appeared that only the center compartment had a lock, and a small key with a silk tassel was in the keyhole.

Connor sighed. "Maybe I'm wrong. But I have the strongest feeling that this desk is important."

"Most of these old pieces had secret compartments," Laura suggested. "Maybe that's what we're looking for."

"That's true," Benjamin agreed. "I've seen a few of these. We even have a similar desk at the house in Potomac. As I recall, there's usually a hidden recess in that compartment just at the rear of the writing surface, inside the place where they kept the quills and ink pots." He slid back the cover of the compartment and felt around inside with his hands until he located a slight indentation. Pressing on it caused a tiny door to open at the rear of the compartment. They all leaned forward, but after reaching in, Benjamin declared it empty. "Besides," he reminded them, "I didn't need a key to open it, and I doubt Gwendolyn would choose a place so obvious to anyone who's ever owned antique furniture of this era."

Connor agreed. "She was too smart to be careless. And if she taped this key under a lamp, she wanted to make sure no one found it."

Laura looked perplexed. "Well, she would have wanted *you* to find it, wouldn't she? There wouldn't be much point in making you her heir and insisting that you needed to follow in her footsteps if she didn't intend to give you access to her knowledge. Are you sure there wasn't any hint in the papers she had her lawyer send you?"

Connor looked indescribably embarrassed. "I didn't really look at them," she admitted. "At least nothing much besides the papers I needed to sign, and the copy of the will."

"But why?" Malcolm asked, his eyes transmitting disbelief. "Didn't it occur to you there might be something important? I mean, weren't you curious?"

Connor was silent for a long moment. "I couldn't...that is, I didn't want to...read whatever she'd written to me. It hurt too much knowing I'd never see her again. And I didn't want to think that when she came to New Mexico, she already knew she wasn't coming back here. Don't you see," she said, "my grandmother took care of everything *before* she left England. All her affairs were in perfect order. And she'd left a long letter to me. Her solicitor sent it along. But I couldn't...I was—"

"Afraid?" Laura asked softly, her eyes fixed on Connor.

"Yes, God help me, I was afraid of what that letter would say, of what she wanted me to do, or believe, or...become. And if I never read it, I wouldn't have to really *know*." Connor's voice broke, and Laura immediately wrapped her arms around her lover's trembling shoulders.

"I understand, sweetheart. We all do." Her glance took in Malcolm and Benjamin, who both nodded. "But I don't see how you can get around it anymore. There's too much going on that we don't understand, and I have a feeling you're the only one who can untangle all of this. Whatever she wanted to say to you, maybe it's time you heard it. And we're all here to help you no matter what."

Connor gave Laura a good, hard squeeze, then stepped back a pace, still staring at the desk as if waiting for her memory to cooperate. She took a deep breath. "I know you're right. I'll get the envelope. It's in my briefcase with the other estate papers."

She left the room and quickly returned with a long, thick, white envelope clutched in her hand. But only Laura remained in the library. "We thought it would be better if you had time alone to read it. Then, if there's anything you want to share with us, anything we need to know, you can call us. We'll be in the kitchen."

Connor sighed. She'd known it should be this way, but the thought of being alone still wasn't terribly appealing. "I wouldn't mind if you stayed."

Laura smiled and brushed Connor's bangs out of her eyes. "I know, darling. And I appreciate it. But I can't imagine that Gwendolyn intended the text of that letter for anyone but you. And although I really don't know exactly where she is these days, I'd still prefer *not* to piss her off. That's one old lady who can take care of business."

Connor's smile was tinged with sadness. "She was the strongest woman I've ever known. She never wavered from what she thought was right. When I was little, I imagined that sparks flew right out of her eyes. Yet, there was such warmth and love there when she sat me down and tended my cuts and scrapes, and read to me from all these books, and..." Connor's voice thickened with emotion, and she gulped hard. "Oh, God, I miss her."

"I know you do, honey. But I have a feeling she's not far way. Now you sit down in Gwendolyn's chair and find out what she had to tell you. I'm hoping that letter will clear up a lot of pressing questions." Laura kissed Connor gently, then closed the door behind her as she left.

Chapter Twenty

Rejoice, ye dead, where'er your spirits dwell,
Rejoice that yet on earth your fame is bright,
And that your names, remembered day and night,
Live on the lips of those who love you well.
—Robert Bridges
Ode to Music

[December, two years earlier]
My dearest granddaughter,

I am no longer with you on the Earth plane, but rest assured I have not ceased to exist. I suppose you could think of me as having gone elsewhere. The exact nature of that "elsewhere" is difficult to explain to you at this time in your life, so I'll simply let it suffice to tell you that I am well and conscious of my Self and my existence. In the morning I shall set out for America, for that place I found in one of my atlases, New Mexico, which to me still seems an odd name for one of the United States. Still, there it is. Perhaps Americans find the naming of our counties and towns equally strange.

I think you already know at some level, even if you have chosen to ignore that knowledge, that I am able to travel on the astral planes when necessary.

Thus, I have seen you in that lonely desert place with your friend, who appears as a blazing star in the astral firmament, though her life energy is seeping away. I trust, however, that she will survive this ordeal, though there is little I can do to help her. I see others nearby, however, who are actively embracing her life force to keep it intact until more can be done.

Tears trickled down Connor's cheeks. So, her grandmother had known everything that had transpired in the desert—the shooting at the arroyo, Laura's seemingly mortal wound, her own raging anger and fear. Connor had to admit she'd been aware of Gwendolyn's presence, that she'd had a startlingly clear vision of her grandmother, a vision she was later so willing to discount as nothing but a dream. She reached for a tissue from the lace-covered tissue box and for moment breathed in the scent of lavender and spice that had been Gwendolyn. Connor closed her eyes and felt her grandmother's presence so strongly, her chest constricted with grief.

"Go on, my child."

Connor sprang up from the chair, staring wildly around the room. But she was alone. The slanting sunlight picked out tiny dust motes in the air before bathing the muted tones of the old oriental rug in a warm glow. All was silence, all was peacefulness. Connor felt as if she were standing in the one calm place in the universe, in the eye of a storm that had begun to envelop all of them. Yet she felt safe here, at this moment. She sat down again and resumed her reading.

Still, despite this assistance already in place, I know I am called to join you there (in the physical realm) for reasons not yet entirely clear to me. But the Ancient Ones of Light, who have guided me always, have added their voice to the summons, along with that of a quite remarkable being who appeared on the astral with me. She, I do not doubt, is the spiritual projection of someone you are about to meet. As always, I will obey the guidance of the Ancient Ones, though indeed I would have come there in any event once I realized you were in danger. I have projected my image to you, and my energy as well, so that you may draw some sustenance and hope from me in these hours of travail that you are facing. I have no fear that you will be taken from us, however, for I would certainly know if this were the case. You and I are too closely connected from past-life journeys together for me to remain ignorant of your future. This is one reason I know you are destined to accomplish a great deal during this particular incarnation of your spirit.

This scares you, my dear child, does it not? You wonder if more will be expected of you than you believe you could accomplish, if you will find yourself summoned just as I was long ago. I regret that I was not able to teach you more when you were young so that you would be better prepared to meet your destiny. But even I was unsure of how much was too much. And your mother was highly suspicious of my "peculiar tendencies" as she called them. Even when she allowed you to visit me in England, she interrogated you at length when you came home to see if I had taught you anything she considered "unsuitable." Later, after your unhappy marriage, you immersed yourself entirely in your career and raising Katy, and I felt the time was not right for broaching the subject of spiritual matters. Now, of course, I know that I waited too long. I will not be able to teach you those things which it was my duty to teach you. At least I cannot do so in person.

So, dear Connor, here is the basic history of our spiritual family, and a few facts you must understand. I will be brief, for I have only a few hours before the taxi will come to take me to the train station and on to the airport. I will post this to my solicitor, along with some other papers, so that you, and you alone, will receive it. There are others who would go to some lengths to prise this information from you, thus I admonish you to keep it safe.

A cloud passed over the sun, and the room grew suddenly dim. Connor was aware that the sensation of warmth she'd felt was gone, replaced by an inexplicable chill. She clutched the letter to her chest, feeling an overwhelming desire to...what? Absorb it? Protect it? Hide from it? Then the moment passed, and the warm glow reasserted itself around her. Connor let herself breathe again. She stared at the strong, elegant handwriting, but the words blurred into illegibility. Without understanding why, she knew she stood at a crossroads. She could put the letter down, tuck it away somewhere, perhaps even burn it. She could choose not to read the words that could so easily herald an end to her normal way of life. She could walk away from this house, leave the unsolved murders to the police. She could take Laura to visit Katy at Oxford and let the two of the most important people in her life get to know each other. They would sit in a pub and laugh and talk about nothing more sinister than the eccentricities of the dons and the stress of examinations. The images of what had happened on the Tor would simply fade away.

She and Laura would go back to New Mexico, back to the house Laura had built on the reservation. They would ride and explore and make love, and Connor would write and...and what? Connor could almost *see* herself in this idyll her mind had constructed; she could almost reach out and touch the homespun comfort of it. But not quite. The letter in her hand would not let her. Even now it vibrated with energy, as if a mild charge of electricity flowed from it. The words shimmered on the pages.

She looked around the room. Nothing had changed. It was the same comforting, familiar place she'd always known. And Gwendolyn's presence was everywhere.

Connor sank into the depths of the chair. Laura was right. This was something she had to do on her own, a decision she would make for herself. She sensed that the people who loved her would want to protect her from whatever secrets this letter would reveal. Well, perhaps not Laura. Within Connor's lover possessed a sensibility Connor almost envied, a willingness to remain open to even the most outrageous possibilities. Laura, granddaughter of an ancient Native American shaman and medicine woman, wasn't afraid of the unseen. She simply accepted that there were things in this world (and apparently out of it) that she did not fully understand. But that didn't make them any less real. *Why,* thought Connor, *is it so hard for me to do the same?*

Now that you've decided to read on, granddaughter...

Connor frowned. Now how on earth had Gwendolyn known that Connor would stop reading right there, that she would choose that moment to wrestle her fears to the mat? She sighed. The answer didn't bear thinking about, at least not yet.

...I hope you will hear me out before making a final decision. I do not want to give you the impression that you have no choice in this matter. All human beings are created with the God-given right to choose. This is our greatest gift, because in choosing we make the conscious decision to live in Darkness or to live in the Light. Each step we take on the pathway delivers us from the grip of our unconscious desires and redirects our potential to consciously achieve harmony and balance, both in the world and in ourselves.

Connor shook her head over that last part. She wasn't sure she understood it really, and it reminded her of some of that New Age drivel she'd run across from time to time. But surely Gwendolyn Broadhurst, in her profound wisdom, was beyond that sort of silliness. Or was dismissing something as silly the sort of judgment Connor invoked to protect herself from what she didn't understand?

I know this may seem a bit incomprehensible to you now, but I assure you that if you choose to serve the Truth, the Truth will serve you. The difficult part, of course, comes in discerning Truth. One of the most oft-ignored principles taught by Jesus was right judgment. By this, of course, he did not mean judging your fellow human beings, but rather properly discerning what is real and what is not real. I know, these statements still do not satisfy your lawyer's mind. But be patient, child; be patient, as I relate a few morsels of history—very ancient history.

Many millennia ago before time was first reckoned by human calendars, there was on this planet an era of great abundance and enlightenment and peace. The beings of Light who dwelt here were able to converse with the angels and archangels as easily as you might speak with a person standing right in front of you. It was a golden time of spiritual advancement for all who incarnated here. Some might even think of it as the Garden of Eden. And, to carry forward with that metaphor, into this sacred place came a serpent. Not a Bible-story snake, or a devil, or any-

thing of that sort. No, into this place came falsehood, doubt, and fear. This was the time of Darkness, and the great civilizations crumbled or sank beneath the sea. Knowledge was lost. The connection with the Creator was forgotten. The angels and archangels retreated to another part of the cosmos and left Earth to deal with itself.

Thousands of years later, life began again, but this time it was quite a different experience for those who chose to incarnate on the little planet. Even though the Darkness receded, there was much fear and ignorance. Humans developed all sorts of explanations for natural events, and religions in many forms arose, mostly polytheistic ones based on multiple gods and goddesses who controlled humankind. These deities, interestingly enough, were imbued by their worshipers with all sorts of "human" short-comings—jealousy, anger, lust, need, and so forth. This was simply an instance of humanity seeing itself reflected in the heavens. Of course, later on, established religions rallied to the notion of one God and then made the somewhat irrational decision to worship other men's words and holy relics, and follow politically motivated dogma rather than the actual teachings that prophets and messengers had brought to the physical realm. The old religions of goddess and Earth spirits, which still retained vestiges of Truth, gave way to the patriarchal religions, which then usurped the rituals and the observances and led the world in a far less peaceful direction. You've seen the results in these past two millennia.

To Connor's surprise, some of this actually made perfect sense. She had always marveled at Gwendolyn's ability to happily and reverently attend the local Anglican church while remaining deeply committed to her studies of pagan religions and witchcraft. At least Connor had *thought* Gwendolyn's interests had been purely scholarly. But the events of the past couple of years, especially the past couple of weeks, had shaken this comfortable assumption.

At this point, I shall skip forward several millennia, for I do not have the time to do otherwise. If you choose to heed my advice and follow my direction, you will find all the information you need in the books in my library, and most especially in the unbound manuscript pages—documents that are

concerned primarily with our family's history and with the history of
Glastonbury. You will also find one other item, and I will give you the clues
to its location at the end of this letter. I hope you will forgive me for being so
cautious, but as I said, there are others who are seeking this information.

Anxiety clutched at Connor's heart. The pages Gwendolyn spoke of
were gone. Connor was almost tempted to feel guilty. If only she'd
come back here sooner, before someone had gotten wind of
Gwendolyn's absence from her own funeral. If she'd read the letter, she
would have known something important had been kept in this room.
If...Connor sighed. All this "what if" was useless.

Once you accept that there is Darkness and there is Light, that this
physical realm is based on the notion of duality—good and evil, past and
future, up and down, and so forth—you can also recognize that without
one half of each pairing, there can be no other half. I hope that makes
sense, as in my haste I try to compress into a few words what I would pre-
fer to have spent a lifetime teaching you. Now there is no time for a lecture
in metaphysics or the mystical nature of our universe. What I say must
suffice for now, and the most important principle for you to understand is
that a balance must be preserved. Yes, there are times when the pendulum
swings too far and great sorrow is visited upon humankind. But, for the
most part, a tenuous balance reasserts itself, not simply because universal
laws demand it, but because for centuries upon centuries there are those
whose work it is to see the balance restored. They have sometimes been
revered, at other times reviled. They have been called priestesses and
priests, and they have been called witches and warlocks. Humanity has
confused metaphysics and mysticism with some individuals' pathetic
attempts at casting spells and evoking the Darkness. This does not mean,
however, that there IS no one capable of spreading Darkness. There cer-
tainly are any number of powerful figures who do just that. But opposing
them are people like me and those in my circle.
   I don't wish to alarm you, but I am one of those individuals who has
actively maintained a defense against the encroaching Darkness. It has
been, if you will, my sacred duty, and one that I have undertaken willingly.

Now, my days in this incarnation draw to a close, I must pass on this respon-
sibility. And in this exigency of haste, I must be blunt. You, my child, are the
one we believe is destined to assume my place.

The pages slipped from her fingers and her breath came in short
gasps. She'd almost known this was coming, but not quite. Nor had she
really considered what "this" might be. There had been one slim
chance to avoid this knowledge, and she had let it slip away. If she had
tossed this letter into the fire, she would never have known. Connor
closed her eyes and stilled her breathing, without being consciously
aware that she was using a technique her grandmother had taught her
for those times when anxiety welled up inside her. She thought of the
dreams, the times she'd felt Gwendolyn so close to her. The night she'd
learned of Ariana's murder and felt the world crash down around her.
Gwendolyn's voice, her presence, had soothed Connor while she
floundered in a morass of pain and despair.

But those were dreams.

A thought flared inside her mind. Gwendolyn had said "We
believe..." Why the switch to the first-person plural? Connor snatched
up the letter. If Gwendolyn had not been acting alone, assuming what
she said wasn't pure craziness, then there was someone else who could
explain all of it, someone else who could help.

Knowing you as I do, I am aware that this pronouncement will not
be pleasing. You were never one to like being told what to do. Even when
you were a very small child, I recognized your spirited strength.
Naturally, your mother thought of you as simply willful and disobedient.
But, as you can no doubt surmise, she was afraid, not of you, but rather
of your connection with those things she could never bring herself to
understand or accept. I sometimes regretted that my daughter turned
out to be rather a young soul with little experience or wisdom. Yet I loved
her despite her anger and resentment. It pained me when she rejected
you so heartlessly, when she refused to see that you are constitutionally
incapable of living a lie, of being anything other than what you truly
are—a woman who prefers the love and companionship of women. Her

prejudices would simply not let her see past the absurd dictates of what passes nowadays for religion.

When you were born, my dear, I knew full well that you were a special individual. I did not know then, however, who you were. By that I mean I had not yet been granted permission to consult the Akashic Records and was not privy to your true identity. This identity of which I speak is your Soul Self, the true being that you are, shorn of worldly trappings and the physical body. When I did learn the truth, I admit even I was taken aback, for she (that is to say, you) had not incarnated here for over thousands of years. And your return could be seen as both a blessing and a cause for some concern. There could be only one reason why she (you) would return now. And I determined that you had chosen this association with me as your grandmother so that you would one day have access to my knowledge and be drawn to the one place in the world where you would be able to put right an evil deed that was done long, long ago.

To be honest, dear child, I think once this is accomplished, you may no longer feel the need to continue with the sort of work I have spent much of life doing. This does not mean I would discourage you from taking up my post permanently, residing here in what is now your house, and living out your life with Laura. Oh, yes, I know she will be in your life, because she is more closely linked to your spiritual self than you can imagine. But I don't know when you will be able to come to terms with that and with the fact that you must go on living your life even after you lose someone you love to the inevitability of physical death.

Connor's jaw dropped. This letter had been written almost two years earlier, before she'd so much as considered Laura Nez as someone she might love. It occurred to her that Gwendolyn must have been pretty damned clairvoyant. But what if Connor had read this letter immediately? Would her relationship with Laura have developed the same way or at all? Would she have run away from Laura and have needed to be coaxed back, or would she have taken her grandmother's advice? Not that any of that was relevant. But still, how did that endearing if aggravating old lady seem to know everything? And if she was right about that, Connor had the uneasy feeling she was right about everything, even the crazy ideas in this letter. She was only just getting comfortable with the whole idea of reincarnation, for crying out loud. Now she was being set up for some vaguely described, yet seemingly critical task she couldn't even begin to understand. Why? And she still didn't know who "we" might include.

If you have "wised up," as they say in America, and taken up residence with that remarkable young woman, I know you will be thinking of reasons not to risk this potential happiness, and responding to the importuning of a crazy old woman (as I may appear to be) might seem wildly unreasonable. But I beg you to consider. As I have said, you may not choose this duty for the rest of your life. But I have come to understand that there is one task that you and only you can perform. Nor is it by any means a minor undertaking. Your response to this challenge is vital to that balance of which I spoke. You hold the threads of the future in your hands, even though I imagine you are not entirely comfortable with the responsibility. I cannot help that. You chose this life, and I believe we all serve our Creator in whatever way is given us.

Once you have reached England, and Rosewood House, you will be drawn to Glastonbury. There is good reason for this, but I shall not enumerate specifics in this letter. Even with my precautions, there is always the chance that it could fall into the hands of someone who would use our secrets to their own, possibly dark ends.

Thus, I have secreted the information in a place only you can find. To be doubly secure, the container is locked. But the key is available. Simply ask your father about a gift I received from your mother two years ago. With that information, you will be able to locate the key. Once you have that in hand, sit down and think. That's right. Think, Connor; use that powerful intellect of yours. When you were young, about eleven years old, you had a favourite book, part of a series. (I couldn't understand the attraction myself. But perhaps your interest was a harbinger of things to come.) If you consider this book, you will be able to deduce where the final piece of the puzzle lies.

I shall be watching over you every moment, my dear granddaughter. Odd in a way that knowing full well who you are in the spiritual sense, I still think of you most often as my granddaughter. But that is my human side, and who could blame me for being proud that you are of my flesh and blood?

Please be careful in making your decision. I cannot stress to you enough the importance of the work we were doing and the work that will now fall to you. But you're quite intelligent enough to decipher this puzzle. And I know full well you will have others at your side. That handsome and loyal young man, the policeman from Washington, he is a part of this. And Benjamin will lend his valuable assistance if you ask him. Speak to them, speak to Laura. If she is willing to look deep inside herself, to practice some of what her grandmother taught her, she will see the Truth of this and know her role as well. When you are ready, there will be allies of my own who stand prepared to assist.

Good-bye for now. I miss you, and I know that you miss me. But we shall meet again; this much I can promise. And I shall always be near if you need me.

Affectionately,
Gwendolyn

She read her grandmother's last words and closed her eyes. A minute or two later, she saw that the sunlight in the room had shifted. How long had she been sitting there? Her watch insisted that more than an hour had passed, but that was impossible. She got up from the chair and noted with some chagrin the stiffness in her limbs. Her joints believed she'd been sitting for quite a while. At least she hadn't been wandering about the house doing things she couldn't remember. "Must be getting old," she muttered, folding the letter and stuffing it back into the envelope. She started toward her grandmother's desk, intending to tuck the letter inside, perhaps even in the secret compartment her father had discovered. But just as she reached to pull open the sliding cover, she heard a noise and whirled around.

There was no one there.

Could the noise have come from outside? Connor went quickly to the front windows where she and Laura had caught sight of the hapless vicar, and peered into the shrubbery. Nothing stirred in the deepening shadows. And yet she had the undeniable sensation of being watched, almost as if there were someone just beyond the very limits of her peripheral vision, there, in the corner near the side window, perhaps just outside. Something. If she could only turn her head very, very slowly, would she see...it? Him? *Oh, for crying out loud,* she thought. *Get a grip, Connor. There's no one else in this room and no one peeking through the window. You're making yourself crazy. And you've got enough to worry about as it is.*

Still, Connor felt unusually vulnerable. The house no longer seemed safe. She stuffed the letter into the pocket of her jeans and went in search of her companions. The kitchen was empty, and she might have been alarmed if not for the fact that so much time had passed since she'd been left in the library to read Gwendolyn's letter.

"Anyone home?" she called out, embarrassed that her voice sounded so weak and tentative. What was happening to the bold district attorney in her? Where was that voice that could shout down a weasely defense counsel?

"Hey! Where is everyone?" That came out better, and a voice immediately answered.

"We're out here in the garden, honey," Benjamin answered.

She went out the back door beside the kitchen and around to the side garden. Her father, Malcolm, and Laura were seated in comfortable lawn chairs, sipping glasses of iced tea. She smiled at them and was pleased to see a wave of relief pass over her three friends. Clearly they'd been worried.

Connor pulled a chair closer and sat, still clutching the letter. "I guess you're wondering what took so long."

Laura smiled. "It had occurred to us that you didn't get through law school or become a best-selling author by being the slowest reader in the class, so, yes, we did get to wondering."

"I'm surprised you didn't all come to check on me."

"I did," said Laura. "Just a quick peek to make sure you were still there."

Connor's face tightened. "You mean to make sure I hadn't gone wandering off to the Tor in a daze?"

Laura didn't react to the resentment in Connor's tone. "Partly, yes. Since we haven't found out what we're dealing with, it seemed reasonable to assume that other...odd...things could happen. And there is the small matter of the break-in. Someone might think there's still something here worth having. Don't you agree?"

This jibed so perfectly with Connor's eerie sensation of being watched, she didn't even bother to argue. Maybe Laura was right. But what the hell was going on? Nothing in her grandmother's letter specifically explained what this situation meant. She'd said to keep the information safe. Safe from whom? Why did anyone else care if Connor Hawthorne was some sort of reincarnated "something"? And what did "preserving the balance" really mean? It was like some sort of foreign language she wished someone could decode for her. She looked at her friends. Maybe they could do just that.

"I'm sorry if I sounded a wee bit testy. But I'm so damn confused by all this, and Gwendolyn's letter didn't exactly shed a lot of light on the situation. Hell, I don't know if there is a situation. But I do know she wouldn't have minded me sharing this with you. I was going to try to summarize it, but I think it's better if you all read it. I wish there were some way to make copies of it." She glanced around her as if a Kinko's might materialize at the foot of the garden.

"Is there a fax machine here?" asked Malcolm. "We could use that to make copies."

Connor shook her head. "Gwendolyn was somewhat of a Luddite really. She hated technology. Wouldn't even have push-button phones in the house—and no answering machine. She said if people wanted to speak with her, they could keep calling until they found her at home."

"I've got a portable fax in my luggage," Benjamin offered.

"Dad, you have got to be the techno junkie of all time. I'll just bet you've also got a laptop and a satellite phone and a printer."

"A tiny printer," he said, grinning. "Let's go inside to the kitchen and I'll get the fax."

Several minutes later the machine was slowly churning out copies of Gwendolyn's letter on thermal paper that exhibited an unfortunate tendency to curl up immediately. But Malcolm showed them how to slide each page over the edge of the table, creating a bend in the opposite direction. "At my office we're still using the equipment we've had since the eighties," he explained. "We order thermal paper by the truckload. Frankly, I hate the stuff."

One by one, the sets of copies were complete. Benjamin returned the original to Connor's keeping, and they all sat down. Connor wasn't sure she could read the entire letter again, at least not yet, but she skimmed over it, seeing phrases she couldn't even remember having read the first time through. It occurred to her once more that she really could be losing her mind. What might that feel like? her brain inquired. The irony was that she probably wouldn't know until it was too late.

Benjamin finished first, followed a few moments later by Malcolm, who excused himself for a call of nature. Laura flipped back a couple of pages and was still reading when he returned, but a minute or two later, she turned over the last page and placed it facedown on the stack of copies, which Connor began shredding manually.

Connor looked at their faces and saw they shared her confusion. If anything, Benjamin looked the most nonplussed of all; he was the first to speak. "I'm not saying I don't believe what's in here. Actually, I probably could, if given some time to think about it. But there are clearly grave risks involved. She as much as says there are other people who are after information she had, that she's left for you to find. I don't like the idea of you being saddled with some...holy mission or whatever."

Connor was tempted to smile at her father's protectiveness, but she didn't. He was perfectly serious. "Dad, I know it sounds pretty weird. But do you really think my grandmother would, as you say, 'saddle' me with this responsibility if it weren't damned important?"

Benjamin shrugged. His agreement would not come easily. "Her idea of what's important, and our idea of what's important might be entirely different. And what if, and I'm only saying what *if*, this is all just her imagination?"

Laura spoke up instantly, her tone crisp. "Not possible. You knew her a lot better than I did, but even I don't think for one second that this lady is...or was...anything but sharp as a tack."

Connor agreed. "You're kind of clutching at straws, Dad. But thanks for wanting to. Whatever we decide from here on in, we can't base it on risks to me. Okay? I want everyone's promise on that."

One by one they nodded about as enthusiastically as school children who have just been told recess is canceled and they're going to have a quiz that will be lots more fun.

"That doesn't mean we aren't going to look out for you," Malcolm countered.

"I wouldn't want it any other way. We're a team after all, aren't we?"

He smiled. "Yes, but on our last team outing we had serious casualties, something I'd like to avoid this time. And," he added, "what exactly does she mean when she says *I'm* involved in this. At least I assume she's talking about me, except for the 'young' part."

Benjamin patted his shoulder. "She meant you. To Gwendolyn, anyone under fifty is young."

"But where do I come in? Is she saying I'm some old friend of yours reincarnated as the scourge of crime in metropolitan Washington?"

Connor chuckled. "Scourge? Where do you get this stuff?"

"He's been reading too much," said Laura.

"Did year hear a noise?" said Connor suddenly. They all stared at her and then dashed to the doors and windows.

"Nothing here," Malcolm reported from the hallway.

Laura added an all-clear from the door to the garden while Benjamin, who had walked along the side of the house, came back into the kitchen. "Nothing outside, no footprints in the mulch, or signs of anyone having been there." He turned to his daughter. "What did you hear?"

Connor shook her head, feeling altogether sheepish. "It must have been a tree branch or something, scraping the side of the house. I've just had this weird feeling of being watched. I guess paranoia is finally having its way with me."

"I seriously doubt that, sweetheart," Laura insisted, sitting down beside Connor and wrapping an arm around her. "We're all getting a little spooked by this stuff. But I think it's a good idea to keep an eye out."

"So what about this reincarnation thing?" asked Malcolm, indicating to the others that this was one of the harder parts for him to deal with.

Laura patted his hand. "Gwendolyn is saying that all of us are connected from other lifetimes. And I also have a feeling it explains what happened on the Tor."

"You mean last night?" asked Connor.

"Yes, and also before, when you and I went up there. The images we saw, the other people, they were all part of a past life. I'm almost sure of it. I tend to think we sort of 'tuned in' on more than one lifetime's events until we focused on the most relevant one, the one that's brought us here now."

Connor closed her eyes and tried to remember the sequence of events. It came to her in bits and pieces. "The Tor, but without the tower. The circles and lines of torches coming up the hill."

"Exactly, and I wasn't able to break through to that lifetime until the last second. I spent most of my efforts trapped outside the tower, which wasn't even there in your vision."

"But why?"

Laura shrugged. "I think because someone doesn't want us reunited at that level, doesn't want us on the same wavelength, so to speak."

Benjamin interrupted. "But how could someone else actively intervene to prevent that?"

"I think there are ways, but we don't yet understand enough about what's going on to come up with a theory. So even if we accept everything Gwendolyn's said in this letter, we're still missing big pieces of the picture. This," said Laura, tilting her chin toward the paper, "is sort of like the appetizer, I think. The main course still hasn't been served up. Do you have any idea what this hint means? Or how it will lead us to the cache of information?"

"We already found the key by accident," Benjamin remarked. "But it certainly must be the one she had in mind."

"So we have to find what the key fits," said Malcolm. "Only I think we're right back where we started hours ago."

"Not necessarily," said Connor. "Because I think I know which book she's talking about, and if that's the case, I also know exactly where we're going to start looking."

Chapter Twenty-One

A man cannot be too careful in the choice of his enemies.
—Oscar Wilde
The Picture of Dorian Gray

Conrad slammed the gearshift on the Jag into fourth and increased his speed along the M4. Today he didn't find any pleasure at all in the surge of the powerful engine, the gleaming wood trim, the leather-wrapped wheel beneath his fingers. As he swung to the right to pass yet another slow-moving car, he experienced a sensation he almost hadn't recognized at first. But then he hadn't been insecure or nervous since the first time he'd killed someone. And that had been decades ago.

His best friend, Layne, had tried to cheat him out of his share of the robbery takings. Poor stupid Layne hadn't thought a skinny twelve-year-old would have the guts to slip a blade into a boy four years his senior and a head taller. Conrad had done precisely that and had sliced hard enough to kill the older boy within seconds. Layne had underestimated Conrad, and the other two boys hadn't even argued when he demanded Layne's share as well. Perhaps it was the dead look in Conrad's eyes, in such stark contrast to the tight smile he wore when he said it.

He'd never been nervous since; there hadn't been a day in his life he didn't believe he could handle anyone or anything, particularly since he'd never been the least bit picky about the methods he used. But now he was definitely off his feed. Something was wrong with his stomach; the pain was enough to have him swallowing handfuls of digestive aids. And that goddamned little man was still out there, still stalking him. The man who'd taunted him, stolen his papers, and then had the fucking nerve to buy him a drink and disappear again. How he hated the little creep. And what the hell did he want from Conrad? Whose side was he on? Even more to the point, what did he know about Conrad's plans for the future, a future beginning right here in England and then spreading out to encompass who knew how much of the world's economy? He believed that once he had the right elements in place, nothing could really stop him.

Conrad knew what most of the idiots in the world did not know. Power was never about guns and rockets and tanks and missiles. He sold those to the people who were under that impression because it made him all the wealthier and thus able to pursue the real source of power: money. His fellow businessmen might scoff, and there were countless do-gooders who took delight in preaching about the evils of money. But he didn't care. Let the businessmen laugh and the ministers preach. The only real power to be had in the world was economic. The man who controlled the purse strings controlled the governments. To Conrad, politicians were laughable. They had no real control over anything, so they bent and swayed from one position to another and licked boots in the meantime, depending on the political climate.

But no one had elected Conrad Thackeray to anything. His world was just that—*his*. He decided what happened within it, and he didn't have to answer to a damn soul. For some years now, everything had been going his way, and not because of luck. His success was founded in meticulous planning and supreme confidence. And just now, when the fruits of his labors were almost within reach, that confidence was eroding.

Conrad angrily swerved around a battered Citroën sedan and cut back sharply in front, noting with some satisfaction the startled look on the driver's face as the Jag cleared the Citroën's front bumper by mere inches. He pressed the accelerator and shot away, passing cars in the first and second lanes as if they were parked.

Ordinarily, he would have stayed on the motorway to the junction of the A46, then turned south to pass through Bath and eventually veered off on the A361 to Glastonbury. But one look at his speedometer, where the needle rested just over the 110 miles-per-hour mark, shocked him back to reality. At this rate he'd likely kill himself, and all because he couldn't control his seething anger.

The junction for Swindon and Salisbury loomed up suddenly, and he shot across three lanes, from the far right, high-speed lane to the exit lane, downshifting through the gears with practiced ease. He ignored the bleat of the horn behind him, swung his car through the roundabout, and shot down the A346 in the direction of Salisbury, where tourists were no longer permitted to wander at will through Stonehenge, but must instead view the ancient stones from a distance. Not that Conrad gave much thought to the mystical origins of the place. His only consideration of the attraction was that it could prove a gold mine if the National Trust only had the sense to charge substantial fees, and rent the site out to all those absurd New Age groups that insisted the site was the focus of magical forces. Conrad smiled to himself at the thought. One more group of loonies who didn't understand power.

In any event, Conrad had no intention of visiting Stonehenge. Keeping the Jag to a sedate sixty miles per hour, he turned west once more at Marlborough and followed the sometimes obscure A361 signs through the countryside. He passed the turnoff for Avebury, where stood a more sprawling henge, encompassing a village within its circle, and he continued on through Devizes to Semington, where, to his satisfaction, the road improved somewhat before meandering south and west again.

The signs for the turning to Shepton Mallet aroused him from his musings. He was almost there. On the outskirts of Glastonbury, he turned into the farm lane that led to Gillian's new lodgings. Two miles farther on, he spied the driveway, almost hidden by the high hedgerows. In the growing dusk, he'd switched on the headlamps to avoid a collision with an oncoming car in the narrow lane, and as the lights swept across the front of the cottage, a sharp pang of annoyance lanced through him. Another car was drawn up next to Gillian's. It wasn't one of Gerald's as far as he knew. As a matter of fact, the black Rover sedan had the distinct look of officialdom about it. For an instant he considered leaving, but he was quite sure whoever was inside would have heard him arrive and might even have looked out and taken note of his car, possibly the registration number as well. He'd just have to brazen it out.

W

Nicholas Foulsham turned from the window once he was satisfied the silver Jaguar was not leaving. The driver had parked next to Lady Fenwycke's car and doused the headlamps. "You've a visitor, it seems," he said innocently, though from the look on her face, he was fairly sure this particular caller had been expected. And he could also make a reasonable guess as to whose car it was. The timing, as far as the inspector was concerned, was perfect. He'd had a difficult time getting so much as five minutes of Conrad Thackeray's time, given the man's "very busy schedule" as Thackeray's secretary had reminded him frequently. But here, in a quiet cottage in the country, away from his office and his host of minions and security guards, Conrad would find it rather more difficult to dodge questions. Foulsham almost allowed himself to smile.

The silence was broken by a firm knock. Lady Fenwycke went to answer, and Foulsham didn't know what amused him more, that Thackeray had knocked as if he were a casual guest, or that the hostess went through the motions of being surprised at his appearance on her doorstep. Neither pretense was particularly convincing.

"Hello, Conrad. What brings you all the way out here from London?" she asked, her back to Foulsham, who imagined she was trying to signal Thackeray with all manner of winking and eyebrow raising. He almost wished he could see it. But Conrad's expression was sufficiently entertaining—a tight smile pasted over an angry scowl, the former utterly failing to disguise the latter. It gave the man's face a rather crazed look, Foulsham thought.

"I was planning to look at some property in Taunton," he replied, taking off his mac. "Thought I'd swing by here, see how you were holding up."

"How thoughtful of you, Conrad. Please do sit down, and I'll make some tea. You'll remember Chief Inspector Foulsham, of course."

Foulsham nodded, almost gleefully willing to assume his assigned role in this farcical scene right out of an Oscar Wilde comedy. Conrad knew Foulsham wasn't buying the pretense, and Foulsham knew that Conrad knew. Gillian obviously wasn't sure what to believe, so she kept on making tea. And, meanwhile, no one was willing to drop the entire charade. Thus Foulsham inquired about the weather in London, the state of the business community, the traffic on the M4, and which route Thackeray had taken. Unfortunately, once those subjects were sufficiently well mined, Conrad had nothing left to fall back on. The chief inspector correctly guessed that the man would as soon bite his tongue as allow himself to ask how Foulsham's business was going. That would be tantamount to inviting an interrogation on the spot. But Foulsham had no intention of rescuing him, or letting him off the hook by leaving. Instead, he stood by the mantelpiece and waited.

Gillian's voice, brittle as glass, startled them both. "Do you both take cream and sugar, or would you prefer lemon?"

Foulsham looked at her curiously. If anything, she appeared even more nervous than she had when she'd opened the door to him an hour earlier, when she had given a remarkably unconvincing performance of nonchalance. But now there was something else there, something furious in the way she slapped the saucers down on a small tray with enough force to crack them in half. The milk sloshed over as she poured it into a small pitcher and Gillian swore under her breath. So much for the gracious lady of the manor, thought Foulsham.

Gillian handed round the tea, then perched herself on the edge of an upholstered armchair, her spine rigid. The chief inspector observed that her paisley silk skirt rather clashed with the homey chintz flowers of the chair fabric, then turned to Conrad. "Last time we met, Mr.

Thackeray, you were engaged in some rather pressing business. Now that you're here, perhaps you wouldn't mind if I asked you a few more questions we weren't able to get to earlier."

Conrad glanced at his watch, which even he knew was foolish. It was after seven o'clock on a Friday evening in the bucolic countryside of Somerset County, miles from any metropolitan area. It was hardly likely that critical business decisions hung in the balance at that very moment. Despite his discomfiture, Thackeray could hardly plead a pressing engagement.

"Why, of course," he said, with little enthusiasm. "Though I hardly see what help I can give you. I was only at that party by coincidence. Haven't the least notion who did for that poor girl."

Foulsham smiled. "Nothing so dramatic, Mr. Thackeray, as asking you to name a suspect. But you seem an observant sort of man, and you might have noticed something out of the ordinary, something no one else might have paid attention to."

Conrad frowned and steepled his fingers as if in deep thought. Foulsham was fairly sure the only thing the man was considering was how to extricate himself from this room, and from under the policeman's scrutiny.

"No," he finally said. "I didn't see anything unusual, unless, of course, you count a headless body hanging from a ladder."

Gillian Fenwycke gasped and dropped her teacup.

For an instant, no one moved. Then Foulsham knelt to pick up the china. The saucer was unharmed, but the cup had bounced once on the fitted carpet, then landed on the edge of the brick hearth where its handle had broken off. But even as he gathered up the pieces, he quickly peered at Gillian, and what he saw made the tiny hairs on his neck stand up. For the instant she thought his attention was fixed on the carpet, she'd let down her guard. What he saw in Gillian Fenwycke's blazing eyes was most assuredly not hysteria, nor even distress. It was rage that Foulsham glimpsed, a rage that made him feel as if he had fallen into an icy river. Within a fraction of a second, though, the moment had passed, and he was not entirely sure he had seen anything at all. Gillian leaped from her chair and returned quickly with a small broom and dustpan. "Please, Chief Inspector, you'll cut yourself. Let me do that. I'm so awfully clumsy sometimes."

Conrad hadn't so much as stirred from his chair, and he stared disgustedly at the stain on the carpet as if he'd just seen someone ruin an Aubusson tapestry through sheer stupidity. Foulsham sensed that the man probably considered it beneath him to help anyone, particularly a woman, clean up a mess. Nor did he apologize to Lady Fenwycke for his brutally callous reference to the murdered woman. For that reason alone, Foulsham glanced up and said, "Would you be good enough to get us a dish towel from the kitchen, Mr. Thackeray?" He was secretly pleased to note the flush of color on Conrad's pale cheeks. The man didn't like being ordered about, now did he?

Thackeray couldn't refuse a perfectly reasonable request without appearing inordinately rude, and Foulsham was convinced that, for some reason he had not yet fathomed, Conrad definitely did *not* want to antagonize him. That in itself was odd. Thackeray had a number of friends in high places, or so it was said in various circles. He seemed much more the sort to bluster and shout and tell inconsequential policemen to sod off. But since the moment he'd walked into the cottage, he hadn't acted particularly aggressive at all. Why? He was fairly sure of what was going on between Thackeray and Lady Fenwycke, but there again, the situation was puzzling. Considering all the women a rich bachelor could have for the asking, why choose a married one? Why choose the wife of a peer of the realm and risk a pitiless raking-over from the tabloids? No, there was much more to this than a sordid affair. And he'd have to get Thackeray alone before asking whether he knew of Lady Fenwycke's dalliance with Patricia Frome.

He took the towel from Thackeray, mopped the carpet, then waited while Gillian took the shards of china and the tea tray back into the kitchen. Foulsham remained standing when she returned and resumed her seat. Both of them sat there, looking neither at each other nor at him. If he were a sadistic sort of man, he thought, he could keep wait there, silently, until one of them exploded. But he wasn't, and besides, he had felt the onset of a new train of reasoning in this case. He wanted some time alone to mull it over. And he also intended to take another trip to Haslemere. There was more to his "love" triangle than met the eye. Or would that be "quadrangle," counting the deceased Ms. Frome?

"I really must be toddling along," he said in his friendliest "Uncle Nick" tone. "Of course, I may well need to see you both again at some point, though," he paused, "not necessarily at the same time." He smiled and left that ominous intention hanging in the air as he shut the wooden door behind him. What he wouldn't give to be a fly on that wall tonight. Foulsham also wondered whether he should park down the lane and find out how long Mr. Thackeray intended to stay or, in the alternative, where they might go together. But given the geography, he soon saw there was no place from which he could see the end of the driveway and still be out of sight. If he waited at the end of the lane where it came out on the main road, he might miss them entirely if they went the other direction. Besides, it was only a matter of curiosity as yet, not firm grounds for suspicion. He had no proof at all that either of them was actually involved in the murder. Yet Foulsham, for all his emphatic belief in facts and reason, was not averse to following up the occasional hunch. And he had one.

Chapter Twenty-Two

Thou has left behind
Powers that will work for thee; air, earth, and skies;
There's not a breathing of the common wind
That will forget thee; thou has great allies;
Thy friends are exultations, agonies,
And love, and man's unconquerable mind.
—William Wordsworth
"Toussaint L'Ouverture"

Connor led her companions up the stairs to the first floor where their bedrooms were located, then down the long hallway to the back of the house to a narrow door, almost hidden in the woodwork. With no sun filtering through the windows, the hall was shrouded and gloomy. The door, which had no regular knob or handle, was invisible unless you knew where to look for it. Connor pushed hard on the left edge once, then again. The door swung toward them. "A spring-loaded catch," she explained. "When I was little, I thought this was my secret hideaway."

She pressed the light switch, and they trooped up the narrow

staircase to find themselves in an enormous attic filled with old furniture, boxes, and shelves of cast-off odds and ends.

"There's enough here to fill up two or three antique shops,"
Benjamin commented as Connor found her way to another light
switch. "The dealers in London would be drooling if they knew."

"I guess I'll have to spend some time going through it all," Connor
sighed, looking around her. "But right now there's only one antique I'm
interested in." She made her way to the far end of the attic at the rear of
the house, where the pitch of the roof made it necessary to stoop slightly. In one corner stood an ancient steamer trunk from which the leather
had peeled away in several places. "If I understand what Gwendolyn
was hinting at, this should be what we're looking for."

Laura frowned at the thick layer of dust on the trunk. "But this
looks as if it hasn't been opened in twenty years."

"I know, but I still think this is where she wanted me to look."

Malcolm, who, like the others, hadn't understood Gwendolyn's
oblique references to Connor's childhood, asked, "What makes you so
sure?"

Connor smiled. "When I was a kid, Gwendolyn was always trying to
get me to read what she considered to be real 'literature.'" She crooked
her fingers to emphasize the last word. "But when I was about nine, I
couldn't stand reading about all those depressing Dickens characters
and the trials and tribulations the Brontë sisters thought were so fascinating. So I'd bring my own books from the States when I came to visit.
And I'd hide them in various places where Gwendolyn invariably found
them." Connor scratched her head. "Now that I think about it, she must
have been psychic, because she always *knew* things."

She knelt in front of the trunk and tugged at the brass hasp. "So one
day she told me if I wanted a mystery to solve, I should try to figure out
where she'd hidden my favorite book of the moment. At first I was
angry because I thought she was being mean, but then I realized she
was actually humoring me. And it only took me about two hours to
find it."

Connor flung back the lid, sending up a cloud of dust that made
Laura sneeze. Inside were dolls and various other toys. She scooped

them out, pausing only a moment to spin an old-fashioned wooden whirligig, which she handed to Laura. Beneath the toys were books, and it took her only a few seconds to spot the one she wanted. "This is it," she announced gleefully, and held it up for them to see.

"Well, I'll be damned," Benjamin laughed. "I'd completely forgotten your childhood obsession."

In Connor's hand lay a very old and worn blue-gray hardback book. On the cover, the silhouette of a woman holding a magnifying glass bent slightly forward to examine the title: *The Secret in the Old Attic.*

Laura chuckled. "A Nancy Drew mystery? That was your childhood obsession?"

Connor looked a little sheepish. "If you must know, every now and then I still get the urge to read one."

"But what's the clue?" Malcolm inquired with his usual practicality.

Connor's smile faded. "I'm not sure. But this must be what she wanted me to find. Funny that it seems to be the only one here, though. I had a lot of others."

"Should have been *The Secret of the Brass-Bound Trunk,* don't you think?" Laura asked impishly.

Connor stared at her. "How would you know that?"

"You think you were the only kid who ever read those books?"

"And you were giving *me* a hard time."

"Just teasing, love. I still have the entire set in storage."

"You're kidding. I never did manage to get every book in the series all together at one time. I'd love to—"

"Um...ladies," Benjamin interrupted with a smile. "I hate to interfere in this Nancy Drew fan club meeting, but shouldn't we get back to deciphering the mystery of Rosewood House?"

"Spoilsport," Laura answered. "But you're right. What's next?"

Connor looked at the book in her hand and gently opened it. On the flyleaf, in a careful child's hand was written, L. CONNOR HAWTHORNE.

Laura smiled. "You hated the name Lydia even when you were nine?"

"I hated it from first grade onward," Connor answered. "But my mother wouldn't let anyone use my middle name. Gwendolyn didn't care, though. She liked the name Lydia, but she understood that it just didn't fit me." Connor gently flipped through the pages, with their large, old-fashioned type, the paper yellowed at the edges. "Doesn't seem to be anything in here," she said, baffled.

"Let me have a look at it," suggested Benjamin. "Why don't you search through the rest of what's in there. Maybe the book itself isn't the clue."

Connor handed him the book, and he went to stand under one of the attic lights with Malcolm close behind him, apparently intent on seeing what methods the ex-spy might put to use in examining the book. Meanwhile, Laura and Connor knelt by the chest and began removing more items.

Laura picked up a much-the-worse-for-wear Raggedy Ann doll. "Yours?" she asked, smoothing out its faded dress.

Connor nodded but didn't answer, and Laura reached for her hand. "Don't tell me you're embarrassed that you liked dolls?"

"Well, sort of."

"Why? Does it clash with that handsome, slightly butch, "lesbian about town" image you project to the world?"

Connor sat back on her haunches and scrutinized Laura's expression. She couldn't quite tell whether her lover was teasing or serious, so she decided to answer honestly. "I guess maybe it does."

"Even the biggest, toughest dyke on earth started out life as a little girl."

Connor chuckled. "I know. And you know I'm not into stereotypes. It's just that I was always at war with myself, even when I was little. Part of me wanted to be G.I. Joe, and part of me wanted to be—"

Laura held up both hands as if to ward off a blow. "Please don't say Barbie."

"Don't be absurd. It was my mother who wanted Barbie for a daughter. Why do you think I had to suffer through a debutante season and an excruciating marriage? But, believe me, even if I couldn't figure out whether I wanted to be Cinderella or sleep with her, it never occurred to me to want to emulate a doll with pointy boobs, no waist, and the human equivalent of seven-foot legs."

"Thank heaven for that. But what did you mean about being Cinderella or her Prince Charming?"

"Well, it's kind of hard to explain. But I had this yearning to be the knight in shining armor, to *be* James West, or James Bond, or even Jonathan Hart, with Jennifer at my side."

"Ah, yes," Laura smiled. "The lovely Stefanie Powers."

"Exactly my point," Connor nodded with a grin. "I wanted to be the other half of a perfect couple. But, on the other hand, I never wanted to be a *man*."

"Surely you don't subscribe to that absurd theory, that all butch lesbians want to be men?"

"Of course not," Connor retorted. "That *is* absurd. Some women may be transgendered, but I've always felt right at home in a woman's body."

Laura brushed Connor's bangs out of her eyes. "And I'm damn glad you're in it. Because, quite frankly, I chose girls over boys a long time ago, and I might have missed you completely if you were otherwise equipped."

Connor grinned and leaned over for a quick kiss before they went back to the task of emptying out Connor's childhood mementos.

"How was your grandmother about it?" Laura asked, pulling more items out of the trunk.

"You mean me being gay?"

"Even before you decided that you were. Like when you were little."

"The nice thing was that even though she was very stern about some things, like what I read or whether I used correct grammar, she didn't make a practice of criticizing my personal choices. I knew I had to appear in a dress to go to church with her on Sunday, but the rest of the time she let me wear what I wanted. And if I played war games with my dolls, she'd simply inquire who was fighting whom and for what reason. Half the time she'd turn whatever game I had going into some sort of history lesson." Connor tugged an old teddy bear out from under a pile of old manila folders. "Do you know that this particular bear was once introduced to me as Winston Churchill?"

Laura reached out to stroke the nubby fur. "Does look sort of like him."

"Before I knew it, I was going around spouting 'Never have so few given so much that so many...,' et cetera, et cetera."

"What a gift she was to you," said Laura wistfully.

Connor felt warm tears trickle down her cheeks. She reached to wipe them away, but Laura's gentle fingers were already there.

"You still miss her, sweetheart, and you will for a long time. But I don't think she was kidding when she said she'd be close by. I can feel her presence."

Connor thought about that for a moment. "I think you're right."

"Right about what?" said Malcolm, who had wandered back over to where they were sorting through everything.

"Oh, nothing really. You and my dad having any luck with the book?"

"I don't know. He took it downstairs and said to come down when we were ready."

Connor surveyed the pile of detritus from her childhood. "I guess we're done then. There isn't anything else here that could be of help."

"You want to put all this back in the trunk?"

"No, I'll come back up in a day or two and sort it out."

Turning the lights off behind them, they all descended to the first floor, and seeing no sign of Benjamin, they continued to the ground floor. Connor's father was in the kitchen, standing in front of the stove. In one hand he held the Nancy Drew book, in the other the old-fashioned teakettle that had stood on the stove for as long as Connor could remember. Benjamin was directing the steam from the kettle's spout to the inside surface of the book's back cover.

"What are you doing?" asked Connor.

"Conducting a little experiment. And I'm just about done."

Connor glanced at the endpaper, which was curling up and back. "I think the book is about done, at any rate."

Benjamin shrugged. "Sorry about that, but I think it can be glued back together. There wasn't any other way to get at it."

"Get at what?" they all said in unison.

"This," said Benjamin with a flourish, reaching beneath the curled paper to extract an extremely thin piece of parchment paper that clearly had not been part of the book's original design. Carefully, he unfolded it and discovered it was much the same consistency as onion skin.

The other three stared at him as if he were a magician who had just plucked out the proverbial rabbit. Laura was the first to move closer, peering at the paper.

"But it's blank," she announced, her voice conveying puzzlement. "Someone went to all that trouble to hide a little blank piece of paper?"

"Ah, but I have a feeling it isn't. You see, if it did have writing on it, the ink would probably have shown through the endpaper. But it didn't. So I suspect our Gwendolyn decided on employing a touch of the melodramatic in her efforts at misdirection." He peered at his daughter for a moment, and her bafflement instantly gave way to understanding.

"Invisible ink," she exclaimed, and began to laugh. "My dear old grandmother actually used invisible ink to leave me a message. She must have been reading spy novels or maybe hanging out with her son-in-law too much," Connor said with a grin.

Benjamin huffed in mock offense. "I've never used it in my life," he retorted. "But it wasn't a bad idea."

"Do you think heat will bring it up?" asked Laura. "Although it may also be in some sort of code." She had worked for Benjamin several years, and it occurred to Connor there probably was very little that Laura did not know about codes, cryptic messages, and espionage. She also realized she couldn't have handpicked a better team to help her solve the puzzle Gwendolyn Broadhurst had left her.

"We'll try heat first. I think we can assume Gwendolyn used something simple, maybe even a household concoction with lemon juice or something."

Benjamin was right. Mrs. Broadhurst hadn't wanted to make the task too difficult or time consuming. Besides, the ink ploy was only designed to protect the brief document from detection by a casual observer. And it would have worked. The book could have changed hands a dozen times in the years to come, and no one would have been the wiser.

The words she committed to paper began to emerge as soon as Benjamin held the parchment over the gas burner with a pair of salad tongs, careful not to let it get hot enough to burn. The balance was tricky since the paper was extremely dry. "I'd swear this parchment is antique," he muttered, carefully moving it back and forth. "It's positively brittle."

"Maybe there's a reason for that," suggested Laura. "Other than the fact that it's extremely thin and wouldn't make much of a bulge. By the way, how did you discover it was there?"

"Just a hunch. I checked the spine, and then turned each and every page to see if there were any pages stuck together, or any sentences that didn't seem to run from one page to the next. Then I carefully felt the end papers, and the back one seemed slightly thicker."

Malcolm nodded approvingly. "We could use more people with your brains on the D.C. police."

Benjamin smiled slightly. "Actually, I'd drive you insane. I'm always looking for conspiracies, always picking at the tiniest details. And let's face it, in your job a crime is often just what it looks like, with no embellishment or hidden motivations."

"Not always," murmured Connor, her voice tight.

No one spoke for a moment. The murder of Connor's ex-lover, Ariana, had certainly not been what it seemed, a senseless murder on the banks of the C&O Canal in D.C.

"No, honey. You're right. Not always. Now let's see what Gwendolyn had to tell us, or should I say, tell *you*. This is addressed to 'my dear granddaughter.'"

Connor took the paper from her father and peered at the neat, formal script. Then she read aloud.

My dear granddaughter,

It doesn't surprise me that you've found this message. You have an excellent memory and a great deal of native intelligence. I hope you won't be disappointed that you have not quite reached the end of your search.

Connor allowed herself a sigh of frustration. "I don't understand why she's so intent on all this cloak-and-dagger stuff."

"Maybe what we're looking for is a lot more important than we realize," Benjamin said. "I don't think Gwendolyn ever did anything just on a whim."

"No, she didn't," Connor agreed, turning back to the note.

But I won't keep you in suspense much longer, and I assume you are all there. If my meditations have been fruitful, and the course of future events has not already been substantially altered, I assume that the image I saw clearly—of you and your father, as well as Miss Nez and Mr. Jefferson standing in my kitchen reading this—is accurate.

Connor's scalp prickled as she looked up and observed the expressions of the other three. Malcolm's astonishment was plain to see. Benjamin's shrug of incomprehension was eloquent. And Laura, the first to speak, sounded more amused than surprised. "She's even better than I thought, although Grandmother Klah would think of it as business as usual. She was always doing things like that, describing scenes and events before they'd happened."

"How could she know we'd be here?" asked Malcolm. "Hell, *I* didn't even know I'd be here until a couple of days ago. Jeez, I really hate this stuff." He scrubbed at his eyes with one hand, as if he could clear up the mystery.

"You didn't hate it when it saved our lives," Connor reminded him.

"Well, yeah. But how did your grandmother *know?*"

"If I knew that, Malcolm, I'd sit down and meditate and get to the bottom of all this right now."

"But why didn't *she?*"

"Why didn't she what?" asked Laura.

"Get to the bottom of all this before she died. I mean if she knew that we were all going to be here, then she must have also known why, and what was going to happen to you and Connor up on that hill, and she should have known about that murder at Lord what's-his-name's house..."

Connor, who had begun reading again, held up her hand. "Whoa, there. I think she explains that. Listen."

Without a doubt, you are asking yourselves why I would have to resort to all this subterfuge rather than simply writing you a nice long letter and sending it by registered post. That way I could tell you the entire story and also warn you in advance of the obstacles you might face. Unfortunately, my gift does not work quite that way, although there have been times of late when I wished precisely that, if for no other reason than I might avoid any risk to you and those you love. For there is, without doubt, grave risk here. The problem is, my "sight" is not perfect, nor does it reach much beyond my own family and my own "group." (I trust you will understand the need for the euphemism.) Those who oppose the power of Light, or the power of good, if you will, are shrouded in veils of secrecy which my sight cannot penetrate. My faith tells me this is as it should be. But time is short, and you must get on with your work.

"I would if you'd get to the point, grandmother dear," Connor sighed.

"Kind of odd, though, isn't it, how she keeps anticipating our questions," Laura commented.

"*Odd* doesn't even begin to describe my grandmother."

"I notice you're still in the present tense."

Connor stared at her. "Yeah, I keep doing that." She turned back to the letter.

Is there anything you've ever wanted to do, but didn't have the courage to try? For most of us, there is some pursuit that falls into that category. While one can overcome fear through sheer determination, sometimes it's much better to simply pretend at first. Then all that's LEFT is to TURN the Fantasy into Reality.

Connor looked up, bewilderment clouding her eyes. She turned the parchment over and then back again. "That's it, that's where it ends. But that doesn't make any—"

"Hey!"

Malcolm's shout startled Connor so badly she dropped the parchment and spun around, cannoning into her father and Laura just as they turned in the direction Malcolm was already moving. This left them tangled with each other as Malcolm, with only three long strides, reached the door leading from the kitchen into the rear yard and flung it open. They were close on his heels, but Malcolm had already disappeared around the corner of the house by the time they reached the garden. They heard him shout again and ran pell-mell toward the front garden. But when they reached him, Malcolm was alone, staring down the driveway, his fists clenched.

Laura reached him first. "What did you see?"

He was panting hard, given the fact that it took some energy to move his 265 pounds on a dead run. "That little creep from the bar."

"Who?" said Connor.

"The little guy, the one Benjamin said he'd seen before."

"Our leprechaun?" asked Connor in disbelief.

"Yeah. Guy wouldn't come up to my belt buckle, and looks about a hundred years old. But he must be in great shape. He took off so fast, it's like he disappeared."

"You know, I'm getting damn tired of hearing that," said Benjamin. "This disappearing into thin air thing."

"Doesn't exactly thrill me either, Dad. But you've got to admit it's weird the way he's right in front of you one minute and gone the next."

"I think he's just very good at making himself scarce. Or maybe blending into the background."

Malcolm scowled. "But this time he didn't have time to go anywhere. Once you get around the house, you can see all the way down the driveway, and other than the trees along the sides of the house, there's no cover. It's just lawn. If he went down the drive and into the road, I would've been able to see him."

They stood there for a moment. Connor suddenly grabbed Laura's arm. "Unless he didn't go down the road. Is the front door of the house locked?"

"Yes," said Benjamin. "I locked it when we came home last night, and no one's gone out today."

But Connor wasn't listening. She darted away toward the front porch with Laura right behind her. Malcolm and Benjamin stared at them, then at each other.

"What is she talking about?" asked Malcolm. "Why would—"

His words were cut off by a shout from Connor. "It's open. The damn door is..." The rest of her sentence was swallowed up as she continued on into the house.

The two men found Connor and Laura in the kitchen where Connor was in the process of slamming the Nancy Drew book down on the table.

"The parchment is gone!"

Laura was on her knees, peering under the edge of the stove. Malcolm began pulling the chairs out and looking under the table.

"Don't bother," said Connor, her voice chastened by defeat. "It isn't here. He took it." She flopped down in one of the kitchen chairs. "The son of a bitch took it."

No one spoke for several long moments. Malcolm's jaw was visibly clenched, but he had apparently chosen to keep his anger to himself. The look on Connor's face defied any attempts at sympathy or rationalizing.

Laura was the first to break the silence. "But he doesn't know what it means."

Connor glanced at her. "What?"

"Whoever he is, he doesn't know what the letter means. We don't even understand it, and Connor is her granddaughter. So how is this complete stranger going to decipher one cryptic note that only Connor is meant to understand in the first place?"

The dark cloud over Connor seemed to lift slightly. She pursed her lips. "Hmm. You know, you might be right. Everything Gwendolyn has left behind has been pretty much couched in terms that only I would be able to translate. Even the letter...oh, shit! The letter."

The three of them stared in amazement as Connor flew out of the room and down the hall, and then they followed, like a group of Keystone cops, tripping over each other in the process. If the situation weren't so serious, it would have been funny.

When they reached the library, Connor was already bent over the open desk, her hand thrust into the inner compartment. Then she turned around, bewildered and angry.

"Honey," said her father. "You didn't put the letter back there. After we copied it, you put it in your pocket. And we destroyed all the copies."

Connor's hand flew to the back pocket of her jeans. She felt the outline of the thick folded document. "Phew! But I thought for a minute—"

"You were right to be worried," said Benjamin. "Last time I looked, that window was closed and locked." They turned to see that the sash of one of the tall Palladian windows had been pushed up, leaving an opening through which only a child would fit.

"Then he *did* come into this room. But he didn't find what he was looking for," said Laura.

"Assuming your grandmother's first letter is what he was seeking," mused Benjamin. "But I don't think so. He didn't really have time to search if he came straight into the house when Malcolm chased him. Though I'm wondering how he evaded the lock on the front door so quickly."

"He probably had already picked it," the big cop answered. "I think he saw us getting the parchment out of the book and then had every intention of letting himself be seen so we would chase him out the back door. He planned to come through the front."

"But how could he be so sure that Connor wouldn't take the message with her?" asked Laura.

"He couldn't be. But his timing might have been a little off. Maybe he planned to wait until she actually put it on the table before he showed himself. But it happened a little early. Unfortunately, with me and my big mouth, I startled Connor so much she dropped it. Worked out great for that little creep."

Connor took his large hand in both of hers and squeezed it gently. She knew how much he wanted to make things right for her. "Don't start blaming yourself. We're all doing about the best we can right now, and I'm grateful to have you here. Believe me."

Malcolm looked down at her and smiled ruefully. "Well, right now I feel like they should take away my cop degree. Two brushes with this jerk, and I haven't even gotten a close look at him."

"You will. I have a feeling that before long I'm going to see our leprechaun friend dangling from your right hand with his feet well off the ground."

They all grinned at the comic image, and even Malcolm seemed to relax a bit at the thought of getting his hands on the thief.

"Besides," Connor continued. "I don't need the parchment. I know exactly what Gwendolyn had in mind. It just came to me when I reached into the desk and found her letter. Feeling around in that dark little recess triggered something in my memory." She turned to her father. "Dad, you remember when I was about ten years old and Gwendolyn let me call you at your office because I had what I thought was earth-shattering news?"

Benjamin tilted his head to one side and absentmindedly stroked a finger along his jaw. It made Connor smile, as this was always the mannerism he adopted when he was struggling to remember something. Usually it didn't take him long, and this was no exception. "You mean the summer you got over your fear of water and you learned to swim?"

Connor grinned. "Exactly! And Gwendolyn started me out learning the 'dead man's float' in the smallest amount of water you could imagine."

Chapter Twenty-Three

Turn the key deftly in the oiled wards,
And seal the hushed casket of my soul.
—John Keats
"To Sleep"

Malcolm, Laura, and Benjamin all started to talk at once, but Connor was gone before they could so much as finish any of their questions. Laura turned to Benjamin. "Do you have any idea what she's talking about?"

Connor's father shook his head. "I can't begin to imagine what's got her all fired up. I remember her calling me and going on and on the way kids do, but I don't recall what exactly happened. I was probably only half-listening."

"Whatever it is," interrupted Malcolm. "She's upstairs."

They heard the sound of footsteps passing overhead.

"Then perhaps we'd better join her," prompted Laura. "Before she solves this entire puzzle by herself."

After a quick glance into the rooms along the hallway, they found Connor in the bathroom adjoining the large, sunny front bedroom. She was lying beside the enormous claw-foot tub which stood several inches off the floor. The interior was easily big enough to bathe at least two medium-size people at a time. At first Laura was alarmed to see Connor's head wedged underneath the edge of it.

"Are you okay?" she gasped. "What's the matter?"

"The only thing the matter is, I'm too big." Connor's voice was muffled.

Laura shook her head. "I tend to think of you as exactly the right size, sweetheart. But I'm assuming this isn't some sort of new diet fad, crawling under bathroom fixtures."

Connor slid away from the opening. "Very funny. What I meant was that getting under here was a lot easier when I was a skinny kid."

"What's under there?" asked Malcolm. "Maybe I can reach it." Connor looked at him dubiously, and he shrugged. "I'm big, but my arms are a lot longer than yours."

"You can give it a try. Most of the space underneath the tub is open, but under the side closest to the wall there is a long, flat wooden box, almost like a platform, because it's attached to the floor itself. It's about four inches high, three feet long, and maybe six inches deep. I don't remember why it was originally built, or maybe it was left there when the tub was installed. But the side facing us is a hinged door that lifts up. And that's where we'll find what we're looking for."

Benjamin cocked his head to one side. "You're sounding awfully confident about this. Why?"

"I'll tell you once we get inside that box. Go ahead, Malcolm? If you can't reach it, we'll have to think of something else."

Malcolm obligingly got down on the tile floor, and the others moved back to allow him room to maneuver his large frame. He tried it once lying facedown, but even though he could feel the wood under his fingertips, he couldn't get any leverage. "Maybe I'd better try lying on my back. I think I could reach farther."

They backed away again as he repositioned himself. A few moments later, his efforts were rewarded as a loud *thunk* reverberated.

"The front panel's open," he said, "but I can't feel anything inside...no, wait a second. Something smooth and metallic." He groaned as he tried to force himself farther into the opening. "Damn, I can't get it."

Laura knelt and tugged at his other arm. "You're going to end up stuck under there, my friend. And I don't relish the thought of having to call a plumber to get you unstuck."

Malcolm grudgingly extricated himself and sat up. "I could barely touch it, but there's something there."

Laura lay down flat and peered under the tub. "I see a glimmer of a reflection. What we need is something with a long handle, a tool or..."

Connor was out the door in a flash.

"I wish she'd stop doing that," Malcolm grumbled, and went after her.

Benjamin smiled. "I think our tall friend has reappointed himself Connor's bodyguard and full-time shadow."

Laura sat up, dusting off her hands. "I know."

Benjamin leaned against the sink. "That doesn't bother you, does it? I mean that he's so intent on protecting her?"

"Why would I be bothered? Oh, you mean because I love her, I'm thinking that should be *my* job."

He smiled. "I suppose. After all, I've known you a long time. I think if I were in your shoes, I'd want to be the one dogging her steps every minute."

Laura thought about that for a moment. "I suppose part of me does want just that. But as much as I want to protect her from harm, she'd hate the idea of having a lover who was trying to double as a bodyguard, don't you think? Somehow that would make it seem as if we weren't equals."

"Did you know you're one of the wisest youngsters I've ever known?" Benjamin quipped, wrapping an arm around her shoulders and giving her a quick hug.

"Nice to know you can be over forty and still thought of as a youngster," she smiled. But almost instantly a shadow passed over her face.

"What is it?"

Laura sat down on the edge of the tub. "I was thinking it's just as well to have Malcolm 'on the job,' so to speak. I didn't do a very good job of protecting your daughter the first time."

Benjamin squatted down beside her, his expression stern. "Don't even think that. You risked your life out there in the desert, and you saved both your lives when that hit man ran you off the road. You couldn't have known what else was waiting for you. Stop beating up on yourself."

She sighed. "If Malcolm hadn't come along right when he did—"

"My daughter would be dead, and so would you, and I'd be one of the saddest men alive. But he did, and you're not, and I couldn't be happier to see the two of you together."

"Does this mean we have your blessing?"

"You have to *ask*?" he teased.

"No, I guess if you didn't like the idea, I'd know about it. But I can't help worry how it almost didn't happen for us. I was afraid when she left the rez all those weeks ago that she'd never come back. And I was amazed at how empty I felt without her. I knew there would never be anyone else for me but Connor Hawthorne, as silly as that sounds."

"It isn't silly at all. I think people really are made for one specific partner, but they often end up cruising through life with the wrong one."

"Don't tell me you believe in soul mates?"

"I'm likely to be drummed out of my position as president of the National Society of Professional Cynics, but yes, I do believe in that. I never found mine in this lifetime, but that's just how it is. I certainly don't regret my marriage, if only because it produced my daughter."

"In which case I certainly don't regret it," Laura smiled. "And that soul-mate thing pretty much describes how I feel about her. But if she sensed that, it's hard to figure out why she ran away from me. I almost think she would have stayed away if I hadn't forced the issue."

"She was afraid, Laura. I think you know that. Connor's never been very comfortable with her feelings. Loving you probably seemed like too great a risk. I'm thankful she came to her senses, though I imagine you had to do a little coaxing."

She met his eyes. "I did have to insist on getting at the truth, and let me tell you, you raised one remarkably honest and loving woman."

He nodded and a gentle smile lit up his face, stretching all the way to his eyes. "I can't take a lot of the credit for how she turned out, but you're right about her. She's got an incredible capacity for love when she lets herself break free of all the internal restrictions." He took Laura's hand in his. "From what I've seen so far, I think you bring out the best in my daughter. And besides—"

The sound of clanking and approaching footsteps interrupted him. Benjamin stood up and leaned against the wall as Connor and Malcolm appeared at the bathroom door carrying an assortment of garden tools and miscellaneous household objects with which to carry out the removal of Gwendolyn's hidden cache.

Fortunately it took only a few minutes of experimenting with rakes and a long-handled garden claw to identify the correct technique to drag the item from its hiding place. Slowly they pulled it forward until the leading edge protruded and Laura was able to grasp it with her hands and finish the extrication. Laura sensed as she did so that it wasn't what any of them had expected.

This small casket was no antique object. If anything, it appeared extremely modern, almost high-tech in appearance. The rectangular, brushed-aluminum container was some twelve inches wide, four inches deep, and a little more than two inches tall. The corners were rounded off, and it was surprisingly heavy for its size. An almost imperceptible crack ran around it, indicating the presence of a lid, but there were no visible hinges.

Laura tried to lift the lid but couldn't budge it. "I guess getting it out of that hidey hole wasn't the hard part."

Connor had pulled the odd-looking key from her pocket in anticipation of opening the box, but stopped when she looked closely at it. "I can't believe it. There's no keyhole."

Laura turned the casket over and ran her hands along the bottom side. "Nothing here either," she said glumly. "So, what do we do, try a hammer and chisel?"

"Not if you want to avoid destroying what's inside," said Benjamin, from the doorway to which he'd retreated when they'd started poking under the tub with the long-handled tools.

"What do you mean?" asked Connor. "Why would opening it destroy anything?"

Benjamin shook his head. "If it's what I think it is, any attempt to open it without following the correct procedure will probably incinerate the contents."

Connor stared at him. "Oh, come *on*, Dad. This is Grandma Gwendolyn we're talking about, not some master spy from one of your classified files."

He shook his head. "You think just because she was old-fashioned about certain things, she'd refuse to use whatever she needed to protect herself, and you?"

"But why? This is all so...weird."

"I'll agree with you on that, but I'm pretty sure this container is of the same design as one I saw in Germany a few years ago. Of course, when I saw it, we were too late to get the documents that had been inside it. An overzealous Brit agent had tried to pry it open. He got acid burns on his hands and a pile of smoking ashes as his reward for haste."

"So you're saying this key has nothing to do with it?" she asked, holding up the tiny piece of metal.

"No, indeed. It's precisely what we need. The trick is finding the keyhole."

Laura looked down at the box. "I don't know. This is about as smooth a surface as I've ever seen."

Benjamin stepped forward and held out his hands. "Let's take this into my room. I think we're better off staying up here. Even if our leprechaun is adept at disappearing, I'm willing to wager he's no good at floating in midair."

He took the box to a writing table that stood near the largest of the windows. Malcolm, newly reminded of their recent intruder, paced from window to window, checking out the front of the house and the road beyond, while trying to keep an eye on what Benjamin was doing.

The ex-senator sat down and rested his hands on top of the box. "We spent some time analyzing the one we found. And, as with all magician's tricks or baffling brain teasers, it isn't hard once you know the solution. The construction of the casket is based on ancient Asian puzzle boxes. It's a matter of placement and finger pressure even where it seems there are no moving parts."

They watched in fascinated silence as he probed the metal surface with gentle yet firm pressure. Finally, he took hold of the sides of the box, his fingers curled around all four corners, and worked his thumbs back and forth from side to side. In a moment, they heard a distinctive click, and the bottom front edge of the casket protruded slightly. Benjamin worked his fingers farther down and pressed again. The base of the casket slid forward again. Gently he turned it on its back side and there was now a visible channel where the base of the box had opened up along the back edge. Very carefully, Benjamin picked up a letter opener and used it to pry the sliding base farther forward toward the front of the box. About halfway along, the base stopped sliding, and Benjamin immediately stopped pushing on it. "That's where our Brit friend made his mistake," explained Benjamin. "He kept going."

"Then what's the next step?" asked Laura. "Is this a series of movements of different pieces of the box?"

Benjamin took a deep breath and let go of the casket. "No," he said, with a slight smile. "This is where we use the key." He pointed to a thin slot that had been revealed as the base moved. "And that's really all there is to it."

Connor instantly produced the key, Benjamin signaled for her to wait. "You should know that there's the slightest chance that there's one last booby trap. Turning the key the wrong way might—"

"Might what?" asked Malcolm.

"I don't know. Might destroy the contents or—"

"Blow up?" the big man scowled. "Then there's no way she's opening that thing."

Connor bristled visibly. "I'm perfectly capable of figuring this out, and I don't need—"

"Hey," Laura interjected. "Let's not get carried away. Gwendolyn wouldn't do anything to jeopardize Connor's life. So I think maybe Benjamin's—"

"Been watching too many spy movies," her former boss finished the sentence, and his joke vanquished the tension in the room. "Laura's right. The only risk is to the contents, but I doubt Gwendolyn would want us to get this far and fail."

Connor moved closer to the box and four people held a collective breath as she eased it into the hole. Encountering resistance, she withdrew it and turned it over. This time, it slid in easily.

Benjamin laid his hand gently over hers. "Do you think it matters which way the key is turned?"

"I think it does," said Connor thoughtfully. "And I'm going to turn it left." Without waiting for any feedback on her decision, she twisted the key counterclockwise. They heard a soft click, and the top of the box raised a centimeter. Removing the key, she placed the box flat on its base and lifted the lid. Inside, resting on dark velvet, were two scrolled pieces of yellowed parchment. After only a moment's hesitation, she carefully removed them and laid them on the table.

She chose one scroll and slowly unrolled it. They all leaned in for a closer look.

"I think it's written in English," Connor said after several moments. "But it's a very old form, dating back several centuries, I should think."

"Can you read it?" asked Benjamin.

She stared at it again and shook her head. "Only a few words here and there. Between the odd characters, and the vastly different spelling in use then, and the cramped handwriting, I don't know if I could decipher it at all, let alone any time soon."

"What about the other scroll?" suggested Laura. "Maybe it'll tell us more."

Connor repeated the process with the second parchment. Rather than a document, this turned out to be a map, or at least some sort of diagram. They peered at it. "Those are probably buildings," said Benjamin, pointing to various blocks indicated on the paper. "And maybe roads. But the text isn't any easier to understand than what's in that first one. About the only thing I can be sure of is this circular symbol with tiny letters—I'd say it has to be a compass with directional indicators."

"But what's the map for?" asked Laura, with her usual cut-to-the-chase approach. "This scavenger hunt is already sufficiently bizarre without some sort of Middle Ages treasure hunt cropping up."

Connor shook her head in frustration. "I can't believe we've gotten this far, and all we have to show for it are two pieces of paper we can't decipher. But I'm not willing to believe for a minute that Gwendolyn was just leading us a merry chase for the fun of it."

"I agree," said Benjamin. "Your grandmother never did anything without good reason, and from what she said in her letter, these are bound to be of the utmost importance."

"But what about—" Laura's question ended abruptly when the doorbell rang. They all stood perfectly still for a moment, and then Connor threw up her hands in mock disgust. "I think we're all getting a little gun-shy. It's the *doorbell,* for crying out loud. How many bad guys ring the doorbell first? And it's probably that poor vicar we almost killed."

She placed the parchments back in the casket, closed it, and shoved it under the bed. Then she dashed through the hall and down the stairs, but as she started to open the door, she realized the others were right behind her. "Do you suppose we could look a little less like a commando team lying in wait," she said. "Maybe disperse a little."

Malcolm, who had been coiled into a human spring, ready to charge into action, grinned a little sheepishly. "Sorry. Reflex reaction." He moved back into the doorway leading to the library, and Benjamin sat on the bottom step of the stairs, leaving Laura and Connor to answer the door together. He couldn't see who it was from his vantage point and stifled an urge to jump to his feet when he heard a pleasantly deep voice announce itself. "Good afternoon. I'm William Carlisle and this is my wife, Ellen. You must be Connor."

Chapter Twenty-Four

I have heard
That guilty creatures sitting at a play
Have by the very cunning of the scene
Been struck so to the soul that presently
They have proclaim'd their malefactions;
For murder, though it have no tongue, will speak
With most miraculous organ.
—William Shakespeare
Hamlet, Act 2, Scene 2

Surely there were better ways to earn a living, thought Peter Garrett as he burrowed deeper into the tall grass beside the hedgerow. He was quite sure there were insects crawling into his pants and invading parts of his anatomy he rather favored. But he didn't dare stand up and investigate the situation, at least not while two of the men he'd been detailed to watch were loitering within twenty yards of his hiding place. They'd been standing there on the road for the past half hour, smoking and talking in so low a tone he could only occasionally make out what they were saying. He had no wish to draw their attention. He wasn't armed, and he doubted that the bulges under their dark jackets were oversized wallets.

He peered through his binoculars at the storage buildings on the other side of the road and about 150 yards away. Since his predawn arrival, removal vans had come and gone almost every two hours. He'd tried to determine from the way the vehicles sat on their suspension whether they were full or empty. At the very least he hoped his surveillance would reveal whether something was being brought to the out-buildings on Lord Fenwycke's land, or taken away. But if his guess were correct, the stream of vans had both picked up and dropped off. He imagined this might make some sense to his guv'nor, Nicholas Foulsham, but he, himself, wasn't in the mood for theorizing. It was almost dark, he hadn't learned anything important, and he was starving. What he needed was a brimming pint of cool lager and a plate of liver and onions and gravy. As it was, he didn't even dare reach into his pocket for the packet of crisps he'd brought along.

The sound of an engine alerted him that another van was approaching. He heaved a sigh of relief. Dusk had fallen, and the noise of the van's motor would drown out his cautious retreat. He waited until it had drawn even with the two guards, and then slowly crawled backward, crabwise, careful to disturb the tall grass as little as possible, lest its movement be detected. Still, the two men were on the driver's side of the van, and Garrett was hidden on the left side of the road. With the vehicle between them, and the growing darkness, he doubted they would notice anything less than a bull elephant tramping through the field of unmown hay. Nonetheless, his tours of duty in Her Majesty's army had taught him caution.

He'd wriggled backward at least thirty yards before he allowed himself the luxury of turning around and facing in the direction he wanted to go. Then he belly crawled another 200 yards before cautiously raising his head above the grass to triangulate his position. His car was still a half mile away, across the field and through a small copse of trees that bordered Haslemere on the west. However, knowing that warmth, comfort, and his wife's solicitousness were less than an hour away, he didn't even resent the long walk. It would do him good to work out the kinks in his back and neck he'd gotten from lying there for so many hours.

And what a waste it had been. Clearly the men he'd observed were up to no good, but what exactly? Without a better theory, it was going to be damned difficult to procure a warrant to search anything belonging to Gerald Fenwycke. What would Foulsham say? That Detective Sergeant Garrett had seen half a dozen vans come and go, four or five unknown individuals moving back and forth between two buildings, and two men with suspicious bulges under their jackets. Now that was certainly cause to call out the troops, wasn't it?

Garrett judged he was far enough away, and sufficiently shrouded in darkness, to risk standing up. Satisfied that no one had detected his presence, he began to make his way on foot, pausing now and then to get his bearings. As he went through the trees and came out in the lane, he realized he'd slanted too far south. His car was farther along, hidden behind a screen of thorn bushes. He turned to his left and was pleased to feel the breeze in his face freshening as he neared the car. Feeling almost benevolent enough to forgive Foulsham for this miserable assignment, he reached into his jacket pocket for the car keys. Not there. He tried the other one. No. Next, he felt in the pockets of his trousers. Nothing but some coins and a pencil.

With growing alarm he went through the entire procedure again until he was forced to admit the unthinkable. He'd lost the car keys while he was crawling through the field, and he had one chance in several million of finding them in the dark. "Damn!" he swore softly. Now what? He stood for a few moments considering his options. There weren't many, and the most obvious ones entailed a considerable amount of personal embarrassment. He could walk to the village some three miles distant and find a garage willing to tow his car back to the station, all of which would draw unnecessary attention to his presence and jeopardize the surveillance. He could, instead, leave the car and come back the next day with another set of keys. Both of these possibilities, however, meant admitting to Foulsham what had happened, and enduring the taunts from his fellow officers.

Garrett stood with his hands in his jacket pockets, which is when he finally noticed he could put his fingers straight through the left one. In near darkness, he felt the outside of his coat and found the tear in the fabric. So that was it! Hope flared ever so slightly in his heart. He remembered exactly when he'd done the damage. Just before dawn, after he'd hidden the car and was about to cross the lane and slip into the woods, he'd heard a car coming. Not wishing to take the chance that it was someone associated with the goings-on at Haslemere, he'd virtually dived into the cover. There'd been some tangles of brush on the verge where the trees ran closest to the road. It was behind these that he'd hidden himself as a long, silver Mercedes swept past, its engine whining in too low a gear. When he'd shifted his position, he'd caught his jacket on a branch and had to tug away. No doubt the sounds of the vehicle passing had prevented him from hearing the jingle of keys falling to the ground.

He walked slowly back toward the spot he remembered, but now he was hampered by the darkness. All around him the land was pitch black, and he could barely see his hand in front of his face. How was he ever going to find the keys? Perhaps he could risk just a moment's light. He took out the tiny pocket torch he always carried and pointed it at the ground, flicking it on for just a moment. He twisted the cap to narrow the beam and switched it on again. At first his eyes were too dazzled by the artificial light to see anything at all. Then he moved along, pointing the torch at the ground until he saw the edges of what must be the brush pile.

Cautiously moving around behind it, he swept the tiny beam back and forth in a slow, methodical pattern. For several minutes, he searched, trying to remember exactly where he'd stood up, which branch had torn his jacket. Still, not even a glimmer of metal caught his eye. After a while, when he was tempted to discard the absurd notion of finding his keys in the dark, the potential humiliation of returning to the station on foot renewed his determination to succeed. And that's when it happened. A tiny flash. Yes! His key ring dangled from a bit of thorn bush that had been hacked out of the hedge and left to dry with the other leavings.

The sergeant smiled. So the day hadn't turned out so badly after all.

It seemed that fate, which in Garrett's experience rarely favored hard-working coppers, was smiling on him for once. He stepped out into the road, gripping the keys tightly, not daring to let go of them for an instant until he was safe in the car. He turned off the flashlight, waiting a moment to let his eyes readjust. But they didn't. Instead, he saw flashes, streaks of white light everywhere. Then he realized the lights weren't outside, they were in his head...oh, God, his skull was on fire. He slumped to his knees, still trying to understand the blinding pain. He thought he heard laughter, and then he felt himself falling, falling, into a deep pool, sinking under the warm, welcoming darkness.

W

Chief Inspector Nicholas Foulsham had never in his recollection acted anything less than professional when examining a crime scene, at least not since he'd been a callow and eager constable. Today was an exception. He could not muster the self-control he needed. He could not switch over to that emotionless state where his mental faculties functioned like a well-oiled machine and his feelings were kept locked up tight. He couldn't do it because this wasn't business, this was personal.

He stood there, ten feet away from the gray Rover and clenched his teeth over and over until his jaw ached. But it was the only way he could manage to keep silent. He'd already shouted at the Scenes of Crime officers and Inspector Rathbone. He'd been rude, unreasonable, and angry. But there was no helping it. Peter Garrett didn't deserve to die like that.

"We're ready to move the body, sir," announced one of the SOC officers, and Foulsham simply nodded. He would wait until Garrett was removed from the vehicle, until the lashings that tied the man's wrists to the steering wheel of his car were finally cut, with care being taken to preserve the knots. His hands couldn't have rested on the center bar of the wheel because the man no longer *had* any hands. Bloody stumps. Foulsham felt the rising in his gorge and fought to swallow.

The morgue attendants laid Garrett gently on a stretcher, with a strap over his chest to hold his arms in place. At least he still has his head, thought Foulsham, over and over, trying to ignore the circle of thorns wrapped tightly around Garrett's forehead, cutting deep into the skin, and the blood that had gushed down his face and into the eyes that were open and staring. Garrett had been alive when the murderer had prepared his body in an obscene parody of Christ's ordeal on the cross. He had been alive because he had bled from the thorns. And he had probably been alive when the murdering bastard took his hands.

Foulsham felt himself tremble violently, and in his distraction he failed to hear someone call his name. Too late he turned to see DC Mary Fitch coming toward him. She looked past Foulsham to the stretcher just as the covering was being pulled over those sightless eyes.

"Dear mother of God," she breathed as the blood drained from her face. "What have they done to Peter?"

$\mathcal{W}^o$

Four hours later, Foulsham and DC Fitch left the Garrett home. A woman police constable remained behind to sit with Glenda Garrett. Superintendent Hollis had offered to send someone else to make the necessary notification to Peter Garrett's family, but Foulsham had refused to abdicate that responsibility, and Mary had likewise insisted that she would be there too. It had been worse than they'd anticipated. At first Glenda Garrett had flatly refused to believe them, even though she'd been frantic over her husband's failure to return the previous evening. Then she'd begun smashing things in the parlor; she'd had to be physically restrained while a doctor was sent for.

Another officer was dispatched to collect the Garrett children, who attended the local comprehensive, and take them to their aunt's house. No one was quite sure if Glenda Garrett would be up to caring for the children, let alone herself. Foulsham had made other such notifications in his career, but he didn't know when he'd seen any human being more thoroughly, and perhaps irreparably, shattered by the loss of a loved one. He didn't envy the WPC her job in looking after the woman whose pain made him all the angrier, and all the more determined.

"All right, Fitch. I want warrants to search the buildings on Fenwycke's property. And I want them fast. In the meantime, detail at least four constables to watch both ends of the lane that runs alongside that property. I don't care who sees them, and they're to get registration numbers off every vehicle that comes and goes." He slammed his hand on the desk. "Not that there will be anything there. They've had hours to clear out."

W

Foulsham's pessimism regarding the result of a search was well-founded. The outbuildings were completely empty, swept clean. Although there was clear evidence of thorough and recent use—fresh scrape marks on the wooden floors, the wheel tracks of what was probably a forklift, and tire marks of numerous vehicles coming and going—there was nothing to indicate what had been stored there.

Frustrated by the lack of evidence, Foulsham tackled Gerald Fenwycke. Compared to the results of the search, he hit pay dirt.

"So you have no idea what Mr. Thackeray wanted to store on your property, Lord Fenwycke?" Foulsham's allowed his skepticism to show clearly, and Gerald had the good grace to look embarrassed.

"He said it was merely temporary. Said he needed someplace out of the way to test some sort of new technology or something."

"But surely you asked about the nature of the 'experiment' or whether there would be any risk to anyone nearby?"

Gerald's face took on a pinker hue. "Not precisely, no. Don't like to interrogate a man about his business, don't you know? Besides, it was...it was...er..."

"Yes?"

"Well, my wife had sort of promised Thackeray he could rent that part of the property and I didn't like to go back on something she'd agree to. That is I..."

Foulsham suddenly saw the situation in a slightly new perspective, and he could almost feel sorry for this idiot. Gillian Fenwycke was involved in all this, whatever *this* was, up to her pretty little eyebrows. She was likely in it for money, and was perfectly willing to let Gerald cuckolded into the bargain. It wasn't simply another sordid affair that he'd witnessed at the cottage in Glastonbury. Now it took on the characteristics of a meeting of conspirators. Both Thackeray and Lady Fenwycke had been on edge. And Gillian had been enraged by Foulsham's presence. Or was it Thackeray who had angered her? Perhaps a falling out among thieves. He turned his attention back to the somewhat pitiful Lord Fenwycke.

"So, as I understand it, you paid no attention whatever to activities taking place on your property."

"Well, not precisely. I mean I did..."

"Did what, sir?"

"I did pass by there a couple of days ago. I was out on Blazing Star, and thought I'd check in."

"And what did you see?"

"Um, nothing actually. Everything looked quiet, and the chap I spoke to said that, um, said that they hadn't actually started work or anything so there wasn't much to see."

In other words, thought Foulsham, one of Thackeray's goons had run him off his own land. The chief inspector would have been tempted to smile if it weren't for the image burned into his retinas of Peter Garrett and his crown of bloody thorns. He doubted he'd find reason to smile for a long time to come.

"Then what, if anything, did you see at a distance, Lord Fenwycke?"

"Um...some panel vans, and a lorry sitting by one of the outbuildings."

"Anything identifiable about these vehicles?"

"Had some sort of writing on the side. Assume it was that World Technology Partners firm of Thackeray's, but I couldn't say for sure."

Is there anything on earth you could say for sure? thought Foulsham, but he restrained himself from asking the question aloud. He did allow himself a parting jab, though.

"Any idea of when Lady Fenwycke will be returning? I'd like to ask her a few questions."

Gerald's face suffused with blood. "I...I'm not quite sure. She's having a bit of rest, don't you know. I expect she'll be in touch. I mean, I expect she'll be returning shortly."

Foulsham nodded and let himself out. So the little bugger hadn't even heard from his dear wife. That hardly came as a surprise, nor would he be the least bit shocked to learn that Lady Fenwycke would provide an alibi for Conrad Thackeray. His intuition (something he would never admit aloud to having), told him there must be more to that particular relationship than adultery. Was it possible that Gillian Fenwycke knew the details of Thackeray's business, at least the part that had been carried out at Haslemere? Was she a pawn or a player?

Sensing it was time to get the truth out of someone, Foulsham turned his car toward Glastonbury. But what would Hollis say, he wondered, if he started hauling the local nobility into the station for interviews? Probably nothing Foulsham wanted to hear right now. For that matter, he hadn't actually gotten the go-ahead from Hollis to begin investigating Garrett's death. He'd assumed he'd be in charge, and if for some reason Hollis wanted to hand it off to someone else, well, it would be time to call in a few favors. He wasn't about to let go of this now, not with the obvious connection between the Frome murder and this one.

Foulsham downshifted at the roundabout and barely noticed that he'd been cut off by another driver who'd failed to yield the right of way. The teenager sped on around in front of him. On another day Foulsham would have been annoyed, but today he didn't particularly care about the peccadilloes of stupid drivers. He only cared that a man he'd worked with for more than five years was dead because he'd been following Nicholas Foulsham's orders.

Chapter Twenty-Five

Wherein they shall find many joyous and pleasant histories,
and noble and renowned acts of humanity, gentleness, and chivalries.
For herein may be seen chivalry, courtesy, humanity, friendliness,
hardiness, love, friendship, cowardice, murder, hate, virtue, and sin.
Do after the good and leave the evil,
and it shall bring you to good fame and renown.
—Sir Thomas Malory
Le Morte D'Arthur (Caxton's Original Preface)

If the Carlisles had expected a warm reception in respect of their long-standing friendship with Gwendolyn Broadhurst, they were definitely disappointed. Connor was polite but distinctly chilly as she effected introductions, and Laura followed her lead. Benjamin Hawthorne was taciturn in the extreme. Of Malcolm Jefferson they could make nothing, for he barely spoke at all.

After some awkward moments spent standing in the entrance hall, Connor suggested they go into the drawing room, much more formal in its furnishings and arrangement than the library. It had an unused air about it, as if Gwendolyn had done little entertaining in several years. But the graceful Queen Anne furniture gleamed in the afternoon sun, and the accessories and objets d'art scattered about the room were well-dusted, as were the paintings that hung above the chair rail running along the walls.

Ellen consulted her husband with a glance and noted his almost imperceptible shrug. Apparently he had no better idea than she about what was going on here. But given their sensitivity, they both knew they were not welcome, for reasons that had yet to be discovered. It would require careful digging, and she left it to William to begin the excavation.

"Senator Hawthorne," he began, choosing formality as a balm for the vague hostility he sensed in all of them. Well, not Laura Nez perhaps. She regarded them both with a certain neutrality, as if she had not quite sorted them into a category of friend or foe.

"Just 'Benjamin' is fine," Connor's father responded. "I know you were friends of Gwendolyn's, and you've known my daughter since she was a child."

Ellen felt a wave of protectiveness emanating from the man when he looked at Connor. And just as easily she sensed that Benjamin had been both father and mother to the girl as well as protector. Getting between him and his child would be akin to getting between a mother bear and her cub—in both cases a highly dangerous proposition.

"Well, then, Benjamin. I wish this were purely a social call, but under the rather unusual circumstances, there were certain facts about Gwendolyn that we felt we should discuss with Connor, and given the events of the past few weeks, we didn't think it could wait."

Connor answered. "What exactly did you wish to tell me about my grandmother?"

William paused, looking from Connor to her father, to Laura, then to Malcolm. "I don't wish to seem rude, but I think Ellen and I should discuss these things with you in private first, then if you wish to—"

"No."

William blinked and fell silent. Ellen, who rarely had the experience of seeing her husband nonplussed by a situation, was tempted to be amused by his discomfiture, but this was hardly an appropriate venue for humor. Instead, she gently intervened.

"Connor, are you quite sure you wish for everyone present to be privy to your grandmother's life story? There are facets of it she may have wanted to remain unknown except to you."

"I doubt that," Connor answered, with remarkable conviction. "She knew everyone in this room, and they knew her." She glanced at Laura and Malcolm. "Even if only for a short while."

"During her last trip to America," prompted William.

"Yes."

"And she died there," said Ellen, though there was something in the tone of her voice that belied the certainty of that statement.

"Not exactly."

Ellen sighed. This was getting them nowhere. Perhaps it was time for less fencing and more truth. "Connor, we both sense your lack of trust in us. But may we ask why you choose to distrust us right from the start? If you could answer that, perhaps we will be able to put your minds at ease. Otherwise the work we have to do will be next to impossible."

"What kind of work are you talking about?" asked Benjamin.

"The kind that Gwendolyn and William and I, along with a few others, have been doing for years. But first, let's hear your concerns. Why have you all got the wind up about us?" Everyone but Connor appeared puzzled by the question. "I mean, why are you looking at us as if we're suspicious characters?"

Benjamin leaned forward in his seat, and Ellen knew he'd come to some sort of decision. He was either going to throw them out or tell them what was going on. When he spoke, she thanked God it was the latter.

"After I spoke to you, William, I learned that you are involved with a highly questionable multinational corporation. So questionable, in fact, that I've asked some former colleagues to look into it."

William's eyes narrowed slightly. "And what corporation is it that has you up in arms?"

"Funny you should put it that way," answered Benjamin. "The transactions I've been tracing all involve weapons and armaments, including some heavy-duty technology, surface-to-air missiles, and nuclear capability. And they were traced back to World Technology Partners, a company controlled by one of your party guests."

William nodded, the tension gone from his expression. "Conrad Thackeray, of course."

"You don't seem surprised. May I assume you're well aware of the scope of Thackeray's activities?"

"You may indeed. And before you ask this policeman to show us the door because of our seeming association with him, perhaps you would do me the courtesy of ringing up Fenton Carstairs."

Ellen saw that the name didn't mean anything to Laura, Connor, or Malcolm, but it clearly struck a chord with Benjamin Hawthorne.

"You're talking about the Fenton Carstairs with MI-6?" he queried.

"Can't imagine there are too many chaps saddled with a dime-novel moniker like that," William answered with a smile, "though I suppose I shouldn't talk considering the family name I inherited."

"And how would you happen to know Fenton?"

"Our fathers were friends, and there are some family connections," William explained. "Fenton used that acquaintanceship to ask me a favor, one I was happy to grant."

Ellen spoke up. "Are you quite sure you should be discussing this, William? I mean, Fenton made it very clear that—"

William held up a hand. "I understand your reservations, my love, but I don't think there's room here for anything less than complete honesty. Otherwise, we're never going to be able to accomplish what must be accomplished." He looked Benjamin squarely in the eye. "Our mutual acquaintance, Mr. Carstairs, is as concerned as you apparently are over the movement of not only small arms and war materiel, but also the components to construct weapons of mass destruction. And he has strong misgivings about Mr. Thackeray, but insufficient cause to ask MI-5 to conduct an investigation. Instead he prevailed upon me to use my social standing to strike up a business relationship with Thackeray on the pretext of wishing to invest in his company."

"But Thackeray has huge cash reserves from what I can tell," Benjamin interrupted. "Why should he seek out any investors at all?"

"Purely to promote the appearance of legitimacy. What better way than to list a few peers and bankers on the list of stockholders? Makes it seem much more aboveboard. Not that I think he's particularly concerned about appearances of late."

"What makes you say that?"

"Perhaps my wife could better answer."

"The current gossip in the county has Thackeray involved with the wife of one of our neighbors, Lord Gerald Fenwycke."

"Affairs are hardly newsworthy," Benjamin shrugged, clearly unimpressed.

"Yes, but Gillian Fenwycke has never put herself in a position to be criticized, let alone held up to public ridicule."

"Why should she be?" asked Connor. "Lots of people cheat on their spouses. I would imagine that's the case even among the lords and ladies of England," she added dryly.

Ellen smiled. "Naturally. We're hardly immune to human error, even though it's been said that the upper-crust accent gives our occasional tawdriness a certain touch of class."

It took the four Americans an extra half-second to realize she was teasing, and when they did none of them could resist returning her smile. The room itself seemed to expand and lighten. Ellen breathed a small sigh of relief. There was still hope for this situation after all.

"So, as I understand it, Fenton asked you to get closer to Thackeray?"

"Not close, precisely," said William. "That might have seemed a bit suspicious since Thackeray's much more accustomed to Brit bluebloods turning up their noses at him since he's just a multimillionaire by effort, not birth. And since he knows he has ten times the net worth of most of them, he couldn't care less what they think. It would have been distinctly out of character if I'd attempted to form a friendship of any sort. Instead, I intimated that I was interested in making very substantial returns on investments, no matter how much risk was involved. He likes that—taking risks, that is. So he let me in."

"Has it done any good?"

"In small ways. I've managed to obtain a few pieces of information that would not have been available to the public since World

Technology Partners is privately held. Thackeray's accounting division does issue sanitized financial statements, but Fenton has managed to read between the lines of the documents I've turned over to him."

"And his conclusions?" asked Benjamin.

William shook his head. "That's something you'll have to ask Fenton. I don't mind coming clean with my side of it, but I'm not at liberty to discuss his views or his intentions."

Benjamin nodded slowly, and Ellen saw that he had markedly relaxed his defensive posture, an easing mirrored in the demeanor of his three companions. She allowed herself to breathe more freely as the hostility in the room melted away.

"If you'd been willing to spill your guts about Fenton," said Benjamin, "I'd have been very unwilling to trust you at all. But as it is..." He stopped, apparently considering what to think. "If you will excuse me for a few minutes." With a meaningful nod at Malcolm, he left the room. Ellen read into the gesture precisely what Benjamin had meant—keep an eye on things until I get back. She had no doubt this particular copper would be a formidable adversary if provoked. If only she and William could convince these people that they were all on the same side, the right side. In the meantime, the silence was getting oppressive.

"So, Connor. It's been more than thirty years since I first met you. And now you've become a world-renowned author."

Connor had the good grace to blush slightly. "I think that might be a bit of an overstatement, but I have had some success as a writer."

"I know Gwendolyn took a great deal of pride in your accomplishments," William added. "She wasn't the sort to put herself forward, as they say, but she didn't mind showing off your latest novel whenever a new one was released."

Ellen saw the stricken look in Connor's eyes and knew that Gwendolyn's love for her granddaughter had been entirely reciprocated. This young woman was still grieving the loss. *So*, thought Ellen, *Gwendolyn is truly gone from this plane, but where had she gotten to? And what did these people know about her departure?*

Her attention was drawn to the young Navajo woman, who stood abruptly and announced she was going to prepare some tea. Ellen was on the verge of volunteering to help when she happened to take notice of the watchfulness in the eyes of the policeman, and decided that Malcolm Jefferson would be much happier if she remained in the room with her husband. It was an odd sensation, she thought, being on trial so to speak, but it was a means to an end, and she could hardly blame them for their caution. Gwendolyn's warnings to her and to William about what forces might be at work once she departed had been frustratingly nonspecific, but nonetheless dire enough to make them equally as cautious.

She examined Gwendolyn's granddaughter in a covert, glancing way and saw the lines of strain and fatigue around the younger woman's eyes and mouth. Something was already haunting her, Ellen concluded. And it wasn't dear old Gwendolyn. She had just opened her mouth to frame an innocuous comment about the gardens at Rosewood House when the door opened to admit Benjamin. He was almost smiling. With some relief, she concluded that they had been properly vetted by Fenton Carstairs. Thank the angels their one acquaintance in MI-6 should turn out to be someone Benjamin Hawthorne knew and apparently trusted.

He looked around the room. "Where's Laura?" he asked.

"In the kitchen, Dad. Making some tea."

"Good, we'll need it. I think we all have a great deal to discuss."

Connor looked at her father quizzically. "We do?"

"Yes, I'm afraid I've done what Sherlock Holmes often cautioned against...theorizing ahead of my facts. Fenton vouches unequivocally for the Carlisles, and what's more, he suggested that anything we uncover may be of material value in nailing Conrad Thackeray for any number of crimes, large and small."

Connor shook her head. "It's getting hard to tell the players without a game card."

Benjamin smiled. "That's pretty much the way it's always been in my job, honey. Maybe I'm just used to it." He turned to the visitors. "I apologize for your chilly reception, but considering what's been going on around here, we had to be absolutely convinced of your trustworthiness.

And given what I had discovered about your involvement with that company, well, you can understand my caution."

"No need to apologize, Senator. We'd have done the same had it been the other way round. But I'm glad we could get past that awkwardness without wasting a great deal of time. Old Carstairs was a heaven-sent coincidence."

"First off, please call me Benjamin. It's been a long time since I stood on the senate floor. And secondly, if I've learned one thing over the past couple of years," said Benjamin, "there's no such thing as coincidence."

William said, with a twinkle in his eye, "Sounds as though you've been hanging about with our friend Gwendolyn."

"Yes, but not nearly enough as it turns out." He walked over and rested his hand gently on his daughter's shoulder. "It wasn't until too late that I started learning some extremely important things from my mother-in-law. I wish I'd had more time with her."

The door opened, and Laura appeared with a tray of teacups, teapot, and utensils. William jumped to his feet and gallantly relieved her of the tray, a gesture she didn't protest. If anything, she seemed perfectly at ease when William's hands brushed hers as he took the heavy tray. Ellen realized, to her delight, that this young woman was as extraordinary in her own way as Connor was in hers. Laura had read the changes in the energy in the room the moment she entered, detected the cessation of hostility, and was behaving accordingly. Ellen knew she must be extremely sensitive. Small wonder she and Connor had been attracted to each other, that they had been thrown together under difficult circumstances. Yet something niggled at the back of Ellen's mind. If these two were, in some way, soul mates, then the eventual destiny of which Gwendolyn had spoken must somehow involve Laura Nez as well. But how? And why Malcolm Jefferson and Benjamin Hawthorne? Neither of them were known to be psychically sensitive or metaphysically adept. Yet they were here, which could only mean that they too had a purpose. She took a deep breath. What a pity she couldn't see anywhere near as much of the future as Gwendolyn had.

Shaking herself out of the reverie, she scooted her chair closer to the butler's tray on which William had placed the tea things. "Shall I be mother?" she asked with a smile, picking up the teapot. "Connor, do you take lemon or milk and sugar?"

Once they'd all been served, Malcolm dispatched himself to the kitchen in search of snacks. He returned with some "cookies," which Ellen recalled was American for biscuits, and they sipped in peaceful silence for a few moments.

"You knew my grandmother well, didn't you, Lady Carlisle?" Connor said, placing her cup on the small table beside her chair.

Ellen nodded, adding, "Yes, indeed. But I think we must all be on a first-name basis here. We're William and Ellen, please."

"Then perhaps you can tell me more about what my grandmother was really up to...in her spare time."

Ellen consulted William with a quick glance. "We could, but it's difficult to know exactly what she would have wanted us to say."

"I don't think we have much choice except to put our cards on the table," interjected Benjamin. "I don't understand much of this situation, but I do know that we haven't got a great deal of time to straighten it out. Some pretty odd things have been happening."

Ellen shuddered as an icy chill ran up her spine. Damn, she thought, why hadn't she and her husband come to Rosewood House sooner? All this kid-glove approach had gotten them was into trouble. "What exactly has been going on?" she asked.

All eyes turned to Connor.

"The reason I asked you about my grandmother is because I'm totally confused about why she was so intent on my coming here, and why she left me this house, and, most of all, why she's led me on this scavenger hunt for clues to find her last instructions to me."

"And have you found them?" asked William, his eyes intent.

Ellen saw Connor recoil from the question. Clearly, trust hadn't fully blossomed.

"William, why don't we start with our end? Then we'll see if Connor wants to share her discoveries." He nodded, and she saw in his eyes the understanding that he'd been too eager to hear news of Gwendolyn.

"You may find some of this difficult to believe," Ellen began. "I'm not sure where each of you stands on metaphysical theory and, more specifically, what is called pagan spirituality. But let me assure you that we are not pagans in the sense that is conveyed in most books, and we are firmly committed to God's work." She smiled. "I know that sounds a trifle odd coming from a priestess of what is sometimes called the 'old' religion. But, truth to tell, much of what you have gleaned in the later writings is not accurate. To those of our faith there has always been the one God/Goddess/All That Is. And our commitment requires that we not simply believe, but that we actively nurture the God energy in ourselves and our world." She stopped. "I'm losing you, aren't I?" she asked a bit sheepishly. But to her surprise, no one looked confused or bored.

"Go on," said Connor. "You'd be amazed at how many times we've discussed this sort of thing with each other at various times. Does it surprise you that a politician, a cop, a novelist, and a..." She stopped and looked at Laura. "What career category do you think you'd fit into, love?"

Laura smiled. "I've been everything from chauffeur to bodyguard to spy to medicine woman in training...and now I suppose I'm just me."

"Well, I'm glad you're you. So my question is, Ellen, did you think we wouldn't be able to absorb the more esoteric elements of New Age spirituality?"

Ellen blushed. "Guilty as charged. And if I ever sound the least bit patronizing, give me a good, sound thrashing, will you?"

They all laughed. "Hardly," said Connor. "But you can take it as a given that we know some of what Gwendolyn believed, and she taught me in particular to have a healthy respect for God, although it wasn't the God most people learned about or talked about. Gwendolyn's supreme deity was not the Sunday school version, rife with some of the least desirable human qualities. Her God wasn't jealous, angry, judgmental, vengeful, or temperamental. Her God also wasn't encompassed by a male pronoun. She said she used 'Goddess' more frequently in private to balance the energy, but that gender wasn't even a consideration at the highest levels of understanding."

"Then she taught you well," Ellen smiled warmly. "I always suspected she had made it her job to bring you up properly, to let you know there was more to the universe than catechism and dogma."

"There was a time, to be honest, when I had rejected everything she taught me, and for that matter, I'd rejected just about every sort of spiritual belief. But then some things started happening, and I couldn't be the ostrich with my head in the sand anymore. Some things you can't explain."

Laura leaned over to fill her teacup. "I think the saying is, 'my dogma got run over by my karma.' "

Connor chuckled softly. "Yes, that's it. I used to think I was in complete control of every part of my life. Then, little by little, I found out I wasn't. Well, that's not exactly right. I mean, I believe we all have free choice, but we can't begin to understand where those choices might lead."

"And you relied a great deal on Gwendolyn to help you with that?" asked William softly.

Connor looked a little startled. "I suppose I did. More than I thought. But I realized far too late that I needed her guidance, and then she was gone."

"Can you explain that to us?" asked Ellen. "It's really bothered us dreadfully not knowing. When we heard about her death and the funeral plans, we naturally expected to hear from her."

Malcolm was the only one who looked askance when she said that, but she had a feeling he was still a bit resistant to all this "hocus-pocus." She could read those words in his mind.

"By 'hear from her,' I take it you mean connecting with her presence in the Dreamtime," promoted Laura, causing Ellen to wonder just how extensive her shamanistic training had been.

"Yes, you could put it that way. But we've heard nothing at all. Our first concern was that we had inadequately prepared a communication channel, but after repeated efforts we were even more alarmed that she had been caught in some kind of energy vortex and was trapped, unable to move in either direction."

"You mean heaven or hell?" asked Malcolm, his incredulity plain to see.

"Not exactly, Mr. Jefferson," William answered. "To us there is no 'hell' such as you may have been taught. There is only the Darkness and the Light. For those like us, the only approximation of hell would be if we were plunged into Darkness, if we were deprived of the pure Light of Divinity."

"But what exactly do you people *do*?" he persisted. "And what does all this have to do with the things that have been happening here: the murders, the burglary, the little creep who got into the house and snatched Mrs. Broadhurst's message?" Malcolm's anger was palpable.

"Something of Gwendolyn's was stolen?" William asked sharply.

"More than one thing," Connor answered, closing her eyes for a moment. "Someone rifled through the library and took some documents about family history and about ancient religious practices, at least that's what I think they were. And just today someone diverted our attention long enough to snatch a note that Gwendolyn had left for me hidden in the binding of a book."

Ellen almost felt faint. Dear God, what had they done? Not taking even the most basic precautions. But she kept herself from blurting out her annoyance. Recriminations were pointless. She a took a long, centering breath to maintain control of her rampaging emotions.

"But what was stolen today won't do anyone any good," said Connor.

"What do you mean?" Ellen retorted. "There could be irreparable damage done by the others."

"Because the message was something only I would understand, sort of a like a personal code. The clue may have been lost, but I still solved the puzzle." She smiled at her friends. "At least the first part. Then I had some very competent advice at the end of the search."

"And what was it?" Ellen barely dared to ask.

"We'll get to that," said Connor firmly. "First, please finish telling me about Gwendolyn's role in your group or whatever you call it? Then we'll share what we've learned."

Ellen knew she'd met her match in Connor. This was no shrinking violet willing to be victimized. "All right then. Gwendolyn held the position of leadership in our circle. She was the equivalent of what you might call a high priestess. She was, or is, one of the greatest adepts ever to appear in England, or in the world. It was her task and her commitment to lead us all in 'missions,' if you will, both on this plane and in the astral, to counteract the insurgent Darkness in so many places in our world. You may think of it in terms of battle. I know it sounds a bit melodramatic, but we don't see it that way. It's a job we're born to do, lifetime after lifetime. In this case, Gwendolyn's illness took her from us long before she would have become too old to carry out her responsibilities. Though I don't suppose that's a coincidence either. Still, we feel a little lost without the guidance of our Mistress Gwendolyn. Still she often assured us that..."

"She assured you that what?" asked Connor, her face darkening slightly.

Ellen fought her way past a mountain of indecision. Was this what Gwendolyn would want her to say? Was this her proper job? Or should it be left to fate? She felt for the gentle old voice in her mind, but could not hear Gwendolyn. Ellen would have to take this plunge herself or withdraw altogether.

"She assured us that you would take her place when the time came."

Connor looked stricken at the news, then grew increasingly angry. "You mean take her place *here*, spend all my time sitting around in a circle, chanting and performing rituals? You can't be serious. Even if I believe that what you say is true, Gwendolyn's made it clear I have a choice in the matter."

In that instant Ellen knew that Gwendolyn had been right. This woman was the natural heir. Even in the throes of rejecting the faith, Connor was strong and forceful. This was the type of woman they needed, the sort of human being who never backed down once she'd taken a stand. Ellen felt extremely grateful that Connor's principles would never allow her to abandon the task Gwendolyn must have set her.

"I don't believe Gwendolyn intended you to devote your *life* to us and the work we do. Instead I believe she left this plane, somehow or other...and I hope you'll tell us about that...because she knew she wasn't strong enough to stand against whatever this current threat might be. William and I know something is going on, but we can't pin down what it is or put a face to the disruptions we feel in the spiritual balance. Yet the disruption is strong and very real."

"The body you found in your library was real enough," said Benjamin, so quietly that at first Ellen didn't know if she'd heard him at all. She shuddered at the thought of that young girl's headless body.

"Yes, it was. Along with the desecration of Gwendolyn's grave and the murder of a policeman at Haslemere."

"Haslemere," Benjamin echoed. "What has that got to do with this situation?"

William held up one hand and began ticking off items on his fingers. "First, the grave diggers are murdered and one of them turns out to have been employed at odd jobs at Haslemere. Second, the body of Patricia Frome turns up in our library. Third, Gillian Fenwycke, mistress of Haslemere, was having an, er, relationship with Miss Frome."

Ellen noticed that he blushed slightly and remembered what a prude her dear husband could be. He'd never quite gotten used to the idea that people nowadays talked about sex as carelessly as they discussed the weather.

"And, fourth," William concluded, "the policeman who was killed sometime last night was found this morning just on the edge of the grounds at Haslemere. He'd been detailed to surveil some activities on the property, which not so incidentally are connected to our friend, Mr. Thackeray. And, saving the worst news for last, when they found the man's body, his hands had been removed."

Ellen watched them all carefully. Benjamin's expression was somber and thoughtful. Connor looked stunned. Laura was more concerned with Connor's reaction than her own. And Malcolm looked angry, something she would have expected from a man who would feel a great deal of empathy for a fellow officer killed in the line of duty.

Benjamin finally spoke. "It's pretty horrible that the man was mutilated, but you still haven't explained how these events are connected in a substantive way. Simply because this Haslemere place plays a role in most of them..."

"There's more to it than that," Ellen assured him.

"And what is the 'more' then?" he frowned.

Ellen started to answer, and changed her mind. She decided this information-sharing game needed to be conducted on an alternating basis. Plus, she wanted to firm up her evaluations of these people. Could they or could they not do whatever would be required of them?

"First I'd like to know one thing: Where is Gwendolyn?"

For the next few minutes, the four Americans did an admirable job of trying to answer Ellen's question. The only difficulty lay in that none of them knew her actual current location, if that word even applied in the nonphysical realms. But they did explain briefly what had transpired on the Navajo reservation, how close Laura and Connor had come to dying, how Malcolm had been guided to show up at the right place at the right time despite being in the middle of a vast desert, and how Gwendolyn had been summoned there to meet them by someone on the astral. There, the account faltered, and Ellen decided that they weren't quite ready or able to explain the rest.

"All right, very well," she said. "Now it's my turn."

"You've mentioned that Gwendolyn often spoke of her heritage. She didn't mean, at least not precisely, her physical, that is to say, genetic heritage. She was speaking more of her spiritual heritage, of a series of incarnations that brought her here to this place at this time. She also believed that you, Connor, were the reincarnation of someone in particular. But she was never willing to share that with us. She said it might someday bring too much pressure to bear on you to fill a role you might not want."

"I know that feeling," said Connor. "With all the weird things that have been happening lately. Then there was the letter from Gwendolyn, and the—"

"Wait, you mentioned that before. What letter?" Ellen interrupted.

"One I received by way of her solicitor. But I hadn't opened it. I only read it today as a matter of fact."

Once again, Ellen fought to swallow her impatience. She couldn't imagine not rushing to open any sort of missive that their beloved Gwendolyn had left behind. But then she silently chided herself for judging the girl. Maybe Connor had simply had enough of mourning her lost loved ones.

"Did she explain everything to you?"

"I can't honestly say she explained anything to me, at least not completely or in a way I could completely grasp."

Ellen valiantly attempted to disguise her disappointment. "I'd hoped—"

"You can read it for yourself," Connor said abruptly, leaning forward in her chair and reaching into her pocket.

She hesitated only an instant before handing the envelope to Ellen, who positioned her chair so that William could read over her shoulder. They quickly read through the long letter, with only the sounds of clinking teaspoons punctuating the silence. Finally she folded it up, stood, and returned it to Connor. She looked at Gwendolyn's granddaughter for a long time.

"I can see why you don't understand what she was talking about. She purposefully kept it vague. But I think we can shed a little more light on it."

Ellen returned to her seat and William to his. They sat there side by side, and Ellen wondered if she were doing the right thing, speaking of secrets that had been guarded by so few for so long.

"As mistress of our circle, Gwendolyn was in possession of certain knowledge that could not, for safety's sake, be shared with anyone else in the group. The information had been passed to her by Althea Carruthers, the former mistress of the circle, although she made her transition long before William and I were born."

Benjamin cleared his throat. "Wasn't Althea Carruthers a relative of Gwendolyn's?" he asked.

"Why, yes," Ellen responded. "But I'm surprised you would know that."

"Genealogy's been a hobby of mine over the years. I did a little research of the family tree."

"Hmm," said Ellen, masking the skepticism she felt. She doubted there was anything Benjamin Hawthorne did that was without a specific purpose. He was a man whose mind never stopped analyzing everything that went on around him. She sense that research was a firm habit, not a hobby, and one that must have served him well in his less publicized activities.

"My father was acquainted with Althea," offered William. "He was the one who stepped forward to confirm that her choice of replacement was Gwendolyn Broadhurst."

"And Althea would have given the information into Gwendolyn's keeping," added Ellen.

Connor gestured impatiently. "This history lesson is all well and good, but for the sake of brevity, could we get to the point? What exactly is it that my grandmother was keeping, or protecting?"

Ellen looked at William, he at her. She closed her eyes for a moment. The unspoken communication passed between them as easily as if they had spoken aloud.

Do we have the right to disclose this, William?

I don't see that we have a choice. And we have Gwendolyn's own words. She's chosen Connor.

If only we could be absolutely certain.

Almost nothing in life is absolute, my love.

Except this commitment we share?

Except that.

Ellen opened her eyes to find the them all staring at her. Most amazing of all, though, was the expression on Connor's face. In an instant, she knew Connor had somehow heard the brief silent exchange, even if she was not quite aware of it. But it was close to her consciousness. And her next words confirmed Ellen's assessment.

"So you have my grandmother's own words to guide you. What else do you need?"

"Nothing really. It's just that secrecy has been so much a part of our lives where the circle is concerned. It has existed in some form or another for many, many centuries, though most of the records we have go only as far back as the fifth century B.C., according to the modern calendar."

"You have actual documentary historical records of this group from that long before the Christian era?" asked Connor, her disbelief plain to see.

"Yes, and some fragmentary material that is somewhat earlier, from as long as 3,000 years ago. But that's mostly indecipherable to us. Still, we keep it, guard it, not knowing when it may be of use in our work."

"And you've described your work as 'defending the faith,' I believe," said Connor. "Sounds suspiciously like the Crusades."

Ellen shook her head. "Nothing like that, I'm happy to say. No, the threats we perceive and respond to are almost entirely on the astral planes. Surely you've heard about the groups that formed and combined efforts during World War II."

Benjamin was the first to nod his agreement. "I've seen reports on it, classified reports. There was some serious speculation that the groups around that time, especially ones involved with Dion Fortune, were actually the reason the Nazis were never able to occupy Britain."

"And I imagine you found that fairly amusing, did you not?" said William. "That a bunch of loonies might actually have contributed to the war effort?"

"Well, yes. I did have my doubts about it. But on the other hand, there were reports from some respected intelligence gathering organizations that more or less admitted the possibility."

"Our circle is one that was in existence then," said Ellen. "Once upon a time, Dion Fortune joined us quite briefly. Not that I'm old enough to remember it myself, but William's father spoke of it from time to time."

Laura sat beside Gwendolyn's granddaughter on one of the brocaded loveseats and laid her hand across Connor's. "I think what we need to focus on," she said quietly, "is what Connor is supposed to do now. And what exactly is the threat that your circle perceives?"

Ellen turned to her husband. "William, you know this part of our history rather better than I do. Perhaps you should explain."

He nodded and spoke without hesitation. "You've all heard many of the stories associated with this area. The county is probably best known to tourists for the town of Glastonbury and the Tor."

Ellen noted Laura's hand tighten perceptibly where she gripped Connor's, and a sensation prickled at the back of her neck, but she didn't interrupt her husband.

"The historical aspects are interspersed with hearsay, legend, myths and so forth. And you already know, of course, that Glastonbury was also once referred to as the Isle of Avalon." Ellen could see that William's audience was growing impatient. They knew all this.

Cut to the chase, darling. They're ready to hear this.

"And almost every schoolchild has, at some time or another, heard the legend of King Arthur and the Knights of the Round Table, and of course, about the sword, Excalibur, which was reputed to be the source of Arthur's power and strength."

"The sword in the stone," suggested Malcolm, and Ellen read in him a fascination with all things chivalrous and gallant. He would have been an extraordinary knight, she thought. Perhaps he had been just that.

William nodded at Malcolm. "Yes, that was part of the legend."

"But you're calling it a legend too. As far as I know, that means it isn't actually true. It's some sort of story that's been embellished over time."

William shrugged. "I say 'legend,' because there's no doubt that parts of the story were fabricated by historians and poets and minstrels and various politically motivated individuals throughout history. And many prominent scholars have decided there is little or no fact to the story."

"You're saying they're wrong?" asked Malcolm.

"Yes, I am. Arthur did exist, and so did Guinevere. There was indeed an association of knights, but they were more likely the part of the society which gave birth to the Knights Templar of later centuries. But, anyway, to get back to Excalibur, this is what we and our predecessors have kept to ourselves for so many centuries—the heart of Arthur's kingdom was not the magic of the sword he wielded. Yes, it was a powerful and magical tool given to him at a time when the land was rife with violence and discord. He was given the sword as a talisman, an symbol upon which the warring factions could fix their attention and allegiance. But it wasn't the power source itself."

"Wasn't there something about the scabbard?" volunteered Benjamin. "That it had curative powers of some sort?"

Just as William opened his mouth to respond, Connor's voice sliced through the room, even though she'd spoken barely above a whisper. "It was the sword belt, and it wasn't Arthur's—it was Guinevere's."

A profound silence had fallen over the six people sitting in the drawing room at Rosewood House as if no one dared breach it. Thus it was a full minute before Ellen managed to say anything at all.

"How do you know that?" she asked more sharply than she'd intended. But the young woman's words had come as a distinct shock.

When Connor looked at Ellen, she seemed to be attempting to focus from a great distance. "Because I saw it, I saw the belt that she once wore. She gave it to Arthur."

"And do you know why she possessed it in the first place? Who gave it to her?"

Connor's eyes closed. "It was a gift, a powerful talisman from the gods," she said in a voice not quite her own.

"A gift from a guardian spirit to be more precise," corrected Ellen. "Though at the time the belt first appeared in the world, those who received it would have believed it to be a gift from their pantheon of gods or creators. Arthur and Guinevere inherited it because they were meant to use its power to join the old religions with the new, with the teachings of the one they called Jesus."

"Yes," said Connor. "That was the gift."

Ellen saw that Laura was aware of Connor's unease. The young woman had begun rubbing Connor's hands between her own. Catching Laura's eye, Ellen smiled to reassure her. "It's all right," she said. "Connor is making some connections at a superconscious level, but she's in no danger."

"I'm counting on you being right," Laura frowned. "I don't think I know how to cope with what's been happening, with what happened on the Tor."

"What happened on the Tor?" asked William, and Ellen heard the underlying alarm in his voice.

Laura shook her head. "Let's not talk about it right this minute. We'll explain that when you're done. I don't understand what you meant about the teachings of Jesus. What has Jesus to do with medieval Britain?"

"Quite a lot actually. He visited here when he was young and studied with the Druids and the followers of the old Goddess faith. Joseph brought him, the one later known as Joseph of Arimathea."

"So you're saying this object was a source of power, and that it was intended to draw the followers of both Christianity and non-Christian religions. Seems unlikely to me."

William intervened. "I understand your skepticism, and I could cite a wealth of historical material available right in Glastonbury that would eventually help you see the entire picture of the times. You'll recall that it was Arthur who tried to bridge the gap between the old religion and the new until he was seduced by the newly powerful class of bishops and priests who demanded his allegiance to Christianity."

"But wasn't he forever sending people out looking for the Holy Grail?" asked Laura.

"He knew the Grail was within the borders of his kingdom, brought by Joseph on his last trip to Britain, and since Arthur had lost faith in the talisman of the Light beings, he believed that only the Cup could preserve his reign. But the talisman is the object of which we speak. It was the crystal and gold belt once given to Guinevere. It has its origins much, much further back, and it is an object of great value—not intrinsic value, mind you—although its historical significance would probably fetch a staggering price at Sotheby's. But for our purposes, its value lies in its power. And our circle has been entrusted with keeping its whereabouts secret for more than a dozen centuries."

"Why keep it hidden?" asked Malcolm. "Why not lock it up in a museum under guard, with high-tech alarm systems?"

"Because that would not keep it safe. Those who understand its power would stop at nothing to procure it, and the belt itself actually emanates power when it is out in the world, so to speak, a power so profoundly potent that it cannot simply exist without someone to control it and direct it."

"I thought this was something the 'good guys' used," asserted Malcolm, crooking his fingers around the words.

"Ah, yes, Mr. Jefferson. That is the crux of the matter, isn't it? What is good and what is evil?"

"I think I'm pretty clear on that," he bristled. "I know because it's my job to know."

William smiled. "And I imagine you do your job exceedingly well, rather better I suppose than the ones trying to solve Miss Frome's murder. But you see—and this is harder to explain—there's a bigger picture here and it has to do with some rather confusing concepts with which Ellen and I still struggle, even though we've been studying and learning for a long time." He paused a moment to gather his thoughts. Ellen glanced at Connor and was relieved to see that her eyes were open, and she was listening to the conversation.

"In our everyday world there are always two opposites—good and evil, up and down, love and fear, Light and Dark, and on and on. You see, we live in duality. That's how human life is supposed to be. But if you think about it, or at least if you look at it the way *we* choose to, at the level of consciousness where only God exists in pure divinity, there *is* no duality. God is only good. God created everything, thus everything is God. Even the bad guys."

Malcolm shook his head, and Ellen could tell from his mulish expression that he wasn't going to buy this metaphysical theory, especially since William was trying to do it all in shorthand to save time.

"Mr. Jefferson, I know this seems implausible to you, but could you just bear with us for a while, and when there's more time, we can sit down and discuss it at length. Believe me, I don't want to try to convince you of anything that's uncomfortable for you, and I'm not trying to undermine your faith and your beliefs. But this is the only way we can explain what's going on. So, could we have a theological truce?"

Malcolm sighed. "Okay. I'll agree, but only for Connor's sake. I doubt you'll ever be able to convince me that there's any sign of God in the scumbags that cops usually deal with every hour of the day."

She smiled. "Believe me, I do understand what you're saying. This was hard for me too. But please let William finish, and then we'll go from there."

The big cop fell silent, but Ellen still felt his disapproval from across the room. She let it pass over her. Whatever role the man was intended to play would become clear soon enough. And she sensed that his loyalty to Connor and Benjamin and Laura was absolute, no matter what his personal beliefs. That could be a great boon to them in the days to come.

William waited until his wife had mediated the disagreement, and then went on briskly, as if trying to fit in as many words as possible in a short amount of time.

"So, if you accept that there is such a phenomenon as raw, undifferentiated power, the sort perhaps that created this entire universe and everything in it, then you can see that such a power can be turned to any use, for good or evil as we perceive it."

"But surely," said Laura, "some objects or talismans exist purely to augment the power of one or the other."

William smiled. "A hopeful view. And in some instances, it may be true. But only in the dual world. Take the Grail for example. It is said that Joseph brought the Lord's cup from the Last Supper to England and hid it right here in this area. There are those who believe that the Grail is the ultimate symbol of pure goodness. That is why Arthur became obsessed with finding it, to the exclusion of all other concerns, and to the exclusion of his wife, Guinevere, a powerful and wise priestess, from his decisions. And yet I will tell you that without the existence of opposing symbols of Darkness, neither the Grail nor even the talisman of which we speak would have any power at all."

As far as Ellen could tell, Connor was the first of the four to grasp what she and William were trying (she thought somewhat badly) to explain. "You're saying," Connor nodded, "that without one, there cannot be the other, which makes perfect sense to me for some reason. But this belt...whose was it before it was Guinevere's, by the way?"

William exhaled. "That, you see, is the crux of the matter. The documents we have, which predate Guinevere and Arthur by a fair margin, still don't give us the full story of the belt. But it is referred to obliquely, and there are those few ancient scraps of manuscript and copies of markings from stones that give us a few clues."

"Such as?" she asked. Ellen saw that Connor was completely in control of herself now, but there was something added, a certain edge to her voice, an overtone or an echo oddly incompatible with her basic personality. Or was it? The question gave Ellen pause. Under any other circumstances, she would have called a halt to the discussion and gone into meditation to discover what was happening with Connor. But there was no time for caution.

"One of the few pieces we've deciphered is that the belt was originally given to the priestess Cerydwynn more than three millennia ago by one of the Light beings of the cosmos."

"Light beings?"

"Some people think of them as angels."

Connor frowned. "So an angel gave this Cerydwynn the belt. I have to tell you this is getting a little far-fetched. I have this image of Della Reese visiting some Celtic priestess and telling her to get her priestess act together."

Ellen laughed out loud. "I adore that show, and to be quite honest, I have no idea what angels really do look like. But we have theorized that the particular angel in our story was—and is, of course—one of the archangels. We think of them as upper management in the divine realm."

"Which archangel?"

"Rafael or Michael. We're not sure."

"So where was this belt for 1500 years or so, perhaps more, between the time this Cerydwynn got hold of it and Guinevere ended up with it?"

"Well," William continued, unable to fully disguise his discomfort. "It was lost for a time, until it was recovered by the priestess eventually known in literature as the Lady of the Lake, from a time long ago when the Isle of Avalon truly was surrounded by water, or at least could be made to appear as if it were."

"I'm not even going to tackle that last part of it, but why would this Cerydwynn ever give up a gift from an archangel?" Connor insisted. "I'd think she'd have passed it along to her successor when the time came and so on and so forth. I imagine such an object, if it possesses half the 'power' you claim would have protected her and her tribe or civilization, or whatever. But from what you've said, there aren't any records of her people having survived."

"No, other than what we have, there aren't. It's as if Cerydwynn's people were wiped from the face of the earth. And only legend and mystery remain."

"Why?"

"Because Cerydwyyn was betrayed by her closest allies, and the belt was taken from her. From that day, until the time of the Lady of the Lake, we don't know exactly what happened to it. But we do know that great harm came to the followers of Cerydwynn. Within a relatively short time, they were all dead, and there was talk of a strange plague, which then moved across the continents in a wave of sickness and terror."

"And what became of the priestess herself?"

William paused, and Ellen knew how difficult this was for him. His sight in matters of the past was stronger than hers. He'd seen bits and pieces that left him shaken. But he'd told her the truth, and now she felt it was incumbent upon her to share it with Connor.

"Cerydwynn died on what is now called Glastonbury Tor. She was surrounded by enemies, and even the power of the angel's gift could not save her."

"How did she die?" asked Connor in a soft, yet insistent, voice.

"She was beheaded and...and mutilated."

"How?"

"Her hands were removed, we think because those who killed her believed she could thus be prevented from using her power in the afterlife. For the same reason, her head was placed in a wooden container with stones and sunk at sea. Without her hands to work and her eyes to see, she would be forever powerless."

The old clock in the hall ticked relentlessly. As if hypnotized by the sound, no one spoke. Ellen was about to stir herself to ask if they should turn on the lamps against the growing darkness when Connor's voice brought her up short. It was unexpectedly loud and tinged with hysteria.

"That's who I'm supposed to be, isn't it? The great priestess

Cerydwynn. That's why it happened. I was there, on the Tor; I saw the people moving up the hill, I felt the disruption in the energy field around me. And I looked down at the gold links and discs of metal, and the crystals, all shining up at me in the torchlight and...I looked down and I saw..."

She didn't finish the sentence. Connor had fainted.

Chapter Twenty-Six

Integrity without knowledge is weak and useless;
knowledge without integrity is dangerous and dreadful.
—Samuel Johnson
Rasselas

When Nicholas Foulsham arrived at the cottage in Glastonbury, Gillian Fenwycke was gone, not just temporarily but permanently, the landlord informed him. "Not so much as a 'by your leave,' " the old man grumbled. "Left in the night. Was booked for a fortnight, possibly more, said her ladyship."

"She left early then?" said Foulsham. "Did she not pay you for the full time?"

"Yes, she paid me in advance. Still, me and the missus don't hold with guests sneakin' out like, in the middle of the night besides. This is a respectable place."

"What time was it she left, do you recall?"

"T'was half three in the morning. Sound of the car along the gravel in the drive's what woke me. Came near to calling the police, I did, thinkin' it might be burglars."

Foulsham doubted that thieves would announce their presence by casually motoring up the gravel drive, but he kept his observations to himself lest he alienate his only witness to the time of Lady Fenwycke's departure.

"Did you happen to notice if anyone was with her?" he asked.

The old man, whom Foulsham rightly judged to be in his eighties, gawped at him. "I told you t'were the middle of the night. Meanin' it were dark out. And with them black windows on the car, how would I know if her ladyship was drivin' alone or not?"

Foulsham sighed, trying to keep his tone patient and courteous. "Perhaps she had visitors last evening?"

"Just the one as we've seen hangin' about a time or two."

"And which one would that be, Mr. Tuggle?"

"Not as if we was introduced," he snorted. "The tall, dark-haired bloke with the fancy car."

Foulsham was sure the man was referring to Thackeray, but he hadn't a picture to show for confirmation. Not that it mattered, at least not yet, not until he had enough evidence to charge the man with murder and the woman as an accessory. He didn't believe for a moment that she hadn't known what was going on at Haslemere.

"And what time did he leave?"

Tuggle shrugged dramatically. "Can't say. Musta been during the news program since I can't see the drive from the lounge."

Foulsham sighed. Another veritable fountain of useful information. "Mind if I have a look in the cottage?" he suggested as casually as he could. With Gillian Fenwycke permanently departed, he would be on firm ground in searching the Tuggle's property with their consent.

"She took all her things," said Tuggle.

"Still, if you wouldn't mind. Just take a few minutes."

"Well, if you're so set on it, though I can't imagine what for." Inspiration slowly dawned on his craggy features, his scowl rearranging itself into a leer of curiosity, something Foulsham saw time and again in those who began to scent a scandal brewing. "This something to do with that body what was found at Lord Carlisle's house? The one with no head on it?"

Foulsham felt a shudder of anger run through him and resisted the urge to shout in the old man's face, "That 'body' was a girl named Patricia, you stupid old fool!" Instead, he lowered his voice. "I had a few more questions for Lady Fenwycke regarding the timing of events at the party where the crime was discovered. It happens that she was among the first to see the, er, deceased."

"If it's questions you've got, why go lookin' about the cottage? Told you she's left."

The shrewdness of the man's question threw Foulsham off for an instant. He'd been lulled into thinking the fellow wasn't all that bright or at least preoccupied with his own troubles.

"Lady Fenwycke assured me she had made some notes in her day-book about potential witnesses, said I could come by for the information, and it occurred to me she might have left it behind for me." He knew the excuse was as feeble as they came, but there was a chance an elderly complainer like Tuggle would accept it at face value. Apparently, he did.

"I don't have time to be givin' tours of the place," he grunted, scratching at his scraggly white beard. "Mind you, the place is still paid for, and I reckon if her ladyship left anything behind that the missus didn't see, well, it better be left where it is. I won't be accused of theft and have my character took away, you understand."

"Of course, Mr. Tuggle," Foulsham assured him hastily. "If there's anything at all that I think was left for me, I'd be happy to give you a receipt for it. Now, if I could just have the key, I won't trouble you to show me around."

"Key, what key?" Tuggle erupted. "Took the bloody key and all, didn't she? The gentry don't take no notice of inconveniencing working people, do they? Left the door open so's anyone could walk right in, then took the only key. Have to have another one made, and keys like that don't come cheap, now do they?"

Foulsham backed away from the tirade and made his way around the owner's house to the dirt car park overlooked by Gillian Fenwycke's rental cottage. As Tuggle had promised, the door was unlocked and he noted with some annoyance that the lock was of the plain, old-fashioned type that could be opened with a skeleton key. No doubt Tuggle would find one in his own house that would fit.

The cottage felt empty, and other than the original furnishings, it was. The lounge was untidy, littered with newspapers and glasses. In the kitchen, dishes lay in the sink under a steady drip from the cold water tap. Foulsham stood in the silence for a moment, then mounted the stairs to the bedroom. The sheets were in disarray, but Foulsham had no desire to inspect them closely enough to determine why. He could guess easily enough. One by one, he opened the drawers in the old dresser, the doors of the armoire, and the cupboards. Towels were strewn over the floor of the bathroom, but there was no sign of any personal items. Fenwycke's keen sense of smell detected the lingering scent of the perfume Gillian Fenwycke wore. It had seemed overwhelming the first time he'd interviewed her. Now there was only enough of it in the air to remind him that she'd been there.

For a moment his shoulders sagged and he scrubbed at his face with both hands. Foulsham hated to admit that he was lost, but he could think of no other way to describe the sensation. There were pieces floating around him in a maelstrom of confusion and lies, and nothing he could take hold of, nothing on which he could build a case against anyone. For all his determination, his comforting self-delusion of clapping the malefactors in irons, there wasn't one tangible shred of indisputable evidence he could use. For that matter, there was little that could be described as strongly circumstantial. He had only Gerald Fenwycke's word that Thackeray was using the outbuildings, that and an odd anonymous tip that had convinced him Garrett's surveillance would yield results. When you looked at the case objectively, all he really had were suggestive bits and pieces swirling around in the ether; he had his absurd hunches, his innate mistrust of Conrad Thackeray, his contempt for Gillian and Gerald Fenwycke, his conviction that something much worse was going on than he could possibly imagine, and he had the images he couldn't get out of his head—Peter Garrett's bloody face and butchered stumps, Patricia Frome's decapitated body, two harmless village ne'er-do-wells lying in someone else's grave.

If he didn't come up with something, they'd replace him with someone whom he knew, without any egotism at all, wouldn't get any further. The cases would never be solved, and Nicholas Foulsham could not bear that. Another man might have been worried about the state of his professional career. For reasons he could not have explained in words, DCI Foulsham was much more worried about the state of his soul.

$\mathcal{W}$

While the police scraped the ground around the outbuildings at Haslemere, with a view to finding something that would justify their presence, and explain the murder of Sergeant Peter Garrett, the man suspected as somehow being involved in it was rapidly turning into a raving lunatic. Conrad Thackeray, soon to be under the intense scrutiny of the authorities, and beset by the grotesque little man who was there dogging his steps every time he turned around, felt his self-control ebbing away as surely as if it had been a slippery rope running through his hands. At the moment, he didn't even feel safe in his own office.

"What do you mean, you don't *know?*" he screamed at his security chief, spraying the man with spittle. "How can a man be murdered, and have his hands cut off, not 500 yards from where your stupid fucking guards are stationed, and you don't know anything about it."

"But, sir—"

"Don't even say a fucking word!" he shouted. "My sources have already told me this dead copper was on an assignment. And what was the assignment? He was watching your men, you bloody goddamn moron, yes, *watching,* doing *surveillance,* taking registration numbers, probably taking fucking *pictures* for all you know. And not one of your low-life thugs even noticed him."

The security chief opened his mouth, hesitated, then spoke in defense of his security force. "We couldn't have known he was there. Our sources on the police force didn't know either."

"Didn't know...didn't know. Is that all you have to say for yourself? And what about that stupid maneuver in Washington? As if it wasn't bad enough that you left two dead bodies in the grave in St. Giles instead of covering it up, then you send a complete buggering idiot to try and strong-arm a fucking U.S. senator. How smart is that?"

"He's an *ex*-senator. And you know we always respond to any intrusions into our databases. He was—"

"An *ex*-senator. Oh, that's rich, that is. Also an *ex*-presidential advisor, *ex*-intelligence officer, *ex*-counterintelligence specialist. Man's a goddamn fucking spymaster right out of some bloody James Bond movie, and you send someone with a peashooter to tell him go away and play like a good boy." Conrad grabbed hold of the man's lapels. "What I said goes. You're a complete fucking moron!"

Conrad shoved him away and began striding back and forth, slamming pieces of furniture as he went. A Chinese porcelain vase crashed to the ground, and he kicked the pieces of it in the direction of his victim. "You see that," he roared. "Cost fucking 10,000 pounds, it did, and that's nothing compared to what your stupid, bloody mistakes are going to cost me. I ought to shove the pieces up your goddamn arse!"

The security chief blinked rapidly for several seconds, his face a frozen mask of fury. Then he reached for the security badge he wore on his tailored blazer and yanked it off. Finally, he bent down and picked up the largest shard of porcelain. "Tell you what, *Conrad*," he said, using his employer's name for the first time in his tenure as chief, "why don't you shove it up *your* bloody arse!" He slammed the piece down on the massive mahogany desk, and shoved it toward Thackeray, leaving a long, jagged scar across the polished wooden top. He flung the badge at Thackeray's face and stalked out of the office.

W

An hour later Conrad sat motionless in his comfortable executive chair where he'd virtually collapsed when the security chief left. "Under control," he muttered, "got to stay under control, got to figure this out." But what was there really to figure out? The police already knew about his involvement with as-yet-unspecified activities at Haslemere. He was sure Gerald had been more than eager to share that little tidbit. He'd hoped Gillian would firmly deny it, and make Gerald look the fool that he was, but she was nowhere to be found. Probably legged it to Spain by now, he thought bitterly. Why had he ever bothered with the stupid bitch? No loyalty there now that his enterprise stood on shaky ground.

He breathed deeply, over and over. *Yes, that's better. Calm yourself. All is not lost. You've got resources.* And he did. With business interests all over the globe, the loss of his British base of operations would hardly do more than inconvenience him in the short term. So why had he gotten so angry? He never got visibly angry. He simply got even. He'd sliced up an enemy when he was only twelve and gotten away with it. This...why, this was nothing. He'd had nothing to do with the policeman, but why was the man there in the first place? Who'd talked? Who'd leaked information?

No, it didn't matter now. He'd have to get out of England until the publicity died down. Maybe he'd never be able to come back, which didn't matter, did it? He kicked the wastebasket. Bloody hell! This was his home! He was Sir Conrad Thackeray, confidante to prime ministers and members of parliament, immune to the speculations of plodding coppers. But not anymore perhaps. And now, more than anything, he wanted to find out what bastard son of a whore had done this to him.

With a sense of being dragged against his will, Conrad stood up and walked to the window, looking down on the London he'd grown to think of as his personal playground. There, amidst the rush of traffic, the knots of hurrying pedestrians, the din of a frenetic city that pulsed with life...the little man stood grinning up at him.

Conrad shut his eyes and beat his fists against the sealed, unbreakable glass. But no one out there could hear him.

Chapter Twenty-Seven

What if earth
Be but the shadow of Heaven, and things therein
Each to other like, more than on earth is thought.
—John Milton
Paradise Lost

"Good God, what's happened?" cried William Carlisle, leaping to his feet to lend aid to Gwendolyn's granddaughter, who had crumpled in her seat as if all the starch had gone out of her. His good intentions were thwarted by the headlong rush of Malcolm and Benjamin, and he collided with them in the middle of the room. William stepped back, and the other two men followed suit. Laura ignored them as she grabbed her lover's arm to keep Connor from sliding off the settee. As if by unspoken agreement, the three men retreated several paces.

Laura stroked her cheek. "Connor, sweetheart, are you there? Can you hear my voice?"

At first there was no response, and Laura felt twinges of panic. She fought them down. This was hardly the time to give in to fear, not when Connor needed just the opposite. She took Connor's hand in her own and squeezed it gently, then raised it to her lips and kissed the tips of the fingers softly. "Connor, come back to us, please. Come back. There's nothing to be afraid of now. I'm here." Connor's eyelids fluttered briefly, giving Laura some hope that her words might be filtering through whatever mental defenses had closed down around Connor's mind.

Laura felt a light touch on her shoulder, and looked up into Ellen's dark eyes. "She hasn't gone far, you know," said Ellen softly. "She's assimilating so much, and it's difficult for her conscious mind to comprehend. This, I think, is just a brief retreat, from the truth."

"But what *is* the truth?" Laura snapped at her, making a valiant effort not to shout the question at the top of her lungs. "She isn't the type to faint. Believe me, I know. She's been through things you can't begin to imagine."

Ellen's mouth curved up at the corners. "I think perhaps you do me an injustice in that regard, Miss Nez, for there are many things I cannot only imagine, but have seen with my own eyes, or through the eyes of others. Let me assure you that I am not trying to diminish in any way what your companion is going through. If anything, it is more fearful than you already suspect."

"And the truth?"

"I doubt I could explain it all to you, and right now isn't the best time for it. We can't be sure of what her consciousness is able to hear and understand. For the moment, she should have a lie-down in a quiet room."

"I'm not leaving her," Laura asserted fiercely. "Not for a minute."

"Nor should you," said Ellen. "She needs you more than anyone. And not simply because you love each other. There's much more to it, which," she said, raising a hand to ward off the question on Laura's lips, "we will get to as soon as possible. But that is a part of the story that Connor must hear too."

She reached out and placed her hand on Connor's brow. Within seconds the pained scowl on the young woman's face relaxed.

"What are you doing?" Laura asked at once.

"Simply easing her fear. I'm giving her images to replace the ones that shocked her psychically. That's what it is, you know. Some shocks are physical, some mental, this one is psychic." After a minute or two, Ellen took her hand away. "I think you'll find that she will be able to walk with you upstairs and will be amenable to the suggestion of resting."

Laura looked at Connor skeptically but saw that her lover's face was now peaceful. "Sweetheart," she said in a low voice, reaching for her lover's arm. "Why don't you come with me?"

Much to her surprise, Connor stood up immediately, opened her eyes, and moved toward the door. Laura linked her arm through Connor's, and together they left the room.

Benjamin was at Ellen's side in an instant. "I think it's time you were entirely honest with us about what you know, or even what you suspect, is happening here. If you think I'm going to accept vague New Age theories and half-baked answers when my daughter's well-being is in jeopardy, then you don't know me very well."

"All right, Senator, let's talk turkey, as you Americans say."

W

Laura eased down on the bed beside Connor and propped herself up on one elbow so that she could keep watch. The way things were going, even a change of expression on her face might mean something. She reached out and stroked Connor's cheek, brushed back a lock of hair that lay across her forehead.

"Oh, my sweet love, what's happening to you? I can't bear the thought of you being hurt or being afraid for your life. Not again, not after everything that's happened. I can't lose you just when I've finally found you."

Laura couldn't stop the tears that trickled down her cheeks, and she didn't try. Her Grandmother Klah had always told her that some tears were meant to be shed, and holding them in didn't do anyone any good. But Laura had always fought the impulse, just as she knew Connor had done. Both of them had worked for years in a "man's world," where tears, however justified, would always be a target of ridicule from those who were too afraid of emotion to dare understand it.

Moving closer, Laura put her head on the pillow next to Connor's, one arm across Connor's waist, and the other arm she slid beneath her neck, holding her in a safe embrace. She'd always heard that talking to people in a coma was a good idea—because they could hear you even if they gave no outer sign. This wasn't a coma exactly, but even with all she'd seen in the world, Laura was hard-pressed to put a name to it. Catatonia? No, that didn't fit. Connor was vaguely responsive, after all, and able to move. Though since she'd laid down on the bed, she hadn't stirred at all. Still, talking couldn't hurt, could it?

She lay there in the half-light, whispering softly in her lover's ear, nothing earth-shatteringly profound, nothing perhaps worth quoting in one's memoirs, but simply thoughts that came straight from her heart, formed into words that tried in all their inadequacy to express the love she felt for the woman who lay in her arms. She could not have known, of course, that the murmured words of love and hope were actually less important than the feelings from which they were born. Laura's fierce and uncompromising love was weaving the words into a strong silken thread to which Connor's heart and mind were desperately clinging.

$\mathcal{W}$

"Is it true?" asked Benjamin. "Is my daughter supposed to be some reincarnation of a 3,000-year-old priestess whom we don't even know existed?"

"Oh, she existed, all right. And even if I'm not entirely convinced that Connor is she, it's obvious that Gwendolyn was sure." Ellen tapped the letter which now lay on the side table. "I never knew the woman to jump to any conclusion whatsoever. If anything she was more cautious than any member of the circle, sometimes to the point of making the rest of us somewhat impatient. She would not have written this to her granddaughter if she'd had the least doubt."

Malcolm stirred in his chair. "You keep talking about this circle. Who exactly is involved? And what about these 'others' you mention? I assume they're what I would think of as the 'bad guys'?"

William smiled. "Yes, I think for our purposes that would serve. But on the other hand, keep in mind that those who have chosen the Darkness, who have committed to it with their very souls, are just as convinced that they are in the right and we are the ones to be 'conquered,' shall we say. As for our circle, there would ordinarily be thirteen of us, and no, it isn't an unlucky number despite what you may have been taught. But now, of course, we are twelve without Gwendolyn."

"And why don't you promote from within?" said Malcolm wryly. "And draft a new member to fill the ranks? Why do you act as if Connor is obligated to have something to do with all this?"

"We aren't foisting any obligations on your friend," Ellen answered. "Even Gwendolyn, while carefully explaining why she hoped Connor would assume a certain degree of responsibility in the circle, did not *demand* that she do so. If you read it again, you'll see Gwendolyn is careful not to override Connor's free will. What has me worried is that before she's even had a chance to consider what the request means, she's already acting in what you have described as strange and unpredictable ways."

"This behavior then is not what you would expect?" Benjamin asked. "I'm sorry, but I'm really out of my depth here."

"I know you are, sir," said William courteously. "Your skills and talents are not unknown to me, but they are part of the physical world, the third-dimensional reality you perceive with your human senses. This playing field—and sometimes battlefield—on which we strive is completely different. The tools, the weapons, the strategies, they are all imperceptible except with the psychic senses. And to answer your question, no, this is not what we would expect."

"Do you have any idea why this is happening?"

William glanced at Ellen. "Before we try to explain, we would like to beg your indulgence for a few moments while we set up a shield around this house."

"A shield?" said Benjamin, raising an eyebrow. "You mean some sort of security device?"

"Not in the way you mean. But it works just as well," William explained. "We protect ourselves and the environment on a psychic level." He shrugged. "I know it sounds crazy, but it's highly effective.

Ellen and I will know at once if someone is trying to approach the house, physically that is. And we'll also know if anyone is attempting to interfere with any of us on a psychic level."

Benjamin and Malcolm watched the Carlisles prepare themselves. From a viewer's perspective, they simply closed their eyes and held hands. On the inner planes, Ellen and William were doing a great deal more. Drawing on the assistance of the divine force and the others of their circle who had been on almost continual standby over the past few weeks, together they constructed a dome of light that entirely covered Rosewood House. Invisible to the naked eye, it was a solid energy field controlled by the sheer will of William and Ellen. Anyone passing through it would be detected as quickly as if he'd broken the beam of an electric eye, or been caught on a security camera. But as William had explained, the field was also intended to identify and lock out more subtle intruders, those who would launch a foray via the astral planes.

Before returning his awareness to the drawing room of Rosewood House, William looked around him with some satisfaction. Ranged around the perimeter of the dome were the astral bodies of their ten allies, each of them alert and ready. In the silent, entirely mental communication they all shared, he thanked them and briefly explained the events happening on the physical plane. Then, feeling Ellen's summons, he allowed himself to be drawn back into his physical body.

"Now that that's taken care of," he said, "we can answer your questions, at least as far as we are able."

Ellen spoke up. "First, though, if you could give us a brief summary of what exactly has happened to Connor since she's been here. There was some mention of an incident at the Tor. I think it would help us to untangle the puzzle if we knew."

"It seems to me we're the ones giving information here, and you're not telling us much of anything," said Malcolm.

Benjamin sighed. "I agree, my friend. But the request is not unreasonable." He looked William and then Ellen right in the eye. "But I suggest that neither of you continue to try our patience. There is just so much accommodation that either Captain Jefferson or I will prove willing to make."

"Understood," William replied.

Benjamin drew a swift but vivid picture of the night Connor had driven them all to the Tor. "She had no memory of any of it," said Benjamin. When Laura asked her about it, apparently she thought Laura was talking about the first time they'd climbed up there, when they both found themselves..."

"Found themselves what?" prodded Ellen.

"In some sort of dream or something," said Benjamin, shaking his head. "I don't pretend to understand the phenomenon they both described, but I know my daughter, and I know Laura Nez. I'd trust either of them with my life. If they say they were caught up in some kind of time warp, then I'm willing to believe."

"Did you say time warp? Do you mean they both had the sense of being in another time, or in another place?"

"The place didn't change, at least the location, although the Tor that Connor described was empty. There was no tower on it at all, whereas Laura did see the tower and was trying to get inside of it to find Connor. And according to them, they got separated initially in a downpour of rain."

Ellen sensed there was more. "And why was that part strange?"

Benjamin pursed his lips. "Because that day there *was* no rain. And when they came down the hill, they were the only ones soaking wet."

William nodded. "The connection between Connor and the distant past must be exceedingly strong to breach the veils between the dimensions of time. Had you told me she simply experienced within herself the events of another time, that would be not altogether uncommon. But you describe *physical* phenomena. That is most troubling."

Malcolm stood abruptly and shoved his hands into his pockets, "But what about last night? When she drove the car to that hill and doesn't even remember doing it? There weren't any weird manifestations, just Connor acting as if she were somewhere else entirely."

Ellen answered him. "I know you are deeply concerned over Connor's mental state, but let me assure you that she is not, how shall I put it, mentally ill, at least not in the standard sense."

"What other sense is there?" Malcolm growled, his skepticism painfully obvious to Ellen.

"Well, quite frankly, it may sometimes be difficult to tell the difference. And there are those who theorize that all mental illness is the result of being out of synch with this dimension, or is related in some way to the solidity of the individual's connection with the generally accepted view of reality."

"As in the collective hunch?" said Benjamin.

"Pardon?" Ellen queried, looking puzzled.

"Oh, sorry. It's something in a book, and a play based on the book. One of Lily Tomlin's characters refers to reality as a 'collective hunch.' I always thought there was something to that."

"Ah, I see what you mean. And that's actually a good way of looking at it. You see, most of what we think is 'real' is only a product of our perceptions, and often those perceptions are strongly shaded by the opinions or beliefs of our fellow humans. What you often find is that the great inventors and artists and philosophers of our civilization are those who see things differently, who are born with the ability to perceive what most do not."

"Sort of 'thinking outside the box' in a way."

"Precisely," William answered. "And what we do could be seen as thinking quite far outside the box. We use meditation and our honed talents to use parts of the mind that are not normally accessed by most human beings. We have learned how to expand our awareness and use it outside the confines of our bodies."

"Is that what's happening to Connor then?"

"Not exactly," said Ellen. "Because she isn't consciously aware of her ability to move between planes in her astral form. And she certainly isn't consciously aware of other lifetimes she has led, at least not until now."

"You're talking about the reincarnation angle?" asked Malcolm.

"Yes, you could call it that," Ellen smiled. "You Yanks certainly have a way of putting things. And in this case I think it particularly appropriate. You see, third-dimensional reality is so straightforward. It either is or it isn't. You come at events head-on, as it were. But expanded awareness naturally makes you look at events differently, sort of from an angle."

"So Connor is a reincarnation of someone, or at least that's what Gwendolyn thought," said Benjamin. "But assuming the fact of reincarnation, I thought people weren't supposed to remember their past lives."

"Not as a matter of course," said William. "But as you well know, there are people who go looking for those lives."

"Not Connor," Benjamin replied. "She's tried to disassociate herself as much as possible from most of what Gwendolyn wanted to teach her."

"Understandable," William agreed. "A great deal of what we study and practice is not easily accepted by the average person. And let's face it, this life seems complicated enough without confronting the questions that past lives can bring up. But for those who wish to look, those lives may provide answers to nagging difficulties the person is experiencing. Not always, mind you. Some people go completely round the bend with the pursuit of the past and never learn to cope with the present."

"True. But Connor hasn't pursued the past at all. She's had a difficult life in some ways, particularly the past couple of years."

"Yes, I understood from Gwendolyn that Connor's former lover was killed and that Connor herself was targeted for death."

"And she almost bought it," commented Malcolm. "Laura too. I can see why neither of them would want to go through hell again. Far as I'm concerned they've already been there."

Ellen's expression was grave. "I understand. But ironically, that very experience is part of what set all this in motion. Gwendolyn left us before we were ready and before Connor had learned what she needed to know. We are somewhat in the dark as well since Gwendolyn never returned from her journey to where all these events took place. Please," she said, turning to Benjamin, "you've beat around the bush on the topic of Gwendolyn's trip. Would please you tell us what happened to her there?"

Benjamin studied his fingernails for the longest time, and Ellen sensed there were conflicting loyalties that made his decision extremely difficult. When he opened his mouth to speak, she was half-dreading that he would refuse to tell them anything at all.

"Connor, Laura, Malcolm, and I, and only two other people whom you don't know, are aware of the circumstances surrounding

Gwendolyn's, um, departure from, I guess you would call it 'this plane' of existence. And we're sworn not to reveal those circumstances to anyone. So you see I have quite a dilemma. On the one hand is my promise, and on the other is the need, greater than any you can imagine, to help my daughter to understand what she is going through and help protect her from harm. Yes, she's a grown woman, and she doesn't particularly need anyone's protection, but that's how I feel."

"You're wrong, Benjamin," Ellen said. "Everyone needs friends and family, and sometimes even protection. I don't think for a moment that your daughter believes your desire to keep her from harm reflects a lack of faith in her strength and courage. Indeed, Gwendolyn believed you were instrumental in teaching her to be independent and think for herself."

"Thank you for that," he said, clearing his throat. "I have to say that it's hard to be caught so often between opposing beliefs. And here is another situation that defies an easy solution. Still," he paused, rolling his head on his neck, "if I'm any judge of character at all, I believe you folks are on our side, and if Gwendolyn saw fit to call you her friends and allies, then I suppose I should too. But I want Malcolm's opinion on this. He is bound by the same promises I am."

Ellen swung her gaze to the policeman, who'd been markedly reticent throughout much of the afternoon. But she sensed that he preferred actions to words and was more comfortable when he could *do* something to express his feelings rather than talk about them.

"Benjamin's right. We promised a particular person that we'd keep this quiet. And it would have stayed that way if someone hadn't gone messing around with Mrs. Broadhurst's grave, and now the whole world knows there's nothing but stones in that coffin. But I still thought we could ignore it, since no one else knows a damn thing about what happened out there in the desert. At least I don't *think* anyone else does." His eyes narrowed, and Ellen had the distinct feeling that the piercing glance he directed at William and herself had skewered more than a few criminals under his interrogation.

"No, Captain Jefferson, we don't know. There was a major disturbance of sorts on the astral plane before Gwendolyn left England. She sent us a message the old-fashioned way, through the post, but didn't explain the details of why she was going. She merely said that she had been specifically summoned, that her granddaughter needed her, and that we should await her further instructions." Ellen paused, her voice suddenly softer. "There was never any...word...from her."

"She didn't exactly die," said Benjamin, and the force of his statement took Ellen completely by surprise. She felt William's body stiffen with shock. He leaned forward beside her.

"Good God, man, you mean she's alive?"

W

An hour or so later, Benjamin showed the Carlisles to one of the guest bedrooms on the first floor and then went back downstairs to the library where Malcolm was waiting.

"Are you sure we did the right thing?" he asked the ex-senator.

"Not sure, maybe. But I think we did what we had to. Maybe they can make more sense of it than we ever did."

"How's Connor?"

"I peeked in. She and Laura are both asleep. At least I hope Connor's asleep. But one way or the other, Laura's with her."

Malcolm smiled. "I was beginning to worry that my old friend was going to blow that relationship."

"Me too. Connor has always had a tendency to run away from the good things."

"What do you mean?"

"You know how most people want to avoid unpleasantness, confrontations, things like that? Not Connor. She's a fighter. She was one hell of a district attorney, never backed down, very rarely compromised. Put up with death threats from the creeps she convicted."

"Tell me about it," Malcolm agreed. "She flatly refused to have a security detail when that serial killer Denny Pring was on trial and swore he had friends who were gonna cut her into pieces. I was ready to lock her in a cell."

"She's stubborn—not proud, mind you, but definitely stubborn.

Like with her writing. When she was wrong about something she admitted it, but when she believed in what she wrote, all the publishers on earth couldn't have changed her mind. I imagine she gave some editors ulcers over the past few years."

"But she's probably sold a million books by now."

"True, but I don't think it much matters to her anymore. Don't ask me why. It's just a feeling I get. My daughter's changing somehow."

"I get the same feeling, but I'm not sure I like it."

Benjamin smiled at the man who'd been Connor's friend for so many years. "Hey, we never want the people we love to change. But they do, and usually for the better, at least from their perspective."

"Yeah, I suppose. I was worried after Ariana died. Connor closed in on herself, like a turtle hiding in its shell. If it hadn't been for Laura—"

"Connor would be dead now," said Benjamin flatly. "And if not for you, both of them would be."

The two men sat in the quiet for several minutes until Malcolm asked, "So what did you mean about her running away from the good things?"

"There's something inside her...it's hard to explain. Maybe it's all those years of Amanda's disapproval and my inattention when I thought I was too busy saving the world from itself to spend time at home, but Connor's always had this little part of her that doesn't think she's good enough, or thinks that good things never last. It's as if she left all the dreams behind when she stopped being a child."

"You don't think she looks forward to anything at all?"

"No, I think she does. But she's always half-prepared for disappointment. The situation with Ariana just made it worse. Connor was so angry and grief-stricken and betrayed. She didn't know how to deal with all that pain, so she did what you said: She crawled into a shell."

"Until Laura came along."

"Yes, indeed. It's amazing now that I think of it. I've got to hand it to her, even when Connor took off, Laura didn't give up. She gave her room to run, but not enough to go back into hiding."

"You think it'll last, what's between them?"

Benjamin almost grinned. "This isn't something I usually say, because I've always been superstitious about inviting bad luck, but after seeing the way they look at each other, I'd bet my life on it."

W

In the guest room, William and Ellen Carlisle sat in the comfortable brocaded slipper chairs near the window and talked quietly.

"If what they say is true, my dear, then where on earth is she right now, and why hasn't she made some effort to communicate with us?"

Ellen shook her heard and allowed herself a rueful smile. "I don't think 'on earth' covers enough territory. Frankly, I have no idea where she is because I've never known of anyone making a transition like that, but I'm beginning to think that her silence is no accident. I have a strong hunch Gwendolyn knows precisely what is going on and has chosen not to intervene, or she is in some way precluded from intervening."

"And where does that leave the circle?"

"Still intact for the moment. And once Gwendolyn's granddaughter recovers from the fugue state she's in, then it will be time for us to meet with her and her friends and her father and explain the entire story of Cerydwynn as we know it."

"But what about this message they say was stolen? They haven't yet told us what was in it and whether it has led them to...well, to anything else."

Ellen gave her husband a rueful smile. "I know, it seems like bad luck to even speak of it until we know for sure. Almost as if the walls have ears. If they do, I just hope they belong to Gwendolyn Broadhurst."

W

Upstairs, Laura dozed off and on, keeping at least one hand in contact with Connor at all times. She didn't know if it helped, but she was sure it couldn't hurt.

Chapter Twenty-Eight

*"She's the sort of woman now," said Mould..."one would
almost feel disposed to bury for nothing,
and do it neatly too!"*
—Charles Dickens
Martin Chuzzlewit

"Gillian, is that you?" Gerald's question echoed through the entry hall, and Lady Fenwycke was instantly reminded of how much she hated her husband and his whiny tone of voice.

"Of course it is I, you great idiot. Whom were you expecting?"

"Why, no one really. I thought—"

"Thought what? That I'd planned to be in Glastonbury for a fortnight, and now here I am showing up in my very own home unexpectedly. Come now, Gerald, surely this isn't a complete surprise. Or were you quite sure Conrad had me so completely *satisfied*," she slowly drew out the word, "that I'd never come home again."

Gerald's face went bright red and she laughed. "Am I embarrassing you, dear husband? Not much of a challenge doing that, you know.

You're so easily rendered speechless, and, I might add, dickless. Now, if you'll excuse me, I'm going to unpack and then dress. I have plans this evening."

"B-b-b-ut," Gerald spluttered. "We need to talk."

"About what?"

"Well, certainly about what's gone on these past few days. Surely there's been some misunderstanding."

Gillian laughed merrily. "Misunderstanding? Rather an understatement, wouldn't you say? Our marriage has been a joke of the most deadly kind."

"What do...I mean...how could you say such a thing? We've been—"

"Been what? Married all these years? Not exactly. And if you think for a moment that your pathetic attempts at passion have been enough to satisfy me...ever...then you're more foolish than I thought."

Gerald's eye widened. "What do you mean...'ever'?"

"Just what it sounds like. Good lord, Gerald, you really don't know, do you?

"Know what?"

"That I've been consistently, constantly and gleefully unfaithful to you...such a dramatic word, isn't it, for such a prosaic activity as fucking. But at any rate, I've been unfaithful since about two hours after our wedding ceremony."

Gerald was rapidly turning purple. "T-two...two..."

"You're stammering again, Gerald. Yes, two hours, and I hiked up my dress so that your pal Horace Dieters could slip me one." She stared at him with undisguised contempt. "You really thought your Victorian 'lie back, dear, and I'll be done in a moment,' was really going to do it for me?"

Her husband's whole body shook. She had the rather pleasant thought that he might drop dead from a stroke or heart attack and save her a great deal of trouble. "Then what they've said about this serving girl, that she and you had been—"

"Spit it out, Gerald. We'd been fucking too. Although I don't suppose that's quite the right term, perhaps not even politically correct. But you're right about the serving part anyway, she gave service of the most satisfactory sort—lip service, shall we say."

He stood there, his jaw working, while Gillian waited for him to collapse. Finally he managed to squawk a question. "And you...you did the same for her?"

Gillian suspected that his apoplectic rage had been augmented by a hint of salacious curiosity. Men were so bloody predictable.

"Why, of course. Rather a tasty indulgence, though you wouldn't know anything about that, would you? Such a chaste and honorable man is Lord Fenwycke. Although, come to think of it, I've always rather thought that your tastes ran more to diddling the stable boy. You do spend a lot of time down there at the horse barn. Of course, the boy is rather handsome in a smarmy sort of way."

"Th...th...that's preposterous. How could you even think such a thing?"

"Doesn't matter, does it? But I imagine it will make for some juicy headlines in the tabloids during the divorce. I used to worry about all that, but you know, lately, I've come to realize that being married to you is much more painful than scandal."

The blood completely drained from his face, leaving him looking ghostlike and old. The sight of him sickened her.

"But you can't possibly mean that? We can't...I mean, no one in my family has ever..."

"Ever what?"

"You know perfectly well what I mean. You're just upset right now, what with this awful crime at Bannister House. And there's been another murder practically on our own doorstep."

"Hmm," she said, starting up the stairs. "So I've heard. Perfectly ghastly what some people will do. But you know, when I think about it, that's the first exciting thing that's happened at this National Trust-listed mausoleum since we got married. Lots more publicity I imagine, but our divorce proceedings will make better reading." Her laughter floated up the stairs in her wake.

W

Gerald was in shock and more frightened than he'd ever been in his life. He'd wanted her to come home, certainly. But he'd expected a suitably chastened Gillian to show up on the doorstep. She'd be embarrassed by her behavior, and perhaps (and this is what he'd especially hoped for) she'd be miserable at having been used and rejected by that cad Thackeray. At the very least, he'd assumed things would get back to life as usual, which wasn't ideal but certainly bearable for the most part.

The last thing he'd anticipated was this bizarre attitude and her overt cruelty. Publicity, by God. She didn't care about his reputation, about the family name, about the sanctity of Haslemere. And she'd come home, not to stay and work things out with him (preferably by apologizing abjectly) but to attack him with vile accusations and damnable lies, then calmly bathe and change her clothes. How dare she!

Gerald fumed and paced and fumed some more. He tried to decide what his father would have done in this situation, or his father's father, or even his elder brother. But miserable as the truth was, it came to him that this never would have happened to the previous Lord Fenwycke, or probably any other Lord Fenwycke who'd ever lived. Somewhere beneath the bluster and belligerence, Gerald knew he was horribly inept and insubstantial and without a backbone, and now the wife he'd chosen was going to drag his family name into the muck. Who knew what she'd say or do?

He went back into his study, closed the door, and poured himself an enormous snifter full of brandy with just a touch of soda. Should he call his solicitor? But what if she'd only been baiting him? What if she had no intention of divorcing him, but only wanted to hurt him? What if she'd meant every word she'd said? He could see the bold, black headlines: PEER'S WIFE REVEALS HUSBAND'S DALLIANCE WITH STABLE BOY; FENWYCKE DENIES AFFAIR WITH TEENAGER. He would be ruined; his business interests would go up in flames, and he'd lose Haslemere. Gerald leaned back in his chair and closed his eyes against the hot tears that spilled over and down his cheeks.

W°

Gillian sank into the steaming tub and allowed herself to revel in the feeling of invincibility and power that had recently asserted itself within her. Gerald was a sniveling, sanctimonious boor, and she'd decided putting up with him was no longer strictly necessary. The situation had changed. There were other, better options available. There were other men, men who could give a woman a proper "seeing to" one moment and make a million or two screwing over the general public the next. She liked that about Conrad. He had no scruples to speak of— a favorable attribute in her eyes. She'd always found morality somewhat constrictive and principles unduly expensive. Image was important to her, but only because it translated into privileges of which she was fond. Conrad might be extremely useful to her once he learned to keep that nasty temper in check.

She was fully aware that leaving Gerald did have a few drawbacks, but avoiding them was not worth the price of tolerating him anymore. And she was actually rather excited about spreading lots of unsavory rumors, making him the butt of jokes in every pub in England. Instead of paying that odious little journalist any more blackmail, she'd give him an exclusive story instead. Then she'd probably have Conrad get rid of him for good.

Gillian heard a sound outside her bedroom door. She tensed, listening. No, no one there.

Yes, Newbury would have to go. Who knew what he had squirreled away in those "archives" of his? But ridding the world of the extortionist wouldn't be difficult. There were people who would do anything for a few pounds, even murder. Gillian laughed. She, too, could be bought, but the price was higher...ever so much higher.

𝒲°

"No, sir, I do not have a list of suspects in mind" Foulsham did his best to keep his anger in check. "No, I don't believe we need to call in any assistance from the Yard... Yes, sir, that's true, of course, but I think we ought to give ourselves a few days to sort it out ourselves."

He looked up and met Mary Fitch's eyes as he held the receiver in a death grip, Hollis's voice whining out of it like a cloud of angry mosquitoes. She tapped the side of her head and smiled. She was right.

Hollis was a nutter, interested in little else besides the efficiency rating of his station and making sure that in his corner of Somerset, violent crimes simply did not happen, at least for reporting purposes.

"I'll be questioning people today," he said firmly into one of the rare lapses of noise from the earpiece. "Yes, there are several, um, Conrad Thackeray, of course, and the Fenwyckes, and..." He pulled the receiver away to protect his eardrums from the ensuing blast, and stared at the ceiling. As if four murders on his patch inside of a month weren't enough, he had holier-than-thou Hollis bleating his litany of reasons why he should "tread very carefully" with the local gentry.

"Of course, sir. I'll keep you apprised of our progress. No, that won't be necessary. I have DC Fitch in my office now. No, thank you, sir. DS Crandall is busy with the lorry hijackings... Yes, I agree that murders are rather more serious than stolen lorries full of stereos. Yes, but Fitch is more than capable, sir...yes, I will, sir."

Foulsham crashed the receiver back into its cradle and exhaled harshly. "God save us from men like that," he said, then flicked a glance at his aide. "Sorry. Not good form, is it, to criticize one's superiors?"

"Superior in rank only, sir," she said, with the faintest of smiles.

"Thank you. But let's get down to cases here. If we don't make an arrest for these murders, especially Peter's, Hollis will have the entire staff of the Yard down here inside of forty-eight hours."

"That means we have to work fast," she agreed. "But why not pull in more bodies to help us. DS Crandall isn't a bad sort really."

"No, I suppose not. But he's got all the imagination of a trout. It's ones like him make the public refer to us as 'the plod,' you know."

"He is a bit procedural, sir, but as long as it's only knocking on doors, he's relentless."

"All right then, page him and leave him a message to get back to the station. When he gets here, draw up a grid around the murder scene for at least a square mile search area, then tell him to..." He stopped when he saw the expression on Fitch's face. "What?"

"He may be a plodder, sir, but he knows that detective constables don't give assignments to detective sergeants."

"Yes, I suppose you're right. It would be like him to resent it. Then tell him that I've asked you to pass along my instructions. I'm going to make some phone calls, and then go make myself unwelcome at Haslemere."

"You suppose Lady Fenwycke's back there?"

"I have no idea. But somehow I doubt she's with Thackeray. In any event, we'll find her. I wager she knows a great deal more than she's telling. After I leave there, I'll be at Bannister House interviewing the Carlisles again."

"You don't actually think they're involved in this?"

Foulsham eyed her shrewdly. "Not in the way you mean—that is, I don't think they're involved with the Frome girl's murder. But I do believe they know more about the circumstances of the murder than they've been willing to share. Well, I'll be buggered if I let them give me the runaround again." He slammed his hand on the desk to punctuate his determination, and Fitch smiled.

"Whatever you say, sir. Will you be wanting me to go with you for any of the interviewing?"

"Later, yes. And if I end up inviting anyone to help us with our enquiries here at the station, I'll want you present. Now go along and get hold of Crandall."

"If you bring in any of the people you've mentioned, sir, I think you'll want your very *own* solicitor present." She stood up smartly, gave him a grim smile, and was out the door almost at a trot.

Foulsham shook his head and sighed. She was right, of course. If he started meddling with people who had the chief constable's ear or, God forbid, the ear of anyone at Scotland Yard, well, he probably would need a solicitor.

Chapter Twenty-Nine

That willing suspension of disbelief for the moment,
which constitutes poetic faith.
—Samuel Taylor Coleridge
Biographia Literaria

"We've got to stop meeting like this."

Laura raised her head from the pillow and focused on the pair of eyes that was becoming almost as familiar to her as the ones she saw in the mirror every morning.

"I hope you don't mean in bed."

Connor sat up. "No, I intend to meet you frequently and at length in the boudoir, my darling woman. But it's disorienting to awaken and find you watching over me, especially when I don't remember coming upstairs or lying down."

Laura rolled into a kneeling position and rested her hand on Connor's cheek. "I know you don't. But I'm convinced we can get to the bottom of it. Ellen and William have yet to give us the whole story, but when they do..."

"Then what? I go around playing some 3,000-year-old priestess, waving a magic wand maybe and dancing in circles in the moonlight? That ought to get me committed if nothing else."

"Oh, come on. Lots of people dance in the moonlight these days, and some of them even dance naked."

"Is that meant to reassure me?"

"Not exactly, but I wouldn't necessarily mind dancing with you naked...indoors or outdoors."

"Thanks, sweetheart. I'll let you know when my natural reserve is sufficiently eroded by sheer insanity to take you up on the idea of engaging in public nudity."

"Which is probably never?" Laura grinned.

"Not in this lifetime anyway."

"Speaking of which..."

"Oh, no," Connor groaned. "I didn't mean to be speaking about it all."

"Not much choice, I'm afraid. Something tells me these episodes you're having aren't going to simply stop because you won't join the club."

"Club?"

"You know what I mean, this circle or whatever it is."

Connor sighed heavily. "So what do you think of the Carlisles?"

"At first I wasn't sure. They seemed pretty stiff and formal. But if I go with my gut instinct, I like them, and I believe them. The question, though, is what *you* think. Do you trust them?"

"That's hard for me. Given my life to date, trust isn't the easiest attitude for me to adopt toward anyone I hardly know."

"I know. And you've had the pins knocked out from under you a lot these last couple of years. But you can't give up on the human race."

"You mean don't throw the baby out with the bath water?"

"Or...if at first you don't succeed, try, try again."

"Hope springs eternal," Connor chuckled.

"A stitch in time saves nine."

"Wait a second, that doesn't fit at all."

"I know," admitted Laura. "I'm running out of clichés."

"That's impossible. There are more clichés than people on planet Earth."

"But not on the tip of my tongue."

"Then how about if I give you something else to do with the tip of your tongue?" asked Connor.

Laura slipped into her lover's embrace, and their lips met. She found the suggestion extremely agreeable, so much so that it was another ten minutes before they went downstairs.

$\mathcal{W}$

The doors to the drawing room were open, and Connor heard a low murmur of voices as they descended the stairs. William and Ellen Carlisle were once again seated on the loveseat in the center of the room, and Malcolm and Benjamin each occupied two of the half-dozen armchairs. Connor addressed herself first to their guests.

"I apologize for my absence, in more ways than one," she said graciously. "And I hope we can have a normal conversation without me wandering off. There are some things I need to know, and I'm hoping the two of you can help."

"Indeed we can," said Ellen. "Do you suppose that works both ways?"

Connor looked at her quizzically. "Meaning?"

"Will you share with us whatever information Gwendolyn left behind? We have to tell you that we've been in quite a state of agitation wondering why she didn't make better preparations in case something like this should happen. There are certain, well, certain facts we truly need to know if our circle is to continue functioning, at least if it's going to do any good at all. But..."

Connor knew immediately that the documents she and her companions had found earlier that afternoon were, in all likelihood, exactly what Ellen and William were seeking. But she also knew there was some reason her grandmother had left them hidden in Rosewood House where only Connor could find them. She didn't sense it was due to Gwendolyn's mistrust of William and Ellen, but because she, Connor, had to be involved in the resolution of whatever this was.

"I'll be as candid with you as possible," she said. "But first tell me about Cerydwynn."

The tale, as it unfolded, was and was not what Connor expected to hear. She hadn't paid enough attention over the years to the history her grandmother had tried to teach her, but certain elements were familiar, so she'd learned something, at least by osmosis. Still, the cold "crawlies," as she called them, skittered up and down her spine as the Carlisles carefully laid out the story of a powerful priestess who had been betrayed by her rivals.

Thousands of years before, Cerydwynn had been the unchallenged leader of her people, a tribe of extremely civilized artists, craftspeople, inventors, and musicians. Their culture formed a figurative island amidst a sea of ignorance and savagery, and it was said that their ancestors were not of the world on which they now lived. It was appropriate then, that the home of Cerydwynn's people was literally an island, and this fact alone had kept them safe from the predations of their fellow human beings. In fact, until the water receded completely or other peoples turned to seafaring, Cerydwynn's tribe should have prospered and remained content. Their physical needs were met in every way, and Cerydwynn herself was honored as the most powerful magician and priestess they had ever known.

"And this was three millennia ago?" asked Connor.

"Actually, the dates of these events aren't known to us with any certainty," Ellen responded. "The record we have is at least that old, but we believe the stories it summarizes occurred much earlier. How early, we don't know." Her expression was one of earnest frustration.

"Any idea when the waters around Avalon receded?" Laura inquired.

"There are differing estimates, but you see we also don't know if this description of a land surrounded by water might not actually refer to England itself. Added to that is another theory that Avalon was protected by an *illusion* of being a solitary island in the midst of a small sea."

"All right," said Connor, frowning. "I don't suppose it much matters at this point. Please, go on."

"At any rate, the downfall of this civilization came not from the aggressions of a conqueror from outside, but from a faction within the tribe led by two people who wished to wrest power away from Cerydwynn."

"You mentioned that before, and frankly, I seem to be, um, remembering some of it myself, for reasons I don't even want to think about. But who were they, these people who betrayed her?"

"We don't know. The fragments we have are silent on that rather important point. But we were hoping that Gwendolyn might have been guarding some additional information that would help us know what to do."

Connor took a deep breath. "You said earlier, if I recall, that Cerydwynn was put to death and her body mutilated."

"Yes," said William. "Hopefully in that order."

"I'd hope so too," said Connor, carefully keeping her voice steady. "And you believe these murders in the past couple of weeks are related because of the decapitation of the Frome woman, and the amputations done on the policeman?"

"We can't help but see a parallel. The problem is, we have no idea why someone would re-create those horrible events. Unless of course..." William didn't finish the thought.

Ellen prodded him gently. "You'd better go on."

"Yes, you'd better," said Malcolm, his tone somewhat less than gentle.

"There may be a ritualistic rationale for this that we don't yet understand."

"But surely," said Laura, "the idea would be to reenact the entire incident, and that would mean performing these atrocities on someone standing in for Cerydwynn, and..."

Connor saw the flash of understanding race across Laura's features. "I knew you'd be the first to figure it out," said Connor softly.

"But surely this doesn't mean that you—"

"It means exactly that," affirmed Connor, turning back to William. "Why don't you explain what you're thinking, for everyone's benefit."

William took Ellen's hand in his. "We've come to believe that the person or persons responsible for these murders was, er, practicing in a way, and also using the deaths to draw the attention of Cerydwynn. If what we know of the priestess is accurate, she could not countenance this kind of cruelty. She would respond to it at once, find the guilty parties, put them on trial, so to speak."

"And she would be the judge who passed sentence, would she not?" asked Connor.

"Yes."

For the first time in her life, Connor Hawthorne was utterly adrift, as if she'd been cut off from every facet of life she knew and understood. Everything she'd been told could have come straight from the fevered imagination of a modern-day novelist, but she knew with frightening certainty that it was all true, at least what had been revealed so far. She realized that the rest was locked somewhere in her awareness, and she wasn't entirely sure she could bear the thought of digging into her psyche and finding the reason for the terror she struggled to conceal.

She'd been looking at her hands lying in her lap, and when she glanced up she noted with at least mild amusement that everyone else in the room was looking at her intently.

"No, I'm still here," she announced with a flippant smile. "Not that I'm sure how long that will last. But the more we talk about this, the less I have the sensation of shutting down inside and sinking into darkness."

"Good. Then there is some integration between your conscious, logical mind, and your higher consciousness," explained Ellen. "That is to be desired. I don't think you can accomplish much of anything without both."

"And exactly what is my daughter intended to accomplish?" Benjamin queried sharply.

"We can't know exactly what that is without more input from someone who knows the entire story, who understands the ritual, who may also know the location of the object we've been discussing."

Connor rolled her head around on her shoulders, stretched her arms over her head, and cracked her knuckles. Then she looked from one to another of them until she had met each person's eyes. "All right then, I suppose it's our turn for Show and Tell." They all watched her back as she strode from the room.

Within minutes Connor returned with the metallic box in one hand and the ornate key in the other. Ellen and William looked at it in mute surprise but also, Connor thought, with a degree of recognition. They'd seen this box before, though she didn't know whether they knew precisely what was inside. For that matter, of course, she didn't either, at least she didn't know what it meant. For this reason alone, she'd decided she had no choice but to seek their help. They were perhaps the only people she could even remotely trust to help them decipher the parchment scrolls.

She deftly manipulated the base of the box and inserted the key, then withdrew the scrolls. "We don't understand the language used in either of these," she admitted. "Although clearly this one is a map or diagram. The other is entirely text." She opened the latter one, spread it out on the butler's tray, and weighted it down with two knick-knacks from the console table behind the loveseat.

William leaned over, peering at the ancient parchments as if afraid to so much as touch them. "My God," he said in a whisper. "She really did have it."

"What?" asked Connor, taken aback by the awed expression he wore.

"This," he said, pointing. "It's the, how shall I put it, since the words don't translate well into our language."

"But there's something that looks like a title at the top," Connor insisted. "If you understand the language, what does it mean?"

Ellen interceded. "It's somewhat similar to the Celtic language that's been altered and passed down to us over the centuries. But even the relatively modern Celtic tongue was never intended to be written down. It's a musical, meaningful language that's meant to be sung, to be used in ballads by storytellers. Much of the nuance is in the sound of the words spoken aloud, not the reading of it."

"Well, then, *approximately,* what is the title of this document?" Connor couldn't help notice that an edge had crept into her voice, as if the one-time prosecutor in her lurked just under the surface. Or, she thought, was it someone else entirely who had burrowed into her consciousness?

William frowned and shook his head. Ellen put her hand on his arm. "I know you understand what's written, love. Let your inner awareness take over. Let it flow. There's no such thing here as getting it wrong, and however uncomfortable the truth may be, I can't imagine Gwendolyn would want it any other way."

He closed his eyes for a moment, and when he opened them, his face was calm, his gaze focused and determined.

"This is a ritual," he said in soft, yet firm voice. "Literally, it would be 'The Re-Enlivening of the Priestess' or something along those lines."

Connor felt her scalp and the skin on her arms contract with goose flesh. If she'd ever wondered whether one's blood could run cold, she stopped wondering at that moment. "Enlivening," she repeated almost to herself, then more loudly she suggested, "as in the raising of the dead? Is that what you mean?"

"No, not at all," Ellen hastened to assure her. "We aren't talking about digging up bodies. That's something best left to horror fiction. No, we, as our ancestors before us, believe that the body itself is nothing more than a vessel, a vehicle if you will, that transports the soul on the journeys where it chooses to incarnate. The body disintegrates, as it should. The soul is immortal."

"Which brings us back to our discussion of reincarnation," Laura countered. "And whether or not you, or Connor's grandmother, or anyone else in this room believes Connor is the same person as Cerydwynn."

No one had any immediate comment, although Malcolm looked as if he had a thing or two to say about all this but was biding his time. Connor sat back in her chair, staring at the parchment in front of her. With her usual knack of keeping to the point, she asked, "And the rest of the document. If this is some sort of ritual to bring her back, then what's supposed to be accomplished? And if, by some stretch of my wildest imagination, I am a reincarnation of this particular soul, then why would there be any need for a ritual to facilitate my...return? As far as I can tell, I'm already here."

Ellen questioned William with a glance, and he nodded. "My husband will translate it as closely as possible if it should become necessary. But let me try to explain why we think this ritual exists. First of all, there is no power wielded by those who are of the Light that could force the reincarnation of a soul at any particular time or place. Even the idea of attempting to control the soul choices of any being is abhorrent to us. It would be tantamount to crossing over to the Darkness as far as we are concerned. No, this ritual was only meant to be used if Cerydwynn were able to come back to this particular world, perhaps not entirely aware of her former identity, but in need of assistance in reclaiming her power."

"What power?" asked Connor. "This is beginning to sound like one of those legends about Arthur, that he was alive or somewhere in limbo, just waiting to reclaim the throne of England."

Ellen smiled. "Cerydwynn's power wasn't primarily temporal, although she could produce some remarkable feats of manifestation. The real power she wielded was spiritual, and she was a sort of, how do I put it, an anchor of Light energy in this dimension that we perceive with our usual human senses. She was the penumbra between Dark and Light, a guardian of the shifting divisions between them."

"You make it sound as if she were the queen of the gray area," said Connor, half jokingly, half in earnest.

William nodded. "That's just it. In this dimension there are no absolutes. No matter what people may think about right and wrong, there is no such thing. Human beings exist in a conditional world where every action must be considered in its context. Think about it. It's all right to kill an enemy soldier, it's wrong to kill a stranger on the street. It's all right to drink liquor, but it's wrong to drink more than you can hold and endanger yourself or others. It's acceptable to get a divorce if you're a Protestant, but not if you're a Catholic. You see, it's all about the gray area."

"All right, I get your point. But what has that to do with Cerydwynn?"

"Using the power of the belt which was given to her by one of the Light beings, she literally held at bay the Darkness and created what you might think of as a neutral zone between the two major universal forces."

"What happened when she died?" asked Laura.

"She was attacked by an alliance of Dark energies so powerful she could not withstand it. Her life force, her consciousness, was scattered and no longer sufficiently focused to maintain the barrier completely. It developed 'leaks,' if you will, and through those fissures Darkness poured." He glanced again at the document. "Almost all of Cerydwynn's people were lost. The few that escaped kept alive the ritual they believed would restore their priestess and their civilization, and they guarded the talisman. The words were passed from generation to generation in the form of a song. Eventually, Guinevere heard that song and understood its true meaning. She sought and was given the belt that Cerydwynn had once worn."

"But all this is pure conjecture," said Benjamin, with an asperity that surprised Connor. "You're asking us to believe in something that scholars have completely rejected as having any basis in truth. You act as if King Arthur definitely existed. Ninety-nine percent of the people who would have an opinion on it in the first place would tell you that it's a *story*, just an embellished troubadour's tale from centuries ago. There's no reason to believe it's true."

"Dad, it's okay, please. I know what you're trying to do, and I appreciate it. But remember what you said not long ago, that after meeting Grandmother Klah, you'd been forced to reevaluate your views of what was and wasn't real?"

"Yes," he nodded reluctantly, "I remember."

"Trying to be rational is just our human way of not wanting to admit there are things we can't explain with science or logic or well-defended theories. There's too much *we don't understand at all.* I'm as big a skeptic as you are, and yet I know in my heart that what Ellen and William have told us is true, at least the part of it they understand or know. Besides, if the scholars have learned anything at all, it's that every story, however fanciful, is based in some way on actual events."

Benjamin looked long and hard as his only daughter. "Knowing that you're right doesn't help. I'm being selfish. I don't want to risk your life, not ever again."

Connor smiled. "I'm not particularly fond of the idea myself. So you'd better believe I'm not willing to go too far out on this metaphysical limb." She turned to the Carlisles. "If you would be kind enough to summarize the ritual for me, then we can look at the other parchment."

Slowly but confidently, William Carlisle translated what he could of the document. There were some words, intended to be spoken during the ritual itself, which he insisted he either did not know, or which had no translation into English. He believed, however, that they were meant to represent whole concepts of their spiritual beliefs. "It would be akin to saying that the word *agape* was just the Greek word for *love* without taking into account any of the deeper meaning."

"Very well, then," said Connor. "To the best of your knowledge, what did the authors of this ritual expect to accomplish?"

"The basic purpose of this is to cause the soul of Cerydwyyn to retrieve the memory its true identity, a memory locked behind veils of darkness, even though the soul would be incarnated in an entirely different body with an entirely different mind and heart and fresh set of life memories."

"But if my grandmother's conclusions about me are correct, I'm already remembering events that have no connection at all with my own life, but do sound as if they come from Cerydwynn's. And as far as we know, this ritual has yet to be performed."

William did indeed look perplexed, but not his wife. "I think the authors of this were afraid that whenever Cerydwynn returned she might not remember at all."

Malcolm rolled his eyes. "Then what? They were going to drag whoever they picked up to the top of that hill and keep talking to her until she did remember? Would have been pretty pointless if they were wrong about who someone really was," he said. "And I'm not convinced. I'm not saying Connor didn't see what she said she saw, but that could be something else. I've read somewhere about places having...vibrations, sort of. Some people are sensitive to it, they pick up on traumatic events that have happened in that spot. Maybe that's what's happening here, to both Connor and Laura. They're seeing something that happened to other people."

Connor pondered her friend's theory. "I have to admit that such a possibility hadn't occurred to me, especially since we read Gwendolyn's letter."

Ellen leaned against the back of the loveseat and waited. William followed her example of silence and went to stand by the window. Connor searched her heart and then the faces of her father, her best friend, and her lover. One by one, they nodded. The tacit assurance was simple: "We're with you."

"I know that my father, and Malcolm, and Laura would all rather have me be the recipient of a few stray psychic vibes than the protagonist of some bizarre legend that has, if the Carlisles are correct, led to the murders of at least four people. And I can't say that I wouldn't just as soon drive to Heathrow and catch the next plane home. But," she paused to inhale deeply, "I can't."

"But Connor..." Malcolm began. She gestured for him to be silent.

"Please, don't make this any more difficult or any weirder than it already is. My grandmother once flew 6,000 miles because she thought I might need her. She also knew she was very ill, but she didn't let that stand in the way of doing what she believed was her duty. From what William and Ellen have told us, Gwendolyn spent most of her life in the pursuit of duty. She believed what she and this circle of people did was of utmost importance to the peace of this world. Who am I to start doubting her now?" She waited for their objections, and when none were forthcoming, she continued.

"I don't honestly know if I am the reincarnation of this person, but I will do whatever it takes to accomplish what my grandmother wanted me to. Now, William, if you would be so kind as to outline what the authors of this ritual believed would happen when Cerydwynn returned."

"She would ascend the place we now call the Tor, and there she would speak to the angels and archangels, she would recall all of the souls lost into the void when Cerydwynn was betrayed and the circle was desecrated by violence. She would restore the balance, and..."

"And?" Connor prompted.

"And once her work was done, she would take her place with the beings of Light, never to incarnate again."

Connor saw Laura's face turn pale. "What does that mean exactly?" asked Laura, reaching for Connor's hand and gripping it tightly. "I think I need to know."

Ellen read the distress in Laura's eyes. "We honestly can't be sure whether it means that at the end of her natural life she would then ascend, so to speak, or if her ascension would be immediate, much like saints or martyrs simply being taken up into heaven according to the Christian Bible."

"There's an encouraging thought," said Connor. "Saints and martyrs have never been on my career wish list."

Laura stood up abruptly. "You're saying she might just...leave us...disappear into thin air and..." Her voice choked off in mid-sentence.

"We're saying we simply cannot be sure, without understanding every nuance of this document, and the fact is, we don't. I suspect that Gwendolyn, as the leader of our circle, as the high priestess in effect, may have understood it completely. But we don't."

"There's nothing we can change about what we understand," said Connor. "But since my hunch is that we need this magical belt, we'd better figure out where it is. I've come to the conclusion that the other parchment is going to make that possible."

After she spread it open, Connor looked to their guests for an explanation. She read the instant recognition in their eyes. "What is it?" she asked. "Do you know what this is a map of?"

"Of course," said Ellen softly. "It's Glastonbury Abbey."

W

Once the shock had worn off, the drawing room came alive with voices.

"You mean that place in the middle of town?" said Malcolm.

"There are dozens of buildings on this map," objected Connor.

"There's nothing left now of the Abbey but a few walls and one out-building."

"That place must have been dug up by archaeologists a dozen times over the years," said Laura, to which Benjamin added, "And no one could have kept a discovery like Arthur and Guinevere's talisman under wraps for long."

"Please, please," said William. "You're all right, and yet wrong at the same time. First of all, Connor, this map was drawn when the Abbey was intact, before Richard Whiting, the old Abbot was dragged up the Tor and beheaded when Henry VIII became so disenchanted with the Catholic Church's rules on divorce. Back then the Abbey was the focal point of the entire region and covered thirty-six acres. And yes, Laura, the area has been excavated over and over. I can only assume that the hiding place is so clever as to have been impossible to discover without a map. Last of all, Benjamin is right in assuming that if it ever had been found, eventually word would have gotten out, or at least it would have been passed around in those circles to which I imagine he is privy. The conclusion then, is that the belt is still there, and that we have a chance to retrieve it."

"When do you propose we do so?" asked Benjamin.

"I can't know with any certainty how critical the timing is, but I think we should proceed fairly soon."

"Tonight."

Everyone's eyes fastened on Connor, who did not elaborate on her terse pronouncement.

"But the Abbey is closed now," said Laura. "There's a high wall around the grounds and probably some sort of security. If we go during the daytime, a couple of us could cause some kind of distraction while the others search."

"No. According to this diagram, the casket containing it is within the foundation wall of the apse. We'll need to do some digging first and then we'll have to pry out one stone. And it has to be done tonight, because..."

"Because why, Connor?" Laura insisted. "Why tonight?"

"We've run out of time," she said, "and please don't ask me how I know. I just do." That odd inflection had crept into her voice once more, and her next words emerged in a tone of someone born to command. "William, study the map and be quite sure of the location. We'll leave in an hour." She stood up. "Tomorrow night we shall go to the Tor."

"And then what happens?" asked Benjamin, his eyes riveted on his daughter.

"Then," she answered. "We will ask Gwendolyn."

"And if she remains as silent as she has been to date," said Ellen, "it will all be up to Connor. If indeed you are willing, of course," she added.

"I don't know if 'willing' is quite the right word. We're on a runaway train. We're either going to reach the station at the end of the line or crash right into it."

Chapter Thirty

We are the music makers, we are the dreamers of dreams,
Wandering by lone sea-breakers, and sitting by desolate streams;
World-losers and world-forsakers, on whom the pale moon gleams:
We are the movers and shakers,
of the world forever, it seems.
—Arthur William Edgar O'Shaughnessy
Ode, We Are the Music Makers

It was well after dark when DCI Foulsham pulled his dusty Rover into the long driveway of Haslemere and rolled slowly up to the front of the house. On previous visits after sunset, he'd always found a regular blaze of lights pouring out of the windows and delineating both edges of the drive, but tonight there was only a lone electric lantern suspended over the center of the porch, pooling the light directly in front of the imposing front door.

Foulsham rang the bell and waited the prescribed amount of time, which in his agitated state came to around twenty seconds. He rang again, still nothing. Haslemere appeared completely deserted. He walked around the house to the rear, and shone his pocket torch into the sheds that had been converted into a four-stall garage. In one of them sat the gleaming vintage Deusenberg he'd seen parked in the driveway on a previous visit. In another, a decrepit-looking Volvo estate wagon of the sort he imagined was used for the staff to run errands. Third in line was a fairly new-model Rover sedan, and the fourth stall was empty. None of these was the car he'd seen at Lady Fenwycke's rental cottage. She was gone then, and there was, of course, the possibility that Gerald had gone with her. He strongly doubted the man would be out riding on a night as dark as lampblack.

He made his way to the rear of the house, estimating that he was about even with the kitchen wing. He tried the doors along the side, but all were securely locked. He felt a burning in his stomach, a combination of anger, frustration, and no doubt hunger since he couldn't recall with any certainty the last time he'd eaten. At the moment he longed for an excuse, any excuse, to kick in one of the doors and search the entire house from top to bottom. Of course, his colleagues had already been there, already found absolutely nothing to connect either of the Fenwyckes to the murder of Peter Garrett, but Foulsham, like all perfectionists, was never free of the nagging feeling that he would have done a better job himself, he would have lifted the corner of a rug that had been overlooked or felt underneath a drawer that fit a bit too snugly.

He turned away from the rear doors, and moved around the other side of the house from the way he'd come, picking out the path with his rapidly dimming torch. He shook it and swore softly, then froze as his senses detected another presence somewhere nearby. He instantly switched off the torch, but after a protracted period of listening, his breath held tightly, he heard nothing, felt nothing. Must have been an animal, he thought, and thumbed the switch on his torch, sweeping the beam over the lower windows at the side of the house. To his surprise, one of the tall sash windows stood open, its lower half thrust up as far as it would go. One edge of a drapery protruded onto the sill. Foulsham allowed as how this gave him what one of those American television detectives called a "hinky" feeling. Something not quite right about all this.

He approached the window cautiously, his torch pointed at the ground in front of him. Leaning into the opening, he listened again.

Not a sound. If anything, he noticed the distinct absence of even the expected noises—insects, dogs barking, cars on the road beyond the house. He sniffed the air and grimaced. A smell he'd noticed earlier was much stronger. Casting the light at his feet, he saw that he had stepped into freshly (very freshly) fertilized flower beds. He was up to his ankles in cow manure. "Damn," he muttered, in somewhat of a quandary about tracking all that much inside.

Foulsham climbed through anyway, though the fact that all the windows reached almost to floor level made it more a matter of stepping than climbing. He justified the intrusion in an instant. He'd been checking around the house for the occupants, come upon the open window, and feared a burglar had been at work. Weak, but workable. He didn't check to see how much manure he'd brought with him into the house, and likely onto some fancy carpet, but from the smell, well...

The first item his flashlight picked out was the gun rack fixed to the wall. This, then, was Lord Fenwycke's study. Foulsham had been in the room only a few hours earlier and had thought it ironic that a man who purportedly had never learned to hit a moving target—duck, deer, or grouse—should own two fine hunting rifles. He moved the beam along the wall, then suddenly swung back to the gun rack. There was now only one rifle resting on the pegs. Foulsham hoped for a reasonable, nonviolent explanation, but the churning of his nervous stomach predicted otherwise.

"I don't suppose," he whispered to himself as the torch completed its circuit of the room and fell on Gerald Fenwycke's desk. Foulsham's hand tightened around the torch and instantly the stench of death separated itself, in the policeman's mind, from the bucolic aroma of cow droppings. Apparently Lord Fenwycke's marksmanship had improved. Although how could he have missed with the barrel of the rifle right under his chin?

W

"Too cloudy to show any moon at all," said Malcolm, zipping up his jacket against the cold, clammy air. "You sure this is the best place to go over the wall?" he asked William, who was testing footholds in the old stonework.

"With this shrubbery so close to the wall, and no street lamps nearby, it should do for our purposes. Plus, the spot where we'll come down inside is well away from the visitor center and much less traveled."

"Why do I get the impression you've done this before." Malcolm commented, surveying the wall with his hands.

"When I was much younger," said Lord Carlisle, "I was occasionally given to taking rather silly dares from my schoolmates when they visited me at the holidays. And getting into the Abbey was always a bit of a hobby with teenagers looking for a quiet spot to, er..."

"The Glastonbury equivalent of lovers' lane," smiled Benjamin, his face barely visible in the glow from the nearest light, some fifty yards away. "And I should imagine it's a spot with just the right amount of spookiness to make the girls swoon into your arms at the first noise."

"Exactly," said William, swinging himself up. "But nowadays the Abbey's rather gone out of fashion as a trysting spot."

The rest of them followed, one by one, catching hold of the branches of a conveniently placed tree, and pressing their toes into tiny cracks that had been worn larger over the years by other toes. They all dropped to the ground on the other side without mishap. There had been some argument earlier that only a small delegation should make the attempt; Malcolm had firmly suggested that only he and William enter the Abbey grounds, but Connor had insisted they all go together. William knelt and consulted the map by means of a penlight. "This way," he whispered and they followed single file as he led them across the vast lawns of the Abbey grounds.

"Shouldn't we stick closer to the perimeter?" suggested Malcolm, adhering to the strategic wisdom he'd once learned as a soldier.

"Ordinarily, I'd agree," William answered. "But as it is, we haven't much time to find it and get out of here before dawn. We're all wearing dark clothing, and there aren't any security patrols inside the grounds at night as far as I know."

"Hope you're right because, quite frankly, I'm the only one in this group who blends into the dark."

William swung his head around, not sure if Malcolm was joking, not even sure, as was the case with many people who've had little experience of friendship with those of African descent, whether or not he should laugh. He was spared the need for a decision when Connor herself chuckled, and said, "Yes, and you're also taller, stronger, and can leap tall buildings in a single bound. When those of us with pale complexions have been picked out by the searchlights, you, no doubt, will be escaping smoothly into the shadows."

"Only if it's the police who are after us," he whispered back. "Can you imagine how embarrassing it would be for a cop to get arrested?"

"About as embarrassing as it would be for a famous author, a former U.S. Senator, and a couple of nobles," added Laura. "I, being the only person here without a shred of notoriety, would just be slightly annoyed."

"I always said Yanks had a good sense of humor," said Ellen, who was moving alongside the group. "Now let's find out if you have a good sense of adventure."

As they came closer and closer to the standing ruins, all that remained of the magnificent church that had once stood on that spot, they were also closer to the main gate, the visitors center, and gift shop. Any of these was likely to be either guarded or at least part of nighttime rounds for a watchman. Their earlier propensity for lighthearted banter had faded, and they moved swiftly yet as quietly as possible across the Cloister Garden to the southwestern corner of what had once been the nave. They crouched near the wall.

"To our left is the Lady Chapel," William said softly, pointing in the direction of the one the only semi-intact pieces of the church. "Straight along here to our right," he said softly, "near the pillars is the entrance to the choir. And that's where the bones of Arthur and Guinevere were once buried and dug up by...sorry, sound like a damned tourist guide. Anyway, once we get to the those big pillars, we'll go left toward where the north transept once stood. There's an alcove along there, and we'll need to dig just at the base of the wall on the other side of the alcove."

Within a couple of minutes they had reached what William believed was the location indicated by the map. "I compared this with one of the tourist maps you had in the car," he explained. Most of the elements correspond, though not all. What amazes me is that so little of the Abbey Church remains, and the thing we're seeking is concealed in one of the last bits of foundation that's still here."

"Somehow I don't think it's a coincidence," said Connor. "Shall we start digging?"

William took a folding rule from his pocket carefully measured the distance from the corner to a spot along the base of the wall. Malcolm and Benjamin produced the spades they'd carried in small backpacks. The shafts had been cut down to eighteen inches with the aid of a cross-cut saw in the garden shed. They began digging, being careful not to scrape against the stone loudly enough to draw anyone's attention. William and Ellen stood on either side holding shielded penlights to illuminate the excavation. In the meantime, Laura and Connor had moved several yards away, keeping a close eye on the walkways leading back to the visitors center.

As if on cue, Laura's right hand and Connor's left twined around each other. "Are you scared, sweetheart?" Laura said softly. "You know we don't have to go through with all this." Connor was silent for a while, and Laura saw that her eyes were closed. "Stay with me, girl. This is no time to be shifting dimensions."

Connor opened her eyes and smiled. "Don't worry, I'm still here. Though why I am is a mystery to me."

"Then you don't—"

"No, I don't want to do this, whatever the hell *this* is. But even if I don't believe in the same things my grandmother did, even if chances are this is just a bunch of silly, superstitious people doing absurd things, what if they're absolutely right?" She squeezed Laura's hand. "I know you don't want me to do any of this, do you?"

It was Laura's turn to think, and she took her time answering. "To be honest, I don't. All that talk about Cerydwynn leaving once and for all. Can you imagine how..." Laura's whisper had taken on an added hoarseness, "how much I can't stand the thought of losing you?"

Connor's arms went around Laura and they turned, face to face, their bodies pressed close together. "Yes, my love," Connor said, her voice barely audible in Laura's ear. "I can imagine. Because I feel the same way about you. But I can't run away now. That's all I know for certain. Unless..." she paused and Laura felt Connor's arms tighten around her. "Unless you ask me not to go. I realize I haven't given you much say in this, and you're everything to me. I'm sorry. If you say, 'don't go,' we'll walk away from all of it tonight. William and Ellen can do whatever they like with the belt."

Laura let the words sink in as she stood with her face pressed against the collar of Connor's shirt. Every defensive, possessive instinct she'd ever had was clamoring to be heard—*No! I don't want you to go to the Tor. I don't want to find out I can't protect you. I don't want some ancient ghost to take you away from me. Stay here with me, and we'll be safe.* But would they? And what would Connor feel in a day or a week or a month? What would happen between them if Laura refused now, when so much might be at stake for so many people, to allow Connor the freedom to pursue her instincts, her moral imperatives? Even more important, did Laura herself want that much power over anyone? Instantly, she saw the offer for what it was. Connor was actually volunteering to stop being her true self if that is what it would take to make Laura happy. And Laura absolutely hated the idea.

"Don't *ever* change your mind about doing what you think is right, just because I have an attack of the jitters. You'd never be the same person again, and you wouldn't be the woman I fell in love with. So let's forget about staging a strategic retreat."

Connor pulled away far enough so she could look into Laura's eyes. "You're incredible, you know that?"

A few moments later, a low whisper from William interrupted what might have become a very lengthy kiss.

They moved back to the spot beside the wall where Benjamin and Malcolm had carefully prised out a block of stone with small metal chisels. The stone came easily because it turned out to be much shallower than they'd anticipated. It was, as a matter of fact, only three or four inches deep.

"It's a miracle this has never been found," said Ellen quietly. "But then we have no idea how long it's actually been here."

"True," agreed William. "It's impossible to visually date that parchment, although the language of the first document puts it pretty far back. Still, I'm just as surprised that not one single treasure hunter or archaeologist with a metal detector or ultrasound could find the cavity behind a piece of false foundation stone."

"I don't suppose they were meant to," said Connor cryptically. "But is there anything in there?"

She knelt in front of the opening and was about to thrust her arm in when she paused. "Isn't this where Indiana Jones would advise caution? I wonder if the ancient Celts were into booby traps."

Malcolm immediately dropped to the ground beside her. "Let me do it. Just in case. Remember, my arms are longer."

She squeezed his hand. "That's what you said about getting that box of Gwendolyn's, old pal. Now it's my turn. And I don't think I'll have to reach far, assuming there's something here for us to find."

Connor poked her hand into the opening and felt along the rough surface until her fingers encountered a smooth surface, perpendicular to the "floor" of the hole. She ran her hands across it, trying to gauge its proportions. She shifted position so she could use both hands.

"I've got hold of something," she said. "If I can just manage to get my fingers around the edges."

Inch by inch, with scrapes that sounded far too loud for an ostensibly covert operation, Connor retrieved a smallish wooden casket, ornately carved on the top and sides, smooth on the back and front.

"Well," said Laura. "Is it locked, or can you open it?"

Connor examined it closely and saw the faint line running around the circumference of the box. She braced her thumbs against the top corners and pushed. It barely moved. Switching it around, she cradled it in her left arm and used her right hand to lift the lid. No key was required, but a certain amount of self-control was called for when, in the wash of light from William's small torch, they saw what was inside.

W

Unaware that a mere twenty or so miles away a crime of sorts was taking place inside the walls of Glastonbury Abbey, involving individuals of whom he was increasingly suspicious, DCI Foulsham had enough problems on his mind. He was standing in the fetid gloom of Gerald Fenwycke's study staring at what remained of the man's head. His quandary was that of a police professional who knows he's damned if he does and damned if he doesn't. This room had taken on the status of a crime scene. Foulsham, with his manure-covered feet, was contaminating it with every step he took. Should he double-check to see if Fenwycke was dead? Hardly a difficult question considering the amount of brains spattered over the wall behind him, but still, it was expected. And there was the matter of searching the house to see if any other victims lay within. Foulsham had seen his fair share of murder-suicides and, in his mind, this had all the earmarks of a domestic situation gone bad. Gillian Fenwycke comes home, Gerald tackles her about the affair with Conrad and with the Frome girl. She lashes back at him, saying God knows what. He's provoked, gets the rifle and...He sighed. Hollis would criticize him about something anyway. Whether errors of omission or commission, it mattered little to the blowhard as long as it gave him the chance to call you to his office for a good ticking-off.

Foulsham decided he might as well continue to the hall, find a light switch, and search the rest of the house. He'd touch nothing, and leave a single trail of manure to explain to the SOC officers. He moved through the open doorway into the hall, searching with his torch, now dimmer than ever, for a light he could turn on before the batteries died completely. Then he froze in place. He'd heard something.

What had it been? A footfall, a sigh, the whisper of fabric against something rough? He stood perfectly still, sorting out the sounds and scents around him. But in the instant he realized that what he'd heard was breathing, and that it was very near, and that there was something familiar about...the air parted behind him with an ominous whooshing sound. He was flung forward at the same moment he acknowledged the sizzle of pain across his back. His startled brain took a few milliseconds to work out that he'd been hit with something awfully solid. Another blow, this time to his head, and shards of light pierced his field of vision. His face slammed into the wooden floorboards, and he bit his tongue hard. *Bloody hell, I'm a dead man*, was his last coherent thought.

W

The dawn had barely begun to peek softly through the windows of Rosewood House as the erstwhile commando team reassembled over hot coffee and more of Benjamin Hawthorne's pitiable scrambled eggs. They ate almost ravenously, and, as if by prior agreement, the only words exchanged were mundane requests for condiments and the odd remark about the day's impending weather. Not until every scrap of food had been consumed did Connor clear her throat and gather their attention.

"Tonight I must be at the Tor. But I don't know that everyone here must go with me. It might even be wise for someone to stay behind, just in case."

"In case of what?" asked Laura calmly.

"I don't know," Connor sighed. "But I don't want to leave Gwendolyn's house and her things without the proper care, if you take my meaning."

William and Ellen exchanged glances before she spoke up. "You're quite right my dear, and although my husband's 'sight' regarding past events is much stronger than mine, it falls to me to see possible future outcomes."

"Possible?" asked Malcolm. "I thought psychics and people like that could always see into the future...no offense."

"None taken," she answered. "And anyone who tells you they can see the future unequivocally is either deluded or lying. There are an almost infinite number of possible outcomes to any situation. Every 'next moment,' if you will, hinges on our personal choices in *this* moment. Each course of action we choose presupposes a different set of potential outcomes. My talent is for seeing some of those potential events, based on my knowledge and understanding of the people involved. But I simply can't predict with absolute certainty because all of the factors affecting the future are not mine to control."

"But my wife is being rather modest," protested William. "Her sensitivity to the energies of the people around her, and her amazing grasp of mathematics at a level that completely baffles most of us mortals makes her forecasts remarkably accurate."

"Thank you, love," she said, favoring him with a smile. "But lest we get too carried way with singing my praises, we should keep in mind that we have never attempted a ritual of this nature, nor do we have our high priestess with us. At least not as far as I know," she added, casting an eye around the room as if she might see the formidable Gwendolyn Broadhurst perched on a countertop. "With all those factors, I can't be sure. But I do know there's one person in our group who has never been present on the Tor during any of the future timelines I've followed."

They all waited expectantly. She knew each of Connor's companions was more than willing to stand by their friend no matter the risk, would probably deeply resent being left behind. The expression on Laura's face was of sheer defiance. Thank heavens, thought Ellen, I don't have to ask her to stay behind. But the revelation she did have to make was almost as difficult.

At length she raised her eyes to Connor's father. "Benjamin. I'm afraid you are the one who, as far as I can tell, should stay here at Rosewood House when we go to the Tor."

The ex-senator's face paled. "You can't ask me to do that. Hide out here while my daughter and my friends go up there to face God knows what. No! I won't do it. I don't care what your 'visions' are telling you."

Connor, seated next to her father, took his hand in hers. "Dad. Hold on for a second, okay. If our positions were reversed, I'd feel just the same way. But think about this. If we somehow fail at this mission that Gwendolyn has sent us on, someone has got to be responsible for handling the fallout and protecting this house and Gwendolyn's belongings, the documents we've uncovered. All of that. And if..." she paused, breathed deeply, and controlled the tremor that had threatened to spread to her voice, "if, God forbid, anything should happen to me, I want you and Aunt Jessica to take care of Katy for me. She may think she's all grown up now, but she still needs someone. I can't think of anyone better than her grandfather and Gwendolyn's sister."

"She needs a *mother*," Benjamin's voice was shaking. "And I need a daughter. And Laura and Malcolm, my God, don't start talking like this. All because some crazy old woman decides you're someone you're not, and you go running off to do God knows what on that stupid hill. This is all ridiculous, and we know it." He glared at the Carlisles. "And what business do you have telling me what I can and cannot do where my family is concerned?"

Ellen remained silent, perhaps sensing there was nothing she could do to assuage Benjamin's anger and frustration. William followed his wife's example, knowing full well he would feel exactly the same way if it were one of their own children who was involved in this.

Connor finally broke the tense silence. "Dad, you can't convince me for a minute that you think Gwendolyn was a 'crazy old woman,' and you know it."

His shoulders slumped and for a brief moment, Connor thought he suddenly looked every one of his sixty-eight years and them some.

"I'm going to be all right, and so are Laura and Malcolm. Besides, do you think this big lug," she squeezed her friend's well-muscled arm, "is going to let anything happen to me?"

Benjamin met Malcolm's eyes and an understanding passed between them. Connor thought she could actually hear it, which was absurd from a rational point of view, but not from the perspective she'd been forced to learn these past few days.

Please watch over her, Malcolm.

I'll bring her home safe. You know I'd trade my life for hers if that's what it takes.

Yes, I know.

Benjamin looked at his hands for a long moment, then raised his eyes to meet Connor's. "I'll do as you ask, but I don't have to be pleased about it, do I?"

She smiled at her father. "No, but then you're like me. You hate not having your own way."

W°

Ellen suggested they all get some sleep as they'd already been up for twenty-four hours and none of them knew what the night would bring.

Connor lay awake for a while, the daylight playing havoc with her circadian rhythms despite her overwhelming fatigue. Laura's breathing grew deep and regular, and Connor reached out and gently laid her hand on her lover's back, feeling the reassuring warmth of the life that flowed through her, an energy so tangible that Connor could let herself bask in it, merge with it, float on its current. As never before with another human being, Connor knew she had discovered the meaning of union. Their two selves had become as one, without her having been consciously aware of the transition from lovers in search of love to soul mates in search of each other. Was that what they were then? Soul mates? Despite the intensity of her love for Ariana, she'd always tended to scoff at the concept, though it had been popular enough with many of her friends and acquaintances. But lying here now, knowing herself and Laura to be inseparable spirits, she wondered if all the people who bandied about the term with such recklessness really understood its significance.

Secure in the haven of warmth, Connor slowly let go of the waking world, but sleep did not embrace her. Instead, she floated, suspended in a place that her soul self knew could only be described as nowhere. For in this state there was no up and down, no dark and light, no reference point that could be compared with another. Just as Ellen had tried to explain in words that were wholly inadequate, Connor had come to the place of non-duality, the place that could not be perceived with her physical senses, but only with her spiritual awareness.

For a long time she floated, wondering why she wasn't more worried about being part of what could only be described as formlessness. Perhaps, she thought, this is nothing more than a holding area, a threshold to what Laura often had referred to as the Dreamtime. Connor had only had a glimpse of such a place once in her life, one night in the desert of the Navajo reservation, when she'd looked up at the stars and been engulfed by them. But this experience was quite different, and she knew instinctively that she was waiting.

After a time, hard to judge in a place that has no time, light pierced a corner of consciousness and she was instantly somewhere else. Opening her eyes, she found herself sitting atop a flat rock in the high desert at twilight. She could have sworn she even recognized the precise spot, however unlikely that would be, given the tiny portion of the reservation she'd traveled with Laura. But it seemed familiar. The scent of the juniper and pinon tickled her nose, mingled with the aroma of wood smoke.

A campfire, she thought, and instantly the scene before her changed. Two women asleep beside a fire in the bottom of an arroyo. Connor's heart clenched in her chest when she saw herself stretched out on the blanket, Laura beside her. She knew what was about to happen, knew and tried to look away. But the scene played on and on until the moment Laura lay bleeding in front of her and Connor was staring down the barrel of a gun.

"You acquitted yourself rather well, I thought," said a familiar voice.

"I was scared to death," answered Connor, without taking her eyes from the events transpiring in front of her, as vividly as they had so many months before.

"But you kept your wits about you to the very end," said Mrs. Broadhurst.

Connor wondered if it should seem strange that her long-departed grandmother had dropped into this dream for a chat, but it didn't.

"No, this is a place where anything can happen. But you haven't visited for a long time," said the voice of Gwendolyn, in response to Connor's thoughts.

The memory receded, and Connor found herself once more sitting atop the flat rock.

"Where is here exactly?"

"The place that Laura and her Grandmother Klah have spoken of to you. They call it the Dreamtime, though it has many names."

"Is this where you live?"

"Oh my, no, child," she chuckled. "No one *lives* here. It's only a place of journeying and visioning. And I'm not really here, nor are you. Not in the sense you mean. But we've each sent a part of our consciousness here, so it really amounts to much the same thing for a human being handicapped with three-dimensional awareness."

"And why are you no longer handicapped with it, as you say? Ellen and William don't understand where you've gone or how you got there, and I don't suppose anyone but Grandmother Klah really does. Of course she's not the most forthcoming person in the world."

"No, she is rather meager with explanations, isn't she? But we haven't got much time, dear, at least not in your linear time-driven reality, so—"

"You see, that's just what I mean. You and your friends keep spouting off all this metaphysical gobbledy-gook, and the rest of us mortals haven't got a clue what you're talking about."

"Do you really want a lecture from me on the effects of linear thinking—you concept of past, present, and future—or would you prefer that I show you what you need to know."

Connor felt herself drawing away from the scene in the arroyo, away from her own past, and back toward the quiet place from which she'd come.

"I'm sorry, but this is just a dream after all. And I thought we were in charge of our dreams. At least I think some therapist told me that a long time ago. And why can't I *see* you?"

"I no longer have any form in particular. Does that bother you?"

"Yes. I want you back, just the way you are—tall, silver-haired, marching through the village in your tweedy skirt and jacket. I want..."

"What, my dear?" the voice was gentle, low.

"I want you back in my world where I can talk to you and see your face and you can explain all this. I'm scared, Grandmother. I've been pretending I'm just fine with all this weird witch stuff, but the fact is I need someone who really understands what's happening."

"You don't need my physical presence, Connor. You need to hear my voice, and listen to what I say, and decide for yourself which path you will choose."

"You said all that in your letter. I'm choosing to go along with what you asked. But I still don't understand why, not really. And why should I be stuck with this huge responsibility?"

Connor felt rather than heard her grandmother's soft laughter. "And why shouldn't you? Every human being is, as you like to say, 'stuck' with his or her life. And every one of those lives plays out differently, guided by the choices they made before they were ever born into the body they occupy. Problem is, they don't always remember those choices, or the agreements they made with other souls about the things they wanted to learn. So they get exceedingly resentful if they have chosen to face the challenges of heartache, poverty, illness, violence, and the like."

"I thought we could choose differently, you know, change our thoughts."

"You can, dear. The more enlightened you become, the more you can alter the shape of your experiences and your reality. You're a great deal further along than you imagine, but I don't suppose it's up to me to convince you."

"No, I don't think you could."

"I found myself up against your stubbornness too many times to believe otherwise. For the moment, I'll ask you again if you wish any guidance."

"Yes," Connor sighed. "I do."

For what might have been minutes, or hours, or weeks—Connor had no sense of the passage of time—her grandmother taught her, as Gwendolyn had always taught her. The words were economical yet vividly descriptive. Gwendolyn laid out several thousand years of human history in a few broad strokes that joined a host of seemingly unrelated events into a coherent pattern of human evolution. Soon Connor realized that much of what she heard came not from Gwendolyn's voice but from vivid images that flashed through her mind—of wars and miracles, of witch burnings and pagan celebrations, of devastation and healing, of bold advances and fearful retreats. Always the opposites, the battles.

"Is this how it must always be?" Connor asked. "Why can't good come out on top once and for all?"

"For now, this is the only way in which human beings can grasp the world in which they live. To them it will always be a question of opposites, because it is so terribly difficult for them to accept themselves as God's creations. All this nonsense of original sin and the inherent evil within human beings is simply their way of putting a name and an identity to fear. When fear is rejected once and for all, only love will remain."

"You're beginning to sound like an evangelical infomercial, Grandmother."

Again the soft, melodic laughter. "Thank you for rightly questioning my choice of words, child. Perhaps you are right. When one tries to put the unnameable into words, the words inevitably fall short. But I hadn't intended to convert you to any particular beliefs, simply remind you to look inside yourself for the truth. If one accepts the premise that we are all manifestations of one God, then the truth must be in each of us. You don't have to go on any pilgrimages to find it."

"My truth has always included the concept of good and evil. I don't think I can abandon it."

"Then, for now, that is how your reality will be defined. And thus it is up to those of you who are perched on the edge of enlightenment to maintain the balance for all those who cannot yet discern even a modicum of truth. For them, the balance must be maintained. That is why you've been sent the images created from pure understanding. Now you can grasp the significance of Cerydwynn's return in a world entrenched in duality."

"Then I *am* Cerydwynn?"

"In a sense, my dear, you are. But equally you are Lydia Connor Hawthorne. Your chosen life cannot be subsumed by the lives you have lived before. You are undertaking a task that was left undone, a task intended to put right a mistake that was made long ago. And although I ask you to complete it now, I do not require you to do so."

"When have I ever run away from anything I must do?" Connor asked, with only a trace of bitterness.

"Never, child. And that, more than any other facet of your character, bespeaks the heritage of your soul's journeys through time. You are a strong and courageous being, my dear granddaughter."

Without any audible signal, Connor knew their time together was nearing the end. With the forming of this thought, Gwendolyn's voice became slightly fainter. Desperately, Connor reached out with her mind. "No, please. I don't know enough."

"You will have all the knowledge at your disposal when there is need of it, child. Now it is time for us to return—"

"Wait. I have just two more questions, please."

"Yes?"

"Why did you tell Laura she was my *anam cara?* What does it mean?"

"They are the sacred Celtic words for 'soul friend.' And she has been the friend of your soul and your heart of hearts for many lifetimes. What is your other question?"

"Am I going to die tonight, Grandmother?"

Connor waited in the silence for what seemed an eternity. Finally, the words, reluctantly spoken, echoed in the vastness.

"That, my child, I cannot tell you."

Chapter Thirty-One

See how love and murder will out.
—William Congreve
The Double Dealer, Epistle Dedicatory

Constable Mary Fitch sat uncomfortably behind Nicholas Foulsham's desk, leafing through his appointments calendar. Upstairs, an obstreperous Superintendent Hollis was raging about irresponsibility and insubordination and any other censorious noun he could think of to apply to the absent DCI. For her part, Mary was just plain worried. There'd been no word from her guv'nor all day, and it was already half-two in the afternoon. Small wonder Hollis was in a frenzy. Officers who'd been assigned to question neighbors and conduct searches had been trying to reach Foulsham all day with their reports. At first Mary had tried to cover, but that horse's ass, DS Crandall, had, in his usual sententious way, insisted that adherence to proper procedure required informing the superintendent of Foulsham's nonappearance for work that day.

She'd phoned round to Foulsham's flat and to every place she could think of he might have gone. There'd been no answer at Haslemere, which she thought odd, given that they had one or two servants who should be around. A call to Lord and Lady Carlisle had produced a stiff and uninformative reply from their snooty butler that "his lordship and Her Ladyship are away and have not informed anyone as to their location or expected date of return." Lot of bloody help that was, she'd muttered to herself after slamming down the receiver. Only then did she remember that Foulsham had briefly mentioned a visit to a house in St. Giles on Wyndle, once occupied by Gwendolyn Broadhurst, whose grave had been opened by the two men found murdered in the churchyard. She flipped through his calendar and found a note of the address and phone number. The person who answered the phone sounded American, and assured her that the chief inspector had not been seen there since his initial visit.

The only source of information was the landlord of the cottage that Gillian Fenwycke had rented. Grudgingly he'd supplied the approximate time of DCI Foulsham's visit the day before and then launched into a querulous tirade on being constantly beset with policemen's enquiries. She hung up on him, not really caring if he lodged a complaint, which seemed likely.

Now she'd run out of possibilities. On her own authority, she'd put out an alert for Foulsham's car, hoping Crandall wouldn't get wind of it right away. If she put one more foot wrong, she'd be lucky to keep her job, but she was deeply worried. It was entirely out of character for Foulsham to be anything less than meticulous in his investigative techniques. He'd chided his own subordinates for failing to keep proper notes, failing to check in regularly, and not following established procedure. He would no more run off acting like Rambo than Hollis would ever say a pleasant word to anyone who didn't outrank him.

The phone rang and she snatched it up, praying it would be Foulsham. Instead the switchboard was putting through a call from London. The voice at the other end was brisk yet cordial, and once Mary had assured the caller that Foulsham could not be reached, she was deputed to give her guv'nor an urgent, detailed, and precise message.

She was smart enough to keep it to herself. No sense letting Hollis know that some cloak-and-dagger bloke in the city had been on to someone at the Met who was passing along a polite "suggestion" to Nicholas Foulsham. This was the second intrusion by London police into what was essentially a local matter, and she wouldn't give Hollis, who seized every opportunity to advance his status in the circles of power, the opening to hand over her boss's case. She read over the message again. Its meaning was hardly open to misinterpretation, so why was it so hard for her to trust it? Or was it simply that having heard the content, she realized full well that she was being dragged into something that was almost bound to turn out very badly indeed?

An hour later, with still no word, Fitch finally heeded the growl from her stomach and decided to go down to the canteen and get whatever vile concoctions were on offer that day. But no sooner had she risen from the chair than the phone rang again. This time, the desk officer. There was someone to see her, and the name he gave was startling, if only because she'd written it down so recently. The caller from London had even spelled it.

"Have someone bring him up, then," she said, ignoring the sigh from the desk officer. Detective Constables didn't carry all that much weight with the uniform branch.

Two minutes passed, and there was a knock.

"Come in," she shouted, annoyed that whoever was escorting the visitor hadn't simply opened the door. Then she found herself blushing slightly. The door swung inward and there was no uniformed officer there at all. Instead, she saw a tall, handsome gentleman in a well-cut suit, his raincoat over his arm.

"Good afternoon," he said cordially. "I'm Benjamin Hawthorne."

$\mathcal{W}^o$

The object of Constable Fitch's concern was even more worried than she about his personal safety. He'd awakened in complete darkness, and it took him a long time to decide if it were still night, if he were locked up in some windowless room, or if he were, God forbid, blind. It was a horrifying sensation to hold up his hand in front of his face and see nothing. Rarely could darkness be so profound, thus his fear of blindness began to assume monstrous proportions in his mind. But he willed himself not to give in to the mounting hysteria that plucked at the edges of his mind and squeezed the breath from his chest.

After he'd completed an inventory of the rest of his body and found it reasonably functional, he raised himself to a sitting position and instantly regretted the decision. His head throbbed and pulsed with pain at even the tiniest movement. His exploring fingers discovered a substantial lump just above his right ear. "Hmm, right-handed suspect," was his first thought, which illustrated how ingrained were his instincts to think and act like a police officer. Of course, the conclusion also struck him as absurd since he doubted he would ever have the opportunity to track down his assailant.

Deciding that inaction was bad for his state of mind, Foulsham decided he should try exploring the room—if indeed it *was* a room— in which he was being held. Taking great care to jostle his head as little as possible, he stood up and walked slowly, one careful step at a time, his hands waving back and forth in front of him like dowsing rods. After several paces, panic seeped into his mind, along with the daft notion that he would never find the edges of this place, that there were no walls, just infinite blackness. He sternly rejected this flight of fancy. He was, after all, walking on a *floor*, for heaven's sake. Floors did not go on infinitely. They eventually terminated at their intersection with walls.

Despite his reasoned thinking, Foulsham had almost succumbed to the pounding in his chest, and the desire to curl up in a fetal position until someone came along to rescue him or kill him, when his knuckles scraped across a rough, uneven surface—stone, some sort of stone wall. He paid his palms flat against it, then his cheek. The chill dampness felt wonderfully soothing to his throbbing head, at least until the proximity of moisture triggered an awareness of searing thirst, followed by unmistakable signals from his empty stomach. How long had he been here? Was it still nighttime? And what about...the memory came back to him in one grotesque image—Gerald Fenwycke's disintegrated skull, the stink of cow manure that had disguised for a few moments the much more unpleasant burnt-coppery stench of blood.

And something else, something familiar, but what? He could remember nothing except shining his torch on Fenwycke's body.

Damn, he was thirsty. He felt his way along the walls, wondering if by some miracle there was a sink or a water spigot in the place. He'd made only a few sideways paces when a low rumbling sounded above his head. A pause, then louder. He couldn't identify the sound, even though he was quite sure he should be able to do so. It was this confounded darkness. He felt as if his senses were all wrapped in cotton wool. And, he had to admit, the blow to his head hadn't helped his thought process much. Still, he'd soldier on as best he could. One thought comforted him more than any other. For many years he'd been aware of an odd facet of his character, odd at any rate to most people: he truly was not afraid of dying. It was just something that had to happen eventually. He thought this gave him a slight advantage in dealing with whoever had abducted him. On the other hand, he wasn't particularly fond of the dark, and he sure as hell hoped he wasn't blind.

He stopped in his tracks. His hands had felt something, at least he thought they had. Yes, there it was. Set into the stone wall was a wooden surface. Exploring the edges of it, he judged it to be a panel perhaps two feet square, though he was sure his estimate could be far off the mark, given his disorientation. But having no better ideas, he began to push at the panel, first in the center, then around the edges. After several minutes of effort that left him sweating and dizzy, he felt it give. Not much, less than an inch certainly, but it *had* moved. He pushed again, nothing. And again, still no movement.

Foulsham, whether from the effects of his concussion, or sheer anger, took hold of the unlikely notion that this opening was his escape route, that just on the other side was light and fresh air and freedom. He carefully stepped back, keeping his fingertips on the panel to orient himself. No sense in flinging his body into a stone wall. He didn't think his head could stand it. One more careful pace. He was no longer in contact with the surface of the wood, but he knew where it was. Then, with every scintilla of strength and will he could muster, Foulsham charged at the panel, keeping his head low, his arms in front of him.

Some part of him had expected the maneuver to be completely pointless, resulting in more frustration and certainly more pain. Another part of him was clung to the fantasy of instant escape. The end result of his efforts fell somewhere in between.

The panel did indeed spring open with the weight of his assault on it, but so swiftly and easily that his momentum carried him head-long through the opening. There was no light and warmth on the other side. Foulsham fell forward, and the wind was knocked out of him as he found himself face down on smooth wood. The next thought that surfaced was that his head was pounding, but that was understandable since his sense of gravity told him his feet were well above his head. He was pointing downhill. In the instant it took for his brain to process the situation, however, it got worse. He began to slide in the direction his head was pointing. His fingers scrabbled at the smooth surface to no avail. He slid faster, and to his horror he felt walls on either side, close to his shoulders. He was in some kind of chute, for God's sake.

It was over in a matter of seconds. He'd wisely thrust out his hands to break his fall and protect his head. They came up hard against a bar-rier, and something snapped in his wrist, sending a sharp jolt of pain up his arm. Behind him he heard a scraping sound. He lay panting for minute, then turned over on his back and felt around him. Wooden slats that must have been nailed close together, for he could barely feel the joints between them, everything solid, unyielding. Reluctantly, he reached above his face and encountered another surface no more than a few inches above his face. Foulsham fought against panic. "No," he kept saying. "No, I can get out of this. I can get out of this."

At least now he was lying in a much more level position. He scoot-ed slightly in the direction from which he'd come, hoping against all logic that he could somehow work his way back to the stone room. Even that was infinitely preferable to being trapped this way. But, to his shocked surprise, there was no longer any opening to the chute. His feet hit solid wood. "Dear God," he murmured. "I'm buried alive."

W

Mary Fitch's loyalties were to Nicholas Foulsham. This much was clear to Benjamin as he sat in the visitor's chair across from her and regarded the tense, perhaps even angry, young woman. He liked her, though. She was possessed of a plain, squarish yet kind face, which as yet was only slightly furrowed with the lines and creases that were standard issue for a career police officer. He sensed she was both anxious to talk to him, and suspicious of him at the same time.

"We haven't met, Constable," he said, careful to observe the proper formalities. "But my daughter has met Detective Chief Inspector Foulsham, and mentioned that he visited Rosewood House in St. Giles a few days ago. He's been looking into the incidents at the churchyard, the opening of my mother-in-law's grave."

"Hmm," she nodded, noncommittal in the extreme.

"But the reason I've come here also may be related to the murders that DCI Foulsham has been investigating, I presume with your assistance." He paused, and saw that she wasn't the sort to be swayed by even the smallest flattery.

"And what information do you have?" she said, pulling over a pad of paper.

Benjamin hesitated. He'd expected to come face to face with Foulsham, and he'd also expected Fenton Carstairs to have prepared the ground for him, so to speak.

"Perhaps I should come back at a better time, when the chief inspector is in."

To Benjamin's great surprise, Mary Fitch's face suddenly lost its hard-jawed definition. He had the distinct impression she was valiantly fighting to keep her emotions in check.

"I'm sorry, Constable. Have I said something?"

Benjamin saw that she was reading, or pretending to read, a neatly printed note tucked into the edge of Foulsham's desk blotter.

"Constable?"

"Sorry, sir. Um...this message," she plucked it up and dangled it between her fingers. Someone very high up the ranks has asked that you be extended every courtesy, assured the chief inspector that you can be trusted in every regard, and even hinted that your suggestions about actions we might take should be treated as if they'd come from 10 Downing Street itself. Rather unusual, that."

Benjamin squirmed uncomfortably in his chair. He definitely hadn't wanted Fenton Carstairs to go that far. He'd only suggested the wheels be greased a little. And he'd anticipated appealing to the better nature of Nicholas Foulsham, whom he'd been assured was an intelligent, discerning, and first-rate investigator. But where the hell was he?

He nodded at the detective. "Yes, it is rather. But the situation that brings me here is a little unusual. Perhaps, as I said, I should discuss this with the Chief Inspector. No offense."

"None taken," she replied, "and if I could tell you where the guv'nor was this minute, I'd be glad to have you take it up with him. But as it is..."

A shudder passed through Benjamin. Something was very wrong. "What do you mean, 'as it is,' Constable?"

Her shoulders slumped. "No one has seen or heard from DCI Foulsham since yesterday. He's gone missing."

Benjamin was stunned. Detective chief inspectors, up to their knees in a series of murders, did not simply go off on a lark somewhere. They did not, for that matter, go anywhere without reporting in. He started to ask questions, then stopped himself. These were police officers. They knew what questions to ask and had no doubt made all the necessary inquiries. A cold chill seeped his spine. If, he told himself, the murders were all connected to someone in the Glastonbury area, someone who was intent on having the object they had only just retrieved from the Abbey, the chances were good that Nicholas Foulsham had stumbled on something dangerous enough to get him killed. Benjamin prayed that wasn't the case. The death toll was far too high already.

He looked Constable Fitch in the eye. "Then I'm going to have to ask you a favor," he said. "And I'm going to explain a few things I hope might help you locate your boss."

The phone rang shrilly. Mary Fitch grabbed it. Benjamin saw a spasm of anguish pass over her face. Her replies were terse, the conversation brief.

"It's not..." began Benjamin.

"Don't know. There's a body at Haslemere, it's a place about twenty miles from Glastonbury, other side of Pennard. Local constable hasn't been all the way inside, but says he knows from the smell. Now," she said, gripping the pen in her hand as if it were a life preserver, "what were you going to tell me?"

"I'll tell you on the way, Constable."

"I don't think that would be appropriate, sir."

"Look, we don't have time to observe all the niceties. I don't know what you've been told about me, but I've been around the block a few times."

He could see her running over the list of potential land mines his presence might represent. Apparently her concern for Foulsham overcame her reluctance. She scowled and grabbed her car keys off the desk.

"All right then. You'll go with me. But I want to hear everything you know about this investigation by the time we get to Haslemere."

Benjamin stood and opened the door for her. He knew full well that he wouldn't be sharing everything (much of it was just too weird for the average person to even contemplate), but he would relate enough to make Constable Fitch willing to grant him the one favor he needed.

Chapter Thirty-Two

Twice or thrice had I loved thee,
Before I knew thy face or name.
So, in a voice, so in shapeless flame,
Angels affect us oft, and worshipped be.
—John Donne
Air and Angels

"How many steps did you say there were?" Malcolm panted as he paused beside Connor and Laura halfway up the Tor.

Connor smiled. "You've been sitting behind a desk too long, my friend. I seem to remember there was a time when you could chase a perp for blocks *and* catch him."

"Easy for you to say. These days I need a shovel to get through the damn paperwork. If anyone had told me that being a police captain was going to be all politics, bullshit, and paper-pushing, I'd have told them to take the job and—"

"Yes, we've heard the expression. So quit already if you hate it."

"What else would I do?" he asked with a shrug in his tone, but Connor also heard the unhappiness there. If they got out of this with their skins, she and her friend needed to have a talk about what he really wanted in his future. Then, for the tenth time in as many hours, she thought about his kids. They'd already lost their mother. What right had she to risk their father's life? They had no idea with whom they were dealing. Were they climbing this damn hill again to face off against ghosts, or flesh-and-blood people? And would they be the same ones responsible for the murders and mutilations of innocent people?

"You could get a new career," she said. "Listen. Why don't you wait here, and stand guard. There's only one other way to the top, and we'd be able to see them because the slope is so gradual. If you stay here, you can make sure no one else comes up behind us."

Malcolm huffed angrily. "If you try even one more time to think of a reason why I shouldn't go up there with you, I'm going to get mad as hell."

"But—"

"Ain't no buts about it, girl. This is my fight too. Your grandmother even said that in her letter. And Ellen said she saw me with you on the Tor when she looked in the future."

"That's guesswork. And this might not just be about some weird spirit stuff. Someone's been murdering people and I'm pretty sure, for reasons I can't quite put my finger on, that these 'others' William and Ellen mentioned are behind it."

"Someone called us?" came Ellen's voice behind them as she and her husband came up the steps.

Laura reached for one of the canvas bags Ellen had insisted on shouldering. "Connor wanted to convince Malcolm to act as a rear-guard sentry, and he's not having it. She points out that modern-day murderers are just as likely to show up as ancient Celtic ancestors. He agrees and insists that's why she needs him."

"Oh, but she does," said Ellen, as if proclaiming a fact that every schoolchild should know.

"See," said Malcolm with obvious satisfaction.

"How would you know?" asked Connor sharply; her attempts at containing her tension were less successful with each passing minute.

"I'm fairly sure he's someone that Cerydwynn knew," said Ellen quietly. "I can hear echoes of a name in my mind—Caregyn. He was a warrior spoken of in the old histories."

Connor threw up her hands. "Oh, great, what is this? Some sort of phantom reunion, the graduating class of 3,000 B.C.?"

The group was silent, and Connor knew she'd gone too far. Her own skepticism, fueled by nerves, was running rampant. But there was no sense in making everyone else share it.

"I'm sorry. I *hate* not knowing what I'm doing."

Laura hugged her. "I'm not crazy about that concept either, but then maybe we're just two control freaks having a great big learning experience...right?"

Connor smiled in spite of herself. "I also hate learning things I didn't want to know in the first place."

"Life's a bitch, ain't it?" said Malcolm, as he began to climb the next set of steps. "Friend of mine says every time you turn around, there's another fucking opportunity for growth."

When they reached the top of the hill, and stood next to the tower, the velocity of the wind became much more noticeable, and slightly unpleasant.

"Any idea of what we do next?" asked Connor. "Form a circle, chant, pray, dance? Wait 'til the clock strikes midnight and we all turn into—"

"Connor!"

"Sorry, sweetheart. I'm a little tense."

Ellen spoke up in a brisk and business like tone. "William hasn't had any luck translating the text of the formal ritual into English, and I doubt seriously we would be able to make it work anyway. As we told you before, the sound of the ancient syllables themselves is integral to their power in ritual use. And there's no such thing as a crash course in speaking it."

"Maybe Cerydwynn will show up and do the talking," said Connor, then saw the mild consternation on the faces of Malcolm and Laura. "No," she said, tightening her grip on the casket she carried, "I'm not being a wiseass this time, I'm actually hoping she does."

Laura, Connor, and Malcolm watched as Ellen and William quickly unpacked and donned pale gray robes with metallic threads that shone silver in the light of the full moon which had risen several degrees above the horizon. Ellen retrieved another bundle from her pack and advanced on Connor. "This is for you," she said simply.

Connor shrank back. "Is that really necessary?" she protested. "I don't see why I have to dress the part."

The rest of them were silent, watching her. Ellen held out the roll of fabric again. "I don't know if 'necessary' is quite the right word. 'Appropriate' might be better. This was your grandmother's robe."

A sharp pang of longing and regret knifed through Connor's chest as she thought of Gwendolyn. "All right then," she said, her voice unsteady. "If it was good enough for her, then it's good enough for me." She handed the casket to Laura and pulled the soft, silky cloth over her head. It hung to the ground.

"I'll need some sort of belt," she said, "or I'll be tripping over the hem of this thing."

Ellen raised an eyebrow and pointed to the casket in Laura's hands.

"Wait," said Connor, "no one said anything about me *wearing* it," She instantly regretted the trace of panic in her voice.

"This time the word 'necessary' is definitely appropriate." Ellen responded. "What better time than now? Besides—" She didn't get to finish her sentence. Without warning, thunder boomed so loudly it startled all of them.

"Where the hell did that come from?" asked Laura, who'd been asked by Ellen to keep half an eye on the weather. So far there was not a cloud to be seen. All the stars were still visible.

The thunder sounded again, closer, yet there was no flash of lightning.

"Maybe it's something else," Connor suggested, though aside from military war games, she couldn't imagine what else could cause the sound. She noticed that William and Ellen did not react at all to the second boom. All in all, they were taking this situation awfully well, she thought. Maybe a little too well. And here they were, all kitted out for a witch's circle as if it were the most normal activity in the world for a spring evening in Glastonbury. Just how much could they really trust...She scowled. Great, now she was starting to suspect the people who were on her side. She'd have to get her mind to stop chattering like a panic-stricken child.

Cold air whipped up around them, ballooning the skirts of their robes. Connor heard the rushing sound of rain before she felt it. A frightening flash of déjà vu sent her scrambling to wrap her arms around Laura who had been in the process of removing the belt from its centuries-old resting place.

"Don't let go of me," she gasped. "I'm not going to lose track of you like I did last time."

Laura shouted above the roar. "I thought that was my line. And this does seem way too familiar. Here put this on."

"Let's get inside the tower," she replied, as her fingers wrapped around the cold metal. Then she turned to the others. As loudly as she could, she ordered them all into the structure. "There's no top on it, but at least we'll be out of the wind."

The moon had been devoured by massive clouds, and they stood in the dripping darkness until Malcolm got his flashlight switched on. He shone it against the walls and played it over the stone benches until it came to rest on the object still clutched in Connor's hand. They stood transfixed by the sight of golden disks linked one upon the other, each disk set with magnificent quartz crystals that swirled prisms of light all around them.

"Put it on, Connor," said Ellen softly. "It's time."

Laura, silently, as if in a trance, stepped closer and helped Connor fasten the belt around her silvery robe. She looked in her lover's eyes and Connor knew they'd done this very ritual before, they'd stood here before, together. She closed her eyes and when she opened them, the rain had stopped, the skies above her were brilliantly clear...and she was alone.

Connor wasn't afraid, quite the opposite. She'd never felt more calm, not in this lifetime anyway. The thought, foreign though it was to her everyday consciousness, passed through her mind without a ripple.

Looking down the hill, she saw what she'd expected—shimmering halos of torchlight—though they were less defined than they'd been before, almost as if she were seeing the afterimages of the real events that had taken place here. Fingering the belt of crystal and gold slung loosely about her hips, she swiveled to her right. It was from that direction that the threat would come, up the long, gently graded side of the Tor. How did she know that? Did it matter? No. Past and present had become one. Shadows walked side by side with flesh-and-blood beings.

True to her prescient certainty, a small procession labored up the slope a mere 200 yards below her. The light from the torches was sharp and bright against the night sky. Below them, nothing. Whatever fleeting thoughts she had that there should be a town down there flitted away.

Connor brought her hands up, palms together in front of her face and a prayer came into her mind. The words felt strange on her tongue, yet the meaning was clear to her, not as if they'd been translated into English, but as if they'd been created somewhere in her heart and she knew the meaning without conscious thought.

The many gods that are One God walk the Earth and the form of the One is upon the face of the land and the faces of the people. Praise be to the One.

She raised her eyes to the leader of the procession which had stopped a dozen feet away. "So, you have come at last, Pelwynn. You were expected, of course. But I ask you to turn aside from your purpose. It shall not succeed this time. Because, you see, you have not been able to conjure the beast, have you?" She crossed her arms over her chest and looked into the eyes of her mortal enemy.

W

Laura stumbled and Malcolm grabbed her arm, yanking her upward.

"Ouch."

"Sorry," he gasped. "I didn't mean to—"

"Never mind, just keep going. Are William and Ellen behind us?"

"Yes."

Laura considered shouting for them to keep up, but she didn't think she had the breath.

One moment they'd been standing in the tower, soaked to the skin, and the next they'd been more than half a mile from the base of the Tor, near what should have been the end of Wellhouse Lane. Except that there was no Chalice Garden wall, no cars, nothing but wide-open country and a rutted country lane. In the distance, they could see torchlight climbing the Tor.

"What the hell happened?" Laura had asked.

"What the fuck!" Malcolm had said.

William had stared at the Tor for a moment. "It's begun. Whoever we were then is who we are now. And we must have been this far away when Cerydwynn was attacked before."

Laura didn't stop to hear the rest. She started running, and heard Malcolm's heavy tread right behind her.

It was too far to run nonstop because the path was steeply uphill. None of them was in that kind of physical shape. Perhaps their 'selves' of 3,000 years earlier had been more fit, Laura thought as she pressed a hand to the stitch in her side.

As they neared the gate across the pathway to the Tor, she saw that there *was* no gate, no hedgerow, no asphalt path. This would be a do-it-yourself climb, and she recalled how steeply graded were the sides of the Tor from this approach. But there was no time to sprint around the base of the hill to the shallower slope. She trotted on past the nonexist-ent landmarks and launched herself up the side of the hill. Her feet hit spongy sod, and she slipped, rolling backward. There was no one there to break her fall, and she landed painfully against a boulder.

"Son of a bitch!" she said, springing to her feet, ignoring the sting of where a rock had scraped her face.

"Who?" Malcolm said in the darkness.

"The hill!" Laura growled and started up again.

𝒲°

"Don't be so sure of yourself, Cerydwynn...although I'm not entirely convinced you're the mighty priestess herself. So many weak-minded people end rather pitifully self-deluded, like your grandmother and that silly ragtag Celtic circle of hers."

382

"So you're the one who's been trying to steal the high priestess's secrets."

"All too easily I might add. And to think that only a few years ago I had no idea of my real heritage. But then I happened to overhear something once, and I started digging. I discovered right away that the Carlisles were involved, and Gwendolyn, of course. But just when I was getting close to having everything I needed, she disappeared."

"So you desecrated her *grave*. What were you going to do? Ask her questions?"

Pelwynn's eyes narrowed. "I had someone open it because I was looking for that." She pointed at the belt. "But not only wasn't it there, that stupid old woman wasn't there either. Some sleight of hand, I assume. Maybe you were just a little too anxious to inherit the family manse. Buried the body somewhere beyond prying eyes?"

Cerydwynn ignored the question. "And what do you expect to get from all this? Surely you can't think the talisman will help you."

"Oh, don't I?" Pelwynn smiled again, her lips thin and red against her pale skin. "I may not have found all the information I wanted, but I will. With that lovely trinket you're wearing, I'll be able to get my hands on anything I want. And I'll be answerable to no one. I won't waste the power playing at witches like you and your friends."

"And you're not playing?" said Cerydwynn, her eyes fastened on the small replica of the talisman that hung around her enemy's neck, stark against a long white robe. Her eyes flicked to the people who'd come with Pelwynn. "Speaking of ragtag," she said mockingly, "a poor substitute for the power of the beast, are they not? This motley group hardly inspires admiration."

"Ah, but quality isn't always apparent on the surface, now is it?" She motioned with her left hand, and a short figure slipped from behind her. "My acolyte, whom I believe you've met."

The part of Cerydwynn's consciousness that held Connor Hawthorne awareness recognized the diminutive man she and her friends had dubbed the leprechaun. "So this is one of your spies then."

"I prefer to think of him as my good right hand," Pelwynn smirked. "Even the greatest among us need our minions to take care of tiresome tasks. By the way, where are yours? Surely your precious Daria should be present. I know she'd want to be with you until the end."

Cerydwynn heard the venomous hatred dripping from every word and a new insight flooded into her. Daria was Cerydwynn's lover, her first assistant in the circle, and both places of honor which Pelwynn had wanted. She truly hated Daria.

"Unlike you, I handle my challengers without calling for assistance."

"Oh, and a code of honor too. How very quaint."

"If you understood anything about our people, if you had even an inkling of the role you have assigned yourself, you would not mock the principles by which we are sworn to live."

Pelwynn sneered. "Our people? Our people are dead and gone. There is just you and me now. You may be sworn to live by some moldy old principles, but I'm not. I defeated you when you were Cerydwynn, yet I was robbed of my rightful prize." Her eyes fell on the belt around the other woman's waist. "That is *mine*."

"It does not belong to you, any more than it belongs to me. You know full well that when the time comes, this talisman must be returned from whence it came, in the proper place with the correct words of ritual."

"And you would destroy everything by giving it back," Pelwynn snarled.

"No, I would preserve the will of the One by giving it back."

"No, you won't!"

"There is nothing you can do to stop me, Pelwynn."

Her enemy laughed. "Ah, but I did before. What makes you believe that I cannot do so now?"

"You delayed the inevitable because you were able to summon the beast out of the Darkness, and I admit I was unprepared for your treachery. Surely you did not think to duplicate it this time? If you have, where is it?"

Pelwynn reached for a bag slung over the shoulder of the gnome at her side. Untying the cord around its neck, she tipped it upside down.

Cerydwynn gagged, stepped back, and then fought to regain control. There on the ground lay the partially decomposed head of a young woman, and a man's bloody hands.

"I thought these would serve as a reminder to you of how miserably you failed before."

Cerydwynn was stonily silent, refusing to betray the revulsion she felt. Steeling herself, she glared at Pelwynn. But she felt a twinges of doubt seeping through her body. Connor's awareness reminded their shared soul of what Ellen had said: Cerydwynn had lost this same battle thousands of years ago, had been executed and her head and hands removed. How could Pelwynn have succeeded when Cerydwynn held the reins of power, wore the source of that power around her body? The talisman had not protected her then.

"This time it shall be different," she announced boldly. "This time you shall not prevail. You are nothing but a common murderer. Why would you kill that poor girl, and a man who'd done nothing to you?"

"That's just it. He was nothing. And why not kill her? Surely you've learned that evil is just as reasonable a choice as good. And now I'm giving you a choice."

"I won't give you what you want," said Cerydwynn, her voice strong. "You have no way to force me." In that instant, she knew that the talisman would protect her from simple threats of mortal violence. It was the beast she'd feared, and it was not present on this night.

"Think again, you stupid woman. I admit I haven't discovered all my predecessor's secrets. But there are other ways to snatch victory." Pelwynn swung her arm in a sweeping gesture, and from behind the half-dozen people in her vanguard came four men carrying a long wooden box that very much resembled a coffin. The men sat it down on the ground in front of their mistress. Plucking a blazing torch from the hand of one of her followers, Pelwynn swept it back and forth over the top of the coffin. Bits of pitch on its surface sparked and exploded.

To her horror, Cerydwynn heard thumping coming from within it. Muffled sounds seeped from between the tightly fitted slats of wood.

"I knew that convincing the great Cerydwynn might prove difficult...cold, heartless bitch that she is...but Connor Hawthorne on the other hand..." She kicked the side of the coffin. "I propose a trade. The talisman of the gods for the life of your precious father."

W

"We're almost there," Laura said, sucking air in great gulps. "But who the hell is that?"

Malcolm fell to his knees beside her and peered through the clumps of tall grass behind which they were barely concealed. Moments later, Ellen and William dropped to the ground behind them.

"I told you it had begun," said William. He listened for a moment and his jaw worked furiously. "Mother of God, that woman with the torch, that's Fenwycke's wife, Gillian."

Ellen pushed her forward to look. "It can't be. No. I think you're right. But how on earth did she..."

"You said before, love, that you thought the source of the difficulty lay fairly close to home. You were right. She must have been preparing for this moment for years."

"And spying on us in the meantime."

"I would imagine so."

"Now what do we do?"

"Let's go," Malcolm hissed. "Now."

"Wait," said Laura, placing a restraining hand on his shoulder. "No sense alerting her that we're all here. And you may have noticed that there are ten or twelve people with her. There are only four of us."

"Five, counting Connor."

"True, but who knows what state she's in right now or who she thinks she is? And I'm worried about what's in that box, and why what's-her-name is trying to set it on fire." They watched as Gillian Fenwycke continued to sweep the torch over the top of the coffin-shaped container.

"I have a bad feeling that someone's in it, and that they aren't dead yet," said Malcolm. "Even more reason to go in now. I can take out five or six of those creeps. They don't even look very big, especially that little one."

"Yes, that would be the creepy little leprechaun guy," said Laura. "But listen, we need the element of surprise if we're going to have a chance. You and Ellen and William slide back down the hill a few yards and circle around the perimeter. Get behind them. That way you'll have a better chance if they don't see you coming."

"I wish to God I had my gun," grumbled Malcolm. "That would even things up. Who knows what her little camp followers are carrying."

"This being England, my friend," said William. "The chances are very good they are not armed...with guns anyway."

Malcolm shrugged as if he didn't believe a word of it, but his eyes brightened when he looked down and saw Ellen offering him a long, wicked looking dagger. "This is a sacred ceremonial object. It was never intended as a weapon," she said, releasing it reluctantly. "But I think this situation calls for desperate means. Please only use it if you absolutely have no other choice, if a life depends on it."

"Malcolm gripped the haft of the dagger tightly. "You have my word. Let's go."

"One more thing," Laura whispered to Ellen. "Do you have another one of those robes in your pack?"

Ellen looked at Laura curiously, but thrust her hand into the canvas sack and produced a bundle similar to the one she'd given Connor. "I suppose you know what you're doing," she said.

"Not really," answered Laura. "See you up there."

𝒲

George Stout, whose surname had caused him unceasing grief as a chubby child, was the young and very green uniformed constable assigned the job of guarding absolutely nothing. He thought this a perfect example of how unappreciated were his talents and intelligence. He *could* be vigorously assisting in the investigation of the death of Gerald Fenwycke (which might not be a suicide, even if that's what the scientific muckety-mucks wanted to think); instead he was patrolling the grounds of Haslemere. And for what? There wasn't a single reporter left hanging about the gates; the body had been taken away and the house secured. Everyone had torn off in every direction looking for Lady Fenwycke, and he and half a dozen others had been combing the grounds to see if the wife wasn't perhaps buried somewhere. But not a sign. And what with that and the other CID officers buzzing around where that sergeant had got himself killed, the place had been insane.

The last exciting bit of the afternoon was seeing DC Mary Fitch ticking off that American bloke in the fancy suit what had come down with her in the car. Of course, he hadn't been close enough to tell what had gotten DC Fitch so angry, but she sent the old guy packing, she had. Told off a driver to take him back to the station.

But now the excitement had petered out completely. It was boring beyond the accepted definition of boring. The constable had made the full circuit of the house, noted the trail of footsteps through the garden patch and under the window that had been roped off for the making of plaster impressions. Then he'd swung back around the garage, and sauntered down the rear drive, which extended past the stables and around to the ancient grain elevator, which poked up out of the landscape like one of the turrets of a castle.

He leaned against the fence and lit a cigarette since there wasn't anyone around to tell him he couldn't smoke at a crime scene, though this wasn't, strictly speaking, a crime scene, what with it being so far from the house. After a few minutes of smoking and tossing a few pebbles at the wall of the grain elevator, he crushed the cigarette under his boot and squared his cap on his head. It was going to be a long night.

Then he heard it. A sort of thudding behind him. The constable whirled around. Peering into the shadows cast by the circular stone building, he listened. There it was again. A thumping, thudding.

Part of him wanted to run, that part was sending urgent signals to his feet. But it turned out that under pressure the young man was actually as courageous as he had boasted to his mates. He advanced slowly but steadily, trying not to make any noise at all. The noise had stopped. He waited for it to begin again, dreading that it would, and afraid that it wouldn't, and almost decided to turn around, when there it was, just off to his right, deeply in the shadows. He moved forward and within a few feet, bumped heavily into something. "Damn," he muttered. "They've heard me now."

George wasn't sure who "they" might be, but he did have his truncheon in his hand and his whistle in the other. Though who was to hear

him way out in the middle of the nowhere was a good question he did-
n't care to ask. "At least," he thought, "I can blow it with my dying
breath. Or maybe I'll find this missing lady or a body." Not fully appre-
ciating the melodramatic tendencies of youth, he was savoring the
image of heroism when the thump came again. It was right beneath
him, or in front of him. Daring a bold move, the constable plucked the
torch from his belt and shone it straight ahead. He saw a trapdoor in
front of him. But he would have had to step much farther back to see
what the structure itself was. Having spent most of his life in the city,
his knowledge of farming was minimal at best. Still, he'd heard a sound,
and that was the nearest place it could be coming from. Heaving aside
the sturdy crosspiece that barred the door, the young man flung it wide
open an stepped back. An arm emerged, or, more accurately, fell out of
the opening, and his heart leaped into his throat. It *was* a body. But the
arm moved, which at the moment seemed even more terrifying. Then
he saw a shoulder, then a head.

"Well, it's about bloody time someone found me," said Nicholas
Foulsham.

𝒲°

Focused completely on the present, Connor stared in horror at the
wooden box, easily large enough to hold a man even of Benjamin's
stature. "No," she whispered involuntarily, all thoughts that were purely
Cerydwynn's had disappeared from her mind. Only Connor Hawthorne
was in charge now.

"Oh, yes," Gillian laughed joyously. "It was very easy." She
dropped her voice to a conspiratorial tone. "Of course, I'd really
planned on snatching Daria, well, that one you call Laura Nez. But
your dear Benjamin played right into my hands when I came to the
door of your grandmother's house, insisting I had crucial information about his daughter. He only turned his back for a moment, but
that was sufficient."

"You can't do this," said Connor, her voice no longer ringing clear
in the night.

"Of course I can. I already have. Don't be obtuse, Cerydwynn. Give me the talisman."

Connor's hands flew to her waist. She didn't care about the stupid thing. Her father mattered, not some age-old superstition. But before her fumbling fingers could open the intricate clasp, a voice rang out behind her.

"Don't do it, Connor."

She whirled around. There stood Laura—or was it Daria?—clad in the same silvery fabric. "No," said Connor. "Stay out of this."

"But I have a feeling I am part of it. And who might this be?" she asked, waving a careless hand in Gillian's direction.

"Pretending you don't know me is a rather transparent snub, Daria," she answered for herself. "I don't mind admitting I know exactly who you are."

Laura shrugged, looking to Connor for guidance. She had no idea who Daria was or why Gillian had decided that was Laura's identity.

Connor straightened up, her face no longer a study in panic. "This woman is Pelwynn, the one responsible for the death of Cerydwynn. And she's come to demand the talisman from me. She wants to trade..." her voice trembled, then she took another deep breath. "She wants to trade my father's life for it." Connor's eyes swept over the wooden box.

Laura came to stand beside Connor. Her next comment took Connor completely by surprise. "And how do you know Benjamin is in that box? He doesn't seem the sort to be duped by someone like her."

Gillian bristled with rage. "How dare you speak of me that way. One more word and you'll both die and end up like these two." She pointed to the gory souvenirs at her feet.

Connor heard Laura's sharp intake of breath. Then her lover spoke again. "So what we have here is your basic psychopath who slept with this girl and then killed her, and thinks she can use body parts to work magic spells and witchcraft." She glared at Gillian. "Know what I think?"

Gillian, shaking with rage, said, "I don't care."

"Yes, you do. And what I think is that you give witches *and* lesbians a bad name." The woman moved forward a pace, her eyes locked on

Laura. The little man moved with her, and her followers closed ranks. Gillian swung the torch toward the coffin as Laura raised her voice to a shout. "And I don't think Benjamin Hawthorne is even *in* that box."

Connor, startled by the volume of Laura's voice, almost didn't notice a shadow slipping up behind Gillian's so-called coven. Then another, and another. Yes, she thought. She'd been so wrapped up in the scene in front of her, she hadn't given any thought to Malcolm, Ellen, and William. Her heart thrilled with hope even as the torch swung over the top of the box once more and this time the lid caught.

She lunged toward the hand that held the torch, but Laura stepped in front of her. "No. That might not even be your father in there."

"Someone is," Connor shouted. "Someone who's going to burn alive."

Laura held firm. "Listen to me! Last time she cooked up some kind of monster that consumed you. This time she's bargaining for something you think is worth more than that belt around your waist. She wants fear to consume you. I don't understand all this, but I do know that if you give in, you'll die, and a lot of very bad things will happen. You can't let her win."

Gillian snarled at them and dropped the torch on top of the box; then, as if by sleight of hand, she held a gleaming dagger. She raised it high over her head, the wild heat of insanity in her eyes, and then everything happened at once.

Gillian charged, and Laura stepped slightly to one side, chopping at the arm that held the knife. Connor pushed past Gillian, desperately kicking at the torch. From the corner of her eye she saw two of Gillian's followers go down hard with Malcolm Jefferson on top of them.

Torn between the need to save her father and terror for the safety of the woman she loved, Connor was almost paralyzed. Flames licked at the skirts of her robe. She tried to tear it off, but the belt was tight around her waist. She was trapped. Someone lunged at her from behind, and she tried to fight until a familiar voice barked at her, "Stop it, I'm trying to put out the fire." It was William, a heavy blanket in his hands, beating at the skirt of her robe.

"The coffin," she cried. "Quickly."

He instantly began smothering the flames. Connor turned back and saw Pelwynn and Laura locked together, struggling for the knife, which pointed first at the sky, then swept toward the ground and back again.

"No," she screamed, "this is *my* fight."

In one fluid motion, she plunged between them, her hands grasping at the knife. She felt its keen blade slice her palm, but she would not let go. With the other arm she shoved Laura away as hard as she could, and Laura's robes hampered her completely, causing her to trip and fall. "Take care of my father," Connor shouted and turned away, still trying to get hold of the haft of the knife. She found herself staring directly into the face of Pelwynn, whose features were twisted with rage and bitterness.

"You can't win," Connor hissed in the woman's ear. "Stop this now, before it's too late."

But Gillian wasn't in any state to hear reason. She struggled for the knife one moment, then tried to unfasten the belt from around Connor's waist the next. It was in one of these brief forays to obtain the prize she sought that Connor was finally able to wrest the dagger completely from Gillian's grasp. With a mighty shove, she pushed Gillian away from her and held the knife in her bleeding hand.

Gillian was no longer capable of giving rational thought to her own safety. With a horrible scream of rage, she rushed at Connor, who instinctively tried to step back. But it felt as if an invisible wall had sprung up behind her, blocking her progress. And before she could alter the angle of the dagger, Gillian had run directly onto it. Connor watched in horror as the look on her opponent's face changed from fury to surprise. Blood gurgled between her lips as she tried to speak. Her body slumped, and Connor tried to support her with one arm, immediately letting go of the dagger. Gillian sank to her knees, and her mind had apparently refused to believe she was dead, for her fingers still plucked at the dangling ends of the shining golden talisman that could no longer save her.

After a long moment, Connor became aware of a Laura, standing just behind Gillian, a heavy stone in her hands, poised to strike. But the object of Laura's murderous rage lay dead on the ground. She dropped the stone, and tears flooded her cheeks. Connor turned to see Ellen working frantically at the lid of the coffin, but it was nailed shut. Several yards away, Malcolm and William were struggling with the last of Pelwynn's cohorts, the others having taken to their heels when they saw their erstwhile priestess fall.

Connor moved toward Laura, drained of all sensation. There'd been no ritual, no magic, no completion as Gwendolyn had promised. If there had been a task, Connor was quite sure she had failed to accomplish it. Tears streamed down her face. What if Benjamin were dead?

Suddenly, in the midst of the darkness, there appeared a shaft of blinding light so bright that they all covered their eyes, peering between their fingers. All of them, that is, except Connor. The light did not hurt her eyes. Instead she walked toward it. Laura, afraid of what might happen next, was next to her lover in an instant.

"What are you doing?" she asked.

"I don't know," said Connor.

"You're not going, I mean you're not leaving us...leaving me...you can't"

"I don't know. I don't want to. But something is about to happen."

Gradually the variegated light coalesced into a shape, a vaguely humanoid shape, though it was by no means a human being. And when the shape spoke, Connor was fairly sure that it made no audible sound, yet its voice was pure and clear in her mind.

She said you would prevail, and she was right.

But I haven't done the ritual. And Pelwynn is dead. I killed her.

She killed herself, child. And she has gone home. She is with the One. The ritual is not what you and your companions thought. It was never about words, but about truth. The task you set yourself has been finished. The soul once known as Cerydwynn has completed the journey out of the Darkness.

Who are you?

You know me, and yet you do not. There will come a time for you to see me as I truly am. Now it is time for the talisman to be returned to whence it came.

With the lightest of touches, Connor's trembling fingers released the belt from around her waist. She held it out, and the form of a hand reached out. In the blink of an eye, the belt of Guinevere, the belt that had held Excalibur, the gift of peace from the realms of Light...disappeared.

Must I go with you also?

For the briefest of moments, eyes formed within the hazy figure, and to Connor, those eyes bespoke a love so immense, so infinite, her heart ached to bask in it forever.

No, child. Your life is sacred, and every moment of it must be lived as you intended to live it before you came into this existence. Your soul mate is here with you now. Be at her side, and she will be at yours.

Is Gwendolyn with you?

The one you called grandmother has chosen a path that few have the courage to follow. But she will be watching over you. Be at peace, daughter of creation, and live in joy.

The figure began to lose even the slight definition it had manifested. Once more there was only the shaft of light. Then it too was gone. Where it had been loomed the old stonework of the tower of St. Michael, framed in the new light of dawn.

W

In the distance Connor heard the sound of police whistles. Where on earth had they come from, she wondered, staring around her in bewilderment. Everything was as it had been, and yet everything had changed. Ellen was tugging at her sleeve. "The robe," she said. "Give me the robe." Dazedly, Connor took it off and watched as Ellen retrieved Laura's and William's and stuffed them all into her knapsack.

She looked at her hands, prepared to deal with the blood that was on them. But there was no blood and no evidence at all that she'd cut her hand. It was all too much. An entire night had passed in the space of what seemed like minutes. She felt herself swaying on her feet and then Laura's arms were around her.

"You heard what she said, or he...I'm not sure?" asked Connor.

"Yes, I heard. And I don't think it matters wherever he or she came from," said Laura. "Are you going to be able to make it down all those steps?"

"Oh, God," said Connor. "What about Dad?"

As if in direct answer to her question, Benjamin Hawthorne came up over the crest of the hill and stopped to stare at his daughter.

"Thank you, God," he shouted at the top of his lungs. "Chief Inspector, they're all right."

The tall, thin man Connor vaguely recalled from his visit to Rosewood House had come up behind Benjamin. Foulsham, she thought. She saw that his right forearm was in a splint. "Well, that's good news then," the policeman said. "But what's all this?" His eyes had taken in the wooden coffin, the two robed figures who were forced to lie on the ground because Malcolm Jefferson was sitting on them, and the crumpled body of Gillian Fenwycke.

Connor felt as if she should speak, as if she should try to explain all this, but suddenly she felt her knees buckle. "I didn't know..." she managed, and that was the last thing she remembered.

Chapter Thirty-Three

For night's swift dragons cut the clouds full fast,
And yonder shines Aurora's harbinger;
At whose approach, ghosts, wandering here and there,
Troop home to churchyards.
—William Shakespeare
A Midsummer Night's Dream, Act 3, Scene 1

It took several days for Nicholas Foulsham to sort out what had happened on Glastonbury Tor, and by the time he'd done so, he rather regretted knowing as much as he did. Being a wise man, however, and not entirely resistant to the advice of Benjamin Hawthorne, he saw to it that the supernatural elements of the incident were downplayed, if not omitted entirely from police reports. He was pleased, however, to have finally solved the rash of murders. And he owed much of his success to the ex-senator's carefully crafted arrangements with Mary Fitch to have the police standing by at the foot of the Tor awaiting his signal. It was only Foulsham's great good luck in being found by Constable Stout that allowed him to be in place at the Tor at the appropriate moment.

The hapless occupant of Gillian Fenwycke's coffin turned out to be none other than Conrad Thackeray, who was alive, though suffering from smoke inhalation. The corporate kingpin had been beaten at his own game by his former mistress who'd bribed Clarence Newbury, the dapper blackmailer, to lure Conrad to a deserted farmhouse with the promise of valuable information about the man who'd been following him. Conrad, apparently driven beyond reason by the persistence of the little gray-haired gnome who'd been following him, rushed immediately to meet Newbury and was quickly subdued, tied up, and gagged.

Gillian's violent death was perhaps rather more satisfactory to Foulsham than propriety allowed. But once he'd established, with the aid of statements from Lord and Lady Carlisle, Connor Hawthorne, Laura Nez, and that American cop, Malcolm Jefferson, that Gillian had not only murdered Patricia Frome and Peter Garrett, but had shown every intention of murdering again, he could perhaps be forgiven for taking such an attitude. Then, of course, there was the small matter of her husband's death. The medical chaps still hadn't said one way or the other whether it had definitely been a suicide. He wouldn't have put it past Gillian.

He'd also had the pleasure of arresting Conrad Thackeray for complicity in the murders of the two men in the churchyard. The information had come to him anonymously by mail, and he suspected it had originated with Gillian Fenwycke. According to the squirmy little chap with the Irish brogue, who'd been on Gillian's payroll, she'd convinced the greedy Conrad there was a fortune in salable esoteric objects and historic documents hidden somewhere, probably in Gwendolyn Broadhurst's grave or in her house.

Sadly, Foulsham feared the charges against Thackeray would not stick; the man was already surrounded by a dog pack of solicitors. There was also no way to prove he'd been using the sheds at Haslemere to store and transfer contraband arms as William Carlisle had suggested, but at least he'd had the satisfaction of putting cuffs on Thackeray once he'd been untied and seen to by the medical chaps. And he'd heard that the foreign exchanges were chewing up World Technology Partners stock and spitting it out in shreds. Some pleasures in life were fleeting but nonetheless sweet.

Lady Fenwycke's demise had been ruled a suicide. Other than the single stab wound through the heart, there were no marks of violence on her, and no bloodstains on anyone else who'd been present. Foulsham wondered about it, but the look in Benjamin Hawthorne's eyes, and the word he'd had with a chap named Carstairs in London tended to fade his curiosity about that ceremonial dagger in Lady Carlisle's bag, something she insisted had been brought purely as a precaution. Of course, the whole story about why they were all up there was pure bunkum.

Even though they were all interviewed almost immediately, their stories were perfectly matched. Connor had received an unsigned note telling her that her father was in danger and she must come to the Tor at midnight. Naturally her friends would accompany her, and the Carlisles who happened to be paying a social call, thought perhaps they should come along as well, being more familiar with the area. This did little to explain the knapsacks they carried, and the little carved wooden box lying on the floor inside the tower. But Foulsham let it go. His murders were solved. Clarence Newbury had become extraordinarily cooperative on every conceivable subject except Conrad Thackeray (not that Foulsham blamed him—who would want a man like that for any enemy?). Hollis was no longer ranting up and down the halls, and Foulsham was more than ready to put this case behind him, most especially the part about being let out of a grain chute by a wet-behind-the-ears constable. Some situations were simply too embarrassing to contemplate.

Epilogue

My sweetest Lesbia, let us live and love,
And though the sager sort our deeds reprove,
Let us not weigh them: Heav'n's great lamps do dive
Into their west, and straight again revive,
But as soon as once set is our little light,
Then we must sleep one ever-during night.
    —Thomas Campion
    A Book of Airs

Connor stood at the rental counter, smiling tolerantly at her old friend, the young rental agent, who had not yet gotten over being impressed by her presence. He had also received the personally autographed book, a coup that had, he insisted, sent his partner into paroxysms of joy.

He grinned. "You must have been having a really great time," he said breathlessly. "You were only going to keep the car for a couple of weeks, and you've had it two months."

She put her arm around Laura, possibly scandalizing the other customers behind them, but undoubtedly thrilling the young man on the other side of the counter. "We decided to see a lot of England."

"Oh, I know," he sighed. "There's so-o-o much history. Buildings that go back for centuries and centuries. People are just amazed when they hear stories of what's gone on here."

"Tell me about it," said Connor.

𝒲

They waited until the cabin lights had been turned out and their fellow passengers were engrossed in watching movies or television channels on the personal monitors in business class. They reclined their seats, raised the armrest between the seats, and Connor spread a blanket over them. Beneath it, she took Laura's hand.

"I feel like I could sleep for a week," she said.

"I think we only have about ten hours. But maybe we need a vacation." Connor laughed. "Isn't that what we've been doing?"

"For the last month anyway. And I've got to tell you that the best part was the week in Oxford with Katy. She's one astounding young woman. I love your Aunt Jessica too. But now I'd like for the two of us to take at trip that involves absolutely nothing weird. No ghosts, no crazy old ladies, no witchcraft, no magic talismans," she said, ticking them off on her fingers. "No bodies, no creepy murderers, no voices from pillars of light...have I missed anything?"

"No," Connor smiled. "I think that about covers it."

"Good, I'm ready for plain old-fashioned dull reality as we know it."

"As we make it," prompted Connor whereupon Laura pinched her arm. "Sorry," she said, chuckling. "We'll declare a complete moratorium on metaphysics, at least for the duration of the flight."

"Thank you."

Connor snuggled down in her seat, enjoying the warmth of Laura's body next to hers. "This is good," she sighed. "I'm ready to be home."

A lengthy silence ensued, and Connor thought Laura had fallen asleep. But then Laura spoke in a soft whisper.

"Where is home exactly?"

The question was unexpected, and Connor considered it carefully, her mind lulled by the thrumming of the jet engines. "You know, I'm not sure, at least geographically. I love Santa Fe, and I love your place out on the rez, and there's part of the east that I'm still drawn to. But there's no particular place I have in mind. Why? Does that worry you...that I don't know for sure?"

After another silence, Laura answered. "I guess not. Just wondered if you'd ever feel comfortable calling any place home."

"I guess home is..." Connor hesitated. "Why is it all the best lines are taken?"

"Don't tell me we're in a cliché dilemma again."

"Sort of."

"Something like, 'home is where the heart is'?"

"No, more along the lines of home is wherever *you* are."

Laura had to swallow the mysterious lump in her throat before she could answer. "And you wonder why I love you so much." She leaned her head against Connor's shoulder as they drifted toward sleep.

The plane arrowed swiftly through the night sky, and inside the cabin an almost imperceptible current of air swirled along the aisle.

"Did you feel that?" murmured Connor.

"Feel what, sweetheart?"

"Never mind. Felt like something touched my cheek."

In the cockpit, the tired copilot turned his head quickly to look out the window. A flash of light to starboard? But he saw nothing more. Only stars, and a fat, full moon.